CU00549735

Edgar Wallace was   ch and
adopted by George I   ket. At
eleven, Wallace sold newspapers at Ludgate Circus and on leaving
school took a job with a printer. He enlisted in the Royal West Kent
Regiment, later transferring to the Medical Staff Corps and was sent
to South Africa. In 1898 he published a collection of poems called
The Mission that Failed, left the army and became a correspondent
for Reuters.

Wallace became the South African war correspondent for *The
Daily Mail*. His articles were later published as *Unofficial Dispatches* and
his outspokenness infuriated Kitchener, who banned him as a war
correspondent until the First World War. He edited the *Rand Daily
Mail*, but gambled disastrously on the South African Stock Market,
returning to England to report on crimes and hanging trials. He
became editor of *The Evening News*, then in 1905 founded the Tallis
Press, publishing *Smith*, a collection of soldier stories, and *Four Just
Men*. At various times he worked on *The Standard*, *The Star*, *The Week-
End Racing Supplement* and *The Story Journal*.

In 1917 he became a Special Constable at Lincoln's Inn and also
a special interrogator for the War Office. His first marriage to Ivy
Caldecott, daughter of a missionary, had ended in divorce and he
married his much younger secretary, Violet King.

The Daily Mail sent Wallace to investigate atrocities in the Belgian
Congo, a trip that provided material for his *Sanders of the River* books.
In 1923 he became Chairman of the Press Club and in 1931 stood as
a Liberal candidate at Blackpool. On being offered a scriptwriting
contract at RKO, Wallace went to Hollywood. He died in 1932, on
his way to work on the screenplay for *King Kong*.

The Face
in the Night

HOUSE OF
STRATUS

This edition published in 2001 by House of Stratus, an imprint of Stratus Holdings plc, 24c Old Burlington Street, London, W1X 1RL, UK.

www.houseofstratus.com

Typeset, printed and bound by House of Stratus.

A catalogue record for this book is available from the British Library.

ISBN 1-84232-679-1

THE MAN FROM THE SOUTH

The fog, which was later to descend upon London, blotting out every landmark, was as yet a grey, misty threat. The light had gone from the sky, and the street-lamps made a blurred showing when the man from the South came unsteadily into Portman Square. In spite of the raw cold he wore no overcoat; his shirt was open at his throat. He walked along, peering up at the doors, and presently he stopped before No. 551 and made a survey of the darkened windows. The corner of his scarred mouth lifted in a sardonic smile.

Strong drink magnifies all dominant emotions. The genial man grows more fond of his fellows, the quarrelsome more bitter. But in the man who harbours a sober grievance, booze brings the red haze that enshrouds murder. And Laker had both the grievance and the medium of magnification.

He would teach this old devil he couldn't rob men without a comeback. The dirty skinflint who lived on the risk which his betters were taking. Here was Laker, almost penniless, with a long and painful voyage behind him, and the memory of the close call that had come in Cape Town, when his room had been searched by the police. A dog's life – that was what he was living. Why should old Malpas, who had not so long to exist anyway, live in luxury whilst his best agent roughed it? Laker always felt like this when he was drunk.

He was hardly the type that might be expected to walk boldly up to the front door of 551, Portman Square. His long, unshaven face, the old knife wound that ran diagonally from cheek to point of chin, the

1

low forehead covered with a ragged fringe of hair, taken in con-junction with his outfit, suggested abject poverty.

He stood for a moment, looking down at his awkward-looking boots, and then, mounting the steps, he tapped slowly at the door. Instantly a voice asked: "Who is that?"

"Laker – that's who!" he said loudly.

A little pause, and the door opened noiselessly and he passed through. There was nobody to receive him, nor did he expect to see a servant. Crossing the bare hall, he walked up the stairs, through an open door and a small lobby, into a darkened room. The only light was from a green-shaded lamp on the writing table, at which an old man sat. Laker stood just inside the room and heard the door close behind him.

"Sit down," said the man at the far end of the room.

The visitor had no need for guidance: he knew exactly where the chair and table were, three paces from where he stood, and without a word he seated himself. Again that grin twisted his face, but his repulsive-looking host could not see this.

"When did you come?"

"I came in the *Buluwayo*. We docked this morning," said Laker. "I want some money, and I want it quick, Malpas!"

"Put down what you have brought, on the table," said the old man harshly. "Return in a quarter of an hour and the money will be waiting for you."

"I want it now," said the other with drunken obstinacy.

Malpas turned his hideous face toward the visitor.

"There's only one method in this shop," he said gratingly, "and that's mine! Leave it or take it away. You're drunk, Laker, and when you're drunk you're a fool."

"Maybe I am. But I'm not such a fool that I'm going to take the risks I've been taking anymore! And you're taking some, too, Malpas. You don't know who's living next door to you."

He remembered this item of information, discovered by accident that very morning.

The man he called Malpas drew his padded dressing gown a little closer around his shoulders, and chuckled.

"I don't know, eh? Don't know that Lacy Marshalt is living next door? Why do you think I'm living here, you fool, if it is not to be next to him?"

The drunkard stared open-mouthed.

"Next to him...what for? He's one of the men you're robbing – he's a crook, but you're robbing him! What do you want to get next to him for?"

"That's my business," said the other curtly. "Leave the stuff and go."

"Leave nothing," said Laker, and rose awkwardly to his feet. "And I'm not leaving this place either, till I know all about you, Malpas. I've been thinking things out. You're not what you look. You don't sit at one end of this dark room and keep the likes of me at the other end for nothing. I'm going to have a good look at you, son. And don't move. You can't see the gun in my hand, but you've got my word it's there!"

He took two steps forward, and then something checked him and threw him back. It was a wire, invisible in the darkness, stretched breast-high from wall to wall. Before he could recover his balance, the light went out.

And then there came upon the man a fit of insane fury. With a roar he leaped forward, snapping the wire. A second obstruction, this time a foot from the ground, caught his legs and brought him sprawling.

"Show a light, you old thief!" he screamed as he staggered to his feet, stool in hand. "You've been robbing me for years – living on me, you old devil! I'm going to squeal, Malpas! You pay or I'll squeal!"

"That's the third time you've threatened me."

The voice was behind him, and he spun round and, in a frenzy of fury, fired. The draped walls muffled the explosion, but in the instant's flash of flame he saw a figure creeping toward the door, and, stark mad with anger, fired again. The reek of burnt cordite hung in that airless room like a veil.

"Put on the light; put on the light!" he screamed.

And then the door opened and he saw the figure slip through. In a second he was out on the landing, but the old man had disappeared. Where had he gone? There was another door, and he flung himself against it.

"Come out!" he roared. "Come out and face me, you Judas!"

He heard a click behind him. The door of the room whence he had come had closed. A flight of stairs led to another story, and he put one foot on the lower stair and stopped. He was conscious that he was still holding the little leather bag that he had taken from his pocket when he came into the room, and, realizing that he was going away empty-handed, with his business incomplete, he hammered at the door behind which he guessed his employer was sheltering.

"Aw, come out, Malpas! There'll be no trouble. I'm a bit drunk, I guess."

There was no answer.

"I'm sorry, Malpas."

He saw something at his feet, and, stooping, picked it up. It was a waxen chin, perfectly modelled and coloured, and it had evidently been held in position by two elastic bands, one of which was broken. The sight of this tickled him and he burst into a yell of laughter.

"Say, Malpas! I've got a part of your face!" he said. "Come out, or I'll take this funny chin of yours to the police. Maybe they'll want to recover the rest of you."

No answer came, and, still chuckling, he went down the stairs and sought to open the front door. There was no handle, and the keyhole was tiny, and, squinting through, he could see nothing.

"Malpas!"

His big voice came echoing down from the empty rooms above, and with a curse he flew up the stairs again. He was halfway to the first landing when something dropped. Looking up, he saw the hateful face above, saw the black weight falling, and strove to avoid it. Another second and he was sliding down the stairs, an inert mass.

THE QUEEN OF FINLAND'S NECKLACE

There was a dance at the American Embassy. The sidewalk was spanned by a striped awning, a strip of red carpet ran down the steps to the kerb, and for an hour glittering limousines had been bringing the distinguished and privileged guests to join the throng already gathered in the none too spacious saloons of the Embassy.

When the stream of cars had dried to the merest trickle, a compact, jovial-faced man stepped down from a big machine and walked leisurely past the fringe of sightseers. He nodded genially to the London policeman who kept the passage clear, and passed into the hall.

"Colonel James Bothwell," he said to the footman, and made his slow progress to the saloon.

"Excuse me."

A good-looking man in evening dress took his arm affectionately and diverted him toward a small anteroom fitted as a buffet, and at this early hour deserted.

Colonel Bothwell raised his eyebrows in good-natured surprise at this familiarity. His attitude seemed to say: You are a perfect stranger to me, probably one of these queerly friendly Americans, so I must tolerate your company.

"No," said the stranger gently.

"No?"

Colonel Bothwell's eyebrows could not go any higher, so he reversed his facial processes and frowned.

"No – I think not."

The grey eyes smiling down into the Colonel's were twinkling with amusement.

"My dear American friend," said the Colonel, trying to disengage his arm. "I really do not understand…you have made a mistake."

The other man shook his head slowly.

"I never make mistakes – and I am English, as you very well know, and you are English, too, in spite of your caricature of the New England accent. My poor old Slick, it is too bad!"

Slick Smith sighed, but gave no other evidence of his disappointment.

"If an American citizen can't make a friendly call on his own Ambassador without lashin' the bull-pen to fury, why, sump'n's wrong, that's all. See here, Captain, I got an invitation. And if my Ambassador wants to see me I guess that's no business of yours."

Captain Dick Shannon chuckled softly.

"He doesn't want to see you, Slick. He'd just hate to see a clever English crook around here with a million dollars' worth of diamonds within reach. He might be glad to see Colonel Bothwell of the 94th Cavalry on a visit to London and anxious to shake him by the hand, but he has no use at all for Slick Smith, jewel thief, confidence man, and super-opportunist. Have a drink with me before you go?"

Slick sighed again.

"Grape juice," he said laconically, and indicated the bottle which was otherwise labelled. "And you're wrong if you think I'm here on business. That's a fact, Captain. Curiosity is my vice, and I was curious to see Queen Riena's diamond necklace. Maybe it's the last time I'll see it. Go easy with that water, George – whisky can't swim."

He stared gloomily at the glass in his hand before he swallowed its contents at a gulp.

"But in a way I'm glad you spotted me. I got the invitation through a friend. Knowing what I know, my coming here was the act of one who imagines he is being followed by black dogs and poisoned by his spiritual adviser. But I'm curious. And I'm cursed with the detective instinct. You've heard of them nuts, Jekyll and Hyde? That's me. Every man's got his dreams, Shannon. Even a busy."

"Even a busy," agreed Dick Shannon.

"Some men dream about the way they'd spend a million," Slick went on pensively. "Some men dream of how they'd save a girl from starvation and worse, and be a brother to her until she got to love him...*you* know! Between jobs I dream of how I would unravel deadly mysteries. Like Stormer – the busy thief-taker that gave me away to you. They've got something on me."

It was perfectly true that Shannon had had his first intimation of Slick's character from that famous agency.

"Do we meet now as brother detectives?" he asked, "or are we just plain busy and – ?"

"Say 'thief' – don't worry about my feelings," begged Slick. "Yes, I'm a busy tonight."

"And the Queen's diamonds?"

Slick drew a long breath.

"They're marked," he said. "I'm curious to know how they'll take 'em. There's a clever gang working the job – you won't expect me to give names, will you? If you do you've got a shock coming."

"Are they in the Embassy?" asked Dick quickly.

"I don't know. That's what I came to see. I'm not one of these professionals who take no interest in the game. I'm like a doctor – I like to see other people's operations; you can learn things that you'd never guess if you had nothing to study but your own work."

Shannon thought for a moment.

"Wait here – and keep your hands off the silver," he said, and, leaving the indignant Slick, he hurried into the crowded room, pushing his way through the throng until he came to a clear space where the Ambassador stood talking to a tall, tired-looking woman whose protection was the main reason for his being at the Embassy ball.

From her neck hung a scintillating chain that flashed and glimmered with her every languid movement. Turning to survey the guests, he presently singled out a monocled young man engaged in an animated conversation with one of the secretaries of the Embassy, and, catching his eye, he brought him to his side.

"Steel, Slick Smith is here, and he tells me that there will be an attempt made to pull away the Queen's necklace. You are not to allow her out of your sight. Get an Embassy man to verify the list of guests, and bring any to me that can't be accounted for."

He went back to Slick and found him taking his third free drink.

"Listen, Slick. Why did you come here, if you knew the robbery was planned for tonight? If you are not in it, you'd be suspected right away."

"That certainly occurred to me," said the man. "Hence my feeling of disquiet. That's a new word I learned last week."

From where they stood, the main doorway of the saloon was visible. People were still arriving, and, as he looked, a big-framed man of middle age came in, and with him a girl of such remarkable beauty that even the hardened Slick stared. They were gone out of sight before Dick Shannon could observe them closely.

"That's a good-looker. Martin Elton isn't here, either. That girl goes about a whole lot with Lacy."

"Lacy?"

"The Honourable Lacy Marshalt. He's a millionaire — one of the tough sort that started life in a rough house and is always ready for another. You know the lady, Captain?"

Dick nodded. Most people knew Dora Elton. She was one of the smart people you saw at first nights, or met in the ultrafashionable supper clubs. Lacy Marshalt he did not know save by repute.

"She's a good-looker," said Slick again, wagging his head admiringly. "Lord! What a good-looker! If she were a wife of mine she shouldn't run around with Lacy. No, sir. But they do that sort of thing in London."

"And in New York and Chicago, and in Paris, Madrid and Bagdad," said Shannon. "Now, Percy!"

"You want me to go? Well, you've spoilt my evening, Captain. I came here for information and guidance. I'd never have climbed into a white shirt if I'd guessed you were here."

Dick escorted him to the door and waited until the man's hired car had driven away. Then he returned to the ballroom to watch and wait.

A guest strolling negligently into an unfrequented passage of the Embassy saw a man sitting reading, pipe in mouth.

"Sorry," said the intruder. "I seem to have lost my way."

"I think you have," said the reader coolly, and the guest, a perfectly honest and innocent rambler, retired hastily, wondering why the watcher should have planted his chair beneath the switchboard from which all the lights in the house were controlled. Shannon was taking no risks.

At one o'clock, to his great relief, Her Majesty of Finland made her departure for the hotel in Buckingham Gate, where she was staying incognita. Dick Shannon stood, bareheaded, in the fog till the rear lights had gone out of sight. On the seat by the driver was an armed detective – he had no fear that majesty would not reach its bedroom safely.

"That lets you out, Shannon, eh?"

The smiling Ambassador received his report with as much relief as the detective had felt.

"I heard an attempt was to be made, through my own detective," he said; "but then, one always hears such stories in connection with every function of this character."

Dick Shannon drove his long touring car back to Scotland Yard, and he drove at a snail's pace, for the fog was very thick and the way intersected with confusing crossroads. Twice he found himself on the sidewalk; in Victoria Street he all but collided with a bus that was weather-bound and stationary.

He crawled past Westminster Abbey, and, guided by the booming notes of Big Ben, navigated himself to the Embankment and through the archway of Scotland Yard.

"Get somebody to garage my car," he instructed the policeman on duty. "I shall walk home – it's safer."

"The inspector was asking for you, sir – he's gone down the Embankment."

"A pleasant night for a walk," smiled Dick, wiping his smarting eyes.

"T P are searching for the body of a man who was thrown into the river tonight," was the startling rejoinder.

"Thrown − you mean jumped?"

"No, sir, thrown. A Thames police patrol was rowing under the Embankment wall when the fog was a little thinner than it is now, and they saw the man lifted up to the parapet and pushed over. The sergeant in charge blew his whistle, but none of our men was near, and the chap, whoever it was who did the throwing, got away − they're dragging for the body now. Just this side of the Needle. The inspector asked me to tell you this if you came in."

Dick Shannon did not hesitate. The lure of his comfortable quarters and the cheery fire was a lure no longer. He groped his way across the broad Embankment, and, with the long parapet to guide him, went quickly along the riverside. The fog was black now, and the mournful hoot of the river tugs had ceased as their baffled captains gave up the struggle.

Near the obelisk that records the past glories of Egypt, he found a little knot of men standing, and, recognizing him at close quarters, the uniformed inspector advanced a pace to meet him.

"It is a murder case − T P have just recovered the body."

"Drowned?"

"No, sir: the man was clubbed to death before he was thrown into the water. If you'll come down to the steps you'll see him."

"What time did this happen?"

"At nine o'clock tonight − or rather, last night. It is nearly two now."

Shannon descended the shallow steps that lead to the water on either side of the obelisk. The bow of a rowboat came out of the fog and swung round so that the Thing which lay huddled in the stern was visible in the light of the pocket lamps.

"I've made a rough search," said the sergeant of the patrol. "There's nothing in his pockets, but he ought to be easy to identify − there's an old knife wound across his chin."

"Humph!" said Dick Shannon, looking. "We'll make another search later."

He went back to headquarters with the inspector, and the entrance hall, which he had left silent and deserted, was now bustling with life. For in his absence news had come through which set Scotland Yard humming, and brought from their beds every reserve detective within the Metropolitan Area.

The Queen of Finland's car had been held up in the darkest part of The Mall, the detective had been shot down, and Her Majesty's diamond chain had passed into the fog. Nor was it to be found again until a certain girl, at that moment dreaming uneasily about chickens, came to the glare and sorrow of the great city to visit the sister who hated her.

AUDREY

"Peter and Paul fetched four shillin's each," reported old Mrs Graffitt, peering near-sightedly at the coins as she laid them on the table. "Harriet, Martha, Jenny, Elizabeth, Queenie, and Holga – "

"Olga," corrected the girl sitting at the table, pencil in hand. "Let us be respectful, even to hens."

"They fetched half a crown each from Mr Gribs, the butcher. It's unchristian to call hens by name, anyhow."

Audrey Bedford made a rapid calculation.

"With the furniture that makes thirty-seven pounds ten shillings," she said, "which will about pay the hen-feed man and your wages, and leave me enough to get to London."

"If I had my rights," said Mrs Graffitt, sniffing tearfully, "I'd get more than my wages. I've looked after you ever since before your poor dear mother died, obliging you as no other mortal woman would. And now I'm cast aside without a home, and I've got to live with my eldest son."

"You're lucky to have an eldest son," said Audrey, unmoved.

"If you gave me a pound for luck – "

"Whose luck? Not mine, you dear old humbug," laughed the girl. "Mrs Graffitt, don't be silly! You've been living on this property like a – a fighting cat! Poultry farming doesn't pay and never will pay, when your chief of staff has a private sale for the eggs. I was working it out the other day, and I reckoned that you've had forty pounds' worth of eggs a year."

12

"Nobody have ever said I was a thief," quavered the old woman, her hands trembling. "I've looked after you since you were a bit of a girl, and it's very hard to be told that you're a thief." She wept gulpily into her handkerchief.

"Don't cry," said Audrey; "the cottage is damp enough."

"Where will you be going, miss?" Mrs Graffitt tactfully passed over the question of her honesty.

"I don't know; London, perhaps."

"Got any relations there, miss?"

Perhaps, at this the last moment, the late owner of Beak Farm would be a little communicative. The Bedfords always were closer than oysters.

"Never you mind. Get me a cup of tea and then come for your wages."

"London's a horruble place." Mrs Graffitt shook her head. "Murders and suicides and robberies and what nots. Why, they robbed a real queen the other night!"

"Goodness!" said Audrey mechanically.

She was wondering what had happened to six other chickens that Mrs Graffitt had not reported upon.

"Robbed her of hundreds of thousan's' worth of diamonds," she said impressively. "You ought to read the papers more – you miss life."

"And talking of robbery," said Audrey gently, "what happened to Myrtle and Primrose and Gwen and Bertha – "

"Oh, them?" For a second even Mrs Graffitt was confused. "Didn't I give you the money? It must have slipped through a hole in my pocket. I've lost it."

"Don't bother," said Audrey. "I'll send for the village policeman – he's a wonderful searcher."

Mrs Graffitt found the money almost immediately.

The old woman shuffled into the low-roofed kitchen and Audrey looked around the familiar room. The chair on which her mother had sat, her hard face turned to the blackened fireplace, Audrey had burnt. One charred leg still showed in the fire.

No, there was nothing here of tender memory. It was a room of drudgery and repression. She had never known her father, and Mrs Bedford had never spoken of him. He had been a bad lot, and through his wickedness had forced a woman of gentle birth to submit to the hard life that had been hers.

"Is he dead, Mother?" the child had asked.

"I hope so," was the uncompromising reply.

Dora had never asked such inconvenient questions, but then she was older, nearer in sympathy to the woman, shared her merciless nature and her prejudices.

Mrs Graffitt had brought her tea and counted her money before she wailed her farewell.

"I'll have to kiss you before I go," she sobbed.

"I'll give you an extra shilling not to," said Audrey hastily, and Mrs Graffitt took the shilling.

It was all over. Audrey passed through the December wreckage of the garden, opened a gate, and, taking a short cut to the churchyard, found the grave and stood silently before it, her hands clasped.

"Goodbye," she said evenly, and, dry-eyed, went back to the house.

The end and the beginning. She was not sorry; she was not very glad. Her box of books had already gone to the station and was booked through to the parcels office at Victoria.

As to the future – she was fairly well educated, had read much, thought much, and was acquainted with the rudiments of shorthand – self-taught in the long winter evenings, when Mrs Graffitt thought, and said, that she would be better employed with a knitting needle.

"There's tons of time," growled the village omnibus driver as he threw her bag into the dark and smelly interior. "If it wasn't for these jiggering motorcars I'd cut it finer. But you've got to drive careful in these days."

A prophetic saying.

The girl was stepping into the bus after her bag when the stranger appeared. He looked like a lawyer's middle-aged clerk, having just that lack of sartorial finish.

"Excuse me, Miss Bedford. My name is Willitt. Can I have a few words with you this evening when you return?"

"I am not returning," she said. "Do I owe you anything?" Audrey always asked that question of polite strangers. Usually they said "yes," for Mrs Graffitt had the habit which was locally known as "chalking up."

"No, miss. Not coming back? Could I have your address? I wanted to see you on a – well, an important matter."

He was obviously agitated.

"I can't give you my address, I'm afraid. Give me yours and I will write to you."

He carefully blacked out the description of the business printed on the card, and substituted his own address.

"Now then!" called the aggrieved driver. "If you wait any longer you'll miss that train."

She jumped into the bus and banged the door tight.

It was at the corner of Ledbury Lane that the accident happened. Coming out on to the main road, Dick Shannon took the corner a little too sharply, and the back wheels of his long car performed a graceful skid. The bump that followed was less graceful. The back of the car struck the Fontwell village omnibus just as it was drawing abreast of the car, neatly sliced off the back wheel and robbed that ancient vehicle of such dignity as weather and wear had left to it.

There was a solitary passenger, and she had reached the muddy road before Dick, hat in hand, had reached her, alarm and penitence on his good-looking face.

"I'm most awfully sorry. You're not hurt, I hope?"

He thought she was seventeen, although she was two years older. She was cheaply dressed; her long coat was unmistakably renovated. Even the necklet of fur about her throat was shabby and worn. These facts he did not notice. He looked down into a face that seemed flawless. The curve of eyebrows or set of eyes perhaps, the perfect mouth maybe, or else it was the texture and colouring of the skin... He dreaded that she should speak, and that, in the crude enunciation of the peasant, he should lose the illusion of the princess.

"Thank you – I was a little scared. I shan't catch my train." She looked ruefully at the stricken wheel.

The voice dispelled his fears. The ragged princess was a lady.

"Are you going to Barnham Junction? I am passing there," he said. "And anyway, if I hadn't been going that way, I must go to send relief for this poor lad."

The driver of the bus, to whom he was referring in such compassionate terms, had climbed down from his perch, his grey beard glittering with rain, his rheumy eye gleaming malevolently.

"Why don't you look where you're going?" He wheezed the phrases proper to such an occasion. "Want all the road, dang ye?"

Dick unstrapped his coat and felt for his pocketbook.

"Jehu," he said, "here is my card, a Treasury bill, and my profound apologies."

"My name's Herbert Jiles," said the driver suspiciously as he took the card and the money.

"Jehu is a fanciful name," said Dick, "and refers to the son of Nimshi, who 'driveth furiously.' "

"I was nearly walking," said the indignant Mr Jiles. "It was you as was driving furiously!"

"Help will come from Barnham," said Dick. "Now, young lady, can you trust yourself alone with me in this car of Juggernaut?"

"I think so," she smiled, and, rescuing her bag from the bus, jumped in at his side.

"London is also my destination," said Dick, "but I won't suggest that you come all the way with me, though it would save you a train fare."

She did not answer. He had a feeling that she was being prim, but presently she cleared away that impression.

"I think I will go by train: my sister may come to meet me at the station."

There was no very great confidence in her tone.

"Do you live hereabouts?"

"At Fontwell," she said. "I had a cottage there. It used to be Mother's, until she died. Have you ever tried to live on eggs?"

Dick was startled.

"Not entirely," he said. "They are extremely nutritive, I understand, but – "

"I don't mean eat them; I mean, have you ever tried to get a living by poultry farming?"

He shook his head.

"Well, don't," she said emphatically. "Hens are not what they used to be. Mrs Graffitt – she kept house for me and absorbed my profits – says that a great change has come over hens since the war. She isn't sure whether it's Bolshevism or Spanish influenza."

He laughed.

"So you've given it up?"

She nodded several times.

"I can't say that I've sold the old home: it was sold by bits in the shape of mortgages. That sounds pathetic, doesn't it? Well, it isn't! The old home is ugly and full of odd corners that bumped your head, and smells of a hundred generations of owners who never took baths, except when the roof leaked. And the drainage system goes back to the days of the Early Britons, and none of the windows fits. My sympathies are entirely with the grasping mortgagee – poor soul!"

"You're lucky to have a nice sister to meet you at the station," he said. He was thinking of her as seventeen or perhaps a little younger, and his manner was a trifle paternal.

"I suppose I am," she said without enthusiasm. "This is the beginning of Barnham, isn't it?"

"This is the beginning of Barnham," he agreed, and a few minutes later brought the machine before the station entrance.

He got down after her, carrying her pitiably light baggage to the platform, and insisted upon waiting until the train came in.

"Your sister lives in London, of course?"

"Yes: in Curzon Street."

It was queer that she should have told him that. Nobody in the county was even aware that she had a sister.

Dick did not show his surprise.

"Is she…" It was a delicate question. "Is she – er – working there?"

17

"Oh, no. She is Mrs Martin Elton."

She wondered at herself as she said the words.

"The devil she is!" he was startled into saying.

The train was signalled at that moment, and he hurried off to get her some magazines for the journey.

"It is awfully kind of you, Mr—? My name is Audrey Bedford."

"I shall remember that," he smiled. "I've a wonderful memory for names. Mine is Jackson."

He stood watching the train until the dull red of the tail lamps swung round a curve out of sight. Then he went slowly back to his car and drove to the police station to report his accident.

Mrs Martin Elton, and that was her sister! If he had given her his real name, and she had gone to Curzon Street and told pretty Dora Elton that she had passed the time of day with Captain Richard Shannon, the harmonies of the bijou house in Curzon Street might very well have been disturbed.

And with good reason. Dora Elton was the one crook in London that Dick Shannon was aching to trap.

THE HON. LACY

Lacy Marshalt was once a Senator of the Legislative Council of South Africa, therefore he was by courtesy called "Honourable" – a fact which was, to Mr Tonger, his gentleman, a source of considerable amusement.

He came out of his bath one drear morning, simply attired in trousers and silk singlet, under which the great body muscles showed plainly. Thus, he had less the appearance of a legislator than what his name had stood for in South Africa – the soldier of fortune who had won at least this guerdon of success, a palatial home in Portman Square.

He stood for a long time staring moodily down into the square. Rain had followed the fog as a matter of course; it always rained in England – doleful, continuously, like a melancholic woman. He thought longingly of his sun-washed home at Muizenburg, the broad, league-long beach and the blue seas of False Bay, the spread of his vineyard running up to the slopes of Constantia...

He turned his head back to the bedroom with a jerk. Somebody was tapping softly on the door.

"Come in!"

The door opened and his old valet sidled in with his sly smile.

"Got the mail," he said unceremoniously, and put a handful of letters on the little writing table.

"Say 'sir,' " growled Lacy. "You're getting out of the habit again."

Tonger twisted one side of his face in a grin.

"I'll have to get into it again," he said easily.

"You'd better: I can get a hundred valets in London for a quarter of what I pay you – younger men and twenty times as efficient," threatened his master.

"I dare say, but they wouldn't do what I do for you," he said; "and you couldn't trust 'em. You can't buy loyalty. I read that in a book the other day."

Lacy Marshalt had chosen one letter from the others, a letter enclosed in a pique-blue envelope and addressed in an illiterate hand. He tore it open and read:

O K Breaking down.

There was no signature.

The big man grunted something and tossed the letter to the valet.

"Send him twenty pounds," he said.

Tonger read the scrap of paper without the slightest hesitation.

"Breaking down?" he mused. "H'm! Can he swim?"

Lacy looked round sharply.

"What do you mean?" he demanded, "Of course he can swim – or could. Swim like a seal. Why?"

"Nothing."

Lacy Marshalt looked at him long and hard.

"I think you're getting soft sometimes. Take a look at that envelope. It has the Matjesfontein postmark. So had the last. Why does he write from there, a hundred miles and more from Cape Town?"

"A blind maybe," suggested Tonger. He put the scrap of paper in his waistcoat pocket. "Why don't you winter in the Cape, *baas*?" he asked.

"Because I choose to winter in England."

Marshalt was putting on his shirt as he spoke, and something in his tone riveted the man's attention.

"I'll tell you something, Lacy, hate's fear!"

The other stared at him.

"Hate's fear? What do you mean?"

20

"I mean that you can't hate a man without fearing him. It's the fear that turns dislike into hate. Cut out the fear and it's, well, anything – contempt, anything you like. But it can't be hate."

Marshalt had resumed his dressing.

"Read that in a book, too?" he asked, before the glass.

"That's out of my own nut," said Tonger, taking up a waistcoat and giving it a perfunctory snick with a whisk brush. "Here, Lacy, who's the fellow that lives next door? I've meant to ask you that. Malpas or some such name. I was talking to a copper last night, and he said that it's believed that he's crazy. He lives alone, has no servants, and does all his own housework. There's about six sets of flats in the building, but he won't let any of them. Owns the whole shoot. Who is he?"

Lacy Marshalt growled over his shoulder:

"You seem to know all about it: why ask me?"

Tonger was rubbing his nose absent-mindedly.

"Suppose it's him?" he asked, and his master spun round.

"Suppose you get out of here, you gossiping old fool!"

Tonger, in no wise disconcerted by the magnate's ferocity, laid the waistcoat on the back of a chair.

"That private detective you sent for the other day is waiting," he said, and Lacy cursed him.

"Why didn't you tell me?" he snarled. "You're getting useless, Tonger. One of these days I'll fire you out – and take that grin off your face! Ask him to come up."

The shabby-looking man who was ushered in smiled deferentially at his employer.

"You can go, Tonger," growled Marshalt.

Tonger went leisurely.

"Well?"

"I traced her," said the agent, and, unfolding his pocketbook, took out a snapshot photograph, handing it to the millionaire.

"It is she," he nodded; "but it wasn't difficult to find her once you knew the village. Who is she?"

"Audrey Bedford."

"Bedford? You're sure?" asked the other quickly. "Does her mother live there?"

"Her mother's dead – five years ago," said the agent.

"Is there another daughter?"

The agent shook his head.

"So far as I can discover, she's the only child. I got a picture of her mother. It was taken at a church fair in 1913, one of a group."

This was the flat parcel he was carrying, and the paper about which he now unfolded. Lacy Marshalt carried the picture to the light…

"That is she!" He pointed to a figure.

"God, how wonderful! When I saw the girl I had a feeling…an instinct."

He cut short the sentence.

"You know her, then, sir?"

"No!" The answer was brusque almost to rudeness. "What is she doing? Living alone?"

"She was practically. She had an old woman in the house who assisted her with a poultry farm. She left for London yesterday. From what they tell me in the village, she is broke and had to sell up."

The millionaire stood in his favourite attitude by the window, staring at nothing, his strong, harsh face expressionless.

How wonderful! "Hate is fear," whispered the echo of Tonger's voice – he shook off the reminder with a roll of his broad shoulders.

"A pretty girl, eh?"

"Lovely, I thought," said the detective. "I'm not much of a judge, but she seemed to me to be out of the ordinary."

Lacy grunted his agreement.

"Yes…out of the ordinary."

"I got into a bit of trouble at Fontwell – I don't think anything will come of it, but you ought to know in case it comes back to you." The man showed some signs of discomfort. "We private detectives find we work much better if we give people the idea that we're the regular goods. I had to pretend I was looking for a chicken thief – down at the Crown Inn they thought I was a Yard man."

"There's not much harm in that, Mr Willitt," said the other with his frosty smile.

"Not as a rule," said Willitt, "only, by a bit of bad luck, Captain Shannon happened to stop at the inn to change a tyre."

"Who's Shannon?"

"If you don't know him, don't look for him," said Willitt. "He's the biggest thing they've got at the Yard. The new Executive Commissioner. Up till now the Commissioners have been office men without even the power of arrest. They brought Shannon from the Indian Intelligence because there have been a few scandals lately – bribery cases. He gave me particular hell for describing myself as a regular. And his tongue... Gee! That fellow can sting at a mile!"

"He didn't discover what you were inquiring about – the girl?"

The agent shook his head.

"No. That's about the only thing he didn't discover. You'd think he had all his mind occupied with the Queen of Finland's necklace, wouldn't you?"

Apparently Lacy did not hear him speak. His mind was concentrated upon the girl and the possibilities that followed.

"You allowed her to go without getting her address? That was pretty feeble. Go down and get it. Then follow her up and scrape an acquaintance. You can be a businessman on the lookout for investment – lend her money – all that she requires – but do it in a way that doesn't frighten her."

He took from his pocket-case half a dozen notes, crushed them into a ball and tossed them into the outstretched hand.

"Bring her here to dinner one night," he said softly. "You can be called away on the phone."

Willitt looked hard at him and shook his head in a half-hearted fashion.

"I don't know...that's not my line..."

"I want to talk to her – tell her something she doesn't know. There's five hundred for you."

The private detective blinked quickly.

"Five hundred? I'll see..."

Left alone, Lacy went back to the window and his contemplation of the reeking square.

"Hate is fear!"

It was his boast that he had never feared. Ruthless, remorseless, he had walked over a pavement of human hearts to his goal, and he was not afraid. There were women in three continents who cursed his name and memory. Bitter-hearted men who brooded vengeance by night and day. He did not fear. His hatred of Dan Torrington was...just hate.

So he comforted himself, but deep down in the secret places of his soul the words of the old valet burned and could not be dimmed – "Hate is Fear."

SLICK – PHILOSOPHER

"It is nothing," said Shannon, surveying the battered mudguard.

"Had a collision?" asked Steel, his assistant, interested.

"Yes – a very pleasant one. In fact, the best ever!"

They went into the narrow passage that was the approach to Dick Shannon's apartment.

"No, I haven't been waiting long," said Steel, as Dick unlocked the door of his sitting-room. "I knew you would come back here. Did you see the Bognor man?"

"Yes – he split…after a little persuasion. Steel, do you know anything about the girl Elton's relations?"

"I didn't even know that she had any," said the other.

"Perhaps Slick knows. I've told him to be here at six. I wonder if she got to town all right?"

"Who?" asked the other in surprise, and the Commissioner was for the moment embarrassed.

"I was thinking of…somebody," he said awkwardly, and changed the subject. "Has the body been identified?" he asked.

Steel shook his head.

"The man was from abroad, probably South Africa," he said. "He was wearing *veltshoen*, a native-made boot, very popular among the Boers, and the tobacco in his pouch is undoubtedly Magaliesberg. There's no other tobacco like it. He may have been in England some weeks, but, on the other hand, it is likely that he has just landed. The *Buluwayo* and *Balmoral Castle* arrived last week, and in all probability he came on one of those ships. In fact, they are the only two that have come from South Africa in the past fortnight. Did the Bognor man know anything about the Queen's jewels?"

"Nothing. He said that Elton had quarrelled with him some time ago, and they did no business together. Mainly the talk was, as is usual in these cases, parable and metaphor. You can never get a thief to call a spade a spade."

He stood looking down at the table deep in thought, and then: "I suppose her sister *did* meet her?"

Steel blinked.

"Whose sister, sir?" he asked, and this time Dick Shannon laughed.

"It is certain she did," he said, continuing his train of thought. "At any rate, she'd stop her coming to Curzon Street, and would shepherd her off to some hotel."

A light dawned upon Steel.

"I see, you're talking about Elton?"

"I'm talking about Elton," agreed Captain Shannon, "and another. But the other won't interest you. You're having the house watched?"

"Elton's? Yes. We've had to go very carefully, because Elton's a shrewd fellow."

Dick bit his lip.

"Nothing will happen before a quarter to nine tonight, unless I'm greatly mistaken. At that hour the Queen of Finland's necklace will leave Curzon Street, and I personally will follow it to its destination, because I'm most anxious to meet the fifth member of the gang, who, I guess, is a foreigner."

"And then?" asked Steel when he paused.

"Then I shall take Dora Elton with the goods. And that's just what I've been waiting for for a long time."

"Why not Bunny?" asked Steel, and Dick smiled.

"Bunny's got plenty of courage: I'll give him credit for that; but not that kind of courage. It requires valour of an unimaginative kind to walk through London with stolen property in your pocket and the knowledge that half the police in town are looking for you. That isn't Bunny! No, his wife will do the trick."

He looked at his watch impatiently, then took up a timetable from his writing desk.

"Are you going away?" asked Steel in surprise.

"No," impatiently. "I am seeing what time her train arrives."

He turned the leaves and presently ran his finger down a column, then looked at his watch again as though he had forgotten what he had already seen.

"She arrived half an hour ago. I wonder – "

Steel was wondering, too. He had never seen Dick Shannon in that mood before. But any explanation was denied by the arrival of Mr Slick Smith. He came without diffidence, a very self-possessed, neatly dressed man, whose unlined face, twinkling eye, and expensive cigar advertised his peace with the world. He nodded to Steel, and received a sympathetic grin in reply. Not until he had taken his departure did Dick come to the point.

"I sent for you, Slick, to ask your advice. The robbery came off all right."

"So I see by the morning newspapers," said Slick, "though I do not place too great a credence in the morning press. Personally, I prefer the afternoon variety; they haven't time to think up trimmings, and you get your news without dilution."

"Elton was in it, you know?"

Slick raised his eyebrows.

"You surprise me," he said politely. "Dear me! Mr Elton? He is the last person in the world one would suspect of larcenous proceedings."

"Let's cut out the persiflage and get right down to cases," said Dick, pushing the decanter toward his visitor. "What do you know about Mrs Elton?"

"A most charming lady! A most de–lightful lady! Though it would be an exaggeration to describe her soul as of the white virginal variety. I don't mind confessing that, when I think about souls at all, I prefer them delicately tinted, rose du barri, eau de nil – anything but lemon."

"What was she before she married?"

Slick shrugged his shoulders.

"Gossip and scandal are loathsome to me," he said reluctantly. "All I know about her is that she was a good woman but a bad actress. I think she must have married Elton to reform him. So many of our best women do that sort of thing."

"And has she?" asked Shannon sarcastically.

Again Mr Smith shrugged.

"I heard the other day that he was strong for prohibition. Is that reform? It must be, I suppose."

He poured out a liberal portion of whisky and sent the seltzer sizzling into the glass.

"You can't say anything in favour of booze, however clever you may be. You may say: 'Oh, but I'm a moderate drinker: why should my allowance be curtailed because that horrible grocery man gets drunk and beats his wife?' To which I reply: There are fifty thousand babies in England under the age of six months. Babies who would welcome with infantile joy a nice, bright razor to play with. And you might give them each the razor, Captain, and not more than one in fifty thousand would cut his or her young throat. Must we then deny the other forty-nine thousand and odd the joy and happiness of playing with a hair-mower because one fool baby cut his young head off? Yes, sir, we must. Common sense tells us that what happened to one might just as well happen to the fifty thousand. Do I speak words of wisdom? I do. Thank you – your very good health."

He smacked his lips in critical appreciation.

"Liqueur, and at least twenty years old. Would that all whisky was like that – there would be fewer suicides."

Dick was watching him closely, well aware that he was delicately shifting the conversation into another channel.

"Has she a sister?"

Mr Smith finished the remainder of his glass.

"If she has," he said, "God help her!"

THE SISTERS

Audrey spent a quarter of an hour waiting on Victoria Station, alternately making short excursions in search of Dora and studying the news bills, which were given up to the Robbery of the Queen of Finland and the new clues that had accumulated during the day. Twenty minutes passed, and Dora had not appeared. Mrs Graffitt had an exasperating habit of forgetting to post letters, and she remembered she had entrusted the announcement of her plans to the old woman.

Her stock of spare cash was too small to rise to a taxi, and she sought information from a policeman whose knowledge of bus routes was evidently encyclopaedic. After waiting for some minutes in the drizzle she found one that was bound for Park Lane, from which thoroughfare Curzon Street runs. London was a place of mystery to her; but by diligent searching she at last found the little house and rang the visitors' bell. A short delay, and the door was opened by a smart maidservant, who looked askance at the shabby visitor.

"Mrs Martin Elton is engaged. Have you come from Seville's?"

"No, I've come from Sussex," said the girl with a faint smile. "Will you tell Mrs Elton that it is her sister?"

The maid looked a little dubious, but ushered her into a small, chilly sitting-room and went out, closing the door. Evidently she was not expected, thought Audrey, and the uneasiness with which she had approached the visit was intensified.

Their correspondence had been negligible. Dora was never greatly interested either in her mother or what she magniloquently described to her friends as "the farm"; and when the younger girl had in her desperation written for assistance, there had come, after a long interval, a five-pound note and a plain intimation that Mrs Martin Elton had neither the means nor the inclination for philanthropy.

Dora had gone on to the stage at an early age, and had made, a few weeks before her mother's death, what had all the appearance of a good marriage. In the eyes of that hard, unbending woman, Dora could do no wrong, and even her systematic neglect never altered the older woman's affection, but seemed rather to increase its volume. Day and night, year in and year out, Dora had been the model held before her sister. Dora was successful; that, in Mrs Bedford's eyes, excused all shortcomings. She had been successful even as an actress; her name had appeared large on the bills of touring companies; her photograph had appeared even in the London papers. By what means she had secured her fame and founded her independence, Mrs Bedford did not know and cared less.

The door opened suddenly and a girl came in. She was taller and fairer than her sister, and in some ways as beautiful, though her mouth was straighter and the eyes lacked Audrey's ready humour.

"My dear girl, where on earth have you come from?" she asked in consternation.

She offered a limp, jewelled hand, and, stooping, pecked the girl's cold cheek.

"Didn't you get my letter, Dora?"

Dora Elton shook her head.

"No, I had no letter. You've grown, child. You were a gawky kid when I saw you last."

"One does grow," admitted Audrey gravely. "I've sold the cottage."

The elder girl's eyes opened.

"But why on earth have you done that?"

"It sold itself," said Audrey. "In other words, I pawned it bit by bit until there was nothing of it left; so I disposed of the chickens – probably the only eggless chickens in the country and worth a whole lot of money as biological curiosities."

"And you've come here?"

There was no mistaking the unwelcome in Dora's tone.

"That is very awkward! I can't possibly put you up here, and I don't think it was particularly kind of you, Audrey, to sell the farm. Dear Mother died there, and that in itself should have made the place sacred to you."

"All things associated with Mother are sacred to me," said Audrey quietly, "but I hardly think it is necessary to starve myself to death to prove my love for Mother. I don't want very much from you, Dora – just a place to sleep for a week, until I can find something to do."

Dora was pacing the little room, her hands behind her, her brows knit in a frown. She wore an afternoon frock, the value of which would have kept Audrey in comfort for a month; her diamond ear-rings, the double rope of pearls about her neck, were worth a small fortune.

"I've some people here to tea," she said, "and I'm having a dinner party tonight. I don't know what on earth to do with you, Audrey. You can't come to dinner in that kit."

She looked contemptuously at the girl's uncomely wardrobe. "You had better go to a hotel. There are plenty of cheap places in Bloomsbury. Then make yourself smart and come and see me on Monday."

"It will cost money to make me smart on Monday or Tuesday or any other day in the week," said Audrey calmly, "and two nights at a third-rate hotel will exhaust my supplies."

Dora clicked her lips.

"It's really too bad of you, dropping down from the clouds like this," she said irritably. "I haven't the slightest idea what I can do. Just wait – I'll see Martin."

She flung out of the room, leaving behind her a faint fragrance of quelques fleurs, and Audrey Bedford's lips curled in a faint smile. She was not sorry for herself. Dora had behaved as she had expected her to behave. She waited for a long time; it was nearly half an hour before the door handle turned again and her sister came in. Some magical transformation had occurred, for Dora was almost genial, though her good humour sounded a little unreal.

31

"Martin says you must stay," she said. "Come up with me." She led the way up the narrow stairs, past an entry behind which there was the sound of laughter and talk, and on the second floor stopped and opened a door, switching on the light. Audrey guessed that it was the second-best bedroom in the house, and reserved for the principal partakers of the Elton hospitality.

"You have no friends in London, have you, old girl?" asked Dora carelessly.

She stood watching in the doorway while the girl put down her bag.

"None," said Audrey. "This is a pretty bedroom, Dora."

"Yes, isn't it? Anybody know you've come up?"

"Mrs Graffitt knows I've come to town, but she doesn't know where."

She had expected her sister to leave her as soon as she had been shown into the room, but Dora lingered in the doorway, having apparently something to say.

"I'm afraid I've been rather a brute to you, Audrey," she said, laying her hand on the girl's arm. "But you're going to be a good, sweet angel and forgive me, aren't you? I know you will, because you promised Mother you would do anything for me, darling, didn't you?"

For a second Audrey was touched.

"You know that I would," she said.

"Some day I'll tell you all my secrets," Dora went on. "I can tell you because you're the one person in the world I can trust. Mother used to say that you were so obstinate that the devil couldn't get you to speak if you didn't want to."

Audrey's eyes twinkled in the ghost of a smile.

"Dear Mother was never flattering," she said dryly.

She had loved her mother, but had lived too near to her petty tyrannies and her gross favouritism for love to wear the beautifying veil of tenderness. Dora patted her arm and rose briskly.

"The people are going now. I want you to come down and meet Mr Stanford and Martin. You've never seen Martin?"

"I've seen his photograph," said Audrey.

"He's a good-looker," said Dora carelessly. "You'll probably fall in love with him – 'Bunny' will certainly fall in love with you. He has a weakness for new faces." She turned at the door. "I'm going to trust you, Audrey," she said, and there was an undercurrent of menace in her voice. "Curzon Street has its little skeletons as well as the farm."

"You may say what you like about the farm," said Audrey, her lips twitching, "but the word 'skeleton' can never be applied to those chickens! They ate me to ruin!"

Dora came back to the drawing-room, and the two occupants searched her face.

"Where is she?" asked the taller of the men.

"I've put her in the spare bedroom," said Dora.

Mr Elton stroked his smooth black moustache.

"I'm not sure in my mind whether she ought to be here just now. Give her the money and send her to a hotel."

Dora laughed.

"You've been arguing all afternoon as to how we shall get the stuff to Pierre. Neither of you men want to take the risk of being found with the Queen of Finland's necklace – "

"Not so loud, you fool!" said Martin Elton between his teeth. "Open the window and advertise it, will you?'

"Listen!" commanded Big Bill Stanford. "Go on, Dora. I guess what you say is right enough. It may be a lifer to the man caught with that stuff – but Pierre has got to have it tonight. Who'll take the necklace?"

"Who? Why, my dear little sister!" said Dora coolly. "That girl was born to be useful!"

THE PLOT

Big Bill was no sentimentalist, but in the thing that passed for a soul there was a certain elementary code, the rudiments of what had once been a sense of honour and decent judgement.

"Your sister! Suffering snakes, you couldn't allow a kid like that to take such a risk?"

Dora's smile was her answer. Her husband was biting his nails nervously.

"There may be no risk," he said, "and if there is, isn't it ours, too?"

Stanford stirred uneasily.

"That's so. But we're in this for the profit — and the risk. Suppose they caught her and she squealed?"

"That is the only real risk," said Dora, "and it isn't a big one."

The big man looked thoughtfully at the carpet.

"That stuff has to get out of this house and out of the country — quick!" he said. "It is too big to hold and break up here, and I never pass a newspaper boy but I don't hear the squeal that the papers are putting up. Lock the door, girl."

She obeyed. On the mantelpiece was a beautiful gilt and enamelled clock surmounted by a statuette of a fawn.

Gripping the statuette firmly, he lifted out the greater portion of the clock's interior without in any way affecting the functions of the timepiece, which ticked on. Pressing the spring, one side of the bronze box opened and showed a tightly fitting package of silver paper. This he laid on the baize cloth and unrolled. Instantly there came from the

34

table such a flicker of leaping fires, blue and green and purest white, that Dora's mouth opened in wonder and awe.

"There's seventy thousand pounds there," said Stanford, and thrust out his lower lip thoughtfully. "And there's also ten years for somebody – seven years for the theft and three years for outraged majesty. You cannot rob a visiting queen without putting something on to the sentence."

The dapper man shivered.

"Don't talk about sentences, my dear fellow," he said petulantly. "If Pierre does his part – "

"Pierre will do his part. He'll be waiting at Charing Cross station at nine-fifteen. The question is, who's going to take the stuff?"

There was a silence.

"Audrey will take it," said Dora at last. "I was a fool not to think of it when I saw her. Nobody knows her, and nobody will suspect her. Pierre is easy to recognize. And then, Bunny, out of this business for good." She nodded emphatically. "There's a little old story about a pitcher and a well; and there's Daisy Emming's Life in Prison, published in the *Sunday Globe* – taking them in conjunction I read a Warning to Girls."

"Perhaps Mr Lacy Marshalt will give Martin a directorship," sneered the big man. "When you people get next to what looks like good, easy, honest money, it's surprising how quickly you reform."

"I scarcely know the man," said Dora sharply. "I told you about him, Bunny. He's the man I met at the Denshores' dance. He's a South African and rich, but you couldn't pry loose a red nickel without dynamite."

Martin Elton looked at her suspiciously.

"I didn't know you knew him – " he began.

"Get back to this stuff," snapped Stanford. "There's one thing I want to know – suppose she's caught?"

Another long and painful silence.

"Why not keep it here till the squeal dies down?" asked Elton. "There's no ghost of a suspicion that they connect us with the job."

Stanford looked him straight in the eye.

"Twelve months ago," he said slowly, "when Leyland Hall was cleaned up, you got most of the stuff out of the country through a receiver at Bognor. He gave you a little trouble, didn't he?"

"Yes," said the other shortly; "that is why I hadn't thought of him in connection with this job."

"And you're wise," said Bill, nodding. "Dick Shannon has been spending the greater part of the day with your friend at Bognor!"

Martin Elton's pale face went a shade paler.

"He wouldn't squeal," he said unsteadily.

"I don't know. If a man would squeal to anybody, he'd squeal to Shannon. The English detective service has gone to blue blazes since they introduced gentlemen. I like police whom you can reason with." He jiggled the loose coins in his pocket suggestively. "That's why I say that you can't keep the stuff at this house. Bennett may not have squeaked. On the other hand, he may have emitted squeak-like noises. What do you say, Dora?"

She nodded.

"The stuff ought to go: I've recognized that all along," she said. "Make a parcel of it, Martin."

They watched the man as, wrapping the necklace again in cotton wool, he packed it in an old cigarette box and tied it about with brown paper, and then Stanford asked: "If it comes to squealing, what about your sister?"

Dora considered before she replied.

"I am sure of her," she said.

"Let us see her," said Stanford, when the parcel had been firmly tied and hidden under a sofa cushion, and the top of the clock replaced.

Audrey was sitting in a deep, low chair before the gas-fire, pondering her strange welcome, when she heard Dora's footstep on the stairs.

"You can come down now."

She looked at her sister and made a little face, and, for all her subtlety, could not hide the disparagement in the glance.

"You're a human scarecrow, Audrey! I shall have to buy you some clothes straight away."

Audrey followed her down to the floor below and into the big drawing-room that ran the width of the house. A tall, broad-shouldered man stood with his back to the fire, and on him Audrey's eyes first rested. He was a man of fifty, whose hair was cropped so close that at first she thought he was bald. His deep, forbidding eyes fixed and held her as she entered.

"This is Mr Stanford," introduced Dora. "And this is my little sister."

He held out a huge hand and took hers in a grip that made her wince.

The second man in the room was slight and dapper, and his unusual pallor was emphasized by the small black moustache and the jet black eyebrows. Good-looking, she thought, almost pretty. So this was the great Martin about whom she had heard so many rhapsodies.

"Glad to meet you, Audrey," he said, his admiring eyes never leaving her face. "She's a peach, Dora."

"She's prettier than she was," said Dora indifferently, "but her clothes are terrible."

It was not like Audrey to feel uncomfortable. She was so superior to the trials of poverty that ordinarily she would have laughed good-naturedly at the crude comment. But now, for some reason, she felt embarrassed. It was the unwavering stare of the big man by the fireplace, the cold appraisement of his gaze.

Stanford looked at his watch.

"I'll be going," he said. "I'm glad to have met you, Miss. Perhaps I'll be seeing you again."

She hoped sincerely that he would not.

THE ARREST

Dora signalled to Martin Elton to retire with their guest, and it was when they were left alone that Dora had her story to tell.

It was the story of an injured wife, who had been obliged to fly from the country because of her husband's brutality, leaving behind her the miniature of her child.

"I don't mind confessing to you that we have secured the miniature, Audrey," said Dora, in an outburst of frankness. "I don't think we were strictly legal in our actions – in fact, Martin bribed the servant in Sir John's house to bring it to us. He guesses we have it, and has had us watched day and night, and any attempt we make, either through the post – we are sure he has notified the postal officials – or by messenger, is likely to lead to failure. A friend of this poor dear Lady Nilligan is coming to London tonight, and we have arranged to meet him at the station and hand him the miniature. Now the question is, Audrey, will you be a darling and take it to him? Nobody knows you; his sleuth hounds will not molest you; and you can render this poor woman a great service. Personally, I think there's a little too much sentimentality about it, for I don't see why one miniature should be more valuable than another. But evidently this demented lady thinks it is."

"But what an extraordinary story!" said Audrey, frowning. "Couldn't you send one of your servants? Or couldn't he come here?"

"I tell you the house is watched," said Dora, never the most patient of individuals. "If you don't want to do it – "

"Of course I'll do it," laughed Audrey.

"There is only one point I want to make," her sister interposed, "and it is this: if by any chance this comes out, I want you to promise me that our name shall not come into it. I want you to swear by our dead mother – "

"That is unnecessary," said Audrey, a little coldly. "I will promise – that is enough."

Dora took her in her arms and kissed her.

"You are really a darling," she said; "and you've grown so awfully pretty. I must find a nice man for you."

It was on the tip of Audrey's tongue to suggest that her sister might very well try some other ground of search than that which produced the pallid Martin Elton, for whom she felt an instinctive dislike.

"Of course I'll take it, my dear," she said. "It seems such a little thing to do. And if I meet the grumpy husband, why, I'll just talk to him firmly!"

Apparently Dora's feasts were of a movable kind, for, although Audrey had her dinner in her room, the party of which her sister had spoken did not materialize. At half past eight Dora came up for her, carrying in her hand a small, oblong package, tied and heavily sealed.

"Now remember, you do not know me, you have never been to 508, Curzon Street in your life…" She repeated the admonition, and described in detail the mysterious Pierre. "When you see him, you will go up to him and say: 'This is for Madam' – that, and nothing more."

She repeated the instructions, and made the girl recite them after her. Audrey was at first amused, then a little bored.

"It seems an awful lot of bother to make about so small a thing, but you have succeeded in arousing that conspirator feeling!"

With the package secure in an inside pocket of her coat, she went out into Curzon Street and walked quickly in the direction of Park Lane. She had hardly disappeared before Martin Elton came out. Keeping her in sight, he watched her board a bus, and, hailing a taxicab, followed.

To Audrey the adventure was mildly exciting. She knew neither of the parties of this family quarrel, and found it difficult even to speculate upon their identity. They were probably two very plain, uninteresting people. Family quarrellers usually were. But she was glad of the opportunity of earning her board and keep, and it relieved her of a sense of obligation, for which she was grateful.

The bus put her down opposite Charing Cross station, and, crossing the congested road, she hurried through the courtyard into the station building. There were hundreds of people in the big approach; the night mail was beginning to fill, and passengers and their friends stood in groups before the barriers. She looked for a considerable time before she saw Mr Pierre, a short, stocky man with a square, flaxen beard, who seemed to be wholly absorbed in the animated spectacle. Moving to the other side of him to make absolutely sure, she saw the little mole on his cheek by which she was to identify him. Without further ado, she took the package from her pocket and went up to him.

"This is for Madam," she said.

He started, looked at her searchingly, slipped the package in his pocket, so quickly that she could hardly follow his movements.

"*Bien!*" he said. "Will you thank Monsieur? And – "

He spun round quickly, but the man who had caught his wrist possessed a grip which was not lightly to be shaken. At the same moment somebody slipped an arm in Audrey's.

"I want you, my young friend," said a pleasant voice. "I am Captain Shannon of Scotland Yard."

He stopped, staring down at the frightened face turned up to his.

"My ragged princess!" he gasped.

"Please let me go." She attempted to free herself. She was horribly frightened, and for a second felt physically sick. "I've got to go to – " She checked herself in time.

"To see Mrs Elton, of course," said Shannon, scrutinizing her.

"No, I haven't to see Mrs Elton. I really don't know Mrs Elton," she said breathlessly.

He shook his head.

"I'm afraid we'll have to talk about that. I don't want to hold your arm. Will you come with me?"

"Are you arresting me?" she gasped.

He nodded gravely.

"I'm detaining you – until a little matter is cleared up. I'm perfectly sure you're an innocent agent in this, just as I am equally sure that your sister isn't."

Dora? Was he talking about Dora, she asked herself with a sinking heart. His tone, the hard judgement in the voice, told the girl something she did not want to know. Something that shocked her beyond expression. Then, forcing every word, she said:

"I'll talk the matter over with pleasure, and I won't make any attempt to get away. But I have not come from Mrs Elton's, and she is not my sister. The story I told you this afternoon was untrue."

"But why?" he asked, as they walked together through the stone corridor to the courtyard.

"Because" – she hesitated – "I knew you were a detective."

He signalled a cab, gave directions and helped her inside.

"You're lying to shield your sister and Bunny Elton," he said. "I hate using the word 'lie' to you, but that's what you're doing, my child."

Her mind was in a turmoil, from which one clear fact emerged. It was not a miniature that she was carrying from Dora to the mythical wife; it was something more important. Something horribly serious.

"What was in the parcel?" she asked huskily.

"The Queen of Finland's diamond necklace, unless I'm greatly mistaken. Her carriage was held up in The Mall four nights ago, and the jewels were stolen from her neck."

Audrey sat up with a grimace of pain. It was as though he had struck her. Dora! She had read something of the affair in the newspaper which he had bought for her at Barnham Junction. Mrs Graffitt had spoken of the crime. For a spell she sat, paralysed with horror.

"Of course you didn't know what it was," he said, and he was speaking to himself. "It's a hateful thing to ask you to do, but you must tell me the truth, even if it brings your sister to the place that has been waiting for her these many years."

41

The cab seemed to go round and round; the stream of lights and traffic through the window became a confused blur.

"Do what you can for Dora..." Her mother's insistent lesson, almost forgotten, was ringing in her ears. She was trembling violently; her brain had gone numb and would give her no guidance. All that she knew was that she was under arrest...she, Audrey Bedford of Beak Farm! She licked her dry lips.

"I have no sister," she said, her breath labouring. "I stole the necklace!"

She heard his soft laughter, and could have murdered him.

"You poor, dear baby!" he said. "It was a job carried out by three expert hold-up men. Now let me tell you" – he patted her hand gently – "I'm not going to allow you to do this mad, quixotic thing. Didn't you know that Dora Elton and her husband are two of the most dangerous crooks in London?"

She was weeping, her face in her hands.

"No, no," she sobbed, "I don't know anything... She is not my sister."

Dick Shannon sighed and shrugged his shoulders. There was nothing to do but to charge her.

Pierre had arrived at the station before them, and she watched, with fascinated horror, the process of his searching, saw the package opened on the sergeant's desk, and the flash and glitter of its contents. Presently Shannon took her gently by the arm and led her into the steel pen.

"The name is Audrey Bedford," he said. "The address is Fontwell, West Sussex. The charge" – he hesitated – "is being in possession of stolen property, knowing the same to be stolen. Now tell the truth," he whispered under his breath.

She shook her head.

DISOWNED

Audrey woke from a restless, troubled sleep and, struggling to her unsteady feet, rubbed her shoulders painfully. She had been lying on a bare plank, covered with the thinnest of blankets, and she ached from head to foot.

The sound of a key turning in the cell lock had awakened her; it was the matron, who had come to conduct her to the bathroom. She had returned to her cell a little refreshed, to find coffee and bread and butter waiting for her, and she had finished these when the door opened again, and she looked up to meet the grave eyes of Dick Shannon. He nodded to her.

"I want you," he said.

Her heart sank.

"Am I going before – before a judge?" she faltered.

"Not yet," he said. "I'm afraid that eventually you will go before a judge, unless – "

She waved aside the suggestion with an impatient hand. She had settled that matter definitely in the silence of the night.

The man's heart ached for her. He knew well enough that she was innocent, and he had sent a man into Sussex that morning to prove the matter, as he hoped, beyond question.

"Here's somebody you know, I think," he said, and, opening a door, drew her into a room.

There were two occupants: Dora Elton and her husband. Audrey looked; she had to dig her fingernails into her palms to control herself, and she succeeded wonderfully.

"Do you know this girl?" asked Shannon.

Dora shook her head.

"No, I've never seen her before," she said innocently. "Do you know her, Martin?"

The haggard-faced Martin was equally emphatic.

"Never saw her before in my life," he said.

"I think she is your sister."

Dora smiled.

"How absurd!" she said. "I've only one sister, and she is in Australia."

"Do you know that both your mother and your sister lived at Fontwell?"

"My mother never lived at Fontwell in her life," said Dora calmly, and, in spite of her self-possession, Audrey started. "There were some people who lived at Fontwell, who were" — she shrugged — "pensioners of mine. I helped the woman once or twice. If this is her daughter, she is a perfect stranger to me."

All the time she spoke, her eyes were fixed on Audrey, and the girl thought she read in them a mute appeal. In a flash she realized that what Dora had said might very well be true. She had married in her stage name, and it was quite possible that none of the neighbours identified her with Mrs Bedford's daughter, for she had not visited the place, and Audrey's mother was one of the reticent kind that made no confidences.

"What Mrs Elton says is quite true," she said quietly. "I do not know her, nor does she know me."

Dick Shannon opened the door, and the girl went out again to the waiting matron. When she had gone, he faced the Eltons.

"I don't know how long she'll keep this up," he said. "But if she sticks to the story from first to last, Elton, she'll go to jail." He spoke deliberately. "And I'm going to tell you something. If that child is sent to prison, if you allow her to sacrifice herself, I will never rest night or day until I have brought you both to the penal settlement."

"You seem to forget to whom you're speaking," said Dora, a bright light in her eyes.

"I know I'm speaking to two utterly unscrupulous, utterly depraved, utterly soulless people," said Dick. "Get out!"

Lacy Marshalt sat in his breakfast room. A newspaper was propped up before him; his face was puckered in a frown. He looked again at the picture taken by an enterprising press photographer. It was the portrait of a girl alighting from a taxicab. In the background a blur of curious spectators. A policeman was on one side of her, a broad-shouldered wardress on the other. It was one of those pictures fairly familiar to the newspaper reader. A fleeting snap of a criminal on her way to trial.

There was no need to compare the newspaper with the photograph in his pocket. The name of the prisoner would have told him, even if there had been no photograph.

Tonger came in, slipping through between door and post.

"You didn't ring, did you, Lacy?" he asked.

"I rang ten minutes ago. And I'm telling you for the last time to forget that 'Lacy' of yours. There is a limit to my patience, my friend."

The little man rubbed his hands gleefully.

"Heard from my girl today," he said. "She's doing well in America. Clever kid that, Lacy."

"Is she?" Lacy Marshalt returned to a survey of his newspaper.

"She's got money – always writes from the best hotels. Never thought things would turn out that way."

Lacy folded his paper and dropped it on the floor.

"Mrs Martin Elton will be here in five minutes. She will come through the mews to the back door. Be waiting for her and bring her through the conservatory to the library. When I ring for you, show her out the same way."

Tonger grinned.

"What a lad for the girls!" he said admiringly.

Lacy jerked his head toward the door.

Less than five minutes later Dora Elton pushed open the heavy wicket gate and, crossing the courtyard, mounted the iron stairs to the "conservatory" – a glass annexe thrown out at the back of the house above the kitchen and scullery of the establishment. She was dressed in black and heavily veiled. Tonger detected signs of nervousness as he opened the conservatory door to her.

"Have you come to breakfast?" he asked amiably.

She was too used to his familiarities to resent his manner.

"Where is Mr Marshalt?"

"In the library — readin' *Christie's Old Organ*," suggested Tonger humorously.

Lacy was reading nothing more informative than the fire when she was shown in.

"I had an awful trouble getting here," she said. "Wouldn't it have done this afternoon? I had to tell all sorts of lies to Martin. Aren't you going to kiss me?"

He stooped and brushed her cheek.

"What a kiss!" she scoffed. "Well?"

"This jewel robbery," he said slowly. "There is a girl implicated. I understand that the police are under the impression that she is your sister?"

She was silent.

"I know, of course, that you are on the crook," he went on. "Stanford is an old acquaintance of mine in South Africa, and he's one of your gang. But this girl, is she in it?"

"You know how much she is in it," she said sulkily. She had not come, at some risk, to Portman Square to discuss Audrey. And at the thought of risk...

"There was a man watching this house at the back when I came along the mews," she said. "I saw him by the back door. When he saw me he walked away."

"Watching this house?" he said incredulously. "What sort of a man?"

"He looked a gentleman. I only just saw his face — very thin and refined-looking. He had a limp — "

Lacy took a step toward her, and gripped her by the shoulders. His face was grey, his lip quivered. For a moment he could not speak, then: "You're lying! You're trying to put one over on me!"

She struggled from his grip, terrified.

"Lacy! What is wrong with you?"

He silenced her with a gesture.

"I'm nervous, and you startled me," he muttered. "Go on with what you were saying. That girl is your sister? I want to know."

"My half-sister," she said in a low voice.

He stopped in his pacing.

"You mean...you have different fathers?"

She nodded.

He did not speak again for so long that she began to feel frightened.

"She'll go to jail, of course...and she's shielding you?" he laughed, but there was no mirth in his laughter. "That is best – I can wait," he said.

A month later, on a bright March morning, a pale girl stood in the spacious dock of the Old Bailey, and by her side a square-shouldered Belgian, the first to be sentenced.

Coming out of court toward the end of the case, sick at heart and weary of the solemn machinery of vengeance which was grinding to dust so frail a victim, Shannon saw a familiar figure ensconced in one of the deep-seated benches where, usually, witnesses sat waiting.

"Well, Slick, have you been in court?"

"I have," said the other carefully, "but the illusion of the successful detective wore through, and that big pen was certainly hungry looking. I tore myself away. Other people haven't any sensitive feelings. I saw Stanford amongst the ghouls."

Shannon sat down by his side.

"What do you think?"

"Of the case? Little Miss Quixote – pronounced Key-o-tey, they tell me – is going down." He pointed significantly at the tiled floor.

"I'm afraid she is," Shannon said after a pause, and sighed.

"But that's as far as they'll get her," mused the crook. "She'll come up just as she went down – sweet. That kind doesn't sour easily. Say, Shannon, ever heard of a man called Malpas?"

Dick, who was thinking of something else, started.

"Yes, he's an eccentric old man who lives in Portman Square – why?"

Slick Smith smiled blandly.

"He's in it somewhere," he said. "I am speaking in my capacity as a detective. That case has finished mighty suddenly."

A policeman was beckoning Shannon, and he hurried into court in time to hear the sentence.

"What is your age?" asked the judge, pausing, pen in hand, and looking over his glasses.

"Nineteen, my lord." It was Shannon. "And I may say that the police are perfectly satisfied, in spite of the evidence, that this girl is an innocent victim of other people who are not in custody."

The judge shook his head.

"The evidence does not support that view. It is very dreadful to see a young girl in this position, and I should be failing in my duty to society if I did not deal severely with so dangerous an agent. Audrey Bedford, you will go to prison with hard labour for twelve months."

THE TRUTH

On a gloomy morning in December the wicket gate of Holloway Prison opened, and a slim girl, in an old brown velours coat, came out, and, looking neither to the left nor right, passed through the waiting friends of prisoners to be released, walked quickly up the Holloway Road toward Camden Town. Crossing the road, she boarded a street car, and at that moment Dick Shannon's long machine swept past, and she did not see it. He arrived three minutes too late to intercept her.

She had a few shillings left as the result of her year's work and, getting down at the tram terminus, she went along the Euston Road till she came to a small restaurant.

The face was a little finer-drawn, the eyes graver, but it was the old Audrey who ordered extravagant portions of devilled kidneys and egg. For nine months the prison routine had ground at her soul; for seventy-two hours a week she had associated with the debased dregs of the underworld, and had neither grown down to their level, nor experienced any sense of immeasurable superiority. There were bitter nights when the black treachery to which she had been subjected overwhelmed her, and she closed her eyes to shut out the hideous realities. Nights of torture, when the understanding of her own ruin had driven her to the verge of madness.

Yet it did not seem unnatural that Dora had acted so. It was almost a Dora-like thing to have done, consonant with all that she knew and all that she had heard of the girl. A horrible thought to Audrey (and this alone saddened her) was that the qualities in her sister were those which had been peculiarly noticeable in her mother. With a half-checked sigh, she rose, and, taking her bill, paid at the cashier's little box.

Where should she go now? To Dora, she decided. She must be absolutely sure that she had not wholly misjudged her. She could not go in the daytime; it would not be fair to the girl. She spent the rest of the morning looking for lodgings, finding them at last in a top back room in Gray's Inn Road. Here she rested through the afternoon, straightening the rags of her future. When dark came she made her way to Curzon Street.

The servant who opened the door to her was the same girl that had been there on her first visit.

"What do you want?" she asked tartly.

"I want to see Mrs Elton," said Audrey.

"Well, you can't," said the girl, and tried to shut the door. But Audrey's nine months of manual work had had results. Without an effort she pushed the door open and stepped in.

"Go up and tell your mistress I am here," she said.

The girl flew up the stairs, and Audrey, without hesitation, followed her. As she walked behind the servant into the drawing-room she heard her sister say: "How dare she come here!"

She was in evening dress, looking particularly lovely, her fair hair shining like burnished gold. She stared at the girl as if she were a ghost, and her eyes narrowed.

"How dare you force your way into this house?" she demanded.

"Send away your servant," said Audrey quietly, and, when the girl had gone and she had made sure that she was not listening on the landing, she walked across to Dora, her hands behind her. "I want you to say 'thank you'," she said simply. "I did a mad, foolish thing, because I felt that I wanted to repay Mother for anything that I owed her, and which I had not already paid."

"I don't know what you're talking about," said Dora, flushing. "You've got a nerve to come here, anyway!"

It was the sleek Martin.

"You tried to drag us into your – your crime. You hold your – Mrs Elton up to the scorn of the world, and then you calmly walk into our house without so much as a please or by your leave. Damned nerve!"

"If you want money, write," said Dora, and flung open the door. "If you come here again I'll send for a policeman."

"Send for one now," said the girl coolly. "I'm so well acquainted with policemen and wardresses that you can't frighten me, my dear sister."

Dora closed the door quickly.

"If you want to know, we're not sisters. You're not even English!" she said in a low, malignant voice. "Your father was mother's second husband, an American! He's on the breakwater at Cape Town, serving a sentence of life!"

Audrey caught the back of a chair for support.

"That's not true," she said.

"It is true – it is true!" stormed Dora in a harsh whisper. "Mother told me, and Mr Stanford knows all about it. Your father bought diamonds and shot the man who betrayed him. It is a felony to buy diamonds in South Africa. He disgraced my mother – she changed her name and came home the day after his arrest. Why, you're not even entitled to the name of Bedford. She hated him so much that she changed everything!"

Audrey nodded.

"And, of course, Mother left him," she said, speaking to herself. "She didn't stay near to give him the comfort and sympathy that a wife might give to the vilest of men. She just left him – flat! How like her!"

There was no malice, no bitterness in her voice. Audrey had the trick of seeing things truly. She raised her eyes slowly until they met Dora's.

"I ought not to have gone to prison," she said; "you are not worth it. Nor Mother, I think."

"You dare to speak of my mother!" cried Dora in a fury.

"Yes, she was my mother, too. She's beyond my criticism or your defence. Thank you. What is my name?"

"Find out!" snapped the woman.

"I'll ask Mr Shannon," said the girl.

It was the only malice she showed in the interview. But it was worth the effort to see the change that came to the two faces.

MR MALPAS

Dick Shannon had a flat in the Haymarket, an apartment which served as home and office, for, in the room overlooking one of London's busiest thoroughfares, he got through a considerably larger volume of work than he disposed of in his uninspiring bureau on the Thames Embankment.

Steel, his assistant, christened the flat "Newest Scotland Yard," and certainly had justification, for here, more often than not, were held the conferences which brought the Big Five – an ever-changing quantity – about the council board.

Something in the nature of a sub-committee was sitting on the day that Audrey Bedford was released from prison. Sergeant Steel, who specialized in society cases – it was the Yard's boast that he was the best-dressed man in London – and Inspector Lane, late of Bow Street, now of Marylebone, was the third.

"You didn't see her?" asked the inspector.

Dick Shannon shook his head.

"By the time I got to the Governor and discovered she had been released, it was useless looking for her. I've given instructions to the stations that the moment she reports – she hasn't completed the whole of her sentence – they are to report to me."

He suppressed a sigh.

"There was a miscarriage of justice, if ever there was one!" he said. "And yet, for the life of me, I can't see what other verdict the jury could return."

"But if she was innocent," said Steel, puzzled, "what was easier than for her to speak? It is not innocent to hide the guilty."

"Let us lift this discussion out of the base realm of metaphysics," said Dick testily. "What about Mr Malpas?"

"He's a mystery," said Lane unnecessarily, "and the house is more so. So far as I can find, he has been in occupation of 551 Portman Square since January, 1917, and has been there most of the time. Nobody has seen him. We had a complaint last year from Mr Lacy Marshalt, who lives next door, that he was disturbed by knocking at nights, but we could only advise him to take a summons. He pays his bills regularly, and when he came into the house (which is his own property, by the way) he spent a considerable sum in renovations. A big Italian firm of Turin fitted the house with electric lighting, burglar alarms, and various other gadgets, though I can't trace any furniture going in."

"Are there any servants?"

"None: that's the strangest thing. No food goes into the house, which means that he must eat outside or starve. I've had men to watch the back and front of the house, but he has slipped them every time, though they've seen a few interesting things."

Dick Shannon smoothed his chin.

"It isn't an offence to be a recluse," he said, "but it is an offence to engage in a conspiracy. Bring in the girl, Steel."

Steel went out, to return with an over-powdered young lady, who nodded coolly to the company, and took the chair which Steel, with an air, pushed up to her.

"Miss Neilsen, you are a professional dancer – disengaged?"

"I'm that," she said laconically.

"I want you to tell us about your visit to 551, Portman Square."

She was not particularly anxious or willing to talk.

"If I had known I was speaking to a detective when I got so talkative the other night, I wouldn't have said so much," she admitted frankly. "You haven't any right to question me – "

"You practically accused a gentleman who holds a responsible position of attempting to engage you in a conspiracy," said Dick. "That is a very serious accusation to make."

"I didn't say it was a conspiracy," she denied quickly. "All I said was that the old gentleman, who was a perfect stranger to me, asked me if I would start something at Mr Marshalt's house – that's next door. He wanted me to go to there one evening and make a fuss – to start screaming that Mr Marshalt was a scoundrel, break a window, and get arrested."

"He didn't tell you why?"

She shook her head.

"No. It wasn't my job anyhow. And I was only too glad to get out – the man gave me the creeps." She shivered. "You've heard of ugly men? Well, you don't know what ugliness is. And scared! You have to sit at a table one end of the room while he sits at the other. And the room is all dark except for a little light on the desk where he sits. The house is full of ghosts – that's how it seemed to me. Doors open by themselves and voices talk to you from nowhere. When I got out on to the street again, I could have gone down on my knees and said a prayer of thanksgiving."

"If you were a stranger to him, how did he come to know you?" asked Dick, puzzled and suspicious.

Her explanation was logical.

"He got my name out of a theatrical newspaper – I'm in the 'want engagement' columns," she said.

Lane questioned her closely, but her story held, and presently they let her go.

"Queer," said Dick Shannon thoughtfully. "I should like to see Mr Malpas. You have had other complaints?"

Lane hesitated.

"I wouldn't call them complaints. The inspector of income tax made a little trouble about not being able to see the man. He returned his income at what Inland Revenue thought was too low a figure, and he was summoned to appear before the inspector. And, of course, he did not appear, sending, instead, permission to inspect his banking account. I happened to know of this and took the opportunity of sharing the inspection. It is the simplest account I have ever seen: a thousand five hundred a year paid in – by cash; a thousand five hundred a year paid out. No tradesmen's checks. Nothing but taxes, ground rent, and substantial sums for his current expenses."

"You say he has had visitors?" asked Dick.

"Yes, I was going to tell you about these. At intervals, never longer than two weeks, he has a visitor, sometimes two in the course of the day. Generally it is on a Saturday. The caller never comes until it is dark, and doesn't remain longer than half an hour. So far as we have been able to learn, the same man never comes twice. It was only by accident that we discovered this: one of our officers saw a man go in and come out. The next Saturday, at precisely the same hour, he saw a visitor arrive and, after an interval, take his departure. This was seen again a few weeks later, the caller being a Negro. Our man 'tailed him up,' but could get nothing out of him."

"Malpas must be placed under closer observation," said Dick, and the inspector made a note. "Pull in one of his visitors on some pretext or other – see what he has in his possession. You may find that the old man is nothing more alarming than a dispenser of charity – on the other hand, you may not!"

That almost exhausted the subject of the mysterious Mr Malpas, and they passed to the matter of a providential fire that had saved an insolvent cabinet maker from bankruptcy.

Mr Malpas might not have come up for discussion at all but for the story that the dancer had told to a sympathetic and official listener. That this sinister figure should be associated with the events which, under his eyes, were moving to a climax, that the ragged princess whose image had not left his mind for nine months would shortly come into the old man's ken and find her fate and future linked with his, Dick Shannon could not dream. Mr Malpas was "an inquiry," an arresting circumstance to be questioned and probed. Soon he was to loom upon the scene, blotting out all other objects in Captain Shannon's view.

Audrey Bedford had made an interesting discovery. There was an essential thing in life about which she had never heard. It was a mysterious something called "a character"; sometimes it was more genteelly styled "references."

Without one or the other (and they were really one and the same thing) it was impossible to secure employment. There were leering men who said: "Never mind, little woman, we'll get along without that"; other men who did not leer and were apparently shocked when she told them she had just come from prison, but who bore up well enough to engage her and ask her to come to dinner with them; and there were others (and she liked these best) who said curtly: "We have no opening for you."

Her little stock of money was dwindling. There dawned a Christmas Day when she woke with a healthy appetite to breakfast on water and one very stale slice of bread that she had saved from the night before. And this was to be her luncheon, and would have been her supper, too, only there occurred that night, in a little street off Gray's Inn Road, a fight between two viragoes, one of whom thrust a small and greasy package into the girl's hand that she might deal more effectively with her rival. The police came instantly, there was a wild scrimmage, the battlers were haled off to Theobalds Road Police Station, and Audrey carried the parcel home and supped royally on fried fish and potatoes. It was heavenly.

On Tuesday morning her landlady came up the stairs and Audrey heard the heavy foot of the woman with a sense of blind panic.

"Good morning, Miss. There's a letter for you."

Audrey stared. Nobody knew her address – she had never reached the address stage in any of her essays at finding employment.

"I hope it's good news," said the landlady ominously. "I don't charge much for my apartments, but I like it regular. We've all got to live, and I've had a party after this very room this very morning. Not that I'm going to turn you out. I'd sooner make up a bed for you on the sofa," she added.

Audrey was not listening. She was turning the letter over in her hand. Tearing it open, she found an address and a few lines of pencilled writing. She read the message in bewilderment.

Come at 5 o'clock this evening. I have work for you.

The note was signed "Malpas."

She knit her forehead. Who was "Malpas," and how had he discovered her whereabouts?

THE INTERVIEW

Audrey Bedford held the sodden slip of paper nearer to her eyes to assure herself of the address. The writing, in pencil, was worn now to a faint and almost indecipherable smear. In the failing light of a grey December afternoon it would have been difficult enough to read, but to all other disadvantages was added the drive of wind and sleet. Her old coat was already saturated. It had been wet before she had walked a mile; the brim of her black velvet hat drooped soggily.

She put the paper back in her pocket and looked a little fearfully at the grim door of No. 551, Portman Square. This forbidding house, with its dingy stone front and blank, expressionless windows, might hide interiors of comfort and luxury, but there was little promise in the outward appearance.

What would be the end of this essay? she wondered, with a calmness which seemed strange, even to herself. Would it go with the others and end in dismissal – or, what was worse, an engagement on terms, unspoken but nonetheless clearly understood?

Portman Square was empty of pedestrians. Down one side of the open space the great red buses rumbled and closed taxis and cars sped past at intervals. Drawing a long sigh, she walked up the two steps and looked for the bell. There was none. The door was innocent of knocker – she tapped gently with her knuckles.

"Who is there?"

The voice seemed to come from the side stone door-posts.

"Miss Bedford," she said. "I have an appointment with Mr Malpas."

There was a pause, and then, as the door opened slowly: "Come upstairs – the room on the first landing," said the voice.

It came from a small grating let in the wall. The hall was empty. One yellow globe supplied the illumination. While she was looking around the door closed again, by no obvious agency. For a second she was seized with a sudden unaccountable fear. She sought the handle of the door: there was none. The black, heavy portal was closed upon her irrevocably.

Audrey's hands were trembling; cold and fear combined to break her courage – cold and fear and hunger, for she had taken nothing that day but a piece of bread and the remains of coffee left over from the previous night.

She looked round the hall. Of furniture there was none except an old chair against the wall. The marble floor was thick with dust, the discoloured walls innocent of pictures or hangings.

With an effort she controlled her shaking limbs and walked up the stone stairs. On the second landing was a polished rosewood door – the only interior door she had seen – and, after a pause to summon the reserves of her courage, she knocked.

"Is that Miss Bedford?"

This time the voice came from over her head. Looking up, she saw a second grating in the recessed doorway. It was placed so that any visitor knocking would stand immediately underneath.

"Yes," she answered, holding her anxiety in check.

Instantly the rosewood swung open and she passed into a broad, well lit hall. Facing her was a second door, ajar.

"Come in, please."

This time the voice spoke from the room; it was less distinct.

She hesitated, her heart thumping painfully. The room seemed to be in darkness save for one faint reflection. Pushing open the door, she walked in.

It was a large room, about thirty feet in width, and almost twice that length. The walls, so completely draped by velvet curtains that it was impossible to tell where the windows were hidden, ran up into gloom; the visitor must guess where the black ceiling began and the walls ended. Under her feet was a rich, deep carpet into which her halting feet sank as she took three steps, stopped, and looked open-eyed.

In the far corner of the room a man sat at a desk on which a green-shaded lamp afforded the only illumination the gloomy chamber possessed.

A strangely revolting figure. His head was narrow and bald; his yellow face, innocent of hair, was puckered in a thousand wrinkles and seams; the nose was big and pendulous. His long, pointed chin moved all the time as though he were talking to himself.

"Sit in that chair," he said hollowly.

The chair she saw when her eyes grew accustomed to the darkness; it stood behind a small table, and slowly and painfully she sat down.

"I have sent for you to make your fortune," he said, in his mumbling voice. "Many people have sat in that chair and have gone away rich."

In the green light that fell athwart his face from the lampshade he looked like some hideous imagining of a Chinese artist. She shuddered, and gazed steadily past him.

"On the table — look!" he said.

He must have pressed some button, for instantly a powerful yellow light fell from a bell-shaped shade above and threw a circle of bright radiance on the floor around her. And then she saw on the table a thin package of money.

"Take it!" he said.

After a second's hesitation she stretched out her hand and took the notes, shivering from head to foot. The light above was slowly dimming. Presently it faded altogether, and she sat in the darkness, her hands unconsciously gripping the wealth that had come to her. And a key — she did not realize that until, later, he referred to the fact.

"Audrey Bedford. That is your name?"

She made no reply.

"Three weeks ago you were released from prison, where you served a sentence of a year, or nine months of a year, for being accessory to a robbery?"

"Yes," said the girl quietly. "I should have told you that in any event. I have invariably told that when I have applied for work."

"Innocent, of course?" he asked.

There was no smile on his expressionless face, and she could not judge whether his tone was ironical or not. She guessed it was.

"Yes; I was innocent," she said evenly.

"Faked charge…a frame-up, eh? Elton had it all fixed for you. You knew nothing of the robbery? Just an innocent agent?"

He waited.

"I knew nothing of the robbery," she said quietly.

"Did you say that at the trial?"

She did not answer. He sat so still that she could have believed that he was a waxen figure, worked by some drug-crazy artist.

"You are badly dressed…that offends me. You have money, buy the best. Come this day week at this hour. You will find a key on the table: this will unlock all doors, if the control is released."

Audrey found her voice.

"I must know what my duties are," she said, and her voice sounded dead and lifeless in that draped room. "It is very good of you to trust me with so much money, but you will see how impossible it is to accept unless I know what is expected of me."

Famished as she was, with the prospect of a supperless night, and before her eyes the drab ugliness of her little room and the reproachful face of her landlady, it required more than an ordinary effort to say this. Hunger demoralizes the finest nature, and she was faint for want of food.

He spoke slowly.

"Your task is to break a man's heart," he said.

She almost laughed.

"That sounds…rather alarming. You are not serious?"

He offered no reply. She felt a cold draught behind her, and, turning, experienced a little thrill of fear to see the door opening.

"Good night."

The figure at the end of the room waved a hand toward the door. The interview was over.

She had put one foot on the stairs when the door closed again, and she went down to the hall, her mind in a state of chaos. The front door was not open; evidently he expected her to use the key. With trembling fingers she tried to press it into the microscopic slit which, after a search, she discovered. In her haste the key slipped and fell. It was so small that she could not find it at first. The force of her pressure had sent it into a corner of the hall. She found it after a search, and found something else, too − a pebble, the size of a nut. Attached was a blob of red sealing wax and the clear impression of a tiny seal. It was so unusual an object that she forgot for the moment her very urgent desire to get out of the house. The bizarre has a fascination for the young, and there was something very unusual about that common piece of stone so carefully sealed.

Audrey looked up the stairs, hoping to see the old man and ask him if this queer find of hers had any interest for him. Then she remembered that she would see him again in a week, and she dropped the pebble into her little handbag.

So doing, she became aware that one of her hands was gripping a package of notes. Six hundred pounds! There were three of a hundred, four of fifty, and twenty of five.

Audrey drew a long breath. She thrust the money out of sight and turned the key in the lock − in another second she was facing the realities of a blizzard.

The taxicab that was crawling leisurely toward her had no significance at first. Then it came upon her that she was an enormously rich woman and, her heart beating a little faster, she put up her hand to signal the cab, walking rapidly to meet it as it drew into the curb.

"Take me to − "

Where? First food; then, in the sanity which food might bring, a few minutes of quiet contemplation.

"She's had one over the eight," grinned the driver.

Audrey's first impression was that the man was speaking of her, and she wondered what he meant. But he was looking beyond her, and, following the direction of his eyes, she saw a sight that first sickened and then moved her to pity. Clinging to the rails that bordered the area was a woman. She held tight with one hand, swaying unsteadily, while with the other she was manipulating the knocker of the front door of the house next to that place of mystery which she had left.

Her pathetic finery, the draggling imitation paradise plume of her hat, the wet and matted surface of her fur coat, ludicrously fashionable in cut, made an unforgettable picture. Drunkenness was loathsome to the girl; she realized its horror to the full when she saw it in a woman. Somehow the fighting viragoes of Gray's Inn Road were infinitely less repulsive than the spectacle of this poor creature with her red, swollen face and her maudlin mutterings.

Audrey had withdrawn her foot from the step of the cab, intending to go to her, when the door was flung open violently, and she saw a thin, elderly man appear.

"Here! What's the row? Coming here making this fuss at a gentleman's house. Go away or I'll send for a copper!"

Tonger's voice came down to the girl through the shrill whistle of the wind.

"Going in − " gasped the wreck, and lurched toward the open doorway.

Audrey, watching, saw him try to hold her, but she collapsed on to him.

"Here, hold up!"

There was a little struggle, and suddenly Tonger jerked the woman into the hall and the door slammed.

"That's Mr Marshalt's house," said the cabman. "He's the African millionaire. Where did you say you'd like to go, Miss?"

She was inspired to name a little dressmaker's shop in Shaftesbury Avenue, a shop before whose windows she always lingered when her search for work brought her westward. Later, she would consider the propriety of spending this terrible old man's money. For the moment her creature needs dominated. Opposite the dressmaker's was a shoe shop; two blocks away was a snug hotel.

"I'll come out of this dream some time," said Audrey, looking through the blurred windows at the shops that flashed past, "but I'm coming out with dry clothes and a bed that isn't nobbly!"

BUNNY TALKS STRAIGHT

It is sometimes difficult to rule a line across a human life, and say with exactness, "Here began a career." Martin Elton had become a criminal by a natural sequence of processes, all related one to the other, and all having their foundation in a desire, common to humanity high and low, to live without working.

The product of a great school, he had found himself, at an early period of his life, with no other assets than a charming manner, the ability to converse pleasantly, and a host of exploitable friends. He went where his accomplishments paid the biggest dividends; and being unhampered by a conscience or handicapped with a too stringent sense of honour, he came naturally to the society of men and women who lived by their sharpness of intellect. He had run gambling houses (at one of which he had first met Dora and found in her a partner equally free from stupid scruples); he had manoeuvred intimate robberies that had something of blackmail in them; he had dabbled in racetrack frauds of an unobtrusive character, and had made his many enterprises profitable.

Between the second and third acts of a play to which Dora had taken him, he strolled out into the lobby. There were people who knew him and nodded to him, only one who made any effort to get into conversation, for Martin was not of the gregarious kind. He preferred the company of his own thought at any time, most of all tonight.

" 'Lo, Elton!"

He smiled mechanically and would have moved on, but the man who intercepted him was wilfully blind to his desire for solitude.

"Stanford's gone to Italy, they tell me – that fellow is certainly the bird that's in two places at once. Anything doing?"

"Nothing," replied Martin pointedly. "London has been very dull since Melilla Snowden's rooms at the Albemarle were burgled and her pearls lifted."

Slick Smith laughed softly.

"Not guilty," he said, "and anyway, they were props. The burglary was more genuine, but the scream her press agent raised is just publicity. My opinion of Melilla, both as an actress and a woman, has gone right down to the mezzanine floor. A vamp that can only vamp up Luk-lik-Reels ought to be teaching Sunday School. If you got any kind of work I can do, let me know. But it must be honest."

"Come round one day and fix my kitchen stove," snarled Martin, who was not in the best of humours.

"Stoves are my speciality," said Slick, unperturbed. "Have a good cigar?" He offered his case.

"No!"

"Maybe you're right," agreed the other. "They were a Christmas present. I can't get anybody to try 'em out. It will be tough on me if I have to do the pioneer work. Seen Shannon?"

Martin sighed heavily.

"My dear fellow, I haven't seen Shannon and I don't want to see Shannon. More to the point, I'm not in the mood for conversation."

"That's a pity," said Slick regretfully. "I'm feeling chatty, and I'm tired of talking to myself. I pall on one."

"You're in danger of palling on me." Martin smiled in spite of himself.

"I felt that, too. I'm responsive to atmosphere. There's a whole lot in this aura theory. Lacy Marshalt's not like that."

There was no especial emphasis to his words. He was lighting an experimental cigar as he spoke, painfully and apprehensively.

"I don't know very much about Marshalt," said Martin shortly.

"Don't suppose you do. I know him slightly. He's a thief, too. And the things he steals leave a kind of gap. You're a pretty good fellow, Elton."

The seeming inconsequence of the last remark was not lost upon his hearer.

"I don't think I'd go any farther if I were you," said Martin Elton quietly. "You're trying to be kind, aren't you?"

"Not trying. I do these things naturally." Slick Smith's smile was broad and disarming. "There goes the bell — I wonder if she married the duke and sent her village swain back to the family wood pile? I guess she didn't — they never do in plays."

That raw night, as he was driving home, he thought of Slick. He had not enjoyed the play, neither had Dora, and a sense of restraint had fallen upon both. The drive was unrelieved by any spoken words.

He followed her up to the drawing-room, well prepared for the outburst which was due and, unless he was mistaken, was coming.

"What is the matter with you, Bunny? You've hardly spoken a word this evening. I'm tired of your sulks! You make me so nervous I hardly know what I'm doing!"

He bit off the end of a cigar and lit it, his attention on the match.

"I'm not sulking. I'm just thoughtful, that's all," he said, throwing the stick into the fire before he sat down in a corner of the roomy settee. "Have you heard any more of your sister?"

"No, I haven't," she snapped, "and I hope to God I never hear from her again! The whining little jailbird!"

He took his cigar from his mouth and examined it carefully.

"I don't remember that she whined; and if she's a jailbird, we made her so," he said.

She stared at him in amazement.

"That's a new tone for you to take, Bunny. You practically threw her out of the house last time she was here."

He nodded.

"Yes, I haven't forgotten that," he said quietly. "London is a rotten place for a pretty girl to be alone in, without money or friends. I wish I knew where she was."

A slow smile dawned on her lovely face.

"You seem to have had a visit from R E Morse, Esquire," she said ironically. "But then, you always fell for a pretty face."

He made a gesture of distaste. There were moments when the groundings of Wechester College started up from their sleep and made themselves evident.

"Her prettiness weighs less with me than her helplessness at this moment. She didn't write?"

"Of course she didn't write," said his wife scornfully. "Is that what has been making you so glum? Poor Bunny!" she mocked. "He has a soft heart for beauty in distress!"

He looked at her for a second, a cold scrutiny which aroused her to fury.

"What's wrong?" she demanded, her voice trembling with anger. "Tell me what's in your mind – there's something!"

"Yes, there's something," agreed Bunny Elton; "in fact, there are several somethings, and Audrey is one of them. The girl may be starving. God knows what may have happened to her."

"Let us leave her to His keeping," she said with mock piety, and his eyes narrowed.

"I've been thinking lately," he said, "that, if you behave this way to your own sister, what sort of treatment should I get if things went wrong, and you had to make a quick decision between me and safety?"

"Safety would win," she said coolly. "I'll not deceive you, Bunny. '*Sauve qui peut*' is my family motto."

She kicked off her shoes and was pulling on the red morocco boudoir boots that stood before the fire.

"And is that all? Is it only the thought of the poor little girl driven from home that is worrying you?" she sneered.

"That's one thing," he said. He threw his cigar into the fire and rose. "Dora" – his voice was like ice – "Mr Lacy Marshalt is an undesirable acquaintance."

She looked up, her eyes wide open.

"Isn't he honest?" she asked innocently.

"There are a whole lot of honest people that no respectable lady thief can dine with in a private room at Shavarri's," he said deliberately. "Lacy Marshalt is one."

Her eyes dropped to the fire again; her colour came and went. "You've been watching me, have you? Marshalt may be a very useful man to know in certain eventualities."

"He is no use to me in any eventuality," said Martin Elton; "and he is never so useless as when he is dining furtively with my wife."

A long silence followed.

"I only dined with him once at Shavarri's," she spoke at last. "I intended telling you, but I forgot. Hundreds of people dine privately at Shavarri's," she said defiantly.

He nodded.

"And I'm particularly anxious that you should not be like any of those hundreds," he said. "You've dined with him twice, as a matter of fact – twice, I know about; probably more often. Dora, that isn't to happen again."

She did not answer.

"Do you hear?"

She shrugged her shoulders.

"I get precious little out of life," she said with a little sob. "The only people I meet are Stanford and you and the little crooks you pull into your various games. I like to meet somebody who isn't that way – at times. It's like a breath of fresh air, that makes me forget the rotten atmosphere in which I live."

She did not see his cynical smile, but, knowing him, she could guess how he would receive her excuse.

"Intensely pathetic," he said. "The picture you have drawn of the pure child, striving to regain the memory of her lost innocence, touches me deeply. But if you want to get back to nature, I suggest some other means than tête-à-tête dinners at Shavarri's. They are sophisticated, Dora. You won't go again."

She looked up quickly.

"If I want to go – " she began defiantly.

"You will not go again," he said, his voice little above a whisper. "If you do, I will look up Mr Lacy Marshalt and put three bullets through the pocket in which he carries his excellent cigars. What I shall do to you, I don't know," he said in a matter-of-fact tone. "It depends entirely upon my mood and your – your propinquity. I rather fancy it would be a triple tragedy."

Her face was a ghastly white. She tried to speak, but could not put her words in order. Then, suddenly, she was at his feet, her arms clasping his knees.

"Oh, Bunny, Bunny!" she sobbed. "Don't talk like that; don't look like that! I will do what you wish…there was no harm… I swear there was nothing in it, Bunny… I just went out of devilment."

He touched her golden hair.

"You mean a lot to me, Dora," he said gently. "I haven't given you the very best training, and I guess I've thrown overboard every one of the good old moral maxims that guide most people. But there's one to which I am holding like death – it's 'honour amongst thieves,' Dora…honour amongst thieves!"

She had been in bed two hours, and he still sat before the remains of the fire, the stub of an unlighted cigar between his white teeth, his eyes fixed moodily upon the dull embers. Two bitter hours they had been, when he had stood face to face with the naked truth of things, and had brought his philosophy to join experience in judging the woman he loved. This good-looking young man, with his flawless skin and his dandified attire, was very human.

He rose, unlocked a drawer of the writing table, took out a small Browning, and sat for a quarter of an hour before the fire, the pistol resting on the palm of his hand, his grave eyes fixed upon the weapon. He heard a rustling sound outside, and slipped the gun into his pocket as Dora in her *négligé* came into the room.

"It's past two o'clock, Bunny," she said anxiously. "Aren't you coming to bed?"

He rose stiffly and stretched himself.

"You're not worrying any more, are you, Bunny?" she asked apprehensively.

Her eyes were still red with weeping; the hand she laid on his arm shook. He took it in his and patted it.

"No, I'm not worrying any more," he said. "We'll start afresh."

"But, Bunny," she wailed, "there's no need to start afresh. I swear to you – "

"We'll start afresh," said Bunny, and kissed her.

A CHANCE MEETING

Dick Shannon tapped furiously on the glass of the cab that was carrying him down Regent Street, and, dropping the window, leaned out.

"Turn round and go up the other side. I want to speak to that lady," he said.

The Ragged Princess! It was she – he would have known her anywhere – but a different ragged princess.

"Which lady, sir?"

The taximan screwed his body to shout the query through the open window as he brought the cab to the edge of the opposite sidewalk. But Dick had the door of the cab open and had leaped to the pavement before the car came to a standstill.

"Miss Bedford, I presume?" he laughed. "This is a very pleasant surprise."

It was, in more senses than one. All traces of her poverty had vanished; the girl was well dressed, well shod, and, in the new setting, was so lovely to look upon that she had passed through a lane of turning heads.

The surprise was mutual, and, by the light that came to her eyes, the pleasure was no less.

"I have been searching London for you," he said, falling in by her side and oblivious of the taximan's alarm at the threatened bilk. "By rank bad luck I lost you on the morning you came from Holloway. I arrived a few minutes after you had left. And queerly enough, I made the mistake of thinking that it was necessary that you would have to report to the police."

"Like other dangerous criminals," she smiled. "No – I am spared that. I saw you once or twice in Holloway. You were there on business."

The business that had taken him to the women's prison had been to catch a glimpse of her and to learn of her well-being. There were small privileges that could be obtained for her, an allocation of less unpleasant tasks. She had often wondered why she was so abruptly taken from the drudgery of the laundry and given the more congenial work of librarian, and had not connected the fugitive visits of Dick Shannon with the change of conditions.

They turned into the less congested area of Hanover Square. She had had no intention of going to Hanover Square, and was, in fact, on her way to an Oxford Street store, but she surrendered her will to his in this small matter without exactly realizing why.

"I am going to talk to you like a Dutch uncle," he said, slowing his pace. "You're not a Mason; neither am I. But Masons have confidences and keep one another's secrets and talk 'on the square' with the greatest frankness."

There was laughter in the eyes that she turned to his.

"And from knowledge that I have acquired, in a place that shall be nameless," she said, "policemen are artful! And under the guise of loving-kindness – "

She saw the flush come to his face and the droop of his brows.

"I'm awfully sorry; I didn't really mean to be rude. Go on, be candid – I'll be recklessly truthful, but you mustn't ask me anything about Dora, and you really must not raise the question of that unfortunate Queen's jewellery."

"Dora Elton is your sister, isn't she?"

She was silent for a moment.

"She isn't exactly my sister, but I was under the impression that she was," she said.

He stroked his chin thoughtfully.

"Anyway, it stands to her credit that she's looking after you now."

The girl's soft laughter answered him.

"Do you mean to say that she isn't?" He stopped and frowned down at her.

"Dora and I are no longer on speaking terms," she said, "and very naturally. It isn't good for Dora that she should be on speaking terms with a woman of my low antecedents. Seriously, Captain Shannon, I do not wish to speak about Dora."

"What are you doing?" he asked bluntly.

"I *was* walking up to Daffridge's, only I was arrested and taken – "

"Tell me seriously, what work are you doing?"

She hesitated.

"I don't know, except copying letters for a very unpleasant looking old gentleman, and being paid at extravagant rates for my services."

In spite of the flippancy of her tone he detected the doubt in her voice, and knew that behind her pose of light-heartedness she was worried.

"Hanover Square isn't the quietest place in the world," he said. "I'll drive you to the Park and we'll have a real heart-to-heart talk."

He looked round for a taxicab. There was one crawling behind him, and the driver's face was strangely familiar.

"Oh, Lord! I'd forgotten you," he gasped.

"I hadn't forgotten *you!*" said the taximan grimly. "Where do you want to go to?"

In the desert of Hyde Park they found two dry chairs and a desirable solitude.

"I want first to hear about this unpleasant looking old gentleman," said Dick, and she gave him a brief and vivid narrative of her experience with Mr Malpas.

"I suppose you'll think it was despicable in me to use the money at all; but when a girl is very hungry and very cold, she has neither the time nor the inclination to sit down and work out problems of abstract morality. I certainly had no intention of breaking anybody's heart, but I didn't examine my duties too closely until I was comfortably installed in the Palace Hotel, with two day dresses, three pairs of shoes and a lot of other things that would be complete mysteries to you if I mentioned them! It was not until the next morning that my conscience became awfully busy. I had written the night before to Mr Malpas, telling him my new address, and I was halfway through a second letter in the morning, explaining that, while I was ready and willing to render any service, however menial, I had discovered that heartbreaking was not amongst my accomplishments, when a note came from him. It didn't look like a note: it was a bulky envelope, containing about ten pencilled letters, which he asked me to copy and return to him."

"What kind of letters?" asked Dick curiously.

"They were mostly notes declining invitations to dinners and other social functions, which had evidently come from intimate friends, because he merely signed the letters with his initial. He said they could be written on the hotel notepaper, and that they must not be typewritten."

Dick Shannon was very thoughtful.

"I don't like it very much," he said at last.

"Do you know him?"

"I know of him. In fact, the other day I was having a long talk about him with some – friends. What is your salary?"

She shook her head.

"That we haven't mentioned. He gave me this lump sum, told me to report next week, and since then I've done nothing but copy the documents which come to me every morning by the first post. Today the letters were longer. I had to make a copy of correspondence between the Governor of Bermuda and the British Colonial Office. This time the document was printed – it had evidently been torn from an official Blue Book. What am I to do, Mr Shannon?"

"I'm hanged if I know," he said, puzzled. "One thing you must not do, and that is, to go alone to that queer house next Saturday, or whatever is the day of your appointment. You must let me know the exact hour, and I will be waiting in Portman Square, and when the door opens for you it will be easy for me to slip in." And then, noticing her alarm, he smiled. "I'll remain in the hall within shouting distance, so you need have no qualms that I'm using you for my vile police purposes. We haven't anything against Mr Malpas, except that he is mysterious. And, in spite of all that has been written to the contrary, the police hate mysteries. By the way, were any of the letters you wrote addressed to Mr Lacy Marshalt?"

She shook her head.

"That is the African millionaire, isn't it? He lives next door. The taxi driver told me."

She narrated the queer little comedy she had witnessed on the doorstep of Mr Marshalt's house.

"H'm!" said Dick. "That sounds like one of the old man's petty schemes of annoyance. I think the best thing I can do is to see friend Marshalt and ask him what Malpas has got on him – that there is an enmity between the two is very clear."

A cold wind was blowing, and, warmly clad as she was, he saw her shivering, and jumped up.

"I'm a selfish dog!" he said penitently. "Come and drink a flagon of steaming hot coffee, and I will continue my famous 'Advice to Young Girls Alone in London.'"

"Perhaps at the same time you'll begin it," she said demurely. "So far, we have only had your equally famous lecture on 'How to Get Information from Reformed Criminals'!"

THE MAN WHOM LACY
DID NOT KNOW

Tonger opened the door to Dick Shannon. Tonger had the knack of forestalling the footman and welcoming visitors who had the slightest pretensions to importance, and Dick recognized him by the girl's description. Audrey had said he was bird-like, and certainly there was a strong resemblance in this little old man, with his head perked on one side, his bright eyes, his quick, jerky movements, to an inquisitive sparrow. His keen eyes looked the detective through and through.

"Mr Lacy Marshalt is in – yes," he said, standing square in the doorway. "But you can't see him without an appointment. Nobody can see Mr Lacy Marshalt without an appointment, not while I'm around."

The utter lack of respect amused Dick Shannon. Evidently this was more than an ordinary servant.

"Perhaps you'll take my card to him?"

"Perhaps I will," said the other coolly. "But it's just as likely that I won't! All kinds of queer people want to see Mr Lacy Marshalt, because he's kind and generous and big. That's the sort we train in South Africa, even if we don't breed 'em there. Open-handed, free-hearted – "

He paused to take the card that Dick offered, and read.

"Oh!" he said, a little blankly. "You're a detective, are you? Well, step inside, Captain. Have you come to pinch anybody?"

"Is it possible that anybody requires pinching in this beautifully ordered house, where even the footmen are so polite and deferential that it is painful to trouble them?"

Tonger chuckled.

"I'm not a footman," he said. "You've made a slight error."

"The son of the house?" suggested Dick good-humouredly. "Or perhaps you are Mr Lacy Marshalt?"

"God forbid!" grinned the man. "I shouldn't like to have his money and responsibility. Step this way, Captain."

He ushered the visitor into the drawing-room, and, to Dick's surprise, followed and closed the door.

"There's nothing wrong, is there?" he asked, a note of anxiety in his voice.

"Nothing that I'm aware of," said Dick. "This is a purely friendly call, and you needn't go down to the pantry and count the spoons."

"I'm not the butler either," corrected Tonger. "I'll tell the governor."

He slipped out of the room and in a few minutes returned, preceding Mr Lacy Marshalt. He would have remained, but Marshalt pointedly opened the door for him.

"I hope that fellow hasn't been fresh, Captain Shannon?" he said when they were alone. "Tonger has grown up with me, and has never been wholly civilized in consequence."

"I thought he was rather amusing," said Dick.

Mr Lacy Marshalt grunted.

"He doesn't amuse me at times," he said dourly. "One can pay too big a price for loyalty – there are times when Tonger puts a very heavy strain upon my patience."

He had the detective's card in his hand and now looked at it again.

"You are from Scotland Yard, I see. What can I do for you?"

"First I want to ask you if you know Mr Malpas, your next door neighbour?"

Marshalt shook his head.

"No," he said. "Is this call in reference to a complaint I made some months ago – "

79

"No, I think that was settled by the local police. I've come to see you because I have information that this man Malpas is running some sort of a feud against you. You say you do not know him?"

"I have never seen him, so I can't tell you if I know him or not. Certainly I know nobody whose name is Malpas. Won't you sit down, and will you have a drink?"

Dick refused the drink but pulled up a chair, and the other followed suit.

"What makes you think that Malpas has a grudge against me?" asked Lacy. "It's very likely that he has, because I made a complaint against him, as you evidently know. He was such a noisy beggar that he disturbed my sleep."

"What kind of noise did he make?"

"Hammering, mostly. It sounded as though he were tapping on the wall, though possibly I was mistaken there, and it was more likely that he was closing packing cases."

"You have never seen him?"

"Never."

"Have you had any description of him," asked Dick, "that would enable you even remotely to identify him as somebody you knew in South Africa?"

"No, I know nobody," said Lacy Marshalt, shaking his head. "One has enemies, of course: it is impossible to achieve any measure of success without attaching these disagreeable appendages to life."

Dick considered for a moment. He was dubious about the advisability of taking the millionaire entirely into his confidence, but he decided that, at the risk of subsequently giving himself a great deal of trouble, he would tell Marshalt all he knew.

"Malpas is employing somebody, or is intending to employ somebody, to annoy you, and to cause you inconvenience of a petty character. For example, I am under the impression that the drunken woman who came here a few days ago was sent by him."

"Woman?" Marshalt's brows lowered. "I never heard of any drunken woman coming here."

He got up quickly, rang the bell, and Tonger came in almost immediately.

"Captain Shannon says that a few days ago a drunken woman called at this house and made some sort of disturbance. You never told me."

"Do I tell you everything?" asked Tonger wearily. "A woman certainly did call, and she was certainly oiled."

"Oiled?"

"I mean soused, or, to use a vulgar expression, drunk. What a lady! She fell into the hall, and she fell out again quick. She said she was Mrs Lidderley from Fourteen Streams…"

Dick Shannon was looking at the man's employer as he spoke, and saw Lacy Marshalt's face go grey.

SHANNON PAYS A CALL

"Mrs Lidderley!" said Marshalt slowly. "What sort of a woman was she?"

"She was a little thing," Tonger's eyes were fixed absently on the detective. "But, my word, wasn't she wiry!"

There was relief in Marshalt's sigh.

"A little woman? She was an imposter. Probably she knew the Lidderleys. The last time I heard from South Africa, Mrs Lidderley was very ill." He looked hard at his servant. "You knew the Lidderleys, Tonger?"

"I didn't know Mrs Lidderley. The old chap married after we left the Cape," said Tonger, "if it's Julius Lidderley you mean. Anyway, I pushed her out."

"Did you get her address – where she was staying?"

"Who am I that I should take the address of a soused lady?" asked Tonger, his eyebrows rising. "No, Lacy – "

"Mr Marshalt, damn you!" flamed the other. "How many times am I to tell you, Tonger?"

"It slipped out," said the other, unabashed.

"Follow its example," growled Lacy Marshalt, and slammed the door behind his disrespectful servitor.

"That fellow exasperates me beyond measure," he said. "I've had him so many years, and it is certainly true that we were 'Lacy' and 'Jim' to one another in the old days, and that makes it more difficult. I feel a horrible snob when I insist upon his showing me a little courtesy,

82

but you will see for yourself how extremely embarrassing the volatile Mr Tonger can be!"

Dick laughed. He had been an amused spectator of the scene. Tonger was a type that he had met before in other households – the pet dog that nobody had the heart to destroy, despite its awkward qualities.

"As to Malpas," Marshalt went on, "I don't know anything about him. He may be, and probably is, somebody on whose corns I have stepped at a period of my life, but if I have to pass that category in review, why, I shall be suspicious of a hundred! Have you any description of him?"

"None that you would recognize," said Dick. "The only thing I know is that he's an elderly man, very ugly, and that he commissioned a cabaret singer to molest you, an action which to me seemed hardly worth the trouble, unless you have a peculiar objection to cabaret singers."

Lacy Marshalt paced up and down the big drawing-room, his hands behind him, his chin on his breast.

"The whole thing is inexplicable to me," he said, taking the news with greater calmness than Dick had expected, "and I can only imagine that at some remote period I have done Malpas an injury beyond forgiveness. Why don't you call and see him, Captain Shannon?" he asked, and added quickly: "It is nerve on my part to make suggestions to you! But I'm curious to have this gentleman identified."

But Dick Shannon had already made up his mind that he would see the mysterious Mr Malpas, and the suggestion was unnecessary.

Tonger was waiting in the hall when he came out, and opened the front door for him.

"Is anybody to be pinched?" he asked pleasantly. "We've got a cook we could do without. Come one day and try her pies!"

Dick went out into Portman Square chuckling. He strolled along to the door of the next house and looked up at the blank windows. This was not his first visit to the residence of the eccentric Mr Malpas, but never before had he sought an interview. He looked for the bell, failed to find it, and tapped on the door. There was no answer. He knocked more loudly, and jumped when a voice spoke apparently at his ear.

"Who is that?"

He looked round in bewilderment. There was nobody within twenty yards of him, and yet the voice… And then he saw the small grating let into the stone pillar of the doorway, and found a solution to the mystery. Behind that grating was a loudspeaking telephone.

"I am Captain Richard Shannon from Scotland Yard, and I want to speak to Mr Malpas," he said, addressing the invisible instrument.

"Well, you can't!" snarled the voice, and there was a faint click.

Dick tapped again, but, though he waited for five minutes, no voice spoke to him from the pillar, and the door resisted his pressure. There must be a way to get into touch with this man, and his first act was to search the telephone directory. The name of Malpas, however, did not occur as a resident of Portman Square, and he went back to his flat a little baffled. The day, however, had not been unprofitably spent. He had met the Ragged Princess – ragged no longer – and knew where she was to be found. Dick Shannon was resolved that she should be found, and found as often as he could in common decency call.

TONGER ASSISTS

Few servants enjoyed the freedom and comfort which were Jim
Tonger's. The top floor of the house in Portman Square was his own.
There he had a bedroom, a sitting-room, a bathroom, specially fitted
by his indulgent employer, and here it was his wont to spend long
periods of the evening, engaged in endless mathematical calculations
with the aid of a small roulette wheel; for Tonger had occupied the
greater portion of his life's leisure in perfecting a system which would
one day strike terror and consternation into the hearts of those
responsible for the management of the Casino at Monte Carlo.

He was otherwise engaged that night when the bell over the
doorway shrilled, and he went out of the room hurriedly, locking the
door behind him, and came into the presence of Lacy Marshalt, who
was awaiting him in his study, with greater haste than that gentleman
imagined possible.

"Where the devil have you been?" growled Lacy.

"You rang for me in my room – so I must have been in my room.
I was playing solitaire," said Tonger. "I'm glad you called me, because
I've tried the darned thing thirty times and it hasn't come out. That
means bad luck for me. Have you ever noticed, Lacy, that if you can't
work out a game of solitaire, nothing goes right with you? I
remember the day before I found that diamond patch on Hope River,
I got a 'demon' patience out six times in succession – "

"I want you to let in Mrs Elton at seven forty-five," interrupted
Marshalt. "She'll drive her own car. Be waiting for her in the mews,
and take the machine to the Albert Hall: there's a concert there

tonight. Park it with the others, and after the show is over, bring the car straight back to the mews."

Tonger whistled.

"A bit dangerous, isn't it, after the letter that Elton wrote you?"

Marshalt's eyes narrowed.

"What do you know about the letter that Elton wrote me?" he demanded.

"Oh, you left it about; I couldn't help seeing it," said the servant coolly.

"So far from leaving it about, I put it in the drawer of my desk. I suppose you took it out and read it?"

"It doesn't matter how I saw it – I saw it," said Tonger, "and I tell you that it's dangerous! You don't want to figure in any court case."

"With you as a witness," sneered the other.

Tonger shrugged his thin shoulders.

"You know I'd never go on to the stand and talk against you, Lacy," he said. "That's not my line. But if a fellow like Elton wrote and told me that if I saw his wife again he'd shoot me, why, I guess I'd be interested."

"Mrs Elton and I have certain business to discuss," said Marshalt shortly. "The thing is, I want you to be outside the yard gate at a quarter to eight. As soon as Mrs Elton gets out of her machine, you get in and drive off."

The man nodded.

"So that, if she's being followed and watched, there's the car at the Albert Hall to prove she was there all the time!" he said admiringly. "What a brain! Lacy, what did that busy fellow want?"

"I can't keep track of your slang. What does 'busy' fellow mean?"

"I'm talking about the detective. I take naturally to the argot of the country where I'm living. I wish we were in New York," he said regretfully; "it's a richer language."

Mr Marshalt's lips curled.

"He came to inquire about that crazy man next door," he said. "Apparently he is an enemy of mine."

"Who isn't, Lacy?" asked the other with a sigh. "What have you been doing to *him?*"

"I don't know. I haven't the slightest idea who he is, and I'm not worried, I assure you," said Marshalt carelessly. "Why did you think he called?"

"Over Mrs Elton," said the other coolly. "She's a crook, so is Elton; everybody knows that. You can't touch pitch – not that kind of pitch – without getting your hands black, so black that no Oojah Magic Cleanser can clean it."

A pause.

"I suppose Elton is a crook, but Mrs Elton is quite innocent – "

"So innocent," broke in Tonger, "that angels turn down side streets so as not to feel small when they meet her."

Marshalt checked the angry retort that rose to his lips.

"That is all," he said curtly, and then, as Tonger was going, with unexpected meekness: "I am dining at home tomorrow, and if I have any luck, I shall have rather an interesting guest."

"Who is she?" asked Tonger, himself interested.

"I didn't tell you it was a 'she.'"

"There ain't any other kind of interesting guest," said Tonger coolly. "Have you found that girl?" he asked suddenly. "The girl you set the private detective to find?"

Marshalt started.

"How did you know?"

"I'm a wonderful guesser. Is she to be the belle of the ball tomorrow?"

"I'm hoping she'll come to dinner. And, by the way, you needn't be so much in evidence on that occasion, my friend. I want the parlour maid to be very visible and to wait at table."

"Thus inspiring confidence in the heart of the young and foolish," said Tonger. "All right, governor. What time is this woman coming tonight?"

"Mrs Elton is coming at a quarter to eight: I told you before. And I'd like you to refer to her in those terms, my friend. 'This woman' doesn't sound good to me."

"You're too sensitive, Lacy, that's what's wrong with you," was the valet's parting shot.

He was waiting in the dark mews when the little car came bounding over the cobblestones and jerked to a stop before the door. He helped the slim, muffled passenger to alight, and, contrary to his usual practice, did not speak to her, taking her place in the machine and sending it through the mews to Baker Street.

As he came out into the main road, his sharp eyes detected a watcher standing at the corner of Portman Square, and he grinned to himself. It may have been a casual party to an assignation, but there was something in the patient pose of the figure which suggested private detective. Possibly Mr Elton was not satisfied that his threat would produce the desired effect.

At eleven o'clock he drew out of the phalanx of parked cars, and made his rapid way homeward. Almost as soon as he stopped before the back gate of 551, the door was opened and the girl came out.

"Did you see anybody?" she asked in a low voice. "Anybody you knew?"

"No, ma'am," said Tonger, and then: "I don't think I should do this again if I were you."

She made no reply, slipping into the car and taking her place at the wheel, but Tonger stood with the open door in his hand.

"There are some things that are not worthwhile, ma'am, and this is one of them."

"Shut the door," she said curtly, and he obeyed, and watched the car until its red tail lamps turned the corner. Then he went back to his master.

Lacy Marshalt was in his study, standing before the fire, deep in thought.

"Want me any more?"

Marshalt shook his head.

"Think you're being clever, Lacy?"

The other looked up quickly.

"What do you mean?"

"Do you think it's clever to fly in the face of Providence over a girl you don't care a whole lot about, unless I misunderstand you?"

Instead of the angry reply which Tonger expected, Lacy laughed.

"There is such a thing as wanting the forbidden because it *is* forbidden," he said. "These things are not very palatable without the salt of risk."

"Ever tasted salt – neat?" asked Tonger. "It's rotten! I'm not going to roust you, Lacy, because every man's got his own idea of what's worthwhile. But Elton's the kind that shoots. You can laugh! I know the talkative ones, and I know just how Elton feels, because I've felt that way myself – "

"Get out!" snapped the other, and Tonger went without haste.

Lacy Marshalt's study and bedroom were on the first floor, and were shut off from the rest of the house by a door which cut off a portion of the passage and gave him that complete privacy which his peculiar temperament required. There were moments when he was really unapproachable, and Tonger was quick to recognize the symptoms of that particular mood, and sufficiently wise to leave his sometime friend in peace while the fit was on.

He went back to his room to continue where he had left off that game of patience which would not come out.

Dora Elton got home to find that her husband, who had been out to dinner, had arrived before her.

"Well, was your talk satisfactory?" she asked brightly as she came into the drawing-room.

He looked up from the sofa on which he lay at full length, and shook his head almost imperceptibly.

"No, we shall have to close the establishment. Klein wants too big a share, and he's holding the 'black' up as an inducement. I don't take much notice of that." He pulled at his cigar thoughtfully. "Klein knows that there isn't much money to be had out of the police for shopping a gambling house. There are too many of them. Still, I'd hate to close Pont Street, because it brings steady money and big money, and it's got the kind of clientele that make a straight game profitable."

He looked at his watch. "I was expecting Bob Stanford. Do you want to see him? He's returning from Italy."

She was taking a cigarette from a silver box on the mantelpiece.

"I don't care," she said indifferently. "Do you want a private interview?"

"No," he said after thought. "I saw Audrey tonight."

"Where?" She looked at him in astonishment.

"She was dining at the Carlton Grill."

The match was halfway to the cigarette, and stopped.

"With – ?"

"Shannon – and very cheery. You needn't be afraid. Audrey's not the kind of girl who would give you away."

"I wasn't thinking about that."

"Maybe you were worrying about the impropriety of her dining without a chaperon; and if there was a chaperon there I did not see her," suggested Bunny.

The girl shot a quick, suspicious glance at him.

"I like you least when you're funny," she said. "Was she – well dressed?"

He nodded.

"A most prosperous-looking lady." And added inconsequently, "I never realized she was so beautiful. Shannon hardly took his eyes from her."

"Apparently you were smitten, too," she said with a little smile. "I enjoyed the concert immensely, Bunny. Kessler was wonderful. I don't as a rule like fiddlers – "

"Kessler didn't appear," he said evenly as he blew out a cloud of smoke. He was not looking at her. "He caught a cold and was unable to perform – the fact was announced in the late editions of the evening newspaper: I wonder you didn't see it."

Only for a second was she thrown off her balance.

"I don't know one fiddler from another," she said carelessly. "Anyway, the man they sent in his place plays gorgeously."

"Probably Manz," he nodded.

She was relieved to hear the doorbell ring. What a fool she had been not to make herself completely acquainted with the artists who had appeared that night! Tonger could have attended and made her acquainted with the programme.

Big Bill Stanford came in, a very weary man, for he had spent thirty-six hours in the train, having come direct from Rome. He reported without preliminary.

"The Contessa leaves on Thursday. She breaks her journey in Paris and will be here on Tuesday night. I've got photographs of the tiara and the pearl rope. I think they can both be duplicated in less than a week, and if we can do that the rest will be easy. Stigman has got friendly with the maid – his Italian is grand: you'd think he was a *pukka* wop! She'll give him a chance of 'ringing' the stuff – "

"I thought we weren't going to touch this kind of job again?" said Dora petulantly.

"I'm not," drawled her husband. "We take an outside interest and, Bill, if you bring so much as a pearl into this house I'll brain you!"

"Am I mad?" asked the big man contemptuously. "Did the last job pay so well? No, thank you! Not one link of one platinum chain comes this way. It is going to be easy, Elton."

"I don't want anything to do with it," Dora broke in. "Bunny, why can't we cut this cheap thieving altogether? It is making a nervous wreck of me. I hate it!"

He looked at her.

"Why not?" he asked lazily. "What is ten thousand to you and me? We could live without this kind of work!"

"I could, at any rate," she muttered.

"How? With your needle? Or possibly by giving piano lessons to the musical bourgeoisie? Or perhaps by your art! I forget how much per week you were earning when I drifted across you."

She looked away from him, her lips tightly pressed together.

"Was it three pounds or four pounds a week?" he went on. "I remember that it was some fabulous sum. You were not particular how you climbed into the big type and the principal's salary."

"You might discuss this when we are alone," she said, with a resentful glance at Bill Stanford.

"Bill knows all about it. I've known William longer than I have known Dora, and, speaking generally, he has played the game a little straighter."

She leapt up from her chair, her face white with passion. "How dare you say that!" she stormed. "I have stood by you through thick and thin! You pretend to let bygones rest, and then you throw your beastly suspicions up in my face. Is that *your* idea of playing the game?"

He made no reply, his dark eyes looking at her speculatively.

"I am sorry," he said, but without any great heartiness. "You see how absurd it is to talk about cheap thieving? There isn't any other kind. I am a thief by nature – with talents beyond the ordinary. It sounds as though I am being foolishly boastful, but it is true to say that I am the cleverest burglar in London. There isn't a house I couldn't get into or escape from. I can climb bare walls like a cat – but it isn't necessary that I should. I prefer genteel robbery – which is just robbery, anyway. I stole you into prosperity, and even the price of the wedding ring goes back to a larceny. Lots of men would have got honest just about where that ring had to be bought. Think that out."

She was about to say something but changed her mind and stalked out of the room without a word.

She was in bed when he came into the room, and pretended to be asleep. She saw him gather his pyjamas, dressing gown and slippers, and go out, closing the door softly behind him, and the sound of the second bedroom door opening and closing came to her. Dora sat up in bed suddenly, a panic in her breast. Martin Elton had never done that before.

LACY ENTERTAINS

There came to Audrey Bedford a letter in a strange handwriting. She tore open the envelope, expecting no more than one of those artistic advertisement cards which come inevitably to a hotel guest. Instead she found a letter.

DEAR MISS BEDFORD,
You will be surprised to hear from one who is a stranger to you, but finding your name by chance in the register of the Palace, and thinking that I might be of some service to you, particularly in view of the monstrous miscarriage of justice to which you were a victim, I am writing to ask you if you will come and see me tomorrow evening at 7.30 at the above address. I think I can find you congenial employment – if you are not in need of that, to offer you at least the good offices of a disinterested friend.
            Sincerely,
                        LACY MARSHALT.
PS – Will you send me a wire if you can come?

She puzzled over the letter all the morning. Lacy Marshalt's name was known to her. He belonged to that branch of the politico-social world of people whose names recur in the press. She sent a telegram before lunch, announcing her acceptance of the invitation, after looking up his name in *Who's Who* and discovering that there was a Mrs Marshalt. Mrs Marshalt appeared in all works of reference, but here her tangibility ended. For twenty-five years she had been a most

93

convenient invention. Early in his career, Lacy had discovered that, while the wealthy bachelor might be run after, certain complications followed his attempt to apportion his attentions equally. The wealth of welcome which was his in one quarter was levelled down by the chilling politeness which greeted him elsewhere. "Mrs Marshalt" came into existence to his profit. No longer amongst the eligibles, he retained his place as an amusing companion and gained something in respectability. He never spoke of his wife: when other people made direct or oblique reference to her, he smiled sadly. Without knowing more, the world decided that, if there was an estrangement, Mrs Marshalt was to blame.

Just before half past seven a cab deposited Audrey before the door of Lacy Marshalt's house, and she was admitted by a neatly uniformed maid. She was wearing a simple black dinner frock that she had bought in Shaftesbury Avenue, and, innocent of jewels as she was, there was something so regal in her carriage that Lacy Marshalt stared at her in amazement and admiration. She was infinitely more beautiful than he had thought.

She, for her part, saw a hard-faced, distinguished-looking man, but, what was more to the point, she saw no other guest, and the "Mrs Marshalt" she expected was equally invisible.

"You are Miss Bedford? I am very glad to meet you."

He took her little hand in his, and did not make the mistake of holding it a second longer than was necessary.

"I hope you don't very much object to a *tête-à-tête* dinner. I hate crowds. Twenty years ago, when I was younger, I disliked solitude as intensely."

The subtle emphasis of his age had the effect of quietening the unease in the girl's mind.

"It was very kind of you to ask me, Mr Marshalt," she said with her quick smile. "It isn't everybody who would want to meet a person with my record!"

He shrugged his broad shoulders to indicate his indifference to the opinions of the world.

"You were, of course, perfectly innocent," he said. "Anybody but a congenital idiot knew that. And, what is more, you were screening somebody." He raised his hand. "No, I'm not going to ask you whom, but it was very plucky of you, and I admire you. And I think I can help you, Miss Bedford. A friend of mine needs a secretary – "

"I don't want you to think that I have no work," she smiled. "I am, in fact, employed by a neighbour of yours, though I am not particularly happy about the work."

"A neighbour of mine?" he asked quickly. "Who is that?" And, when she told him: "Malpas? I hadn't the slightest idea that he was human enough to employ anybody. What is he like? – forgive my curiosity, but I'm rather interested in the gentleman."

"He is – not very pretty," she said.

A sense of loyalty made the discussion of her employer a little difficult, and apparently recognizing her embarrassment, he did not press his inquiry.

"If you aren't happy, I think I can get you a position where you'll be most comfortable," he said. "In fact, I can almost promise you the post."

Just then dinner was announced, and they passed out of the drawing-room, along the corridor, through a second door that was opened and which cut off a section of the house, into a small and elegantly furnished dining-room.

As they passed into the room, Lacy stopped to speak to the servant in a low tone, and Audrey heard the murmur of his voice, wondered…and feared.

For a moment she was alone in the room. She looked up and caught a glimpse of her troubled face in the mirror over the mantelshelf.

And then it occurred to her that she was looking at the wall which divided the room from the home of her mysterious employer. Even as this thought came to her –

"*Tap, tap, tap!*"

Somebody in the house of Malpas was rapping on the wall…

"*Tap, tap, tap!*"

It sounded like a warning…yet how could the old man know?

The first part of the meal passed off without any unusual incident. Her host was politeness itself, and when he learnt that she did not drink wine, filled her glass with water. He himself showed no denial in the matter; he drank liberally, without the wine seeming to have the slightest effect upon him, though, when the third bottle of champagne was uncorked by the waiting maid, Audrey began to feel a little uneasy. The sweets came and the coffee, and Lacy pushed a golden box toward her.

"Thank you, I don't smoke," she smiled.

"You have all the virtues, Miss Bedford," he said gallantly. "Mr Malpas does not like you smoking, probably?"

"I have never consulted him," she replied.

"What does he pay you a week?"

She was on the point of answering the question when its cool impertinence came home to her.

"The wage is not settled yet," she said, and looked at the clock on the mantelpiece. "You won't mind if I go early, Mr Marshalt?" she said. "I have some work to do."

The hand that held the big cigar waved impatiently.

"That can wait," he said. "I have a lot to say to you, young lady. I suppose you realize that your job with Malpas will not last forever? He's an eccentric old devil, and the police are after him."

This was news to the girl, though she did not feel the surprise she showed.

"I have reason to believe," Marshalt went on slowly, "that the old man only gave you this job in order to get acquainted with you, and to have an opportunity of studying you, with the idea of a closer acquaintance."

"Mr Marshalt!" she cried indignantly, and came to her feet.

"We were talking as friends," pleaded Marshalt. "I am trying to tell you all I know – "

"You have invented that! You don't even know Mr Malpas; you practically told me so just now."

He smiled.

"I have access to information," he said cryptically, "which puts me beyond the possibility of error. Please sit down, Miss Bedford."

"I must go," she said.

"Wait a little longer. I wanted to talk this matter over with you, and nine o'clock isn't so very late, you know," he laughed.

She sat down again reluctantly.

"I've known you for longer than you can guess. I knew you before this trouble came to you. You probably don't remember seeing me at Fontwell? And it is true that not a day has passed that you have been absent from my thoughts. Audrey, I am very fond of you."

She rose, this time in less haste, and he followed her example.

"I can make life very smooth for you, my dear," he said.

"I prefer a harder road," she answered with quiet dignity, and moved toward the door.

"One moment," he begged.

"You are wasting your time, Mr Marshalt," she said coldly. "I very dimly understand your proposal, and I can only hope that I am mistaken. I very foolishly came here because I thought you were a gentleman who really was anxious to help one who had suffered – unjustly, as you suggested."

And then his tone altered.

"You came here because I sent for you," he said, "and nobody in their senses will suggest that I am dining *tête-à-tête* with you against your will."

She eyed him gravely.

"You seem to forget that you wrote me a letter, and that that letter – " she stopped.

"Is in your handbag," he smiled. "No, my dear young lady, you've got to be sensible. And don't, please, try to go, because this portion of the house is shut off from the rest of the premises, and only one privileged person has the key. If you're a sensible girl, you will be that privileged person."

She ran into the passage. The door leading to the entrance hall was closed. She pulled at the handle, but it did not budge. In another second his arm was round her, and, lifting her as though she were a child, he carried her, struggling, back to the little dining-room.

With all her strength she beat at the face pressed down to hers, and, with a superhuman effort, flung herself free. Her eyes fell upon a sharp-pointed carving-knife that lay upon the buffet, and, snatching it up, she stood at bay.

"I will kill you if you touch me!" she said breathlessly. "Open that door!"

At heart Lacy Marshalt was a coward, and before the threat of the knife he drew back.

"For God's sake don't be a fool," he cried. "I – I only want to help you."

"Open the door!"

He fumbled in his pocket at his key chain, and pulled out a bunch. She heard the click of the lock turning and went out, passing him quickly as he stood with the door in his hand. Beyond was the dimly lit passage.

"Will you forgive me?" he whispered.

She made no reply, but swept past him, dropping the knife on the carpet.

"To the right," he whispered, as if giving her directions.

Obeying him, she turned into a narrow passage, though her instinct and her memory told her that the way to safety lay straight ahead. Before she realized her danger, he was behind her. Only a second she hesitated, and then fled down the narrow corridor. At the end was a flight of stairs, and up these she flew, the man in pursuit. In absolute darkness she was climbing what was evidently a servants' stairway. How many flights she traversed in her terror, she did not know. Suddenly she stopped: the footsteps were no longer following her. Above her head was a skylight, out of reach. There was nothing to do but to retrace her steps, and stealthily she walked down the carpeted stairs. She had reached the landing below when she heard a thin wail of sound, the sound of a woman sobbing.

The acoustic properties of the stairway were such that she could not locate the sound. It might come from underneath, from above; it might be penetrating the partition wall which separated her from the next house — the house of Mr Malpas!

She listened intently. The sobbing died to a low wail, and then was silent. Only for a moment was her attention distracted from her own imminent peril. There was no sound or sign of Lacy Marshalt, and she descended a second flight, peering nervously into the darkness, to which her eyes had now grown so used that she was able to see distinctly. She came to the floor where the little dining-room was situated, and to the narrow hall, beyond the entrance to which lay freedom. Still no sign of Lacy.

And then, as she stepped cautiously into the corridor, a hand came around her waist, another covered her mouth; she was carried bodily back to the dining-room, and the door clicked behind her.

"Now, my little jailbird!" Lacy Marshalt's voice was tremulous with triumph. "You and I will have an intelligent talk!"

He thrust her down into a deep armchair, and she sat, dishevelled, breathless, her unflinching eyes never leaving his face.

"If my servants had not strict orders to confine themselves to the servants' hall, there would have been the beginnings of a scandal. Are you going to see my point of view? If I'd known what a little wildcat I was going to entertain, I should have had a chaperon," he said humorously.

He poured out a glass of wine and pushed it to her.

"Drink this," he ordered.

On the point of collapse, she felt her strength slipping from her, and, risking everything, she drank the wine greedily.

"It's not drugged; you needn't look at it twice," he said. "Audrey, are you going to be a good girl? I want you, my dear. You're the one woman in the world that I have ever wanted, and I never realized that fact until tonight. I can give you everything that heart can desire — money beyond your dreams — "

"You're wasting your time, Mr Marshalt," she said. The wine had steadied her, had given her a new strength. "I won't tell you how greatly you have insulted me: such words would be empty and meaningless to you. I'm going back to the hotel, and I shall call up Captain Shannon, and tell him what has happened."

He laughed.

"In other words, you're going to fetch a policeman! Well, that is a very old-fashioned kind of threat which doesn't frighten me. Shannon's a man of the world; he knows that I wouldn't invite a lady from Holloway to dine with me, unless…well, use your intelligence, my child. And he knows that you wouldn't accept unless you expected to be made love to. You think I'm a brute, but the caveman method saves a lot of time and a lot of stupid preliminaries. Generally speaking, women prefer it to all others."

"Your kind of woman may, but I am not your kind," she said.

"By God, you are!" he said in a low voice. "You are not only my kind, but you are all women to me – the very quintessence of womanhood!"

He stooped and lifted her up, his strong arms about her, one hand behind her head, and she gazed in horrified fascination into the deeps of his black soul. Only for a second, then his lips were pressed to hers. She was helpless; consciousness was slipping from her; life, and all that made life, was going out to the drum beats of her broken heart, when she was faintly conscious of a movement at the lock: somebody was fitting a key. He heard it, too, and, releasing her so suddenly that she dropped to her knees on the floor, spun round as the door opened slowly. A woman in black was standing there, her brooding eyes looking from the man to the dishevelled girl on the floor.

It was Dora Elton, and Audrey, looking up, saw the hate in her sister's eyes and shivered.

THE STORY OF JOSHUA

"I seem to have come at an awkward moment," said Dora Elton in a metallic voice.

She met the blazing fury in Marshalt's eyes without flinching.

"You are rather partial to our family, Lacy," she said.

Audrey had struggled to her feet, and, gathering her wrap, walked unsteadily past her sister into the hall and to the cold, clean air of the night.

Not a word was spoken till the thud of the front door told them that she was gone, and then: "I'm not going to ask you for an explanation, because it is fairly obvious," said Dora.

He poured out a glass of wine with a hand that shook, and gulped it down before he spoke.

"I asked her to come to dinner, and she got a little fresh – that's all. There was nothing to it," he said.

She smiled.

"I can't imagine the gentle Audrey 'getting a little fresh,' but women are queer creatures under your magnetic influence, Lacy." Then she went off at a tangent. "Bunny knew I was here the other night – the night I was supposed to be at the concert."

"I don't care a damn what he knew," growled the man. "If you get so rattled about what Bunny thinks and what Bunny knows, you'd better give up coming here."

Again she smiled.

"And you would like the key, of course? Bunny would find it handy. It opens the back gate and the conservatory door and this dear little *sanctum sanctorum*. Bunny has rather a passion for pass keys."

"I don't want you to think there was anything between your sister – "

"She is not my sister, but that doesn't matter. And as for there being anything between you… Lacy, you beast!"

The air of amused indifference had dropped from her. Rage shook her from head to foot, bereft her of speech for a while, though presently it came in full and spiteful flood.

"I've risked everything for you. I've lied and deceived…oh, you vile thing! I've always hated her. God, how I hate her now! And you want her to take my place? I'll kill you first! I'll shoot you like a dog, Lacy – "

"You shoot me every day," he interrupted with an angry laugh. "Either you or your husband. I'm a human target for the Eltons. Now be sane, Dora."

He took her by the shoulders and drew the head of the sobbing girl to his breast.

"If you think I'm in love with that kid, you're mad. I'm going to make a confession, and you've got to believe me this time."

She murmured something that he could not hear, but he could guess, and he smiled over her shoulder.

"Well, this is the truth – for once! There's one man in the world I hate worse than any other, and that man is Audrey Bedford's father. That makes you jump!"

"Her name is not Bedford," she said with a gulp. She was drying her eyes with a little handkerchief.

"You're right that much. Her name is Torrington, though yours was not. Dan Torrington and I are old enemies. I've got a big score to wipe off, and it's not cleared yet."

"Her father is a convict." There was still a sob in her voice.

Lacy nodded.

"He's on the breakwater at Cape Town, serving a life sentence," he said. "If my gun had thrown straight, he'd have been a dead man. He was lucky; I got his leg and lamed the swine. If the detectives hadn't claimed him at that moment, I'd have been dead, I guess."

"Then you had him arrested?" she said, looking up in surprise.

He nodded.

"Yes, I was running the secret service for the Streams Diamond Mining Corporation, and I discovered that Dan Torrington was engaged in illicit diamond buying. I trapped him, and that's about the whole of the story, except that he got his extra time for shooting at me."

She pushed herself clear of him and, womanlike, walked to the mirror above the mantelpiece.

"Look at my eyes!" she said in dismay. "Oh, what a fool I was to come! I don't know whether to believe you or not, Lacy. How could you revenge yourself upon Torrington by making love to this girl?"

He laughed.

"Well, maybe it isn't as obvious as it looks," he said. "I was a fool, anyway, to try to carry her off her feet. I should have gone slowly and steadily, and then she would have married me."

"Married you?" she gasped.

He nodded.

"That was the general idea."

"But – but you said you would never marry – "

"Here's a story that sounds as if it had been taken from a book," he said. "When Torrington was buying diamonds from the natives, he was the owner of a farm called Graspan. There are thousands of Graspans in South Africa, but this particular Graspan stood on a river, one of those after which Fourteen Streams is named. He had hardly been sent down to penal servitude before a big pipe was discovered on the farm, and by 'pipe' I mean a diamond pipe. I never knew this till a short time ago, because the property has been worked in the name of his lawyers, Hallam and Coold. In fact, it is called the Hallam and Coold Mine today. Dan Torrington is a millionaire; he is also a dying millionaire. Ever since I've been in England I've had one of the warders on the Breakwater send me a monthly report about the man, and the last news I had was that he was slowly sinking."

"Then if you marry Audrey – ?"

He laughed again.

"Exactly! If I marry Audrey, I shall be an extremely wealthy man."

She looked at him, puzzled.

"But you're rich now!"

The smile left his face.

"Yes, I'm rich now," he said brusquely, "but I could be richer."

A tap at the door arrested him.

"Who is that?" he called sharply.

The maid's voice answered:

"A gentleman to see you, sir. He says his business is urgent."

"I can see nobody. Who is it?"

"Captain Shannon, sir."

Dora's mouth opened in an "Oh!" of horror. "He mustn't see me! Where can I go?"

"Through the conservatory and out the back way, the way you came," snapped Lacy.

He had hardly pushed her into the darkened library and returned to his room before Dick Shannon walked through the door. He was in evening dress, and there was a look on his face that was not pleasant to see.

"I want to speak to you, Marshalt."

"Mr Marshalt," snarled the other, sensing the antagonism.

"Mr or Marshalt, it's just the same to me. You invited a lady to dine with you tonight."

A light dawned upon the South African.

"Suppose the lady invited herself to dine with me?" he said coolly.

"You invited a lady to dine with you tonight, and you offered her the deadliest insult a man can offer to any woman."

"My dear fellow," drawled Marshalt, "you're a man of the world. Do you imagine this girl came here with her eyes shut to – to possibilities?"

For a second Dick Shannon stared at him, and then he struck the man across the face with the back of his hand, and Marshalt fell back with a roar of fury.

"That is a lie which must not be repeated," said Dick Shannon in a low voice.

"You call yourself a policeman – is that part of your duty?" screamed Lacy.

"I know the duties of the police very well," said Dick sternly. "They are carved over the face of the Old Bailey. Remember them, Marshalt! 'Protect the children of the poor and punish the wrongdoer.' "

Dick Shannon came out from Marshalt's house a little cooler than he had been when he entered. Glancing up – an almost mechanical act – at the next house, he saw a slit of light in one of the windows, and despite his absorption in Audrey's wrongs and his own murderous feelings toward Lacy Marshalt, he was so struck by the unaccustomed sight that he crossed the road to get a better view. He had been examining the house when Audrey came out and literally ran into him, and there had been no sign of life then. Somebody was peering down through the slit; he saw a vague movement, and then the light went out.

Crossing the road again, he tapped on the door, but there was no answer. Waiting, his mind still occupied with the tearful Audrey, he thought he heard a faint sound in the hall. Was the mystery man coming down, after all? He took a step down to the pavement and drew a little flash-lamp from his pocket. But if the uncouth Mr Malpas had intended to come into the open, he changed his mind.

For ten minutes Dick Shannon waited, and then gave up the vigil. He wanted to see Audrey that night and get from her a statement in greater detail than the incoherent story she had told him.

Walking to the Baker Street side of the square, he glanced left and right for a taxi. There was none in sight, and he looked back along the way he had come. Was it his imagination, or did he see a dark figure emerge from the mystery house and, crossing the road with a curious limping gait, hurry toward the far end of the square? The figure was real enough. The question was, were his eyes tricking him to the belief that it had emerged from the home of Mr Malpas?

He walked swiftly in pursuit, his rubber-soled shoes making no sound. The quarry was making a circuit that would bring him to the Oxford Street end of the square, and had reached the corner of Orchard Street when Shannon came up with him.

"Excuse me."

The limping stranger turned a keen, thin face to the detective. Behind the gold-rimmed spectacles two searching eyes scrutinized the newcomer, and almost imperceptibly his hand had dropped into the depths of his overcoat pocket.

"You're a friend of Mr Malpas, aren't you?" asked Dick. "I saw you coming out of his house!"

Shannon experienced queer flashes of telepathy at odd times – he was conscious of one such manifestation now. As the man looked at him, he read his thoughts as clearly as if he had spoken. The stranger was saying:

"You were a long way off when you first saw me, otherwise you would have overtaken me before. Therefore, you are not certain as to which house I came from."

In actual words he said: "No, I don't know Mr Malpas. The fact is, I am a stranger to London and was trying to find my way to Oxford Circus."

"I didn't see you in the square until a few minutes ago."

The spectacled man smiled.

"Probably because I came in from this end and, finding that I was wrong, retraced my steps. There is a certain amount of amusement to the idle stranger in being lost in a great city."

Dick's eyes never left his face.

"Are you living in town?"

"Yes – at the Ritz-Carlton. I am the president of a South African mine. By the way, you will think I am rather foolish to give this information to a chance acquaintance, but you are a detective – Captain Richard Shannon, unless I am mistaken."

Dick was staggered.

"I don't remember meeting you, Mr – ?" he paused expectantly.

"My name cannot possibly interest you – my passport is in the name of Brown. The Colonial Office will supply you with particulars. No, we have not met before. But I happen to know you."

Dick had to laugh in spite of his chagrin.

"Let me put you in the way of finding Oxford Circus – a taxicab is the quickest method of reaching the place. I will share one with you; I am going to Regent Street."

The old man inclined his head courteously, and at that moment a disengaged taxi came into view and was captured.

"The apparent prosperity of London astounds me," said Mr Brown with a sigh. "When I see these platoons of houses, each inhabited by somebody who must enjoy an income of ten thousand pounds a year, I wonder where the money came from originally."

"It never struck me that way," said Shannon.

With the help of the street lights he had taken a good look at the man. There was little about him that could be regarded as sinister. His hair, which was plentiful, was white, his shoulders were slightly bowed, and although his thin hands were knotted and gnarled like a manual labourer's he had the appearance of a gentleman.

At the corner of the Circus the cab stopped, and the old man alighted painfully.

"I'm afraid I'm rather a cripple," he said good-humouredly. "Thank you, Captain Shannon, for your assistance."

Dick Shannon watched him as he limped into the crowd about the entrance of the tube station.

"I wonder?" he said aloud.

A MESSAGE FROM MALPAS

Audrey was waiting for him in the lounge of the Palace, and all trace of her distress had vanished.

"I hope I haven't kept you from bed," he said apologetically.

All the way down Regent Street he was hoping most devoutly that he had.

She was reluctant to return to her unpleasant experience of the evening, but he was firm on the point.

"No, I'm not going to make any further trouble."

She silently noted the word "further," but wisely did not press him for an explanation.

"Marshalt has a pretty bad private reputation, and had I known that you contemplated meeting him, I should have stopped you."

"I thought he was married," she said ruefully, and he shook his head.

"No. That is his famous 'safety-first' stunt. It prevents his lady friends from resting their hopes too high. He is an unmitigated scoundrel in spite of his wealth, and I'd give a lot to deal with him – adequately! Audrey, you've got to leave Portman Square severely alone."

"Audrey? I don't mind really, though I feel I ought to be a little more grown-up. In Holloway they called me '83,' or, if they were being more than usually kind, just plain 'Bedford' – I think I prefer Audrey from people who aren't likely to hold my hand and get sentimental."

He tried hard to be annoyed and failed.

"You're quaint. I'll call you Audrey, and if ever I grow sentimental, just say 'business,' and I'll behave. And you will leave Portman Square."

She looked up quickly.

"You mean Mr Malpas?"

He nodded.

"I don't know how many of his hundreds you have spent – "

"Sixty pounds," she said.

"I'll give you that, and you can send him back his money."

He felt her resistance to this proposal before she spoke.

"I can't do that, Captain Shannon," she said quickly. "I must make my own arrangements. When I see him on Saturday I will ask him to specify the wage he is paying, and tell him frankly how much I have spent, and that I want to return the balance to him. When that interview is over – "

"And it had better not last long, princess," said Dick grimly, "or I'll be stepping into his grisly drawing-room– "

"Why do you call me princess?" she asked with a little frown, and he went red.

"I don't know... Yes, I do! I'll change my habits and tell the truth! I think of you as the – as the ragged princess. There is an old German legend, or maybe it is Chinese, about a princess who was so beautiful that she was by law compelled to dress in rags to prevent everybody from falling in love with her to the disturbance of domestic peace and happiness, and the first time I saw you I was reminded of the story, and christened you so."

"And that ends your interview," she said severely.

She was by no means annoyed, though he did not know this. In the privacy of her room she laughed long and softly at the story and the compliment it held.

She was preparing for bed when she saw the note which had been left on her dressing table. The scrawled writing she knew at once and tore open the envelope:

I congratulate you on your escape. You should have used the knife.

She gasped. How did Malpas know what had happened behind the locked doors of Lacy's sanctuary?

Audrey had left Dick Shannon in no doubt as to her real mind before he took his departure, for she was a bad actress. Walking home, he arrived at the door of his flat a little after eleven o'clock when the theatres were turning out and the streets were lively with rushing cars, and just as he was going in, he was aware that, standing on the edge of the sidewalk, was a man whom he had met before that evening. He walked back to the motionless loiterer.

"Are you still lost, Mr Brown?" he asked pleasantly.

"No, I'm not," was the cool reply. "It occurred to me after I left you that I would like to have a little talk with you."

A moment's hesitation, then: "Come in," said Dick, and ushered his visitor into his flat. "Now, Mr Brown?" he said, pushing forward a chair, into which his visitor sank with a sigh of relief.

"Standing about or walking is a little painful to me," he said. "Thank you, Captain Shannon. What do you know about Malpas?"

The directness of the question took the detective aback.

"Probably less than you," he said at last.

"I know nothing," was the uncompromising reply, "except that he is a gentleman who keeps himself very much to himself, doesn't interfere with his neighbours, and doesn't invite interference from them."

Was there a challenge in the tone? Dick found it difficult to answer the question.

"The only thing we know about him is that he has strange visitors."

"Who hasn't?" was the reply. "But is anything known to his detriment?"

"Nothing whatever," said Dick frankly, "except that we are constitutionally suspicious of elderly people who live alone. There is always a chance that some day we shall have to force an entrance and discover his tragic remains. Why do you think I know anything about him at all?"

"Because you were watching the house before the young lady came out of Marshalt's and distracted your attention," was the cool reply.

Dick looked hard at him.

"You told me you had just walked into the square and out again?" he said.

"One has to prevaricate," was the calm reply. "Even in your business it is not possible to preserve an even candour. The truth is, I was watching the watcher, and wondering what you had against Malpas."

"You weren't watching from inside the house by any chance?" asked Dick dryly, and the man chuckled.

"It would certainly be the best post of observation," he replied evasively. "I've been wondering, by the way, what happened to that unfortunate girl? Marshalt had a reputation for gallantry in the old days. One supposes that he has not wholly reformed. Have you ever seen anything like this?"

He went off at a tangent, and putting his fingers into his waistcoat pocket, produced a small brown pebble, to which was affixed a red seal. Dick took it in his hand and examined it curiously.

"What is that?" he asked.

"That is a diamond in the rough, and the red seal is the mark of our corporation. We mark all our stones of any size in that way, using a special kind of wax that hasn't to be heated."

Dick looked at the diamond and passed it back.

"No, I've not seen anything like it. Why do you ask?"

"I was wondering." The old man was watching him closely. "You're sure nobody has brought that kind of stone to you – the police come into possession of curious properties."

"No, I have not seen one before. Have you lost a stone?"

The old man licked his lips and nodded.

"Yes, we've lost a stone," he said absent-mindedly. "Have you ever heard of a man called Laker? I see that you haven't. An interesting person. I'd like to have introduced him to you. A clever man, but he drank rather heavily, which meant, of course, that he wasn't clever at

111

all. There is nothing clever about booze, except the people who sell it. Laker, sober, was a genius; drunk, he was the biggest kind of fool. You never saw him?"

The eyes rather than the voice asked the question.

"No, I don't know Laker," confessed Dick Shannon, "which means that officially he is unknown."

"Oh!" The old man seemed disappointed, and rose as abruptly as he had sat down. "You will begin to think that I'm something of a mystery myself," he said, and then, in his brisk way: "Did anything happen to that young lady?"

"Nothing, except that she had a very unpleasant experience."

Mr Brown showed his teeth in a mirthless smile.

"How could one meet the Honourable Lacy and not have an unpleasant experience?" he asked dryly.

"You know him, then?"

Brown nodded.

"Very well?"

"Nobody knows anybody very well," the other said. "Good night, Captain Shannon. Forgive me for intruding upon you. You have my address if you want to find me. Will you please. telephone first, because I spend a considerable time in the country?"

Dick went to the window and watched the limping man pass out of sight. Who was he? What feud was there between Marshalt and him? He almost wished be were on speaking terms with the South African, that he might satisfy his curiosity.

MARTIN ELTON PREDICTS
AN INQUEST

Lacy Marshalt came to breakfast in the blackest mood. The mark of Dick's knuckles still showed redly on his face, his eyes were hollow from want of sleep. Tonger recognized the symptoms and was careful not to draw upon himself the wrath of his employer. Yet, sooner or later, that rage was to burst forth. Something of a philosopher, the valet waited until Marshalt had finished a fairly substantial breakfast, and then:

"Mr Elton called to see you – I told him you weren't up. He's coming back."

Marshalt glowered at him.

"You can tell him I'm out of town," he rasped.

"He happens to know you're in town. It's not for me to give you suggestions, Marshalt, but that's a bad habit you've got into, standing before the window before you're dressed. He saw you."

Lacy Marshalt felt an inward twinge at the mention of Martin's name; but if there was to be any unpleasantness, it were better that it was disposed of while he was in his present mood.

"Bring him in when he comes," he said. "And if he asks you any questions about Mrs Elton – "

"Am I a child?" said the other contemptuously. "Besides, Elton isn't that sort. He was trained as a gentleman, but broke down in training. That kind does not question servants."

If Elton was coming in a truculent mood, he could deal with the matter once and for all. Dora was beginning to bore him. Lacy's ideal woman was self-reliant and free from sentimentality. He had thought Dora was of this type, but she was leaning more and more upon him, bringing problems for his examination which she might dispose of herself, and, worse than all, showing a cloying affection which both alarmed and annoyed him.

He had not long to wait for the advent of Dora's husband. He was halfway through the first leading article of *The Times* when Tonger came in and said, in sepulchral tones: "Mr Elton, sir."

He looked up, trying to read the sphinx-like face of the debonair young man who came into the room, silk hat in one hand, ebony walking stick in the other.

"Good morning, Elton."

"Good morning, Marshalt."

He put down his hat and stripped off his gloves slowly.

"Sorry to interrupt your breakfast." Bunny pulled a chair from the table and sat down. His face was pale, but that was not unusual; his dark eyes were normally bright. "I wrote you a letter some time ago, about Dora," he said, playing with a fork that lay on the table. "It was a little direct; I hope you didn't mind?"

"I don't remember receiving any letter of yours that offended me, Elton," said Marshalt with a smile.

"I hardly think you would forget this particular epistle," said Martin. "It had to do with Dora's little dinner parties; and, if I remember aright, I asked you not to entertain her again."

"But, my dear fellow – " expostulated the other.

"I know it looks stupid and tyrannical and all that sort of thing, but I'm rather fond of Dora. One gets that way with one's wife. And I want to save her from the hideous experience of explaining her relationship with you before a coroner's jury."

He met Lacy's eyes and held them.

"Naturally," he went on with a little smile, "I wouldn't risk a trial for killing you, unless you passed out in such circumstances as threw no suspicion upon me. I wish to avoid, if possible, the vulgarity of *felo de se*, for I have still so much respect for my family that I would spare them the publicity which the more sensational newspapers would give to the case."

"I don't understand you. I'm afraid – " began Lacy.

"That I can't believe," Martin Elton interrupted him. "I'm sorry you make it necessary for me to say this. Dora has visited you twice since that warning came to you. There must be no third visit."

"Your wife came to me last night with her sister," said the inventive Lacy. "She was not here a minute."

The other's eyes opened.

"With her sister? You mean Audrey? Was she here?"

"Yes, she was here. Didn't Dora tell you?"

Lacy Marshalt determined to brazen the matter out. He could telephone to Dora after her husband left and acquaint her with the story he had told.

"Yes, Audrey was dining with me alone, and Dora got to hear of it, and came to fetch her away, thinking that my company would contaminate her." He smiled largely.

Martin thought for a long time.

"That doesn't sound like Dora," he said. "As a matter of fact, she told me she hadn't been here at all, but that little piece of deception I can understand. You know Audrey?"

The South African shrugged.

"I can't say that I know her: I've met her," he said.

"But Audrey was not here on the night of the concert at the Albert Hall, was she?"

Lacy made no reply.

"I don't think you will be able readily to invent a chaperon for that occasion. I think that is all I want to say."

He walked across to where he had put his hat and his stick, and picked them up.

"You're a shrewd fellow, Marshalt – a little on the crook side, unless I'm greatly mistaken, and I'm sure it's not necessary for me to indulge in the heroics proper to this occasion, to impress upon you the advantages of being a live millionaire over – well, other things. The jury will probably pass a resolution of condolence with your relatives, and in that you will have the advantage over me. But it is ever so much more satisfactory to read about somebody else's demise than to be the chief figure in your own. Good morning, Marshalt."

He paused at the door.

"You need not telephone to Dora – I took the precaution of putting the instrument out of order before I left the house," he said, and nodded a grave farewell.

A PROPOSAL

It was a bright wintry morning. A blue sky overhead and yellow sunlight flooding Audrey's room – a day that says, "Come out of doors" and lures the worker to idleness.

Audrey surveyed her task with no great relish. A small pile of pencilled notes, written on every variety of paper, had to be copied and returned by that evening. The work itself was practically nothing: it was the monotony, the seeming uselessness of the task, which distressed her. And she had an uncomfortable feeling, amounting to certainty, that her employer was merely finding little jobs to occupy her time, and that the real service which he had in mind would be revealed in a more unpalatable light.

She opened her window, looked down into the busy street, in a desire to find some attraction that would give her an excuse for putting off a little longer her work. But interest failed, and, with a sigh, she went back to her desk, dipped the pen in the ink, and began. She finished by lunch time, enclosed copies and rough notes in a large envelope, and, addressing them to "A Malpas, Esq., 551 Portman Square," dropped them in the hotel letter box.

Who was Mr Malpas, and what was his business? she wondered. Youth hates the abnormal, and Audrey was true to her age. She was looking forward with some dread to the interview, which might very well end embarrassingly for her; but all her thoughts and her speculations were coloured by one uncomfortable undercurrent which she would not allow herself to put into shape. Not the least of the shocks of the previous evening had been the discovery she had made of Dora's friendship with Marshalt. She was more than shocked; she was horrified. She had a new view of her sister, the ugliest view yet. Had it been she whose sobs she heard? That was unlikely. Audrey had wondered since whether that sound of weeping was not a trick of imagination, conjured by her own terror. Whenever she allowed her mind to halt at the contemplation of Dora, she felt nauseated, and hurried on to a thought less painful.

Then it came to her, as it had come to her in prison, that Dora was almost a stranger to her. She had always regarded their relation as an irrevocable something which gave them, automatically, identical interests. They were two hands of the same body. Yet, if Dora had always belonged elsewhere, the estrangement so violently emphasized had not produced so great a shock as this new discovery.

On her way to the restaurant the hall porter gave her a letter which had just arrived by messenger. One glance at the pencilled address told her that it was from Malpas. He had never before sent a message in the daytime, and she had a little spasm of apprehension that he wished to see her. The note was brief and puzzling:

I forbid your seeing Marshalt again. The offer he is making to you today must be rejected.

She gazed at the peremptory lines in astonishment, resenting alike the tone and the calm assumption of authority. What offer was Marshalt making? It mattered very little; without this order, she would reject the most alluring proposition that the ingenuity of the South African could devise.

The nature of the offer she was to learn. Halfway through luncheon, the page brought her the second letter, and she recognized Lacy Marshalt's flowing hand. The letter began with an abject apology for his boorishness of the previous night. He would never forgive himself (he said), but prayed that she would be more merciful. He had known her for longer than she imagined and…

...I chose the most awkward, the most stupid way of meeting you. Audrey, I love you, sincerely and truly, and if you will consent to be my wife you will make me the happiest man in the world.

An offer of marriage! It was the last thing she expected from Lacy Marshalt, and she lost no time in replying, leaving her lunch unfinished to pen the answer.

DEAR SIR,
I thank you for what is evidently intended as a compliment. I have no regret in refusing to consider your offer.
Sincerely yours,
AUDREY BEDFORD.

"Send that by express messenger," she said, and went back to her luncheon with a feeling that the day, so far, had been well spent.

The offer had had an effect. It had brought from the background of her thoughts a matter which she had partly suppressed. She had a sudden impulse and acted upon it.

A cab dropped her before the little house in Curzon Street, and this time her reception was more gracious than that which had been accorded on her previous visit. And for a good reason: the servant did not recognize her.

"Mrs Elton, Miss? I will see if she is in. What name?"

"Say Miss Audrey."

Evidently the servant did not recognize the name either, for she showed her into the chill room where she had been received before.

Audrey waited until the girl had gone upstairs, and followed her. She had no illusions about Dora's attitude.

"Tell her I am not at home," said Dora's voice. "If she doesn't go, send for a policeman — "

"I'll not keep you long," said Audrey, coming into the room at that moment.

119

For a breathing space Dora stood motionless, her eyes blazing. With an effort she controlled herself and sent away the servant with a gesture.

"Every second you are in my house is a second too long," she said at last. "What do you want?"

Audrey walked slowly to the fireplace and stood with her back to it, her hands behind her.

"Does Martin know about Lacy Marshalt?" she asked.

Dora's eyes narrowed until they were dark slits.

"Oh…it's about Marshalt."

"I want you to give him up, Dora."

"To you?"

The woman's voice was husky; Audrey saw the trembling lips and knew the symptoms. Not for the first time was she watching the gathering of a storm which would presently break in wild, tempestuous fury.

"No. I think he is despicable. I don't know any man that I like less. Dora, you can't love him?"

No answer, then: "Can't I?… Is that all?"

"That isn't all. I'm not going to preach at you, Dora, but Martin is your husband – isn't he?"

The girl nodded.

"Yes, Martin is my husband. Is that all?"

The agony in her voice touched Audrey for a second, and she took a step toward her sister – but Dora drew back with an expression of such loathing and hatred that the girl was stricken motionless.

"Don't come near me… Is that all? You want me to give up a man I love and who loves me. Give him up to you? That is why you have come here today?"

Audrey drew a breath.

"It is useless," she said. "I want you to be happy, Dolly – "

"Call me Dora, you sneak! You jailbird – you…! You've finished, haven't you? You came here for my good? I hate you! I have always hated you! Mother hated you, too – she as good as told me once! Give up Marshalt! What do you mean? I'm going to marry him when I've got rid of – when the time comes. Get out of here!"

She flew to the door and crashed it open. White as death, the rage in her eyes smouldered like live coals.

"I'm going to fix you, Audrey Torrington – "

"Torrington!" gasped the girl.

Dora pointed to the open doorway and with a gesture of despair Audrey walked through. She went down the stairs to the hall, her sister at her heels, and all the time the elder girl was muttering like one demented. Audrey heard snatches of her talk and shivered. The mask was off – all restraint was thrown to the winds.

"You spy, you smug, hypocritical thief! He's going to marry you, is he? Never, never, never!"

Audrey heard the scrape of steel and swung round. On the walls of the hallway hung two trophies of Scottish armour: a steel buckler, a dirk and two crossed pikes.

"Dora – for God's sake!"

In the woman's hand flashed a long steel dirk. She stood at the foot of the stairs, crouched like a wild beast about to spring.

The woman was mad with jealousy and hate. Audrey was conscious that behind her was the scared parlour maid, twittering in her fear. She grasped the handle of the little waiting room, but before she could turn it Dora was on her. She struck savagely; instinct made the girl stoop, and the dirk point buried itself in the wood of the doorpost. Wrenching it free, she stabbed again, and Audrey in her panic stumbled and fell.

"I've got you now!" screamed the maddened woman, and the dirk went up.

And then a hand gripped her wrist, and she wrenched herself round to meet a pair of the most amused eyes that ever shone in a dimpled, dishonest face.

"If I'm interrupting a cinema picture, lady, I'm sorry," said Slick Smith; "but I'm nervous of steel, I am, really!"

SLICK HINTS

The door had closed upon Audrey before Dora Elton recovered some of her normality. She was trembling from head to foot, her head was swimming.

Slick Smith took her arm, led her into the little sitting-room, and pushed her down into a chair, and she did not resist him.

"Get your lady a glass of water," he said to the agitated parlour maid. "These rehearsals of amateur theatricals are certainly fierce."

Dora looked up wonderingly.

"I've been a fool," she said shakily.

"Who hasn't?" asked the sympathetic Mr Smith. "Every woman makes a fool of herself over some man. It's too bad when he's not worth it, lady, too bad!"

The maid came back with the water, and Dora drank greedily. Presently she pushed away the glass that he held.

"She was to blame," she gasped. "She...she...oh, she is hateful!"

"I won't argue with you," said Mr Smith diplomatically; "it would only make you worse. She always seemed to me to be a very nice girl. She went to prison to save you, didn't she?"

Dora looked at the man again and began to realize dimly that he was a stranger. In her elementary passion she had seemed to know him.

"Who are you?" she asked.

"Your husband knows me. I'm Smith – Slick Smith of Boston. Shannon thinks I'm bluffing when I say that I operated in America, but he's wrong. I'm English born and Boston bred; the most elegant

122

combination known to humanity – class and culture. Lady, he's not worth it."

He changed the direction of his speech so quickly that she did not grasp his meaning at first.

"Who…who isn't worth it?"

"Marshalt – he's dead wrong; you don't want me to tell you that? He'd use his first-born for shoe leather if he wanted boots. I like Martin – he's a good fellow. And I'd just hate to see somebody club him just as he was turning his gun on himself. Those kind of accidents happen. And maybe you'd go to the trial and he'd smile at you when the Awful Man put on the black cap before he sent Elton to the death cell. And you'd be sitting there frozen…thinking what a skunk Marshalt was, and how you'd brought both men to the grave. There's only three clear Sundays after a man's sentenced. Three Sundays, and then he toes the T mark on the trap. You'd go and see Martin the day before, and he'd try ever so hard to cheer you up. And then you'd have a night of hell, waiting… And when the clock struck eight – "

"For God's sake, stop!" She jumped up and pushed both her hands across her mouth. "You're driving me mad! Martin sent you – "

"Martin hasn't seen me today and hasn't spoken to me. You don't know what a cur Marshalt is, Dora. I'll say you don't! There's no part of his heart that'd pan a trace of gold."

She lifted her hand to arrest the curiously soothing stream of sound.

"I know…please go now. Did you come to see me about that? How strange! Everybody knows I care for him."

Slick gently closed the door behind him, tiptoed down the passage, and came into the street in time to see Martin alighting from a cab. At the sight of the crook, his brows met.

"What the devil do *you* want?" he asked aggressively.

"I haven't time to tell you – but an income, a grand piano, and a manicure set come nigh top of the list. Elton, you jump too quick. You jump on me because I make a call; you jump on feather-headed young people because they want variety." His bright eyes were fixed on Martin, and he saw the young man change colour. "You jump at easy money from Italy because that big stiff Stanford told you there had never been anything like it…"

Martin was white enough now and without words.

"Mind you don't jump into bad trouble. That just-as-good money was offered to me. Giovanni Strepessi of Genoa makes it, and certainly there's a lot in circulation. As a sideline burglary is less risky, and a little baccarat game a blooming sinecure!"

"I don't know what you're talking about," said Martin at last. "Stanford went to Italy to buy jewellery."

"Maybe there was somebody in the room you didn't want to know when he told you that," said Slick. "Don't go, chauffeur – you can take me home. And, Elton…" He lowered his voice. "Even the graft of the old man Malpas is better than Stanford's new hobby."

"What is his graft?"

"Malpas?" Slick pondered the matter a moment. "I don't know exactly…but never see him in his house alone," he said.

"I saw him once – but he didn't see me. That's why I'm alive, Elton."

THE SWIMMER

Mr Lacy Marshalt had been a very preoccupied man these past few days, and the shrewd Tonger, susceptible to his employer's humours, had not failed to observe the fact. Ordinarily, very little troubled the South African millionaire, and certainly the threat of Martin Elton, who would not hesitate, as he well knew, to give his hatred expression, did not disturb his sleep or trouble his waking mind.

He was not greatly troubled now, only he was very thoughtful. Tonger surprised him half a dozen times a day deep in a reverie. Late on the Saturday night the valet brought a bundle of letters to Lacy Marshalt's study, and put them down on the writing table by his side. The South African turned them over rapidly and frowned.

"There's none from our friend of Matjesfontein," he said. "I haven't heard from that fellow for a month. What do you think is the matter?"

"Maybe he's dead," said Tonger. "People do die, even in South Africa."

Marshalt bit his lip.

"Something might have happened to Torrington," he said. "Perhaps it is he who has died?" and Tonger smiled.

"What the devil are you laughing at?"

"You always were an optimist, Lacy. That's half your charm!" He thought awhile. "Perhaps he can't swim, after all," he said.

Lacy looked up sharply.

"That is the second time you've referred to his swimming. Of course he can swim. I don't suppose even his lame leg would affect him. He was one of the finest swimmers I knew. What do you mean?"

"I was only wondering," said Tonger. He delighted in his mystery, and was loath to reveal it. "A High Commissioner's children should be able to swim, too," he said.

Marshalt turned his suspicious eyes to the man and scrutinized him closely.

"And if they can't swim," Tonger went on, "they shouldn't be allowed to go sailing boats round the Breakwater, especially in the summer, with a southeaster blowing – you know what a rip-snorting wind the old southeaster is?"

Lacy swung round in his chair and faced his servant.

"I've had enough of this," he said. "Just tell me what you're driving at. High Commissioner's children? You mean Lord Gilbury's?"

The man nodded.

"About eighteen months ago, Gilbury's kids took a sailing boat and went out into Table Bay. Off the Breakwater the boat capsized, and they'd have been drowned if one of the convicts who was working on the quay hadn't seen them and, jumping into the water, swum out and rescued them."

Lacy's mouth was wide open.

"Was it Torrington?" he asked quickly.

"I have an idea it was. No name was mentioned, but the Cape newspapers said that the convict who rescued the children was a lame man, and there was some newspaper talk of getting up a petition for his pardon."

Lacy Marshalt began to understand.

"Eighteen months ago?" he said slowly. "You swine! You never told me."

"What could I tell you?" demanded the other, aggrieved. "No names were mentioned, and how could I know? Besides, the warder would have given you the tip if he'd been released, wouldn't he? What are you paying him for?"

The big man made no reply.

"Unless," said Tonger thoughtfully, "unless – "

"Unless what?"

"Unless the warder was pensioned off and was living in Matjesfontein, and didn't want to lose a steady income. In that case he wouldn't know what had happened on the Breakwater, and would go on sending you reports."

Marshalt leapt to his feet and struck the writing table with his fist.

"That is it!" he said between his teeth. "Torrington has been released! I see now what has happened – they wouldn't make a fuss about it, and naturally his lawyers would not advertise his release."

He paced up and down the room, his hands clasped behind him. Suddenly he stopped and confronted the valet.

"This is the last time you play a trick on me, you dog! You knew!"

"I knew nothing," said the aggrieved Tonger. "I only put two and two together and suspected. If he was released he would have come here, wouldn't he? You don't suppose Dan Torrington would leave you alone if he was at liberty?"

That idea had already occurred to the millionaire.

"Besides," Tonger went on, "it's not my business to worry you with all sorts of rumours and alarms, is it? You've been a good friend of mine, Lacy. I dare say I give you a lot of trouble at times, but I owe a whole lot to you. You stood by me in the worst time of my life, and I've not forgotten it. You talk about betraying you! Why, if I wanted to betray you, there are a hundred and one facts stored up there" – he tapped his forehead – "that would put you on the blink. But I'm not that kind. I know the best side of you, and I know the worst. And didn't Torrington play the dirtiest trick on me that any man could play? Wasn't he running away with my little Elsie, the very day you got him pinched? I haven't forgotten. Look here."

He dived his thin hand into his inside pocket and took out a worn notecase. From this he took a letter which had so often been handled that it was almost falling to pieces.

"For years I've read this letter whenever Torrington has come into my mind. It's the first she sent me from New York. Listen:

"DEAR DADDY,
I want you to believe that I'm quite happy. I know that
Torrington has been arrested, and in some ways I am glad that
I carried out his instructions and came on here ahead of him.
Daddy, will you ever forgive me, and will you please believe that
I am happy? I have found new friends in this great city, and the
money Torrington gave me has enabled me to start a little
business which is prospering. Some day, when all this is an
unhappy memory, I will come back to you, and we will forget
all that is past."

He folded the letter, put it carefully back in the case, and replaced
it in his pocket.

"No, I've got no reason to love Torrington," he said steadily. "I'd
plenty for wanting to do him a bad turn."

The big man was staring blankly at the floor.

"Hate's fear," he said slowly. "You're afraid of him, too."

Tonger chuckled.

"No, I don't hate him, and I'm not afraid of him. Maybe it was for
the best. Isn't my little girl doing well in America, with a millinery
store of her own and offering to send me money if I want it?"

Lacy walked slowly back to his desk and sat down, his hands thrust
into his trousers pockets, his moody eyes still staring into vacancy.

"Mrs Elton said she saw a limping man — " he began.

"Mrs Elton gets that way," interrupted the other. "These nervous
women are always seeing things. Lacy, do you think I ought to hate
Torrington? Do you think I ought to feel so mad at him that I'd kill
him? You're a bigger man than me, and take a different view. If you
had a daughter that some fellow had made love to, and got her to run
away with him, would you want to kill him?"

"I don't know," said the other testily. "She seems to have done well
for herself."

"But she mightn't. She might have lived a perfect hell of a life —
what then? For the matter of that," he went on, with his whimsical
smile, "she mightn't have run away at all — what's that?"

He turned as Lacy sprang to his feet and glared at the wall of the room. Muffled and distinct came three slow taps.

"It's that old devil in the next house," said Tonger.

And then a strangled exclamation from his employer made him turn his head. The face of Lacy Marshalt was livid. From his open mouth came strange noises that were hardly human. But it was his eyes that held the valet spellbound, for they held a terror beyond his fathoming.

THE CALL TO PARIS

"What – what is it?" stammered Lacy, his hands trembling, his face ashen.

Tonger was staring owlishly at the wall as though he expected the solid masonry to open and reveal the knocker.

"I don't know – somebody tapping. I've heard it before, a few days ago."

The noise had now ceased, but still Lacy stood transfixed, his head thrust forward, listening.

"You've heard it before, have you?… Somebody knocking?"

"Once or twice," said Tonger. "I heard it the other night. What do you think the old man is doing – hanging up pictures?"

Lacy licked his lips and, with a shake of his broad shoulders, seemed to rid himself of the terror which the noise had inspired. He went reluctantly back to his writing table.

"That will do," he said curtly, and Tonger accepted his dismissal.

He was at the door when Lacy lifted his head and checked him with a word.

"I shall want you to go on an errand for me this afternoon," he said, "to Paris."

"Paris?" The valet's eyebrows rose. "What's the good of sending me to Paris? I don't speak French, and I hate the sea. Haven't you got anybody else? Send a district messenger: they take on jobs of that kind."

"I want somebody I can trust," interrupted his employer. "I'll ring up Croydon and have an aeroplane ready to take you. You will be back before night."

Tonger stood fingering his chin dubiously. The request evidently worried him, for his tone had changed.

"Aeroplanes are not in my line, though I'm willing to try anything once. What time shall I be back – if I ever get back?"

"You'll leave at twelve; you'll be in Paris by two, deliver the letter, and you'll be on your way back by three. That will bring you to London at five."

Still Tonger was undecided. Walking to the window, he looked up at the skies a little fearfully.

"Not much of a day for aeroplane travelling, is it, Lacy?" he grumbled. "It's cloudy and there's a lot of wind... All right, I'll go. Have you got the letter ready?"

"It will be written in an hour," said the other.

After Tonger had gone, he walked to the door and locked it, returned to his table, took up the telephone and put through a call to Paris. When this had been registered, he gave another number.

"Stormer's Detective Agency?... I want to speak to Mr Willitt at once. Mr Lacy Marshalt speaking. Is he in the office?..."

Apparently Mr Willitt was on hand, for presently his voice greeted the millionaire.

"Come round and see me immediately," said Marshalt, and, hanging up the receiver, began to write.

It was a time of crisis for him, as he well knew. Within reach of him was a man whom he had wronged desperately, one who would not hesitate to act, a man cunning and remorseless, waiting his moment. Instinct told Lacy Marshalt that that moment was near at hand.

He finished his letter, addressed an envelope, and heavily sealed the flap. Then he unlocked the door, just in time, for Tonger came to usher in the private detective whom Lacy had previously employed.

"I haven't taken the trouble to inquire before, but I suppose you are the head of this agency?"

Willitt shook his head.

131

"Practically," he answered. "Mr Stormer spends most of his time at the New York branch. In America we hold a much more important position. Stormer's run government inquiries and protect public men. Here – "

"That's the commission I'm giving you," said Lacy grimly. "Have you ever heard of Malpas?"

"The old man who lives next door? Yes, I've heard of him. We had a commission to discover his identity – our clients wanted a photograph of him."

"Who were they?" asked Lacy quickly.

Mr Willitt smiled. "I'm afraid I can't tell you," he said. "It is part of our job to keep our clients' secrets."

Lacy took his inevitable roll of notes from his pocket, stripped two and, laying them on the desk, pushed them across to the detective, who smiled awkwardly as he took them.

"Well, I suppose there's no reason why we should make such a secret about this case. It was on behalf of a man named Laker who disappeared some time ago."

"Laker? I don't know the name. Were you able to get a line on the old man?"

Willitt shook his head.

"No, sir, he's closer than an oyster."

Lacy thought for a long time before he spoke again.

"I want you to have relays of men watching Malpas. I want the front and back of his house under observation day and night; and I want a third man on my roof."

"That will mean six men in all," said Willitt, making a note. "And what do you wish us to do?"

"I want you to follow him, identify him, and let me know who he is. If possible, get a photograph."

Willitt noted his employer's requirements.

"It will be much easier with your co-operation," he said. "The job we had was not big enough to employ so many men. In fact, we only had one detective engaged on the work. When do we start?"

"Right now," said Lacy emphatically. "I'll arrange for the man whom you put on the roof to be admitted – my man Tonger will see after his comfort."

The dismissal of the detective was hurried by the Paris phone call coming through, and for ten minutes Lacy Marshalt was issuing instructions in voluble French.

THE WOMAN IN THE PARK

There were times when Audrey looked back with a certain amount of regretful longing to the days of her chicken farm and the peccant Mrs Graffitt. Chicken-raising had a drawback; for somehow the caprices of the domestic hen, yielding, as they did, a starvation return, were more attractive than those of the unattractive old man who lived and operated in the sinister atmosphere of 551, Portman Square.

She had not seen Dick Shannon for two days, and harboured a wholly unjustifiable grievance against him, though he had given her his telephone number, and a call, as she well knew, would bring him immediately. Once or twice she had taken up the instrument, hesitated with the receiver in her hand, and put it down again.

On one matter she had reached a decision. Her second interview with Mr Malpas was due that night, and she would make an end of their association. Morning after morning his budget had arrived, had been copied and returned to him – she had even carried the letter back to Portman Square in the hope of seeing him before the hour of the interview; but though she had knocked, no reply had come, and she had perforce pushed the letter through the narrow letter slit and heard it thud into the steel letter box.

On the afternoon that Tonger made his reluctant journey to Paris, she went for her favourite walk. Green Park, on a cold January afternoon, was somewhat deserted. The ponds were frozen save near the edges, where the park keepers had broken the ice for the benefit of the winged creatures who live in the little islands and the shelter of the bush-grown banks. The branches of the trees were bare, and only the dull green of laurels and holly bushes remained to justify the park's title.

She walked briskly past the kiosk, following the path that skirts the lake, and came eventually to the footbridge which spans the water. A chill north wind was blowing: the blue sky was flecked by hurrying clouds; snow was coming: she experienced the indescribable smell of it.

She was halfway across the bridge when a heavy gust of wind half turned her, and she decided that this was no day for pedestrian exercise, and, pushing down the skirts that the wind had raised, and with one hand gripping her hat, she turned and walked back the way she had come. Ahead of her she saw a man strolling, a thickset saunterer who twirled a walking stick, and the scent of whose cigar reached her long before she came up with and passed him. A wider sweep of the twirling stick almost struck her, and, glancing round in alarm, the cigar almost dropped from his teeth in his contrition.

"I'm sorry, madam," he said.

She smiled and, uttering some brief commonplace, hurried on. And then, on one of the garden seats that are set at intervals, facing the lake, she saw a woman sitting, and her attitude, even at that distance, was remarkable. She lay back in the seat, her face upturned to the sky, her hands outspread, gripping the seat. Something like fear stirred in the girl's heart. The pose was so unnatural, so queerly disturbing, that she checked her pace, fearful of passing the figure, and, so slowing, the stick-swinging saunterer came up to her. He also had seen.

"That is queer," he said, and she was glad of his company. "What is the matter with that woman?"

"I was wondering," she said.

He quickened his step, and she followed at his heels, for some reason fearful of being alone.

The woman on the seat was between thirty and forty; her eyes were half closed, her face and hands blue with the cold. By her side was a little silver flask, from which the stopper had been removed, so

135

that over the bars of the bench was trickling a tiny pool of liquid that had flowed from the bottle. Audrey looked and shivered.

There was something strangely familiar in that dreadful face, and she racked her brains to identify her. She had seen her somewhere – a glimpse in a crowded street, perhaps? No, it was something more intimate than that.

The stout man had thrown away his cigar, and was sliding his hand tenderly under the head.

"I think you had better go and find a policeman," he said gently, and at that moment a patrolling officer came into view and saved her the search.

"Is she ill?" asked the policeman, bending down.

"Very ill, I guess," said the man quietly. "Miss Bedford, I think you had better go."

She started to hear her name pronounced by the stranger, and looked more closely at him. She had never seen him before within her recollection, but his eyes, as he glanced meaningly along the path, were eloquent; he wanted her to go.

"You'll see another constable on point duty opposite the Horse Guards Parade, Miss," said the policeman. "Do you mind sending him along to me and asking him to ring the ambulance?"

Glad to escape, she hurried off, and was gone before the policeman remembered certain stringent police instructions.

"I forgot to ask her her name. You know her, don't you? Miss – "

"Yes, she's Miss Bradfield. I know her by sight: we used to work in the same office," said Slick Smith glibly.

He picked up the little silver flask, closed the stopper carefully, and handed it to the policeman.

"You may want what's in this," he said; and then, warningly: "I shouldn't let anybody take a sip unless you've got a grudge against them."

"Why?" asked the policeman, aghast. "Do you think it's poison?"

Smith did not reply.

"Can you smell anything?" He sniffed at the woman's lips. "Like almonds…"

The policeman frowned, and then: "You don't think she is dead, do you?"

"As dead as anybody will ever be," said Smith quietly.

"Suicide?" asked the constable.

"I don't know. You'd better take my name – Richard James Smith, known to the police as Slick Smith. They know me at the Yard. I'm on the register."

The man in uniform regarded him with suspicion.

"What are you doing round here?" he asked. He was a dull man and his questions were mechanical.

"Helping you," said Smith laconically.

The second policeman arrived, and soon after the wild clang of the ambulance bell brought a curious crowd. The doctor who came made a brief examination.

"Oh, yes, she's dead. Poison – hydrocyanic or cyanide."

He was a young man, just through the schools, and consequently dogmatic, but here his first diagnosis was to be borne out by subsequent inquiry.

The news came to Dick Shannon by accident, and beyond the interest which the name of Slick Smith aroused, he saw nothing in the matter which called for his personal interference till the officer in charge of the case came to make inquiries about Smith.

"Yes, I know him; he's an American crook. We have nothing on him here, and he has no English record. Who was the woman?"

"Unknown, so far as we can trace."

"Nothing in her clothes or handbag to identify her?"

"Nothing. It looks like a suicide. This is the second we've had in Green Park since Christmas."

That night at dinner, Audrey, glancing through the evening paper, saw a brief paragraph:

The body of an unknown woman was found in Green Park this afternoon. It is believed that she committed suicide by poisoning.

She *was* dead! Audrey went cold at this confirmation of her private fears. How dreadful! It must have been very quick, for the woman had not been there when she had passed along the footpath a minute or two before. Who was she? Audrey was certain she had seen her somewhere…

And then with a gasp she remembered. It was the woman that she had seen a week before, the drunken virago who was hammering at Lacy Marshalt's door!

She left her dinner unfinished and went to the telephone. Here, at any rate, was an excuse for talking to Dick Shannon. The pleasure in his voice when he answered her gave her, for some reason, a warm little feeling of happiness.

"Where have you been? I was expecting you to call me up… Is anything wrong?"

The last words were in a more anxious tone.

"Nothing. I saw in the paper tonight that a woman had been found dead in the Park. I saw her, Captain Shannon – I mean I was there when she was found, and I think I know her."

There was a pause.

"I'll come along now," said Dick.

He was with her in a few minutes, and she told him what she had seen.

"Yes, I knew Slick Smith was there. There was a report that a lady, a Miss Bradfield, was present: that was you, of course? But you say you knew her?"

She nodded.

"You remember my telling you of the woman who knocked at Mr Marshalt's door?"

"The Annoyer?" He whistled. "An agent of Malpas."

"But why – ?"

"He had been employing people to worry Marshalt, for some mysterious reason which I cannot fathom; I rather think that this unfortunate creature was one of them. I made inquiries about her when I was at Portman Square the other day. Apparently Tonger threw her out, and that was the last that was seen of her."

He looked at the girl thoughtfully.

"I don't want you in this case," he said, "either as witness or in any other capacity. You had better remain the unknown witness until the inquest is over. Smith will supply all the evidence we require – I'll see Tonger tonight. By the way," he said suddenly, "when do you visit your ancient boss?"

It was on the tip of her tongue to say that she was going upstairs to dress for the interview at that moment.

"Tomorrow," she said instead.

He looked at her keenly.

"You're not telling the truth, young lady," he said. "You are going tonight."

She laughed.

"I am really," she confessed. "Only I thought you would make a fuss."

"Indeed I shall make a fuss. What time is your interview?"

"Eight o'clock."

He looked at his watch.

"I will kill two birds with one stone," he said. "I'm going to Marshalt's house now, and I will meet you at the north side of Portman Square at three minutes to eight."

"Really, there's no reason why you should, Captain Shannon – " she began, but he stopped her.

"I think there's a good reason," he said; "and what I think goes – for this night only."

She hesitated.

"You promise me you will not go to the house until you have seen me?" he insisted.

She had so intended, but his earnestness was a little impressive.

"I'll promise," she said, not wholly without relief that she would have him on hand during the interview which would follow.

THE BETRAYAL

Martin Elton looked up from the newspaper he was reading, and for the twentieth time his grave eyes fell upon his wife, who had drawn a low chair up to the fire and sat, elbow on knee, her face in her hands, gazing moodily into its red depths. This time she turned with a start and met his scrutiny.

"I thought you were going out?" she said.

"I am."

He folded the paper and put it down. The hands of the clock above the mantelpiece showed twenty minutes after seven.

"What's the matter with you, Dora? You ate nothing at dinner."

"I'm not feeling very well," she said with a shrug, resuming her contemplation of the fire. "What time will you be back?"

"I don't know — about midnight, I suppose."

"You are going to see Stanford?"

"I've seen Stanford once today: I don't want to see him again."

A long interval of silence.

"Did he bring that money here?" she asked, without looking round at him.

"No," said Martin Elton.

She knew him too well to be convinced.

"He brought something in a bag: was it the money that man Smith spoke about?"

This time Martin spoke the truth.

"Yes, he brought three million francs. It's good stuff and there's no danger in it. Klein can get rid of it. And it's all profit."

Her shoulders moved almost imperceptibly.

"It is your funeral, Martin; if you like to take the risk it has nothing to do with me. I'm sick of everything."

"There is no risk," said Martin, and took up the paper again. "The Italian is a genius, and with me it is only a sideline." He was almost apologetic. "I don't intend making a hobby of putting phoney money into circulation."

"Where is it? I want to know."

Her voice was unusually peremptory. She had been suffering from an attack of nerves all that day, and he had done his best to humour her.

"It's in the mattress under my bed," he said. "But don't let it worry you, Dora. I'll have it taken away tomorrow."

He went out of the room and came back presently, wearing his overcoat and gloves.

"Will you go out?" he asked.

"I don't know – I may," she said without looking round.

She heard the street door slam, and returned to her unhappy thoughts. She was afraid of Martin; afraid not, for herself, but for the man she loved. Martin had become an intolerable burden. He was watching her all the time, suspecting her...slighting her. In these past few days she had come to hate him with a malignity which frightened her. It was he who had dragged her down, who had brought her into contact with the underworld, and moulded her in his image. So she thought, forgetting, conveniently, all that he had done for her, and the life from which he had saved her, and his many kindnesses, his invariable generosity.

If Martin were out of the way...!

She sighed at the thought, her unconscious mind moving like a magnet beneath the screen of conscious thought, dragged in its path The Idea, and after a while she found herself thinking deliberately, cold-bloodedly, of a plan that, until then, she had not dared tell, even to herself.

He would kill Lacy Marshalt; she nodded as she considered this certainty. And he was holding the threat over her. She hated him worse for that. And how was she to escape? How might she shake off the burden which Martin had imposed? There was only one way. All day long, all night long, she had been engaged in reconciling herself to the deed of shame.

Martin had been gone a quarter of an hour when she ran up to her room, put on her coat and hat, and came quickly downstairs.

The sergeant in charge at Vine Street Police Station was chatting with Chief Detective Gavon when a pale girl came quickly through the doorway into the bare charge room. Gavon knew her and nodded pleasantly.

"Good evening, Mrs Elton. Do you want to see me?"

She nodded. Her mouth was dry; her tongue seemed to be in a conspiracy against her.

"Yes," she gasped at last. "There is a man in Italy" – her voice was shrill and jerky – "who forges notes on the Bank of France. There's a lot in – circulation."

Gavon nodded.

"Yes, that's true. Why, do you know anybody who has this stuff?"

She swallowed something.

"There's a whole lot in my house," she said. "My husband brought it there. It is in the mattress in his room. There's a little drawer near the head of the bed…it runs into the mattress. You'll find it there."

Gavon nearly collapsed.

"Your husband?" he said incredulously. "Is it his property?"

She nodded.

"What will he get?" She gripped his arm fiercely. "They'll give him seven years for that, won't they, Gavon?"

Inured as he was to the treachery of jealous women, Gavon was shocked. He had seen betrayals before, but never had he dreamt that Dora Elton's name would appear in the secret squeal book at Vine Street.

"You're sure? Wait here."

"No, no, I must go," she said breathlessly. "I must go somewhere…somewhere! My servant will let you into the house. I give you permission."

In another second she was flying down the street.

Fast as she went, someone followed faster, and as she turned up a side street that somebody was at her elbow. She heard the footsteps and turned with a scream.

"Martin!" she cried.

He was looking at her, his eyes blazing, and she shrank back, her hands raised as though to ward off a blow.

"You've been in Vine Street – why?" he asked in a whisper.

"I – I had to go," she stammered, white as death.

"You went to squeal. About the money?"

She looked at him, fascinated.

"You were watching?"

He nodded.

"I was on the other side of the street. I saw you go in – and guessed. I've been waiting for you to do this, though I never dreamt you would. You can save the police a whole lot of trouble by going back and telling them that there's no money there. You've been itching to catch me for a week!"

"Martin!" she whimpered.

"You think that with me out of the way," he went on remorselessly, "things will be easy for you as far as Marshalt is concerned, but you're wrong, my girl. I'm settling with Lacy this night! Go back and tell that to your police friends."

"Where are you going?"

She clung to him, but he thrust her aside and strode along the street, leaving a half-demented woman to stagger to the nearest telephone booth, there to ring in vain Lacy Marshalt's number.

THE HOUSE OF DEATH

Five minutes after his interview with the girl, Shannon's car brought him to the imposing portals of Marshalt's house. Tonger opened the door to him. Usually the valet affected some kind of livery – a tail coat and striped waistcoat – but now he was wearing a tweed suit with a heavy overcoat, and looked as though he had just returned from a journey.

"Marshalt's out," he said brusquely.

"You look pretty sick: what's the matter with you?" asked Dick.

He walked into the hall uninvited, and closed the door behind him; Tonger seemed amused.

"You've said it! Ever been in an aeroplane?"

Dick laughed.

"So that's where you've been, eh? Well, I sympathize with you, if you're a bad sailor – it's a novel but unpleasant experience. I want to see you more than Marshalt. Do you remember a woman who came here a week back – the woman you fired out?"

Tonger nodded.

"Come into the drawing-room, Captain," he said suddenly, and opened the door, switching on the lights. "I've only this minute got back. You almost followed me in. Now what about the lady?"

"This afternoon," said Dick, "a woman was found in the Park, dead. I have reason to believe that it was the same person who made the row."

Tonger was staring at him open-mouthed.

144

"I shouldn't think so," he said. "In the Park, you say? It may have been, of course. But I know nothing about her, where she is or anything."

"You said it was Mrs Somebody from Fourteen Streams."

"That's the name she gave; I didn't know her. Would you like me to see her?"

Dick considered. The man was obviously suffering from the effect of his journey, and it would be unfair to subject him to another ordeal that night.

"Tomorrow will do," he said.

He did not wish to prolong the interview, anxious to keep his appointment with the girl, and Tonger accompanied him to the door.

"Ships are bad," he said, "and little boats are worse, but, my gawd! airplanes are sure hell, Captain! Next time Lacy sends me to Paris, I'll go by boat – all the way if I can! How did she die, that woman?" he asked unexpectedly.

"We think it was a case of suicide by poisoning. A silver flask was found by her side."

He was standing on the doorstep, and as he spoke the door was gently closed on him. Evidently Mr Tonger had merely shown a polite interest in the discovery, and was more concerned with his own inward distress.

"Your manners, my friend, require improvement," said Dick as he went down the steps, half annoyed, half amused.

As he came to the pavement, a woman passed him. He had seen her move through the little halo of light that one of the street lamps threw a dozen yards away, and now, as she came abreast of him, something in her walk arrested him. She was dressed in black; a wide-brimmed hat hid her face. Yet he knew her, and, acting on the impulse of the moment, called her by name.

"Mrs Elton."

She stopped as if she had been shot, and half turned toward him.

"Who is it?" she asked in a quavering voice. "Oh – you!" Then, eagerly: "Have you seen Marshalt?"

"No, I haven't."

145

"I've been trying to get at him, but he must have changed the lock on the back door. Oh, God! Captain Shannon, what will happen?"

"What is likely to happen?" he asked, amazed at the agitation in her voice.

"Martin isn't there, is he? What a fool, oh, what a fool I've been!"

"No, there is nobody there, not even Marshalt."

She stood brooding, her hands at her mouth, her white face drawn and haggard. Then, without warning, she went off at a tangent.

"I hate her, I hate her!" she almost spat the words, and her voice was vibrant with passion. "You would never dream she was that kind, would you? The wretched little hypocrite! I know he is meeting her! I don't care what Martin does, I don't care what he knows; but if Lacy is playing me false – he changed the lock – that proves – " Her voice died to a sob.

"What on earth are you talking about?" he asked, astounded.

The woman was in a pitiable condition of hysteria; he could see her shivering in the intensity of her hopeless fury.

"I'm talking about Lacy and Audrey," she wailed.

And then, without another word, she turned and fled along the way she had come, leaving Dick to stare after her in wonder.

By the time he had reached the end of the square, Audrey was waiting for him.

"To whom were you talking?" she asked as he walked by her side in the direction of 551.

"Nobody – at least, nobody you know," he said.

She would have left him near the house.

"Don't come any farther, please," she begged.

"I'm coming inside that house with you," he insisted, "or else you do not go inside – I certainly have no intention of allowing you to go alone."

She looked at him thoughtfully.

"Perhaps that is best, though I feel that I shouldn't allow you. He may be a dreadful old man, but I owe him something."

"By the way, have you the money with you?"

"All that is left," she said with a little smile. "I've been very mean. I paid my board for a week in advance at the hotel. I suppose you realize that I've got to get another job on Monday, and probably Mr Malpas will send for the police if I do not account for the money I've spent."

"Let him send for me," said Dick.

By this time they were opposite the door of 551, and after a moment's hesitation, Audrey tapped. There was no reply, and she tapped again. Then the hard voice spoke from the door pillar.

"Who is that?"

"It is Miss Bedford."

"Are you alone?"

She hesitated, Dick nodding furiously.

"Yes," she said.

The words were hardly spoken before the door opened slowly, and she slipped in, followed by the detective. A dim light burnt in the hall.

"Wait here," whispered the girl as the door closed behind them.

Dick mutely agreed, though he had no intention of waiting so far out of reach. She had scarcely got to the first landing of the stairway when he was following her, his rubber-soled boots making no sound. She saw him as her hand was raised to knock on the landing door, and frowned him back. Twice she knocked, and her hand was raised for the third time when, from the room within, came the sound of two shots in rapid succession.

Instantly Shannon was by her side, and had pushed her back. Throwing his weight against the door, it opened suddenly. He was in the well-lighted lobby, and ahead of him was the open door of the dark room. And dark it was, for no glimmer of light showed inside.

"Is anybody here?" he called sharply, and heard a stealthy movement.

"What is it?" asked the frightened voice of the girl.

"I don't know."

There was in that room some terrifying influence. He felt the hairs at the back of his neck rise, and a crawling sensation run along his scalp.

"Who is there?" he called again.

And then, most unexpectedly, two lights went on: a table lamp and a heavily shaded light above a small table and a chair within reach of his hand. For a second he saw nothing unusual, and then, lying on the carpet in the very centre of the room, the figure of a man, face downward.

He ran forward. A wire caught his chest, another trip wire nearly brought him down; but his flash-lamp revealed the presence of a third, and he broke it with a kick. In another second he was kneeling by the man's side, and had turned him over on his back.

It was Lacy Marshalt, and above his heart the white shirt front was smudged black with the gases of a pistol fired at close quarters. The out-flung hands were clenched in agony, the eyes, half closed, were fixed glassily on the sombre ceiling, and now a thin ooze of blood reddened the smoke stain on his breast.

"Dead!" gasped Dick.

"What is it, what is it?" asked the terrified voice of the girl.

"Stay where you are," commanded Dick. "Don't move from the room."

He dared not trust her out of his sight in this house of mystery and death. Picking his way to the shadow of the desk, he found, as he expected, within reach of the old man's hand, the little switchboard which controlled the doors. He turned them back one after the other, and then rejoined the girl.

"I think the doors are open now," he said, and, taking her by the arm, hurried her down the stairs.

"What has happened?" she asked again. "Who was that — that man?"

"I'll tell you later."

The front door was wide open, and he ran out into the street. The dim lights of a taxicab were visible in the square, and his shrill whistle brought the machine to the sidewalk.

"Go back to your hotel," he said, "and stay there until I come to you."

"You mustn't go into that house again," she said fearfully. She gripped him by the arm. "Please, please don't! Something will happen to you – I know it will."

He gently loosened her hands.

"There is nothing to worry about," he said. "I'll bring a whole lot of policeman on the scene in a minute, and – "

Crash!

He looked round in time to see the front door close.

"There is somebody still in the house!" she whispered. "For God's sake don't go in! Captain Shannon – Dick! Don't go in!"

He leapt up the steps and flung his weight against the door, but it did not so much as tremble.

"It almost looks as if they've settled the matter for me," he said. "Now go, please."

He hardly waited for the cab to move before he was hammering at the door. He expected no answer. Then his blood went suddenly cold, as in his very ear there sounded a peal of insane laughter.

"*Got him, got him, got him!*" screamed the voice, and then silence.

"Open the door!" cried Dick hoarsely. "Open the door: I want to speak to you."

There was no reply.

A policeman, attracted by the sound of his thunderous knocking, came from the darkness of Baker Street, and he was joined by another man, whom Dick instantly recognized as Willitt, the private detective.

"Anything wrong, Captain Shannon?" asked the latter.

"What are you doing here?" asked Dick.

"I'm watching the house. I have a commission from Mr Marshalt."

This was staggering news.

"Marshalt told you to watch here?" asked Dick quickly, and, when Willitt had replied: "Have you anybody watching the back of the house?"

"Yes, Captain Shannon, and I've got another man on the roof of Mr Marshalt's house."

Dick made his decision.

"Go along to your friend at the back and join him. Have you any kind of weapon?"

The man seemed embarrassed.

"That means you've got a gun without a licence! I won't press the question. Get round to the back, and don't forget that you're dealing with a murderer, an armed murderer who will not think twice about shooting you, as he shot Marshalt."

"Marshalt?" gasped the man. "Is he shot?"

"He's dead," Dick nodded.

He sent the constable away to gather reinforcements and the inevitable police ambulance, and made a quick survey of the front of the house. Separated from the pavement by a wide, spike-railed area were two windows which, as he knew, were shuttered. To reach them would be possible with the aid of a plank, but once he was in the room, the chances were that the door of the hall (he remembered the door) was as difficult to force as the street entrance. He had considered and rejected before that possible method of ingress. Leaving the policeman, who had returned, he went round to the back of the house and joined the two men who were watching.

In the narrow mews behind Portman Square there was little to be seen except a high wall pierced by a door, which apparently had been used, for there was none of the dust and rubbish which so easily accumulates and hardens against the bottom of a door that is not opened.

Willitt's man helped him climb to the top of the wall. By the aid of his flash-lamp he saw a small courtyard and a second door, which he guessed was quite as unmovable as any of the others. He got back to Portman Square as a police taxi, crowded with detectives and uniformed police, came into the square, and the first man to leap out was Sergeant Steel. One of the men carried a big fire axe, but the first blow on the door told Dick that this method must be abandoned.

"The door is faced with steel: we shall have to blow it out," he said.

"Blowing it out," however, presented unusual difficulties. The keyhole was minute, and it looked as though the introduction of explosives into the lock would be complicated and even dangerous business.

And then, when he was consulting the inspector in charge, the miracle happened. There was a click and the door slowly opened.

"Wedge it back," ordered Dick, and raced upstairs into the death room.

The lights were still on; he stood in the doorway, paralyzed with amazement. The body of Lacy Marshalt had disappeared!

MR MALPAS' GOD

"Search every room," ordered Dick. "The man is still in the house. He's been here." He pointed to the desk. The papers which lay about in confusion bore traces of blood.

Dick began his search of the walls for another exit, and: "For the Lord's sake!" he breathed.

At the end of the room near the desk was an alcove which the velvet curtains screened from view. Drawing these aside, Shannon and his companion gazed in amazement at the thing they saw.

It was a great idol of bronze that squatted on a broad pedestal. Behind the figure, and encrested on the wall, was a huge golden sun, the leaping flames of which were set with thousands of tiny rubies that, in the light, gleamed like living fires.

Flanking the obscene idol were two cat-like animals cast, as was the figure, in bronze. Their eyes sparkled greenly in the light of the hand-lamps.

"Emeralds, and genuine emeralds," said Dick. "We seem to have stepped into Ali Baba's cave. The god beats me. He is something between Plutus and the Medusas – look at the snakes in his hair!"

It was a hideous figure. The head was monstrous, the gaping jaws, with their jagged ivory teeth, seemed to move as they looked.

"The old gentleman seems to have added devil worship to his other accomplishments," said Dick, pointing to two small braziers black with smoke that stood on either side of the figure. "That's blood!"

It was Steel who made the discovery. On the black pedestal the rays of his lamp showed a damp impression, and, drawing his finger across it, he displayed a red smear.

"Push the thing and see if it moves."

Three men put their shoulders to the plinth, but it was unmovable. Dick looked at his subordinate.

"Where have they put Marshalt's body?" he asked. "It is somewhere in this house. You take the upper rooms, Steel; I will search the ground floor and cellars."

Steel was sniffing.

"Do you notice any peculiar smell in the room, Chief? It is as though there has been a smoking fire here – the smell that soft coal makes."

Dick had been puzzled by the same phenomenon.

"I detected it when I came in," he began, when one of the uniformed men interrupted him.

"There's something burning on the carpet," he said, and the lamp showed a blue spiral of smoke.

Dick slipped on a glove and lifted it up. It was a hot coal, now dull and lifeless, though the carpet was smouldering.

"How did that get here?" he demanded.

Steel had no solution to offer.

The curtains concealed other points of interest. Behind one, in a corner of the room, he found a little door. Apparently this was not governed by the switch controls, and here the fire axe was brought into play with great effect, and a little stone stairway was revealed. It led downward to the ground floor, through a door into the front room that lay behind the shuttered windows. At some time or other the drawing-room had been a very noble establishment; it was still furnished, though every article was so covered with dust and so moth-eaten as to give the apartment an air of utter wretchedness. Here was stacked in odd corners a medley of incongruous articles. Bundles of skins, stacks of Zulu assegais, and a queer collection of African idols in every degree of ugliness. The skins were moth-eaten, the spearheads red with rust.

153

Last, and not least remarkable, of his finds was a deep Egyptian coffin, brilliantly painted, with a lid carved in the semblance of a man. He lifted the hinged lid – it was empty.

"Lacy Marshalt's body is in the house," he said, as he returned to the room above; "and his murderer is here. Have you looked for communication between the two houses?"

"There is none," said Steel. "The walls are solid: I've tried them on every floor."

Returning to the room where the body had been found, he discovered the police inspector seated at Malpas' desk.

"What do you make of this, sir?"

He handed the paper to Dick. It was a half-sheet of notepaper, and, reading it, Dick Shannon's blood went cold. The paper bore the address of Audrey's hotel, and the handwriting was undoubtedly hers. He read:

Will you come and see me tonight at eight o'clock? Mr M will admit you if you tap at the door.

It was signed "*A*."

Audrey! Only for a second was he thrown off his balance, and then the explanation came to him immediately. This was one of the notes that the old man had asked her to copy. It was the lure that had brought the millionaire to his death.

He took Steel aside and showed him the letter.

"I can explain this," he said; "it is one of the letters which Miss Bedford copied on the old man's instructions." And then: "I'll go along and break the news to Tonger."

He had forgotten all about Tonger and the effect which the news would bring to the house next door.

A small crowd had gathered before the front door when he came out, for the news of the tragedy had spread with that rapidity peculiar to such events. A light showed through the glass panelling in the hall of Marshalt's house, and he rang the bell. Tonger would be shocked. He had grown up with the dead man, fought with him and felt with him. The valet would know some good of his old employer, scoundrel though be had been.

No answer came to his knock. Looking over the area railings, he saw a light in the kitchen downstairs and rang again. And then he heard Steel calling him, and went back to meet his subordinate.

His foot was on the pavement, he had half turned to his subordinate, when, from the interior of Marshalt's house, came a shot, followed by two others in rapid succession.

He was at the door in a second. From somewhere in the basement came the sound of screams, and the kitchen entrance was flung open.

"Murder!" screamed a woman's voice.

In an instant he was running down the steps. A fainting woman fell against him, but he thrust her aside, darted through the kitchen and ran up the stairs which, he guessed, led to the hall. Here he came into a group of three hysterical maidservants and a woman who was evidently the cook, and who proved to be the calmest and most intelligible, though she could give little information except that she had heard shots and the voice of Mr Tonger.

"From there, sir!" A girl pointed with shaking fingers upward. "Mr Marshalt's study!"

Shannon went up the stairs two at a time, and, turning at right angles, saw that the door of the study was wide open. Across the threshold lay the body of Tonger, and he was dead.

Tonger! Passing his hands under the man, he lifted him without an effort and laid him on the sofa. He, too, had been shot at close quarters – there was no need to call a doctor. Death had been instantaneous.

Going to the door, he called one of the maids.

"Bring a policeman in here at once."

This time the unknown murderer should not spirit away the evidence of his deed.

He waited until the body had been removed before he made a rough search of the study. Two exploded shells told him that the murder had been committed with an automatic. But how had the murderer escaped? A thought occurred to him, and he went in search of a maid.

"When I came up from the kitchen the front door was open – who opened it?"

Neither the girl nor any of her fellows knew. The door had been open when they erupted from the basement. A superficial examination of the house told him nothing, but one clear fact emerged: Malpas had a confederate, and if either escaped it was the second man. That Malpas was in his house after the murder of Marshalt, he was certain.

Dick went back to 551 to continue his search there. Every room had been investigated except one on the top floor, which defied the efforts of the police to enter.

"The door must be opened," said Dick decisively. "You must get crowbars. I'll not leave this house till every room has been combed out."

He was alone in the black-draped room where Marshalt had been shot, and was speculating upon the extraordinary character of the disappearance, when he was conscious that somebody was moving behind him, and he spun round. A man was standing in the doorway. The first view of him Dick Shannon had was the gleam of his spectacles. It was "Brown," the limping lover of London whom he had seen that night in Portman Square, and who had been so interested in diamonds. A suspicion shot through Shannon's mind.

"How did you get here?" he asked curtly.

"Through the door," was the bland reply. "It was wide open and, being a member of the crowd bolder than the others, I came in."

"Isn't there a policeman on duty at the door?"

"If there is, I didn't see him," said the other easily. "I'm afraid I'm *de trop*, Captain Shannon."

"I'm afraid you are," said Dick, "but you won't go till I discover how you got in."

The elderly man showed his white teeth in a smile.

"Don't say that I'm suspect," he said mockingly. "That would be too bad! To be suspecting of killing my old friend Lacy Marshalt!"

Dick did not like his sly smile, saw nothing of humour in the tragedy of the evening and, as he accompanied the man downstairs, his mind was busy. The constable on the door had not seen him enter; swore, at any rate, that nobody had passed him while he was on duty.

"What does this mean?" Dick looked at the visitor.

"It means the constable is wrong," said the other coolly. "He will perhaps remember going out on to the sidewalk to move the crowd farther back."

The man admitted he had done this.

"You might have seen that happen from the inside of the hall or from the stairs," said Shannon, unconvinced.

"I saw it from the outside, but I well understand that, if a man is foolish enough to come into a place where a murder has been committed, he has only himself to blame if he is suspected."

"Where are you staying?"

"I am still at the Ritz-Carlton. I will remain here if you wish, but I assure you that the most heinous crime to my discredit is, in this instance, an ungovernable curiosity."

Dick had already verified the man's statement that he was a guest at that fashionable hotel, and the intruder was sent about his business.

"I don't like it at all," said Shannon to his assistant, as they went back to Malpas' room. "He may have come in, as he said; on the other hand, it is quite likely that he was in the house when the murder was committed. How long will they he opening that door? Let me see it."

He followed Steel up to the top landing, where two constables were standing before a stout door which had neither key nor handle.

"How is it made fast?" asked Dick, examining the door curiously.

"From the inside, sir," said one of the policemen. "There's somebody in there now."

"Are you sure?" asked Dick quickly.

"Yes, sir," said the second policeman; "I heard him, too. A sort of thudding noise, and a sound like a table being dragged across the floor."

He raised a finger warningly to his lips, and bent his head. Dick listened; at first he could hear nothing, and then there came to him the faintest of creaks, like a rusty hinge turning.

"We've tried it with the axe," said Steel, pointing to deep gashes in the wood, "but there was no room to swing. Here come the men with the crowbars."

"Hear that?" asked the policeman suddenly.

He would have been deaf had he not: it was the sound of a falling chair, and was followed at an interval by a deep thud as though something was falling.

"Get that door open, quick!" said Shannon.

Taking one of the crowbars in his hand, he forced the thin edge between door and lintel and tugged. The door gave slightly. The second crowbar found a purchase, and as the two were pulled together the door opened with a sharp crack.

The garret into which they burst was empty, and unfurnished except for a chair, which lay overturned on the floor, and a table. Jumping on to the table, Dick pushed at the skylight above his head, but it was fastened. At that moment he flashed a ray from his hand-lamp upward. Staring down at him, he saw, through the blur of the grimy window, the outline of a face. Only for a second, and then it vanished.

A long, pointed chin, a high, bulging forehead, a hideously big nose.

THE CIGARETTE CASE

"The crowbar, quick!" he shouted, and attacked the heavy framework.

In a few minutes it was open, and he had drawn himself up on to the flat, lead-covered roof. He stepped cautiously round a chimney stack, and then:

"Hands up!" called a voice, and, in the light of his flash-lamp, he saw an overcoated man, and remembered that Willitt had told him that a guard had been set on the roof.

"Are you Willitt's man?" he shouted.

"Yes, sir."

"I'm Captain Shannon from headquarters. Have you seen anybody pass here?"

"No, sir."

"Are you sure?" asked Dick incredulously.

"Absolutely sure, sir. I heard a noise of somebody walking before I heard the skylight break – I suppose it was the skylight – but that came from the other end of the roof."

Dick hurried back beyond the opening, taking the opposite direction, until he was brought to a standstill by the wall of the next house, which was a story higher than 551. He threw a ray up to the coping: it was impossible that anybody could have climbed that bare face.

And then he saw, hanging over the low parapet which enclosed the rear of the roof, a knotted rope, its ends secured around a chimney stack. He peered down into the darkness.

"If the fellow went that way, he certainly moved," he said, and went back to interview the sentinel.

The man said he had heard nothing, except a sound which might have been the skylight being opened, and there had been no violent noise of breakage until Dick's crowbar had got busy.

"You're an American?" said Shannon suddenly.

"Yes, sir, I'm an American," said the man. "I've been doing this kind of work on the other side."

There must be some other hiding place on the roof, but though Dick spent a quarter of an hour prying and peering, even hammering at the solid brick chimney stack, he found no place of concealment, and lowered himself down to the little room, leaving Steel to complete the investigation.

Steel's search was leisurely but thorough. With the aid of his hand-lamp he began a systematic examination of the lead. His first discovery was a small brass cylinder, obviously an automatic shell and one recently discharged. The second and the more important find did not appear until he had almost given up the search. It lay in a little rain gutter running on to the parapet, and it was the glitter of its golden edge that betrayed its presence. He fished it out of the stagnant water and brought it down to the top landing.

It was a small gold case and contained three sodden cigarettes. In one corner was an initial. Wiping the case dry, he brought it down to his chief. Dick Shannon read the initials.

"I think we have the man," he said soberly.

MARTIN ELTON COMES HOME

Dora Elton heard her husband's key in the lock and braced herself for the shock of meeting. She was shivering, though she still wore her fur coat and the temperature of the room was above moderate. Tensely strung as she was, all sound was amplified, and she heard him put his walking stick into the hall cupboard, the rustle of his feet on the carpet, and waited. Once she had read of a man (or was it a girl?) who had done the will of a hypnotist, obeying him blindly. And then, one day, the victim felt a joyous sense of freedom and relief and knew that his master was dead.

And Lacy Marshalt was dead. Even if she had not stood on the margin of the crowd and heard the news passed back over the heads, she would have known by that sudden thunderous withdrawal of her obsession. She felt as a murderer feels on the morning of his execution.

The meanness, the stupidity of the crime – the terrific and disproportionate punishment which must be inflicted upon his dearest; the utter futility of past hates –

The handle of the door turned and Martin Elton came in. At the sight of him, her hand went to her mouth to stifle a scream. His face and hands were grimy, his dress suit patched and stained with dust; a strip of cloth hung from one trouser, showing his bruised knee beneath. His face was drawn and old-looking, the bloodless lips twitched convulsively.

For a second he stood by the door, looking at her. Neither malice nor reproach was in his glance.

"Hallo!" he said, closed the door, and came forward. "So the police came, after all?"

"The police?"

"You sent them here to find some money. I saw Gavon; he seemed inclined to make a search. You haven't forgotten, have you?"

She had. So much had happened since then.

"I stopped them. Gavon thought I was hysterical."

He spread his uncleanly hands to the fire.

"I think you were."

Looking down at the dilapidation of his garments, he smiled. "I'll take a bath, change my things, and get rid of these clothes – it was rather a stiff climb."

Suddenly she moved to him, and dropped her hand into the pocket of his jacket. He made no protest, and when the hand came out holding the squat Browning, the sight of it seemed to interest rather than distress him.

With shaking hands, and eyes that saw mistily through tears, she examined the pistol. The chamber was empty, the magazine that should have filled the butt was missing. Smelling at the barrel, her face puckered into a grimace of pain. The pistol had been fired, and recently. The stink of cordite still clung.

"Yes, change, please," she said, and then: "Were you seen?"

He pursed his lips thoughtfully.

"I don't know – I may have been. What are you going to do?"

"You had better change; if there is anything you want, will you call me?"

When he had gone out of the room, she examined the pistol again. There was nothing to distinguish the weapon from a thousand others, except the number that was stamped upon the barrel, and that would not help the police. Bunny had bought it in Belgium, where purchases are not so carefully registered. She slipped the gun into her pocket, and went up to his room and knocked at the door.

"I am going out for a quarter of an hour," she said.

"All right," came the muffled reply.

She knew a terrace turning out of the Edgware Road. The terrace faced a high wall behind which ran the Regent Canal, and halfway along the thoroughfare was a flight of iron stairs to a bridge that spanned the water. A taxi dropped her at the foot of the stairs and was dismissed. From the centre of the bridge she dropped the pistol, and heard a "smack!" as it struck the thin ice.

She came to the corresponding terrace on the other side of the canal and in five minutes had found another taxi.

Martin was in his dressing-gown, sipping a steaming cup of coffee before the drawing-room fire, when she came in. He guessed where she had been.

"I'm afraid I made you look rather a fool – about that money," he said, looking at her across the edge of the cup. "I thought better of it. When Stanford came I made him take the stuff away. Gavon came while we were out – Lucy told me. You didn't know that?"

"She told me something," said Dora indifferently. "I heard, yet didn't hear. What have you done with your clothes?"

"In the furnace," he said briefly.

He had recently installed a system of heating in the house; the furnace was a large one.

"I am going to bed," she said, and came to him to be kissed.

Martin heard the door of her room close and looked thoughtfully at his torn hands.

"Women are queer," he said.

He did not go to bed. His suit was spread in his room ready for the hasty dressing that would follow the expected summons. Throughout the night he sat before the fire, thinking, wondering – but regretting nothing. The grey light of morning found him there, his chin on his breast, sleeping before the cold ashes.

At seven o'clock a sleepy servant woke him.

"There's a gentleman downstairs to see you, sir – Captain Shannon."

Martin rose and shivered.

"Ask him up," he said, and Dick Shannon came almost immediately into the room.

"Morning, Elton. Is this yours?"

He held in his hand a thin gold cigarette case. Martin looked.

"Yes, that is mine," he said.

Dick Shannon put the case in his pocket.

"Will you explain how that came to be found last night near the place where Lacy Marshalt was murdered?" he asked.

"Indeed?" said Elton with great politeness. "At what time was the murder committed?"

"At eight o'clock."

Martin nodded.

"At eight o'clock" – he spoke deliberately – "I was at Vine Street Police Station, explaining to Inspector Gavon that my wife had moments of mental aberration. Moreover, until you told me at this moment, I did not know that Lacy Marshalt was dead."

Dick stared at him.

"You were at Vine Street Police Station? That fact can easily be verified."

"I should have thought it would have been verified before you came," said Martin gravely.

Both men looked at the door as it opened, to admit Dora. The hollow eyes and pallor told of a restless night. She glanced from Shannon to her husband.

"What has happened?" she asked in a low voice.

"Shannon tells me that Lacy Marshalt is dead," said Martin calmly. "This is news to me. Did you know?"

She nodded.

"Yes, I knew. Why has Captain Shannon come?"

Martin smiled.

"I rather fancy he suspects me."

"You!" She glowered at the Commissioner. "My husband did not leave the house last night – "

Martin's low chuckle was one of pure amusement.

"My dear, you are making Captain Shannon suspicious. Of course I left the house. I've just told him that I went to Vine Street, and was at that public institution at the moment the murder was committed.

In some mysterious way my cigarette case spirited itself to the roof of the Malpas establishment."

"I didn't say it was there," interrupted Dick sharply, and for a moment Martin Elton was nonplussed.

"It must have been telepathy – I am psychometric. It was on a roof, at any rate – "

"I didn't even say that," said Dick Shannon quietly.

"Then I must have dreamt it."

Elton was unperturbed by the series of *faux pas*, which would have landed any other man into a welter of embarrassment and confusion.

"I want you to be frank with me, as far as is consistent with your safety, Elton," said Dick. "I can't imagine that you would put up so stupid a bluff as this story of your being at Vine Street at eight o'clock unless there were some substantial grounds for your claim. How came this cigarette case on the roof of 551, Portman Square?"

"I – I put it there." It was Dora. "I borrowed it, Captain Shannon, a few days ago – you know I was a friend of Lacy Marshalt, and that I – I sometimes visited him."

Dick shook his head.

"It was not on Lacy Marshalt's house that it was found. It was on the roof of the Malpas house."

His inquiring eyes sought Elton's.

"I left it there," said Bunny Elton calmly, "earlier in the evening. I intended breaking into Marshalt's place and settling a small account with him. But Marshalt's house is unscalable – it was fairly simple to get to the roof next door. The difficulty began when I tried to find a way into Lacy's castle. It was much more difficult last night because I discovered there was a man – a detective, I imagine – stationed on the roof."

"How did you get down again?" asked Dick.

"That was the astounding thing. Somebody had most providentially provided a rope, which was tied round the chimney stack and knotted at every foot – in fact, it was as easy to negotiate as a ladder."

Shannon considered for a few seconds, and then: "Get dressed," he said. "We will go along to Vine Street and verify your story."

He had no doubt in his mind that the whole statement was untrue; but the first shock of the day came when they reached police headquarters. Not only was Martin's story proved to be true, but in the record book, where all visits were timed with scrupulous accuracy, was the entry: "M Elton called with reference to counterfeit charge," and against this: "Eight o'clock." It was staggering.

"Now," said Martin, enjoying the chief's discomfiture, "perhaps you will ask the night inspector how I was dressed."

"You didn't seem to be dressed at all to me," said that officer. "In fact, I thought you'd come from a fancy dress ball. He was in rags when he arrived. Had you been in a rough house, Elton?"

Martin smiled quietly.

"*On* a rough house, would be more accurate," he said, and then, to Dick: "Are you satisfied?"

The alibi was unimpeachable. Dick looked in his perplexity at the station clock.

"Is that time right?"

"It is now," said the inspector.

"What do you mean?" asked Dick quickly.

"The clock stopped last night; I think it must have been the cold, for it didn't want winding when we started it again. In fact, it stopped round about the time you were here, Elton. It was after you left that the constable drew my attention to it."

"Too bad," murmured Bunny.

He accompanied Dick Shannon back to the house, and no word was spoken until they turned into Curzon Street.

"That fool clock will probably save your neck, my friend," said Shannon. "I've a warrant to search your house, which I'm now going to execute."

"If you find anything that is of the slightest value to you," retorted Martin, "I shall be the first to offer my congratulations!"

THE LETTER

Of all the newspapers the *Globe-Herald* gave the most accurate account of what had happened on the previous night:

Within the space of ten minutes last night, Senator the Hon. Lacy Marshalt of South Africa was shot to death, his body being carried away, and his confidential valet was killed, obviously by the same hand. The first of these tragedies occurred in the Portman Square house of A Malpas, recluse and reputed millionaire. Malpas, a man of eccentric habits, has disappeared, and the police are searching for him.

The story of the crime, gathered by *Globe-Herald* reporters, reads more like a chapter from Edgar Allan Poe than the record of an event which occurred in the fashionable quarter of London last night. At five minutes to eight, Detective Commissioner Shannon accompanied Miss Audrey Bedford, Malpas' secretary, to 551, Portman Square. At this hour Miss Bedford had an appointment with the missing man, and Mr Shannon, having made several futile efforts to interview Malpas, decided that this was an opportunity of gaining admission to a house so carefully guarded. It is now known that the doors and windows of the establishment were operated on an electrical control, and that by means of loud-speaking telephones Malpas was able to interview all callers without their seeing him. At eight o'clock precisely the door opened, and Miss Bedford and the Commissioner entered the house. At that time it is certain that

Malpas was on the premises, for his voice was heard and recognized. Miss Bedford was in the act of knocking on the door of the old man's private apartment, when two shots were heard from within. Gaining admission, Mr Shannon discovered, lying on the floor of Malpas' study, the dead body of Lacy Marshalt...

Here followed a fairly faithful record of all that was discovered subsequently.

The police are face to face with an almost unfathomable mystery, or rather a series of mysteries, which may be briefly summarized.

(1) How came Marshalt in the carefully guarded house of the recluse, who, as it is now known, hated him, and of whom Marshalt was so afraid that he had employed private detectives to protect himself against the old man's machinations? It is clear that some very strong inducement must have been offered to the dead man to come into this house of mystery.

(2) In what manner, after his killing, was the body of Lacy Marshalt removed from No. 551?

(3) Who killed Tonger, the valet, and with what object? The police theory is that the murderer is a man who has been equally injured by both the victims of this terrible outrage.

(4) Where is Malpas, and has he too fallen into the hands of the shadowy criminals?

Dick read the account, and paid a silent tribute to the accuracy of the reporter's record. There were certain points, however, that had been missed, and for this he was grateful.

At ten o'clock he interviewed Marshalt's cook, a stout, middle-aged woman, the least distressed by the tremendous happenings of the previous night.

"What time did Mr Marshalt go out?" was his first question, and she was able to give him exact information.

"At half-past seven, sir. I heard the front door slam, and Milly, who is the first parlour maid, went upstairs to the kitchen thinking that it was Mr Tonger who had come back. Then, deciding it must be the master, she went into the study, and found he had gone."

"Had there been any kind of trouble at all in the house?"

"You mean between Mr Tonger and Mr Marshalt?" She shook her head. "No, sir. Though they were always bickering at one another, Mr Tonger wasn't like an ordinary servant; he knew Mr Marshalt so well that sometimes the maids have heard him call him by his Christian name. They were very good friends."

"Did Tonger have his meals in the kitchen?"

"No, sir, they were all taken up to his room. He had a suite on the top floor, away from the servants' quarters. We slept at the back of the house; he had the front."

Dick consulted the questionnaire he had hastily pencilled.

"Was Tonger an abstemious man? I mean, did he drink at all?"

She hesitated.

"Lately he used to drink a lot," she said. "In the early days I used to send up water or lemon-squash with his lunch and dinner, but for the past few weeks he's had a lot of drink up in his room, though I've never seen him the worse for it."

The woman told him little more than he knew or suspected. He must see Audrey and discover whether she could fill any of the gaps.

She was taking a belated breakfast in the sparsely tenanted dining-room of the hotel when Dick came on the scene.

"I waited up till two o'clock last night, and then, as you didn't arrive, I went to bed."

"Sensible girl," he said. "I promised to come and see you, but I hardly had a second. You know all about it?" he said, glancing at the paper that was folded by the side of her plate.

"Yes," she said quietly. "They seem to have made a lot of discoveries, including the fact that I was with you."

"I told them that," said Dick. "There was nothing to be gained by making a mystery of your presence. Do you remember this?"

He laid a sheet of paper before her – it was the letter that had been found in Malpas' room.

"That is my writing," she said instantly. "I think this was one of the letters I copied for Mr Malpas."

"You don't remember which one? Can you recall the text?"

She shook her head.

"They were all meaningless to me, and I copied them mechanically." She knit her brows in thought. "No – it was not an unusual note. Most of them were a trifle mysterious. Why, where did you get this?"

He did not wish to shock her, so passed on without answering the question.

"Has Malpas any other house? Have any of the letters any reference to a possible hiding place?"

"None," she said, and suddenly: "What have I to do with the money he gave me?"

"You had better keep it until his heir turns up," he said grimly.

"But he's not dead, is he?" she asked in alarm.

"He will be dead seven weeks from the day I lay my hand on the old devil," replied Dick.

He asked her again what the old man was like in appearance, and wrote down the description as she gave it. It was the man whose face he had seen through the skylight!

"He is in London somewhere, probably in the house at Portman Square. The house is full of possible hiding places."

There were at least two he did not know: had he found the second of these, the mystery of Portman Square would have been a mystery no longer.

IN THE OUTER CIRCLE

To say that Audrey was shocked is to describe, in mild and inadequate terms, the emotion which her experience had called into existence. Lying down on the bed after Dick had gone – she was still very tired and sleepy – she recalled, with a rueful smile, the ancient Mrs Graffitt's warning against London. What would that old lady think of her, she wondered. For she did not doubt that the story of her criminal career had lost nothing by repetition. Possibly the farm had already become notorious as the sometime home of a shrewd and ingenious, indeed romantic, law-breaker. Perhaps they would put a tablet on the wall, she mused, half asleep: "Here lived for many years the notorious Audrey Bedford…"

She woke from her doze with a start. Her door was ajar: she was certain she had closed it – equally certain that it had been pushed open by somebody outside. Jumping up from the bed, she walked out into the corridor. There was nobody in sight; she must have been mistaken.

Then she saw on the floor at her feet a letter, and at the first view of the address her breath almost stopped. It was from Malpas!

She tore open the envelope with trembling fingers. Inside was the untidy spread of scrawled lines, three words to the line:

Lacy and his satellite are dead. You will go the same way if you betray my confidence. Meet me without fail tonight at nine o'clock at the entrance of St Dunstan's, Outer Circle. If you tell Shannon, it will be the worse for him and you.

She read the letter again, and the hand that held the paper trembled. St Dunstan's was a landmark in London, a home for blind soldiers, on the loneliest part of the Outer Circle. Should she tell Dick? Her first impulse was to disregard the warning; her second thought was of his safety.

Putting the letter in her handbag, she went out to find the floor clerk. That superior young lady had not seen any man, old or young, in the corridor, except, apparently, people who were well authenticated.

Audrey was so used to mysteries now that this new terror which had been sprung upon her was part of the normal. Who was this mystery man, this grey shadow, that flitted unseen, coming and going at his will? As far as the hotel was concerned, his work was easy. There were two entrances, each leading to a different street (there were stairways and elevators in both wings of the building), and it was, as she knew, a fairly simple matter to slip up and down without observation.

She read the letter again, and liked it less. One thing she must not do, and that was ignore the summons. She must either go to the appointment, or else she must tell Dick and risk what followed. There were many reasons why Dick Shannon should not be taken into her confidence at the moment – he was seeking Malpas, and, though she could lead him direct to the man, she could as easily lead him to his death!

Throughout the day her troubled mind grappled with the problem, to which was added a new discomfort. From the moment she left the hotel in the afternoon until her return, she had the feeling that she was under observation. Somebody was trailing her, watching her every movement. She found herself looking round fearfully, and stepping back with suspicion to stare into the faces of perfectly innocent and unoffending people.

It was characteristic of her that the memory of the tragic sight she had witnessed did not keep her from her favourite walk, though she had to screw up her courage to go along the footpath where she had seen the unknown suicide in her death hour.

The seat was not in view from the far end of the walk; it was placed at the elbow of the path, and came into sight gradually. She stopped dead, her heart thumping fiercely, when she caught her first glimpse. She saw the blue skirt of a woman…and two small feet, motionless.

"You're a fool, Audrey Bedford," she said.

The sound of her own voice drove her forward to discover, sitting in the place of doom, a nursemaid cuddling a rosy-cheeked baby!

The nurse looked up to view with interest a very pretty girl, who laughed aloud as she walked past. Annoyed, the nurse sought the mirror in her handbag to see what the girl was laughing at.

On the way back to the hotel Audrey stopped to buy a weekly devoted to the interests of the poultry keeper – a whimsical thought of hers, but a wise one, for, in the well-remembered jargon of its pages, in the extravagant promise of its advertisements, she found her balance.

She hoped Dick would call that afternoon, but he was far too busy, and in a way she was glad, because she could not have seen him without telling him about her intended errand. Nor did he appear at dinner, and she retired to her room to map out her plans.

First, she would leave all her money behind with the reception clerk in the hotel strong room; and secondly, she would choose the strongest looking taximan she could find, and she would not leave the taxi. That seemed a very sensible and satisfactory plan. If she could only have borrowed a weapon of some kind, her last remaining fears would have been removed; but amongst the mild and innocuous members of the public whom she saw in the lounge there seemed none who would be likely to carry lethal weapons on their persons.

"And I should probably shoot myself!" she thought.

The desirable taxicab driver took a whole lot of finding. Some sort of creeping paralysis appeared to have overtaken the profession, and, standing under the portico of the hotel, she watched fifty decrepit old gentlemen crawl past before a providential giant came her way and was beckoned eagerly.

"I'm going to meet a man in the Outer Circle," she said hurriedly. "I – I don't want to be left alone with him. Do you understand?"

He didn't understand. Most of the young ladies he had driven to the Outer Circle to meet men had desires quite the other way round.

She gave him directions, and sank back in the seat with a sigh of relief that an unpleasant adventure was on its way to completion.

It was a snowy, boisterous night, and the roads of the Circle were black and white, the swaying trees alone refusing to hold the wet flakes that were falling. The Outer Circle excelled itself in gloom – in five minutes' driving she saw no human soul on its sidewalks. For an interminable time the cab continued on its way before it drew up to the kerb.

"Here's St Dunstan's, Miss," said the driver, getting down and standing by the door. "There's nobody here."

"I expect they will come," she said.

She had hardly spoken before a long car came noiselessly into view and slowed a dozen yards behind the cab. She saw a bent figure step painfully to the sidewalk, and waited, her breath coming a little faster.

"Audrey!"

There was no mistaking that voice. She went reluctantly a few paces and looked back at the taximan.

"Will you come here, please?" she asked with an assumption of firmness.

He walked slowly toward her, until she saw, above the white muffler around his neck, the big nose and the long chin she had so graphically described to Dick that morning.

"Come here," he said impatiently. "Send your cabman away."

"He's staying," she said loudly. "I can't remain long with you. You know that the police are looking for you?"

"Send the cabman away," he snapped again, and then: "You've got somebody in that cab! Curse you! I told you – "

She saw the glitter of steel in his hand and shrank back.

"There's nobody there – I swear there's nobody there! Only the taxidriver," she said.

"Come here," he commanded. "Get into my car."

She turned and slipped on the icy sidewalk, and in another second he had gripped her by both arms and was standing behind her.

"Here, what's this?" shouted the cabman, and came threateningly toward him.

"Stand where you are."

Before the muzzle of the pistol the big driver halted.

"Take your cab and go. Here!"

A handful of coins fell almost at his feet, and the driver stooped to recover them. As he did so, the pistol rose once and came down with a crash upon the unprotected head, and the man fell like a log.

All this happened before Audrey realized her extreme danger — happened without her being able to see the face of the murderer, as she knew him to be; for he stood behind her all the time, and struck at the cabman over her shoulder. As the cabman fell, she found herself lifted from her feet.

"If you scream I'll cut your throat!" hissed a voice in her ear. "You're going the way Marshalt went and Tonger — the way Dick Shannon will go, unless you do as I tell you!"

"What do you want of me?" she gasped, struggling hopelessly to free herself from his hold.

"Service!" he hissed. "All that I've paid you for!"

MR BROWN OFFERS ADVICE

The hand of Malpas was over her mouth, as he lifted and dragged her toward the car, and she was fast losing consciousness, when suddenly the grip relaxed, and she fell, half swooning, to the ground. Before she realized what was happening, the lights of Malpas' car flashed past her. She saw three men running, heard a rattle of shots, and then she was lifted to her feet. There was something oddly familiar in the clasp of the arm about her, and she looked up into the face of Dick Shannon.

"You're a wicked girl," said Dick severely. "Lord! But you have given me a fright!"

"Did you — did you see him?"

"Malpas? No, I saw his rear lights, and there's a chance that they may have caught him at one of the gates, but I confess it is a very remote chance. My man missed you; it was only by luck that he picked you up again just as you were driving through Clarence Gate. He got on to me at Marylebone Lane by phone, or else — "

She shuddered.

"Did he tell you anything material?" he asked.

She shook her head.

"No, he made a number of unpleasant promises, which I hope he won't fulfil. Dick, I'm going back to my chickens!"

Shannon laughed softly.

"Even the fiercest of your hens would be inadequate to protect you now, my dear," he said. "Malpas, for some reason or other, thinks it is necessary to remove you. Why he didn't shoot you without any preliminary, I can't for the life of me understand."

And there and then he relieved her mind.

"Yes, you've been followed all day, but not by the sinister Mr Malpas. Two painstaking officers of the CID have been watching your goings-out and comings-in. The nursemaid in the park scared you, they tell me?"

Audrey was human enough to blush.

"I didn't notice anybody following me," she confessed.

"Because you weren't expecting to see those particular people. You were looking for a nasty old man with a long nose."

He saw her safely to her hotel, and went on to the Haymarket. And then for the second time he saw the man Brown. He was standing in exactly the same spot as he had been the night Dick had taken him into his flat.

"My friend, you haunt me," said Shannon. "How long have you been waiting?"

"Four minutes, possibly five," said the other coolly, with a good-natured smile.

"May I suggest that, if you wish to see me, you knock at my door? I employ people who will admit you. I suppose you *do* want to see me?"

"Not particularly," said the other surprisingly. And then: "Did you catch him?"

Dick spun round.

"Catch whom?"

"Malpas. I heard you were chasing him tonight."

"You hear a great deal more than an innocent man should," said Dick.

Mr Brown chuckled.

"Nothing annoys the police worse than to be supplied with information which they fondly imagine is their own private secret! When you remember that your gun play has driven the peaceful inhabitants of Regent's Park into a condition of frenzied alarm, you can hardly say that your unsuccessful attempt to capture the devil-man hasn't been well advertised."

"The devil-man, eh? You know Malpas?"

"Remarkably well," said the other immediately. "Few people know him better."

"And probably you knew the late Mr Lacy Marshalt?"

"More intimately than I knew Malpas," said Brown. "Better acquainted, in fact, than I was with the late Mr Laker."

"Come into my flat," said Dick.

He was not sure that the man was following, he walked so softly, despite his injured leg, until, glancing behind him, he saw him at his heels.

"Laker is a name you have mentioned before: who is he?"

"He was a drunkard, a thief, and a trainer of thieves. He was not so well acquainted with Malpas that he didn't make a mistake. You only make one with Malpas, and his was to call on his boss when he had looked upon red wine – it was the night of Laker's death!"

"His death? Then he's dead?"

Mr Brown nodded.

"His body was taken out of the river some time ago. I thought you would associate the cases."

Dick jumped up from the chair in which he had sat.

"You mean the man who was clubbed and thrown over the Embankment?"

Brown nodded.

"That was the intemperate Laker," he said, "and he was, I imagine, destroyed by Malpas or one of his agents. At the moment I haven't any exact news as to whether such an agent was employed, and I think you'd be on the safe side if you marked Laker down as Malpas' own personal handiwork."

Dick looked at him in silence.

"You're asking yourself whether it is possible that there could be such a – what is the expression? – 'fiend in human shape' is popular – who would murder his way out of all his difficulties? Why not? Commit one murder, and find no cause for remorse, and all the others are not only simple but a natural consequence. I have met many murderers – "

"You have met them?" said Dick incredulously.

The man nodded.

"Yes; I was a convict for many years. That rather startles you, but it is nevertheless true. My name is Torrington. I had a life sentence but was pardoned for saving the lives of two children – the children of the High Commissioner of the Cape. That is why I am allowed a passport in a false name. I am, in fact" – his quick smile came and went – "one of the privileged classes! I am interested in Malpas; I was much more interested in the late Mr Marshalt, but that is a point I need not labour. Criminals interest me, just as a train that has jumped the rails interests one. While it keeps to the rails and carries on its humdrum business, it is hardly worthwhile noticing unless you are a railway engineer; but when it has jumped the rails and becomes a hopeless wreck, or plunges along some track of its own making to destruction, then it becomes a fascinating object."

"You did not like Mr Marshalt?" said Dick, eyeing him keenly.

Brown smiled.

"I did not" – a long pause – "like him. That is true. *De mortuis nil nisi bonum* is a stupid tag. Why shouldn't you speak ill of the dead? For if they die, their acts still circle out on the pool of fate. You want to be careful, Captain Shannon." His hard, bright eyes transfixed the detective.

"Careful about – ?"

"About Malpas. One killing more or less isn't going to bother him, and he has an especial reason for getting at you. Remember, he is a genius, with a deplorable sense of the theatrical." His eyes did not leave Dick's face. "If I were you, I should leave him alone."

Shannon laughed in spite of his irritation.

"That's fine advice to give to an executive police officer," he said.

"It is good advice," said the other, but did not pursue the topic. "Where do you think they have taken the body of Marshalt?"

Dick shook his head.

"It is in the house somewhere. But I don't know why I should give you my theories."

"I don't think it is in the house at all," said Brown. "I have an idea – however, I have said too much already. And now you're coming round to my hotel for a nightcap, Captain."

Shannon declined laughingly.

"Well, at any rate, you'll come along and escort me?" said the other with his tremulous smile. "I am a feeble man and in need of police protection."

Dick sent him down to the street while he telephoned, to discover that no further trace of Malpas had been seen. When he joined his companion he found him in his accustomed place on the edge of the kerb, looking up and down the Haymarket with bright, quick, bird-like jerks of his head.

"Are you expecting anybody?"

"I am," said the other, but did not trouble to explain whom. There was one curious fact that Dick noted on the way to the hotel, and that was that Mr Torrington's limp was not so pronounced sometimes as it was at others. It was almost as though he had lapses of memory, and forgot to drag his foot. Shannon remarked upon it just before they reached their destination.

"I think a great deal of it is habit," said Torrington without embarrassment. "I've been so used to dragging my leg that it has almost become second nature."

He looked past Dick with the same strange intentness that he had shown before.

"You still expect to see somebody!"

Torrington nodded.

"I am looking for the shadow," he said; "he hasn't let up once today, so far as I can discover."

Shannon chuckled.

"You don't like being shadowed – it was smart of you to detect him."

Torrington stared at him.

"You mean the policeman who has been following me? That is he on the corner: I know all about him. No, I was talking of the man who has been trailing you."

"Me?" asked the commissioner, and Torrington's eyebrows rose.

"Didn't you know?" he asked innocently. "Bless my soul – I thought you knew everything!"

THE FEET ON THE STAIRS

Slick Smith lived in lodgings in Bloomsbury. He had the first floor of a house which had been the latest thing in dwellings somewhere around the time when George II was swearing in broken English at his ministers. Now, in spite of improvements introduced by the landlord, No. 204, Doughty Street was a little out of date.

In some respects the archaic arrangements suited Smith remarkably well. There was, for example, a cistern outside his bedroom window, and the constant drip and hiss and gurgle of water would have driven a more sensitive man to madness. Smith, being neither sensitive nor a martyr to nerves, found the noise soothing and the cistern itself a handy getting-off place. Through the window to the cistern support was a step, to the top of a wall was another. An agile man could get from Slick's bedroom to a side street in less time that it would take him to descend the stairs and pass through the front door like a law-abiding citizen. And he could return the same way almost as easily. Therefore he endured the cistern and the low roofs and the twisting stairway where you bumped your head against a three-hundred-year-old beam if you were a stranger. And though the smoke of the kitchen fire occasionally came up to him via the open window of his sleeping apartment, he told the apologetic landlord that on the whole he preferred smoke to the more delicate perfumes.

Nobody in the house knew his business. He was generally regarded as one who had more money than duties. He spent most of his nights away from his rooms and slept the greater part of the day behind a locked door. He had few visitors, and those usually came at the hour the landlord dined, and were admitted by himself. They did not knock or ring – a soft whistle in the street brought him to the door.

When he went out, as he did every evening, he was usually in evening dress, and, almost as though it were part of a ritual, he followed the same route. A bar in Cork Street, a small and not too savoury night club in Soho, a more fashionable club in Coventry Street and so on, to a point where he vanished and left no trace. Night after night expert watchers from Scotland Yard had missed him, and always at the same spot – on the corner of Piccadilly Circus and Shaftesbury Avenue, the best-lighted patch of London.

He had reached the Soho stage of his wanderings on the night that Audrey had made her adventurous journey to meet Malpas, and, seated at a little table at the far end of the room, he listened to the efforts of three instrumentalists who were doing a bad best to keep time with the dancers who thronged a floor as defective in quality as the orchestra.

A little man with a thin, vicious face edged his way to the watcher's side, drew a chair slyly forward and sat down, beckoning the waiter.

"Same as him," he grunted, indicating the bock before Mr Smith, who did not even look round. Until…

"Slick, there's a dame at the Astoria with a carload of stuff. French and divorced. You could straighten the maid for half a monkey…"

"Cease your gibberish, child," said Slick wearily. "What is half a monkey? And which half?"

"Two hundred and fifty…the maid's a Pole…"

"What more appropriate for a monkey than a Pole?" asked Smith. "Or even half a monkey and half a Pole? Tempt me not. You mean Madame Levellier? I guessed so. Her stock's worth twenty thousand – net! And dollars at that. She carries most of it appliquéd to her person. And every cheap grab-it in London knows all about it. You're as interesting as last year's Book of Omens and Prophecies."

The informer was not abashed. He was a "spotter," a gatherer of valuable information, and had never stolen in his life. Keeping to the company of valets and servants, he located rich pockets for other men to mine.

"There's a fellow from the North staying at the British Imperial. He's an ironmaster, and has stacks of money. Today he bought a diamond tarara – "

"Tiara – yes, for his wife," said Slick, still watching the dancers. "His name is Mollins; he paid twelve hundred for the jewel – it is worth nine. He carries a gun, and his bulldog sleeps on the end of his bed – he has a great mistrust of Londoners."

The spotter sighed patiently.

"That's all I know," he said, "but I'll have a good job for you in a day or two. There's a fellow coming from South Africa with a fortune. He's been here before…"

"Let me know about *him*," said Slick, in a changed tone. "I've heard about that guy, and I want to get better acquainted."

He laid his hand palm downward on the table and moved it carelessly in the spotter's direction. That gentleman took what was underneath and was grateful.

Soon after this, Smith left. But at every stage of the journey the same thing happened. Sometimes the spotter was a woman; once it was a hard-faced young girl – and they all told him about the French woman at the Astoria and the ironmaster at the British Imperial, and he listened courteously and helped them out when their information was deficient.

"Listen, Mr Smith." This was at his last place of call, and the informant was an overdressed young man who wore a diamond ring. "I've got it for you. There's a dame at the Astoria – "

"This story must be true," interrupted Slick. "She's got a million dollars of diamonds and a Polish maid, and she's divorced."

"That's right – I thought I had this on my own."

"It will be in the papers tomorrow," said Slick.

It was curious how little was the interest taken by professional circles in the Portman Square murder. Never once did he hear it mentioned, and, when he introduced the topic, they wandered straight away.

"It's like getting a cinema star to talk about someone else," he said to an acquaintance.

"They naturally dislike crime," said that worthy, and had the laugh to himself.

When he finally made his disappearance he was without news. That came later. At two o'clock in the morning a tramp shuffled into the mews at the back of Portman Square, and half an hour later Dick Shannon was called from his bed by telephone.

"Steel, sir... I'm speaking from 551... I wish you would come down – the queerest things are happening here."

"Queer...how?"

"I'd rather you came than explain over the telephone."

Dick knew that his second would not call him from bed at that hour without good cause, and he dressed quickly. When he got to the house, Steel and a policeman were waiting in the open doorway.

"The fact is," confessed the sergeant, "either I have an attack of nerves or else there is something confoundedly wrong."

"What has happened?"

They were in the hall and the door was shut. Steel lowered his voice.

"It started at midnight – the sound of somebody walking up these stairs. I and the constable were in Malpas' room – I was teaching him picquet. We both came out on the landing, expecting to find either you or the inspector from Marylebone Lane. There was nobody. We couldn't both have been mistaken – "

"Did you hear it, too?" asked Shannon, addressing the stolid policeman.

"Yes, sir; it fair gave me the creeps...a sort of stealthy – "

He turned his head and stared up the bare staircase. Dick heard it, and for a second a shiver ran down his spine.

It was the sound of slippered feet on stone steps.

"Sweesh, sweesh..."

Then there floated up to them a muffled laugh.

Shannon crept to the foot of the stairs. Above on the landing, and out of sight, a solitary light was burning, and, as he looked, there passed across the wall the shadow of a monstrous head. He reached the first landing in a second – no sign of head or owner.

185

A VISION OF MARSHALT

"Curious," he mused aloud. "This is the sort of thing calculated to scare Aunt Gertrude."

Steel heard the "Aunt Gertrude." It was the agreed-on code — outside the house and within hail was a policeman specially posted. The man ran across in answer to the flash-lamp signal.

"Phone the Superintendent that the Chief requires all divisional reserves — and a cordon! He will understand if you say 'Gertrude.' "

He came back to find Dick inspecting the big room which Malpas used as an office. The curtains had been removed from the panelled walls — from everywhere except the alcove that concealed the strange bronze god and those that covered the windows. Against the wall facing the window was a long oaken sideboard, the only article of furniture in the room except the two chairs, the little table at which the guests of Malpas had sat, and the writing desk.

"Somebody has been here," said Steel. He pointed to a litter of cards on the floor. "I left those stacked on the desk; I was just going to deal a hand when we heard the footsteps on the stairs. I should think they've gone now."

Suddenly Dick gripped his arm, and the three men waited, straining their ears. Again it came, those shuffling slippered feet on the stone stairs, and this time Dick Shannon signalled them to remain motionless.

Louder and louder, until the feet halted, as it seemed, in the lobby outside. The door was ajar, but, as they looked, it began to open slowly. Shannon's hand dropped to his hip. In another instant the muzzle of

186

his revolver covered the doorway; but nothing else happened, and when he sped softly across the room and dashed out into the lobby, it was empty.

The policeman took off his helmet and wiped his warm forehead.

"Flesh and blood I can stand," he said huskily. "There isn't a man alive that I won't tackle. But this is getting me rattled, sir!"

"Take this lamp and search the rooms up above," said Dick.

The uniformed man took the torch reluctantly.

"And don't hesitate to use your stick."

The policeman pulled his truncheon from his pocket and looked at it with a certain amount of misgiving.

"All right, sir," he said, taking a long breath. "I don't like it, but I'll do it."

"An excellent motto for all police services," said Dick cheerfully. "I don't think there's anything upstairs except empty rooms, but give a shout if you see anything, and I'll be up in two winks."

He heard the heavy-footed policeman walking up the stairs, and if he had been unaware that the man had no heart in the job, his pace would have told him. Suddenly the footsteps ceased, and Dick walked to the foot of the stairs.

"Are you all right?" he called.

There was no answer, only a queer shuffle of feet and a sound such as a roosting chicken would make, a short, throaty growl. And then something round and dark came over the banisters, fell on the stairs and bounded to Dick's feet. It was the policeman's helmet.

Followed by Steel, he ran up the stairs, and, in the light of his lantern, he saw something swaying on the upper landing – something that swung and struggled and kicked impotently. It was the policeman, and he dangled to and fro from the end of a rope noosed about his neck and fastened to the landing above. The man was on the point of collapse when Steel, springing forward, cut the rope above his head. They got him back to Malpas' room and laid him on the floor, while Steel forced brandy between his clenched teeth. It was ten minutes before he had recovered sufficiently to tell what had happened. And of that he knew very little.

"I was turning to go up the next flight when a rope dropped over my head from above. Before I could shout, it was pulled tight, and I could see somebody hauling from the landing. I had the presence of mind to throw my helmet over the banisters, or I'd have been a dead man. Men I can tackle, Mr Shannon, but ghosts…"

"What is your weight, my friend?"

"A hundred and seventy pounds, sir."

Dick nodded.

"Find me the ghost that can lift a hundred and seventy pounds at the end of a rope, and I'll become a spiritualist," he said. "There's the inspector, Steel; go down and let him in."

Steel went to the desk, put his hand on the switch that controlled the door, and withdrew it with a yell.

"What's wrong?"

"There's a short circuit somewhere," said the sergeant. "Lend me your glove, sir."

But Dick saved him the trouble. Reaching out, he turned over the switch, to find that leather was no protection – he felt the paralyzing shock of 250 volts, but the switch was turned.

"There you are," he said. "You needn't go down; they will come in."

They waited, but the knocks were repeated. The men looked at one another.

"The control doesn't seem to be working," said Dick, and at that minute the lights went out.

"Keep to the wall, and don't show any light," said Shannon in an undertone.

But Steel had already pressed the button of his electric torch. No sooner did the light flash than a pencil of flame leapt from the other room, something whistled past his head, and there was a smack as the bullet struck the wall.

Dick fell flat, dragging his subordinates with him. Down below, the hammering on the door echoed thunderously through the bare hall.

Shannon shuffled forward, his lamp in one hand, his gun in the other, and Steel followed his example. The darkness of the room was impenetrable. Shannon stopped to listen.

"He's there, in the corner near the window," he whispered.

"I think he's against the wall," whispered Steel. "My God!"

A queer green oblong of light had appeared in the panelled wall behind and level with the sideboard, and in the strange radiance they saw a figure lying. The light grew in intensity, revealing every horrible detail.

It was a man in evening dress, his shirt-front black with powdered smoke. The face was pallid and waxen; his two hands were clasped on his breast. Motionless, awful... Shannon felt a momentary thrill of fear.

"It's a dead man!" croaked Steel. "My God! It's Marshalt! Look — look, Shannon — it's the body of Marshalt!"

THE BUFFET LIFT

The figure lay motionless, fearful to look upon, and then the green oblong of light dimmed and went out, and to their ears came a hollow rumble of sound like distant thunder.

Dick stumbled to his feet and ran across the room, but his groping hands felt nothing but the carved panelling. The strange apparition had vanished!

As he felt, he heard the sound of feet in the hall below.

"Anybody here?" shouted a voice.

"Come up. Use your lamps: the lights are gone."

As though his words were a signal, the lights flared up again.

"Who opened the street door?" asked Dick quickly.

"I don't know, sir. It just opened."

"There's another set of controls somewhere. Steel, get that axe: it's upstairs. No, one of you men get it: you'll find it in the little room on the top landing. Use your lamps and club anybody you see."

The axe was procured without any untoward incident, and Shannon attacked the panelling. In a few minutes he had laid bare the cavity where he had seen the body of Lacy Marshalt lying.

"A buffet lift," he said. "They have them in some of these houses – the width of the sideboard and on the sideboard level."

He reached in and felt the twin steel cables that operated the elevator. The kitchen was in the basement, and the stout door had to be forced – since Steel had visited the place earlier in the evening, somebody had shot the bolts. When an entrance was made he found, as he expected, the buffet lift at rest. But there was no sign of Marshalt.

"That's how they got the body away in the first case, leaving the lift suspended between this room and the kitchen. I searched this place before. If you notice, Steel, the opening even here is so carefully masked by the panelling."

The detective led the way through the scullery into the little courtyard to the rear of the house. The door behind was open; so, too, was the gate into the mews.

"Marshalt's body is in the house: there's no doubt about that," said Dick. "They couldn't have got it away. Where's your cordon, Inspector?" he asked sharply, looking up and down the deserted mews.

The second half of the cordon were late in arriving, apparently, for they were not on the scene until ten minutes after Dick had returned to Malpas' sanctum.

"This room must never be left without a guard," he said. "If there is one thing clearer than another, it is that the old man isn't playing ghosts from sheer mischief. There is a good, solid reason behind his antics, and the reason is that there is something in this room he wants to get at."

He inspected the narrow stairway that led below to the old drawing-room, but found nothing except clear evidence that this system of serving stairs was general throughout the house.

"You notice there are no servants' stairs at all?" He pointed out the fact to Steel. "Probably this house was built long after that on the left and the right of it, and the architects had to design a method of working in a second staircase without encroaching upon the room space."

"But there are no stairs from the drawing-room to the kitchen," said Steel, and tapped the wall where the stairway ended on the drawing-room level. To his surprise it sounded hollow.

"That's a door with a concrete face," suggested Dick. He put his shoulder against it, and it turned easily. "That is the way our friend came and went. Come up here." He ascended a dozen stairs and stopped. "We are now moving parallel with the main stairway. Listen."

He tapped at the wall.

"You could almost put your finger through it," he said. "That accounts for the slippered feet on the stairs – an old theatrical trick. If you give me two pieces of sandpaper I'll show you how it's produced."

They went back to the big room again.

"And here's a second door." Again Dick tapped at what was apparently a solid wall. "This takes him to the next floor, and he was up there waiting to noose our policeman."

"Where is he now?"

"A sane question," said Dick dryly, "but I'm not prepared to answer you. I should say that he was some miles away. If that cordon had been in its place, there would have been one ghost less in the world." He examined his lamp. "I'm going to have another shot at the roof, though it is unlikely that our bird will be nesting there. By the way, Willitt's detectives have been withdrawn?"

As far as I know, sir. Willitt is still under the orders of Marshalt's lawyers, who have put a caretaker in the house."

A search of the roof revealed no more than that the detective was still on duty. They saw the red glow of his cigar end before he himself was visible.

"Rather unnecessary, isn't it, your being here?" said Shannon.

"From my point of view, yes," was the reply. "But I carry out instructions from my chief as you carry out yours."

"You've seen nobody?"

"No, sir. I'd have been mighty glad to have even a ghost to talk to. This is surely the coldest and most lonesome job on earth."

"You've heard nothing happening below?"

"I heard somebody come out of the back just now: I thought it was you. There has been a big car waiting there for the last hour. I looked over, but I didn't see who it was. He was dragging something heavy. I heard him grunt as he got through the gate and loaded it into the car. I thought it was one of your sleuths."

To Dick Shannon it seemed impossible that one man should have carried the body without assistance; and there was something unnatural about the thing. When he came back to Steel, he found that the sergeant had made a discovery which was eventually to solve the mystery to some extent.

"I found this in the courtyard," he said. "Our friend must have dropped it in his flight."

It was a flat leather case, and, opening it, Dick saw an array of tiny phials, a hypodermic syringe and two needles. The syringe had evidently been put away in a hurry, for it was half filled with a colourless liquid, and the velvet bed on which it lay was wet, where it had leaked.

"It looks as if it had been used recently," said Steel.

"The needle certainly gives that impression," agreed Shannon, examining the thread-like steel. "Send the contents of the syringe straight away for analysis. I am beginning to see daylight!"

STORMER'S

Stormer's Detective Agency occupied the first floor of a new City building. That it was a detective agency at all was not apparent, either from the discreet inscription on its doors, or from the indication in the hall, which said simply "Stormer's," and left the curious to guess in what branch of commerce Stormer's was engaged.

That morning, Mr John Stormer paid one of his fugitive visits to his English headquarters. He came, as usual, through his own private door, and, the first intimation Willitt had that his chief was in the building was when the buzzer on his desk purred angrily. He passed down the corridor, unlocked the door of the sanctum, and went in. Mr Stormer, his derby hat on the back of his head, an unlighted cigar between his strong white teeth, sprawled in his office chair with an open copy of *The Times* in his hand.

"Give me an English newspaper for news every time," he said with a sigh. "Do you know, Willitt, that it will be fair but colder, that there's a depression to the southwest of Ireland and another depression to the northeast of Ireland, that will probably cause rain in the west of England? Do you know that visibility is good, and that the sea crossing is rough? The newspapers over here give more space to the weather than we give to a Presidential election."

He put the newspaper down on the floor, fixed pince-nez on his broad nose, and looked at his subordinate.

"What's doing?" he asked.

"There are five new cases in this morning, sir," said Willitt. "Four of them husband and wife stuff, and one a lady who is being blackmailed by a moneylender."

Stormer lit the stub of his cigar.

"Don't tell me about it; let me guess," he said. "She borrowed the money to save a friend from embarrassment, and her husband doesn't like the friend."

Willitt grinned.

"Very nearly right, sir."

"I should say it was very nearly right," said Mr Stormer with a grimace. "Women never borrow money for themselves: they always borrow it for somebody else. There's never been a bill signed by a woman that didn't have a halo over it. Now what's the latest from Portman Square?"

Willitt gave a long and accurate description of recent developments.

"Last night, eh? Do you know what the trouble was?"

"I don't know, sir. Wilkes reported that Shannon came on the roof, and that the house was surrounded by police."

"Humph!" said Stormer, and there and then dismissed the mystery of Portman Square, and devoted his mind and thoughts to the routine of his business.

He very seldom made his appearance in his London office, but when he did he worked like ten men; and it was not until the City clocks were striking nine that night that he signed his last letter.

"About that business of Malpas," he said; "the old instructions hold until they're cancelled by Marshalt's lawyer. The house is to be watched, a man remaining on the roof, and one of our two best men always to be on the heels of – Slick Smith! You understand?"

"Yes, sir."

"It's too bad Slick should have to be trailed this way, but I'm taking no risks. Cable me if anything develops."

Willitt made a note of the order.

"By the way, how do we come" – Stormer frowned up at the other – "how did we come to be acting for Marshalt at all?"

195

"He wanted a girl traced and came to us – "

Stormer smacked the table with his hand.

"Of course – the girl! Did you ever discover what was behind his interest in Miss Bedford?"

Willitt shook his head.

"No, sir: he was that kind of a man. You remember I told you he wanted me to bring her to dinner with him? I don't think there was any other interest."

"Don't you?" Stormer emphasized the first word. "That is surely strange – wanting that girl located. Her name is Bedford, I suppose?"

Willitt smiled.

"You've asked me that before. Yes, sir. She was very well known in the village of Fontwell – lived there all her life practically."

"And Elton – was her maiden name Bedford?"

"Yes, sir: she was married in that name."

Mr Stormer had a trick of sweeping the palm of his hand across his mouth when he was perplexed.

"I hoped…however. The girl's in town now, eh? Staying at the Regency, your report said…h'm!"

He beat a tattoo on the desk with his pencil.

"Ever thought of pulling her into this business? We want a woman sleuth badly, and she's the kind who'd pay for dressing. Malpas' secretary, too! She's out of a job, isn't she?"

"I've got an idea that Shannon is sweet on her," said Willitt.

"Oh?" Mr Stormer was not impressed. "Any man is sweet on a good-looking girl. There's nothing to it."

He looked at the telephone thoughtfully, and pulled it toward him.

"I'd like to talk to this man Shannon," he said. "Where will I get him?"

Willitt opened a little pocketbook and searched its pages.

"Here are two numbers: the first is his flat, the second is his office. I think you're more likely to get him at the flat."

Stormer called the flat without success. He then tried the Treasury number which connected him with Scotland Yard.

"Captain Shannon has gone home; he has been gone ten minutes."

"We'll try the flat again," said the detective chief, and this time he had better success, for Dick had just come in.

"It's Stormer speaking. That Captain Shannon?"

"Stormer? Oh, yes, the detective agency."

"Yuh. Say, Captain Shannon, I've been able to help you from time to time – you'll remember I put you on to Slick Smith when he came east?"

Dick, who had forgotten that fact, laughed.

"He's been an exemplary criminal since he's been on this side," he said.

"That is how Slick always looks," replied Stormer dryly, "but he's making a living somehow. But that isn't what I wanted to talk to you about, Captain. I understand that my people have got a commission from the late Mr Marshalt to watch his house. Seems fairly foolish, now he's dead, but the instructions hold, I guess; and I'd be ever so much obliged to you if you'd give my men a little consideration. One of them tells me you questioned his right on the roof of this house in Portman Square, and certainly it looks a little unnecessary. What I want to say is that I've given orders that they are to give the police any help they can, and to put no obstacles in their way."

"That is very kind of you, and I quite see your difficulty."

Stormer smiled to himself.

"I guess you don't," he said. "Have you met the caretaker that Marshalt's lawyers have appointed to look after his house?"

"I've seen him."

"Take a good look at him," said Stormer, and rang off before Dick could frame an inquiry.

Mr Stormer was chuckling to himself as at a good joke, all the way back to the restaurant where he dined that night. For he liked his mysteries; liked better the illusion of omnipotence that he was able to create.

He chose to dine that night at the hotel where Audrey Bedford was living, and after dinner strolled from the dining-room to the vestibule, where he interviewed the reception clerk.

"I find I shan't be able to get home tonight," he said. "Could you let me have a room?"

"Certainly, sir," said the clerk, wondering where was the home of this obvious and patent American. He searched the register.

"461."

"That is a little too high for me. I'd like a room somewhere on the second floor."

Again the clerk consulted his register.

"There are two rooms empty, Nos. 255 and 270."

"I guess I'll take 270. Seventy's my lucky number," said Mr Stormer.

The number of Audrey's room was 269.

THE FACE IN THE NIGHT

The girl had spent that day looking for work, and greater success was promised her efforts than in the days when she was the ragged princess, and had nothing but a prison record and a threadbare costume to recommend her. She had not told Dick Shannon of her plans; she was anxious, as far as possible, to dispense with his assistance. The desire for independence is innate in every woman, and her willingness to accept help from a man is in inverse ratio to her regard for him. Audrey Bedford liked him enough to shrink from his help.

There was a certain amount of humour in her ultimate choice of occupation. Once, in the days of Meak Farm, she had written to a weekly journal, which laboured under the cumbersome title, the *Amateur Poultry Farmer and Allotment-Holder*. There had developed between Audrey and the editor a long and intimate correspondence about the diet of sick hens, and it had occurred to her that even the *Amateur Poultry Farmer and Allotment-Holder* did not appear week after week without some professional assistance. She wrote a letter to the editor, was remembered, and summoned to his untidy office, and there and then offered a position on his staff.

"We want somebody to deal with the poultry correspondence," he said.

The theory that professions influence appearances had some support in the fact that he looked rather like an elderly hen himself.

"I think you will be able to tackle that. We want two columns a week for the paper: the rest you can answer privately. If you find yourself up against some proposition that you can't solve, refer to your reply on the subject in our issue of March, 1903. It will give you time."

The salary was not large, certainly insufficient to maintain her in the splendid state which had been hers; but she utilized the remainder of the day to find lodgings, and discovered a very cheery room near to her work. On her way she announced the fact to the assistant manager of the hotel.

"I'm sorry you're leaving us, Miss Bedford," said that gentleman with professional regret. "You'll be giving up your room as from tomorrow at twelve o'clock. We hope to see you again."

She, for her part, hoped he wouldn't. The hotel had unpleasant associations for her, and she was looking forward eagerly to the quietude of her own little room.

Dick had called early to see her, expecting to find her still suffering from the shock of her unpleasant experience of the night before. He was agreeably surprised to learn that she had gone out. Later, one of his men reported that the girl had secured an appointment, and he hurried round to congratulate her.

"You've saved me telephoning for you."

"Why?" he asked quickly. "Has anything happened? You haven't had another communication from – ?"

"No." She shook her head. "I don't think I shall; and if I do, I shall certainly send for you. I've splendid news."

"You're going back to the poultry business – the editorial side."

He laughed at her surprise.

"Of course, your shadow – that is what you call him, isn't it? It's awfully romantic, but a little embarrassing at times, to have a man chasing one. I'd forgotten his existence."

"Why did you want to see me?"

She opened her handbag, took out a little pebble, and laid it on his outstretched hand.

"That," she said. "I meant to have told you before."

He stared at the thing open-mouthed, turned it over, and examined the tiny red seal.

"Where on earth did you get this?"

"Is it important?" she asked. "I meant to have told you before. I found it in the hallway at 551 the first time I went to see Mr Malpas. I dropped the key when I was trying to unlock the door, and, searching for it, I found this little stone."

Dick's mind flashed back to his interview with Brown, or Torrington, who had shown him a similar "stone."

"What is it?" she asked again.

"It is a diamond in the rough. Its value is something like eight hundred pounds."

She gasped.

"Are you sure?"

He nodded. Carrying the diamond to the window, he made a closer inspection of the seal.

"You're certain it's a diamond?"

"It is a diamond all right, and the seal is that of the mining company. May I keep this?"

She was relieved.

"I wish you would."

"Does anybody else know you have it?"

She shook her head.

"Nobody, unless Mr Malpas knew, and that isn't likely, is it?"

Dick considered the possibilities.

"Nobody else has seen it?"

She thought for a long time.

"I don't think so," she said slowly, "unless – yes, I remember. I went the other day to the reception clerk for the key of my room, and it wasn't there, and I turned everything out of my bag on to the counter, and found it – the key, I mean – in the torn lining."

"That's when he saw it – and when I say 'he,' I mean either he or his agent. I should think this partly explains why he tried to get you last night."

Audrey sighed.

"Every day and in every way I am more and more sorry I left my peaceful farm!" she said. "You don't know what a warm feeling I had when my dear poultry editor asked me if I knew how to cure moulting hens!"

She went up to her room that night in a happier frame of mind than she had had in years. She felt that, with her new work, she was leaving behind her the unwholesome atmosphere in which she had moved and lived since her coming to London.

She locked the door of her room, and in her relief was asleep almost as soon as she turned her head on the pillow. And so she slept through the early part of the night, and did not wake till something cold and clammy touched her face.

"Audrey Bedford, I want you," said a hollow voice.

She sat up with a shriek. The room was in complete darkness, except...

Not a yard away from her was a face, suspended, it seemed, in mid-air — a face strangely and dimly illuminated...

She stared at the closed eyes, the pain-creased face of Lacy Marshalt!

THE GUEST WHO DISAPPEARED

"The young lady is in a state of collapse. I've sent for a doctor and a nurse."

"Do you know what happened to her?" asked Dick. He was standing by the side of his bed in his pyjamas, telephone in hand.

"No, sir. The porter, who was on the floor below, heard a shriek. He ran upstairs and found Miss Bedford's door open; he saw she had fainted, and sent for me. I was down in the hall below."

"No sign of Malpas?"

"None whatever, sir. There must have been somebody trying to get at her, because the gentleman in the room next to Miss Bedford's was found at the end of the passage, knocked out. He had evidently been clubbed, probably with a rubber stick, for the skin wasn't broken. He has gone off to hospital to have his head dressed."

Dick was at the hotel in five minutes, and the girl was sufficiently recovered to receive him. She sat before the gas fire in her dressing-gown, very white, but, as usual, perfectly self-possessed.

"There's nothing to tell, except that I saw Mr Marshalt."

"You saw him, too, did you?" Dick bit his lip thoughtfully.

"Have you see him?" she asked in amazement.

He nodded.

"Yes, we had a vision of him last night. Do you remember no more?"

"I'm afraid I fainted," she said ruefully. "It was a dreadfully feminine thing to do, but one gets that way. The porter told me that the man in the next room was badly hurt. Oh, Dick, what does it mean?"

"It means that Marshalt is alive and in the hands of this old devil," said Dick. "Last night we found a hypodermic in the house; we had the stuff analyzed and discovered it to be a drug that would have the result of reducing a man to complete unconsciousness – a mixture of hyoscin, morphia, and another drug that hasn't been identified. Tonight I had a letter from Malpas." He took out a sheet of type-written paper. "This is a copy; the original has gone to the Yard for fingerprint tests."

She took the letter in her hand, and there was no need for her to ask who had written those straggling lines:

Unless you're a fool, you discovered something last night. Lacy Marshalt is not dead. Knowing him, I ought to have realized that he would take no risks. The bullet-proof singlet he wore under his shirt turned the bullet, as you would have discovered if you had made an examination, instead of being concerned with getting the girl out of the house. I am glad he is alive – death was too good for him, and he will die in my time. If you wish him to live, withdraw your watchers and spies from my house.

"Everything I have found in the house confirms the view," said Dick. "Marshalt is being kept under the influence of this drug, and is either taken on his own feet or carried wherever Malpas goes."

"It did not seem like a real face to me," interrupted the girl.

This was a new idea to Dick Shannon.

"You mean, it might have been a mask? That might be an explanation. Yet, if it were so, why should this man write as he does? No, I think his letter is true. The reference to the hypodermic suggests that he was forced into telling the truth by Steel's discovery. It is a quaint case altogether. I'm going now to see after our unknown friend – I presume your scream aroused him and he came upon both Malpas and his burden – if burden it was – and was clubbed for his pains."

The injured visitor had left the hotel, for a hospital, as he said. His name on the register was "Henry Johnson, of South Africa." The clerk who had received him was not on duty, so Dick had to be content with that information; and, leaving instructions that he was to be notified when the unknown guest returned, he went home. He drove on to Portman Square, there to learn that nothing exceptional had happened. The inspector and three men were in the house; he saw Willitt's watcher in the street outside.

Leaving, he remembered Stormer's reference to the caretaker, and, early the next morning, Dick Shannon was a caller at Marshalt's house.

He had had very little time to consider the effect of Marshalt's disappearance upon his household, but he knew, as a matter of fact, that the man had given very exact instructions as to what should happen in the event of his death. Within a few hours of the news being published, a representative from Lacy's lawyer had visited the house, taken complete control, and removed Marshalt's papers. It was on the following day Dick heard that a caretaker had been appointed in accordance with Lacy Marshalt's wishes, but he had had no occasion to call, the police work being in the hands of the local inspector, and, so far as he was concerned, the caretaker had remained invisible.

A servant, whom he remembered, opened the door and showed him into the drawing-room where he had last seen poor old Tonger.

"I suppose things have changed very considerably with you?" he said to the maid.

"Oh, yes, sir. The whole house has been upset; cook has gone, and there are only Milly and I left. Wasn't it dreadful about poor Mr Tonger, and poor Mr Marshalt, too?"

It was evident to Dick that the death of Tonger had distressed the house considerably more than the fate that had overtaken its owner.

"You have a caretaker now?"

The girl hesitated.

"Not exactly a caretaker, sir," she said. "The gentleman was a friend of Mr Marshalt's."

"Indeed?" said Dick, to whom this was news. "I had no idea that Mr Marshalt – " He checked himself, not wishing to speak disparagingly of the woman's employer. "I did not know that. Who is it?"

"A Mr Stanford, sir."

Dick's jaw dropped.

"Not Bill Stanford?"

"Yes, sir; Mr William Stanford. I'll tell him you're here, sir; he's upstairs in Master's study."

"Let me save you the trouble," said Dick with a smile. "Mr Stanford and I are old acquaintances."

Bill was sitting in front of a big fire, his feet on the silver fender, an enormous cigar in the corner of his mouth, and on his knees a sporting newspaper. As he looked round, he rose with an embarrassed smile.

"Good morning, Captain. I was expecting to see you before."

"So you're the caretaker?"

Bill smiled.

"I'm the man in charge," he said. "Nobody was more surprised than I when his lawyers came for me, because he wasn't exactly a friend of mine. We were not in the same set, so to speak."

"You knew him in South Africa, of course?" nodded Dick.

"That's it; that's how I came to know him at all. Why I should have been sent for…but there it was in black and white, with my full name and address written down – William Stanford, of 114, Backenhall Mansions, with the amount I was to be paid and everything."

"A will, one presumes?"

"No, sir, it wasn't a will. It looked as though Marshalt expected to be called away suddenly one of these days. It said nothing about his death; it only said 'if he should disappear from any cause whatsoever, the said William Stanford, etc., etc.' "

Bill Stanford! The friend and, by some considered to be the confederate, of the Eltons! Dick pulled up a chair and sat down.

"What does Martin think of this?"

Stanford shrugged his shoulders.

"I should worry about what Martin thinks," he said, with a curl of his lip. "Martin's a bit sore at me because – " He hesitated. "Well, he thought I knew a lot more than I did know. He got an idea that I was friendly with Lacy and knew all his secrets. I'll give Lacy this credit, that when it came to love affairs, he never told."

Dick didn't ask for any further information on that subject.

"It's dull, especially at night. I'm allowed to go out in the afternoon for a couple of hours, but there's a creepiness about this house that certainly gets on my nerves."

It almost seemed as if he were sincere; his voice dropped to a whisper, and involuntarily he looked round.

"I don't know what your boys get up to next door, but there are some quaint noises on the other side of the wall," he said. "And last night, Moses! I thought the house was coming down. Something happened, too. When I looked out of my bedroom window — that's Lacy's old room — I saw the street full of flatties — I beg your pardon, policemen."

"Call them 'flatties' if it pleases you," said Dick. "Yes, there was something doing. You didn't by any chance have an overflow meeting of ghosts in this house?"

Stanford shivered.

"Don't talk about ghosts, Captain," he begged. "Why, last night I thought I saw — well, that's foolish, anyway."

"You thought you saw Marshalt."

"No — the other man, Malpas. How did you know?" asked the other, surprised.

"Malpas is the busiest ghost in London. Where did you see him?"

"Coming out of the storeroom — at least, standing in the doorway. Only for a second."

"What did you do?"

Bill smiled sheepishly.

"I got upstairs as fast as I could and locked myself in," he said. "Back chat with ghosts ain't in my repertoire."

Shannon got up.

"I'll take a peep at that storeroom if you don't mind."

"You're welcome," said Stanford, pulling out a drawer and taking a large bunch of keys. "It's a fool room that old Tonger used to use for keeping the governor's cartridges and guns, and junk of that kind."

It lay, Dick found, at the end of the hall-passage, and was filled with an indescribable medley of guns, saddles, old boxes, cleaning materials, dilapidated brooms, and all the equipment that untidy cleaners thrust away out of sight. It had one small window, heavily barred, and there was a fireplace, covered up now. At the far end of the room was a rough bench, on which were a gas ring, a small rusty vice, and a few tools. There was nothing remarkable about the apartment except its untidiness, and –

"What are in these boxes?"

"I don't know; I haven't looked," said Stanford.

Shannon pulled back the sliding lid of one of the wooden receptacles, and disclosed a number of small, green-labelled cartons.

"Revolver ammunition," said Dick, "and one package has been removed recently."

The under packet was free from dust, he saw.

"What makes you think it was Malpas?"

"I don't know: it was just the description I've had of him," said Stanford vaguely. "I've never seen him in my life."

He evidently expected Dick to take his departure, and with difficulty concealed his annoyance when the commissioner led the way up the broad stairs to the study. Dick stopped to examine the door which shut off Marshalt's private apartment.

"This still functions?" he asked.

"As far as I know," said the other sulkily. "It's no good asking me questions about this house, Captain Shannon: I'm a lodger."

"So you are," said Shannon sympathetically, and turned as if to go.

The man's relief showed in spite of himself.

"I really believe you are anxious to get rid of me," bantered the detective.

Stanford murmured something about not caring one way or the other.

"And how are our friends the Eltons?"

"I don't know anything about the Eltons," said Stanford, resigned. "They have never been great friends of mine."

And now the unwelcome visitor really took his departure. Stanford went downstairs with him and closed the door with a grimace of satisfaction. He returned to the study, locking the partition door behind him, opened a second door which communicated with the little dining-room, and a man stepped out.

"You've got good ears, Martin," he said.

Martin walked to the window and through the heavy gauze curtain that covered the lower pane followed Dick Shannon with his eyes until he was out of sight.

"Early or late, I fall against that bird," he said without heat. "Yes – I've good hearing. I knew it was he the moment I heard voices in the hall. How long are you staying here? There's a job coming along – "

Stanford spread out his arms in a gesture of regret.

"Can't take it, Martin – sorry. Somehow I feel that I ought to play square with poor Lacy. The money's nothing, but I'll stay here just as long as they want me. I regard it as a duty."

Martin laughed softly.

"What did Lacy leave in the way of money?" he asked.

"So far as I know, nothing," said the other in a grieved tone. "It's not pickings I'm after. I was a friend of Lacy's – "

"You never told me."

"I told you I knew him," protested the other. "Dora knows we were old friends."

"Do you know Malpas?"

The man's eyes narrowed.

"Yes – I know Malpas." He dropped his voice until it was almost inaudible. "And if it comes to pickings, I know just where to pick!"

There were doubt and suspicion in the face turned toward him.

"Where is he?" he asked, and Stanford laughed loudly.

"Think it out, Elton," he said. "Think of all the people who hated Lacy with good reason, think of all the clever men and women who could act an old man at a minute's notice – think it out, boy, and then take three guesses!"

A JOB FOR AUDREY

Mr Stormer arrived at his office at an unusually early hour. He was on the premises long before any of his clerks or his manager put in an appearance; and Willitt was amazed to hear the buzzer sounding as he came to his own desk.

He found his chief lying on a sofa, looking something of a wreck.

"Are you ill, sir?" he asked in alarm.

"Not ill, but dying," growled Stormer. "Get me some strong coffee and a keg of phenacetin. Oh, my head!"

He touched his scalp gingerly and winced.

"My brain capacity has increased to the extent of one cubic foot," he said. "There's a lump here as big as an egg, and no chicken's egg, either. And talking of chickens, go after that girl Bedford. No, sir, this is an ostrich's or a dinosaur's."

"Did you get into trouble last night?"

"Did I get into trouble last night?" repeated his chief wearily. "Would I be lying here like a sick cow if I hadn't been in trouble? Do gaiety and light-heartedness grow eggs on a man's head? Yes, sir, I was in trouble. Get me some vinegar. And listen! You're in a secret. Nobody is to know that this affliction has come upon me, and if anybody makes inquiries, I am in the United States – where I ought to be."

Willitt hastened out and brought all his chief required.

"Now, phone up a barber; go round to the nearest collar shop and get something to make me look respectable."

"Is it cut?"

"No, sir, it isn't cut. I have concussion of the brain, but I am not cut."

He winced as he sat up and took the coffee from the tray where Willitt had placed it.

"You're aching to ask me what happened," he groaned as he sipped the coffee. "Well, I'll tell you. I had a fight with a ghost – at least, he, or somebody who was with him, did all the fighting."

"Who was it?"

"I don't know; I saw nobody. I heard a scream and went out to see what was happening, and saw one, two, three, or maybe it was six people, running down the corridor, and I went after them. The same number of people lammed me on the head, and I came to earth in time to prevent the hotel detective stealing my watch. Maybe he was only opening my collar, but I mistrust hotel detectives. Now, you're not to forget that girl. She's got a job at the *Amateur Poultry Farmer*, a paper run in the interests of introspective fowls, and I guess she's not going to like it. You know her, don't you?"

"Yes, sir; I've met her."

"Well, see her again and offer her a good job. Any salary that seems to her on the generous side which may suggest itself to you, but you've got to fix her – you understand?"

"Yes, sir."

"Here comes the barber, and after he's gone I'm going to sleep, and it will be death to any man who disturbs me. When does Miss Bedford start work?"

"This morning."

"Get to her as soon as you can. She'll probably come out to lunch, and that'll be your opportunity. You can tell her I've got a job that she can do in a cosy chair with her feet on the fender. I want her to watch Torrington, who calls himself Brown. And, believe me, that guy wants watching! Make it appealing – get into your mind that you're giving something away. And, say, Willitt, don't come back here with a tale of failure; I'm that ill I'd be very offensive to you."

It was a novel experience for Audrey to find herself "going to work"; to be one of the crowd that fringed the subway platform, to struggle for her strap or to fight for a place on a bus already overcrowded. The novelty of it did not quite compensate for its discomfort, but she had a very satisfactory feeling when she eventually reached the out-of-the-way office of the little paper and found herself established in a corner of the editorial sanctum.

Mr Hepps gave her a cold and perfunctory greeting, and flung over a heap of letters that had evidently accumulated on his desk for weeks. He was a gaunt, somewhat uncleanly looking man, and, she was to discover, a confirmed grumbler. Apparently he was one of those men who believe that praise given to subordinates would arouse in their bosoms a passionate desire for increase of wages. Indeed, the Mr Hepps she had interviewed the day before and the Mr Hepps who now barked his instructions and wrangled about the length of her paragraphs were two entirely different persons.

She found also that she was expected to work into every answer a small boost for an advertiser.

"Chippers Feed nothing!" he snapped. "What do you want to talk about Chippers Feed for? They don't advertise with us. Cut that out, and tell 'em to use Lowker's."

"Lowker's is poison and death to young chickens," said Audrey firmly. "I would sooner feed them on sawdust."

"What you'd rather do, and what I tell you to do, are two different things," he roared. "I tell you Lowker's – Lowker goes in!"

Audrey looked at the back of his head. There was a jar of paste within reach. For a second she contemplated a violent assault.

The climax came that afternoon when, having mastered the contents of previous numbers, and having discovered that the announcements of the Java Wire Corporation had appeared in the advertisement columns, she recommended its employment in all sincerity. The paragraph came under his notice, and he stormed at the mouth.

"Java netting is out!" he shouted. "I'd sooner close the paper than boost that business."

"But they advertise."

"They don't advertise any more – that's what! Just say wire net. And your paragraphs are too long. And I don't like your handwriting, Miss; can't you use a typewriter? You've got to smarten up if you want to hold this job. Where are you going?" he asked in surprise, as she rose and took down her coat from a peg on the wall.

"Home, Mr Hepps," she said. "You have shaken my faith in chickens. I never thought they could be put to such base uses."

He stared at her.

"I close down here at six."

"I close down at four," said Audrey calmly. "I've had no lunch except a glass of milk and a bun, and the atmosphere of this office is stifling. I'd prefer to work in a hen-house."

"If I'd known you were coming," he said sardonically, "I'd have had – "

"You'd have had the place enlarged – I know. Excuse me if I don't laugh. The fact of the matter is, Mr Hepps, I am through with this job."

"You can go!" boomed Mr Hepps, glaring at her over his lopsided pince-nez. "I'm only sorry I didn't get your character before you came."

"If you did you would have found I'd been in prison," she said.

At his look of horror she gurgled with laughter.

"In prison?" he gasped. "What for?"

"Chicken stealing," she said promptly, and here ended her first day's employment.

She reached the street, feeling famished, and went straight across the road to the popular tea shop at which she had looked longingly through the window of her office many times during the course of the day. A man waited while she bought a newspaper and followed her in, sitting down at the same marble-topped table. Glancing at him out of the corner of her eye, she thought she had met him before, but was immediately absorbed in the newspaper account of "The Strange Affair at the Palace Hotel," and there learnt that the police had been unable to trace a guest who had been wounded in what had been accurately described as "a midnight affray." Her own name, she was

213

glad to see, was not mentioned. She was referred to as "a young lady of wealth," a description which tickled her.

"Excuse me, Miss Bedford."

She looked up with a start. It was the man who had followed her into the tea shop.

"I think we have met before. My name is Willitt; I came down to Fontwell to make a few inquiries."

"Oh, I remember," she smiled. "It wasn't a long interview, was it? I was leaving for London."

"That's right, miss. I represent Stormer's Detective Agency. Maybe you've heard of it?"

She nodded. Stormer's was one of the best known and best respected of these private agencies, which are not very greatly encouraged by the police, and receive little patronage except at the hands of suspicious husbands and wives.

"Mr Stormer sent me along to have a talk with you."

"With me?" she said in surprise.

"Yes, Miss Bedford. You've heard of our agency? It stands pretty high in the matter of credit and respectability."

"I've heard of it, of course; everybody has heard of it," she said. "What does Mr Stormer want of me?"

"Well, Miss Bedford" – Willitt had to proceed cautiously, not knowing how she would accept the suggestion – "the truth is, we're short-handed. A lady who did a great deal of work for us got married and left the business, and we've never been able to replace her. Mr Stormer wondered whether you would like to come into the office?"

"I?" she said incredulously. "You mean, become a woman detective?"

"We shouldn't give you any unpleasant work to do, Miss Bedford," said Willitt earnestly. "We'd put you on to society cases."

"But does Mr Stormer know my record?"

"You mean about the jewel robbery? Yes, Miss, he knows all about that."

The corners of her mouth twitched.

"And is he proceeding on the set-a-thief-to-catch-a-thief principle?"

Even the solemn Willitt laughed.

"No, you'll not be asked to catch thieves. We want you for one special job – to watch a man named Torrington."

Audrey's face fell.

"Watch Torrington? And who is Torrington?" she asked.

"He is a very wealthy man, a South African. You are interested in South Africa?"

He saw her flinch.

"Yes, I am rather interested in South Africa," she said, "if all the stories I have heard…are true."

She never had quite believed Dora's bitter gibe, that her father was an American serving a life sentence on the Breakwater, and yet a doubt had been sown in her mind that had not been entirely dispelled.

"I don't know how to watch people. Does it mean following them wherever they go? Because I'm afraid I'm unsuitable for that kind of work. Besides" – she smiled – "we have one detective in the family."

And then she went very red.

"That's a joke, Mr Willitt," she added hurriedly. "I'm in rather a humorous mood today, having spent the day in the bright atmosphere of a chicken murderer."

She gave a brief but vivid account of her day's work, and in Willitt she found a sympathetic listener. When she came again to his offer, he was in a hurry to assure her.

"You won't be asked to follow Torrington around," he said. "Your job is much easier than that. You will be expected to get acquainted with him – "

"What is he – a burglar?"

"No," confessed Willitt, "he's not exactly a burglar."

"Not exactly!" she said, aghast. "Is he a criminal?"

"That was an unfortunate expression of mine," Willitt hastened to assure her. "No, Miss, he's perfectly honest; only we want to keep tag of the people who come after him, and we feel that we might get you employed in the same capacity as Mr Malpas."

"I can't do it. I'd love the work – it sounds thrilling; and there would be a certain amount of fun in it for other reasons."

He didn't ask the reasons, but he could guess the satisfaction Audrey Bedford would feel in revealing herself to a certain high police official.

"Will you consider it?" he begged. "At any rate, we want you in the office."

"Can I see Mr Stormer?"

"He's gone back to America," said Willitt glibly, "and his last instructions were to secure you at any price."

Audrey laughed.

"I'll try it," she said, and Mr Willitt breathed a sigh of relief, for if there was one thing in the world he didn't wish to do, it was to make excuses to Stormer.

Returning to headquarters, he found John Stormer in a more amiable frame of mind, and reported his success.

"So she kicked at the Torrington job? I guessed she would, but I knew we'd land her!"

Willitt, to whom his employer's prescience was a standing wonder, ventured to put a question.

"You seemed sure of getting her – how did you know that she wouldn't be satisfied with the job? Hepps treated her badly, bullied and found fault with her until she couldn't stick it any longer. The man is a brute!"

"Brute, is he? Well, he's changed considerably since I knew him last. I got his son out of pretty bad trouble once – the usual vamp case, with letters and poetry and everything. And then he was mild enough – he doesn't take three baths a day, but he's mild. I guess he must have been crossed in love – maybe his chickens have turned him down. They're mean creatures. That will do, friend."

When Willitt had gone, he used the telephone.

"That you, Mr Hepps? Stormer speaking. Thank you very much indeed for your help."

"I hated doing it," said the regretful voice of Hepps. "She seems a very nice girl and remarkably capable. I've lost a very good assistant, and, I am afraid, got a very bad name for myself. Personally, I set my face against boosting advertisers in the news columns, and after my treatment of Miss Bedford I feel I can never look a nice girl in the face."

"Maybe they'll be glad," said Stormer.

Mr Hepps evidently missed this point, for he went on: "She said she had been in prison – for chicken stealing. That can't be true, can it?"

"Yuh – that's so," said Stormer. "She's one large hen roost brigand. Yes, sir. Miss anything in your office, let me know."

He hung up with a large and delighted smile.

THE SPOTTER

Mr Torrington's suite at the Ritz-Carlton – he was Mr Brown on the register – was one of the most expensive in a hotel which did not err on the side of cheapness. He saw very few visitors, and, for the matter of that, he was not often visible to the hotel authorities, and, except the manager and the floor waiter who served his meals in his private dining-room, very few of the staff knew him. It was generally understood that he did not wish to see callers; and when a shabby little man came to the reception bureau and asked that his name should be sent up, the clerk in charge favoured him with an uncomplimentary scrutiny.

"You had better write," he said. "Mr Brown doesn't see anybody except by appointment."

"He'll see me," said the little man eagerly. "You ask him if he won't. And I've got an appointment with him, too."

The clerk was obviously sceptical.

"I'll find out," he said curtly. "What is your name?"

The man told him, and the clerk disappeared into the small room behind the counter, where the wishes of a guest could be discovered without the caller overhearing very often an unflattering description of himself. He came back in a few seconds.

"Mr Brown has no appointment with you. Where are you from?"

The little man thought rapidly.

"I'm from…" He named a famous diamond corporation in Kimberley.

Again the clerk disappeared, and, returning, beckoned a page.

"Take this gentleman up to Mr Brown's suite," he said, "and wait in the corridor to bring him down again."

Mr Brown was writing letters when the man was shown in, and he transfixed the visitor through his gleaming glasses.

"You're from De Beers?" he said.

"Well, not exactly De Beers, Mr Brown," said the little man with an ingratiating smile, "but the truth is, I used to know you in South Africa."

Brown pointed to a chair.

"When was this?" he asked.

"Before you got into trouble, Mr Brown."

"You must have been young, then, my friend," said Brown with a half smile.

"I'm older than I look. The fact is, Mr Brown, I'm on my beam ends, and I thought you'd like to help an old friend who's fallen on bad times, if I might use that expression – "

"I'll help you all right, if your story is true; but I confess I don't believe you. I've an excellent memory for faces, and I certainly never forget my friends. Where did we meet?"

The visitor made a shot at random.

"Kimberley," he said. He knew that Kimberley was the centre of the diamond-mining industry.

"I was in Kimberley," said the other; "but then, everybody in the diamond business has been to Kimberley at some time or other. You will, of course, remember my name in those days?"

But the visitor was equal to the occasion.

"I remember it," he said firmly, "but nothing would induce me to say it. If a gentleman wants to be called Mr Brown – well, Mr Brown's good enough for me. The truth is" – here an inspiration came to him – "I was doing a sentence at the same time as you."

"Fellow jailbirds, eh?" said the other good-humouredly, and put his hand in his pocket. "I don't remember you, but I've taken a great deal of trouble to forget a lot of people I met on the Breakwater."

There was a letter on the table which the old man had just finished writing. The visitor saw the flourishing signature, but the notepaper was too far away from him to read. If he could find some excuse for going to the other side of the table, he would be absolutely sure that his information was correct, and, moreover, be in possession of a fact that not even the clever ones knew.

The old man pulled out his case and put a Treasury note upon the table.

"I hope you have better luck," he said.

The little man took the note, rolled it into a ball, and, before the astonished eyes of his benefactor, tossed it into the fireplace that lay directly behind him. Mr Brown turned in amazement, and in that second the signature was read.

"I don't want your money," said the little man. "Do you think I'm only here for what I can get out of you? You can keep your money — Torrington!"

Daniel Torrington looked at him sharply.

"You know my name, then, eh? Pick up that money, man, and don't be a fool. What do you want if you don't want money?"

"A shake of the 'and," whined the other, but nevertheless picked up the crumpled note, which he had been careful to toss no further than was consistent with its safety.

Torrington showed him to the door and closed it upon him. Then he came back to his chair, trying to recall the man's face. Nobody had known him in prison as Torrington; he had had a number for many years, but nothing else, until one of the guards had addressed him as "Brown" in a facetious moment, and that name had stuck. How did this man — ?

Then his eyes fell upon the letter, and he understood. What did he want? What had been the object of the visit? He had never heard of spotters and their audacity, of the risks run by these reporters of the underworld. There were others who found them most useful.

DORA TELLS THE TRUTH

Martin walked home, after his visit to Marshalt's house, outwardly unperturbed. Dora had not come down and he refused breakfast for himself. There were half a dozen letters for his discussion, but he no more than glanced at them, until he turned to their contents for relief. He was making a half-hearted attempt to write a letter, when Dora came into the room. She was in her négligé – she seldom dressed before lunch unless she had very urgent business indeed. One quick glance at her told him that she had not slept very well – there were shadows under her fine eyes and tiny crow's-feet that had never shown before.

He gave her a simple "good morning" and tried to make a job of his letters. He put his pen down at last.

"Dora...what sort of work were you doing before I met you?"

She looked up from the paper she was scanning idly.

"What do you mean? Acting."

"What sort of acting – how did you start? I've never asked you before, my dear."

She returned to the contemplation of the morning news, expecting him to press the question. When he did not:

"I started with Marsh and Bignall on the road: chorus girl. Marsh went broke, and left us flat in a No. 3 town with not enough money to pay our fare back to London. I went with a trick-shooting act for three months, and then got into Jebball's fit-up show. I was everything from leading woman to props! I learnt more about electric wiring than most mechanics know – "

She stopped suddenly.

"I did everything," she said shortly, and then: "Why do you speak of this?"

"I was wondering," he answered. "It is queer, but I never thought of you except as – "

"The clinging ivy? When you met me I was on the way to provincial fame. It wouldn't have got me far. A provincial star doesn't make a lot of money, and I guess I'd never have reached a pretty little house in Curzon Street – honestly. But I was doing well by comparison. Why do you ask?"

"Where did you meet Marshalt?"

She had gone back to her newspaper; he saw her hand tremble and did not press the question. But after a while: "Here in London. I wish I had died before I did."

He was on more painful ground here, no less for himself than for her.

"Dora, are you fond of him?"

She shook her head.

"I hate him – hate him!" she said, with such vehemence that he was taken aback. "You think that means...something? You've got it fixed in your mind that I haven't been a...a good wife to you. I know you feel that. I'll tell you the worst that happened. I loved him. I had ideas of breaking with our life and getting you to let me divorce you. But I was good. I was so good that I wearied him. But I'm old-fashioned in a way. And besides, goodness pays. Easy women are like easy money – they don't last long, and when they're expended a man goes after something new. A woman can only keep a man by his wantings. Bunny, when he died, I knew. I don't mean his death in the flesh – but I was aware of the tremendous change in him..."

He lay back in his chair, looking at her from under his black eyelashes.

"You don't think he is dead?"

The quick, impatient lift of her hands was an answer, even if she had not spoken.

"I don't know. He doesn't feel that way to me. And I care nothing."

She was sincere; he was sure of this.

"Did he ever speak to you of Malpas?"

"The old man? Yes, he often spoke of him. The only time I have seen him really nervous was when he talked about 'the man next door.' Malpas hated him: He used to pretend to the police and people that he knew nothing about him, but he did. He said Malpas and he were partners in the old days and that he ran away with Malpas' wife – I forget all he told me. Did you see Stanford?"

He nodded.

"Did he say anything? Of course, I knew they were acquainted."

"Acquainted?" He laughed. "Bosom friends, I should think. Stanford was never a communicative sort of person, but I should have thought he would have told me that he was a friend of Marshalt's."

He got up, walked across to the back of the settee where she was sitting, and laid his hands on her shoulders.

"Thank you…for all you've said. I think you and I will get straight. How are you feeling toward Audrey?"

She was silent.

"You still feel sore? But why? That is a little unreasonable, isn't it? If this man was the only trouble?"

"I don't know." She shrugged her shoulders. "My dislike of Audrey is ingrained, I'm afraid. I was brought up to dislike her."

"I'm sorry," said Martin, patted her gently on the shoulder again, and went out.

He had an appointment in the City. Funds were running low; one of his gambling houses, the most lucrative, had been raided, and it had cost him the greater part of a thousand pounds to hush up his connection therewith. But the fact that he had been blackmailed by his nominee neither surprised nor shocked him. It was one of those inevitable contingencies for which he was always prepared. There was something like a recognized scale in such cases.

He owed something to Dora in one respect, he remembered, as his car threaded the busy City streets: she had made it impossible to handle the clever handiwork of a certain Italian engraver who specialized in *mille* notes, so perfectly printed that even the Bank of

223

France was deceived. Stanford had passed them on to another purchaser, and that gentleman had been caught with the goods and was now awaiting trial.

Martin lived on "touches," and "touches" had been scarce. It seemed that all the suckers in the world had suddenly been put under lock and key, and it looked, too, as though he were to be reduced to the expedient – the last resort of every crook – of running a bucket-shop and selling those oil shares which look so good on paper. It was not a profession that appealed to him; and though he met his man and settled the preliminaries of the new business, he had no heart in it.

He lunched alone at a restaurant in Soho, and there appeared the inevitable "spotter." At another time he would have shaken off the sly-faced man who sidled up to his table with an apologetic smile and took a seat uninvited. But now Martin's finances were in such a state that he could not afford to miss any chance; and although he expected little from the informer, he wanted to hear what that little was.

The spotter's approach to Martin Elton was slightly different from the direct method he employed with such notorieties as Slick Smith.

"Glad to see you, Mr Elton. Haven't seen you for a long time…thank you, I'll have a brandy. Things are pretty bad round here, Mr Elton."

"Round here" meant round almost any place where men were not troubled with too stringent a regard for mine and thine.

"I thought trade was looking up?" said Martin conventionally.

"Ah, your trade might be." The spotter shook his head sorrowfully. "I'm thinking about the poor hooks and crooks, Mr Elton. Not that I've got any good word for them – they're low people. Even with them, trade wouldn't be so bad if they knew all I know."

"And what do you know?" asked Elton, keeping up the pretence.

The spotter sunk his voice.

"I've got something for you – and I'm the only spotter in town that's got next to it! Found it out myself, too. The Clever Ones are always talking about it, but it took me to clean up the way in!"

He smiled complacently.

"That fellow who is supposed to be coming from South Africa has been here over a year! He's been in 'bird' – got a lifer – but he's as rich as – " He mentioned a number of eminent financiers. "And richer!"

"In 'bird'? What did he do?"

"Shot a fellow or sump'n. But he was released more than a year ago, and I tell you he's worth a million – and more! The Clever Ones got the office that he was coming out, but they didn't know that he was here in England – in London. It shows you that the Clever Ones don't know everything."

"Clever Ones" was a vague description – Martin knew it to signify the gangs that did not depend upon the little man for their information.

"From South Africa, you say?" he asked, suddenly interested. "He's been in prison – on the Breakwater? Was it for I D B?"

"It's something to do with buying diamonds. There's a law in South Africa that sends a man to the Awful Place for years and years if he buys diamonds. I can't understand the Clever Ones not finding him. He's a lame man – "

"Lame?" Martin half rose to his feet. "What is his name?"

"Well, he goes by the name of Brown, but his real name's Torrington – Daniel Torrington. And, Mr Elton, that fellow's easy…"

Martin slipped some money to the man, paid his bill and went home.

Dora was going out, and was on the doorstep when he arrived.

"I want you for one minute, Dora," he said.

He took her up to the drawing-room and closed the door.

"You remember last time Audrey was here? You taunted her with having a name which didn't belong to her; you told her her father was a convict on the Breakwater for diamond stealing. Was that true?"

"Yes," she said in surprise. "Why?"

"I asked you that night about him, and you told me he was shot before his arrest, and was lame. What was the name of Audrey's father?"

She was frowning at him suspiciously.

"Why do you want to know?"

"My dear" – a little impatiently – "it is not caprice that makes me ask. Will you tell me?"

"His name was Daniel Torrington," she said.

Martin whistled.

"Torrington? I wonder! It must be the same man. He's here in London."

"Audrey's father?" she gasped. "But he's in prison: he's there for life! Marshalt told me that. That is why he wanted to marry Audrey."

"He knew that she was Torrington's daughter? You never told me that."

"There are so many things I didn't tell you," she said petulantly, "that it is hardly worthwhile going over them now." And then, in sudden contrition: "I'm sorry I snap so, Martin: I so easily lose patience in these days. Yes, Torrington was serving a life sentence."

"He was released more than a year ago," said Martin, "and has been in London most of that time."

He saw the expression that came to her face, and asked quickly: "Did Marshalt know that?"

She shook her head.

"No; if he had known, he wouldn't have been so happy. Oh!" Her hand went up to her mouth. "Malpas!" she whispered.

He gazed at her in amazement, as there occurred to him the same thought that brought the word to her lips.

"Marshalt must have known, or guessed," she said in an awestricken whisper. "He was in the next house all the time. Bunny, Malpas is Torrington!"

THE NEW HEIRESS

"Torrington! That can't be," said Martin. "What object would he have, a man of Torrington's wealth? A story like that is all right in novels and poetry, but I'm satisfied with the cold statistics of the prison service, which show that crimes of vengeance represent about one in five thousand of the cases that are tried in England. A man doesn't hate so much that he'll spend twenty years of his life planning how to get the better of an enemy. Especially Torrington, who is looking for his daughter."

Her eyes met his.

"Is that why he's here – are you sure?" she asked quickly, and he shrugged his thin shoulders.

"I know nothing; I am merely going on the probabilities of the case. What is more likely than that Torrington has been spending his money to locate your mother and his child?"

She shook her head.

"You're wrong," she said quietly. "Torrington thinks Audrey is dead. Mother told him that, and so did Marshalt. He knew Mother in the old days. She only received one letter from Torrington in prison – it was all about the child. It was on the advice of Marshalt that Mother wrote and said that Audrey had died of scarlet fever. Marshalt wrote at the same time with the news. He never told me what he put into the letter, but he was out to hurt Torrington. Why, there's a tablet up to her memory in a church in Rosebank, in the Cape Peninsula! Torrington arranged with the prison chaplain for the slab to be put up. I am sure because Marshalt told me a whole lot after he discovered that Audrey was my sister. If Torrington isn't Malpas, then Lacy had another enemy." Martin Elton was pacing the room, his hands in his pockets, a faraway look in his eyes.

"What do you think Torrington is worth?"

"Over two million pounds," she said.

"What do you think he'd pay to know – the truth?"

She snapped round on him in a fury.

"Give Audrey – that!" she said between her teeth. "Give her a father and millions to play with, while I'm down here in the gutter, with a crook for a husband, and the riff-raff of the underworld for friends! Are you mad? You're not to do it, Martin!"

She came up to him and brought her face and her hard eyes so close to his that he stepped back a pace.

"Not for all the money in the world would I do it. If Torrington is her father, let him find her. He will have some job!"

"What is her name?"

"Dorothy Audrey Torrington. He doesn't know she is called Audrey. She hadn't been christened when Torrington was taken to prison. He chose Dorothy and wrote of her as Dorothy, but she was never called by that name."

He was looking at her.

"What do you think?"

"She need never have it," he said slowly. "Write to her!"

She stared at him in helpless anger.

"Write to her, or see her – better write to her first. Tell her to come to tea," he said. "Tell her the shock of Marshalt's death has made all the difference, and you want to express your sorrow for all the unkind things you've said and all the – lies you have told."

"I'll never do it, Martin, not for you – "

"Say that twice in your letter – all the lies you have told about her parentage. And when she comes, tell her that what you've said about her was true of yourself."

"I'll see you – "

"Wait – why wasn't she called by the name he chose?"

She made an impatient gesture.

"How could she be? It was mine – he didn't know my second name was Dorothy, and Mother didn't realize it until after Audrey was registered. We couldn't have two Doras in the family."

"And where can I get Audrey's birth certificate?"

She knit her forehead.

"I wonder if I have it," she said. "If I have, I've never seen it; but Mother left a lot of papers that I've never looked at from the day they came into my hands. Get them down, Bunny; they're on the top shelf of my wardrobe."

He came back with an old tin box; it was locked and there was no key, but Bunny opened it without trouble. It was packed full of photographs, old share certificates that in some way or other had come into Mrs Bedford's possession, and which Dora, who knew the woman's story by heart, was well aware were worthless. In a blue envelope at the bottom of the box she found two papers.

"That is my birth certificate," she said, "and this is Audrey's."

He spread it open on the table.

"Dorothy Audrey Torrington," he read, and his eyes were gleaming. "What is your name, Dora?"

"Nina Dorothy Bedford – it was Mother's name before she was married to Torrington."

"I could turn that 'Audrey' into something else – Audrey will not do. Your name would stand. You'll write to her, Dora," he said deliberately, "and you'll tell her, with or without the accompaniment of tears, that she is your elder sister."

"But that is impossible – " she began.

"You'll tell her this. Age isn't provable. And if she remembers too distinctly – " His face was set and hard. "I've got a soft place in my heart for a girl in trouble, and I'll tell you that, if I could have helped Audrey, if I could help her now, I would. But there's a million in this, and I'm going out for it."

"You mean – " Her voice was scarcely above a whisper.

"I mean, you're Dorothy Torrington."

"But suppose she does remember? And she will, Bunny. Why, I had my hair up long before she!"

He nodded.

"Then she's got to go somewhere and forget," he said. "Nobody knows that Audrey is Torrington's daughter – "

There was a tap at the door and the maid came in.

"Will you see Mr Smith, sir?" she said. "Mr S Smith of Chicago?"

MR S SMITH BRINGS NEWS

There was a silence, and then Martin said: "Show him up here. You know this fellow, don't you?" he asked.

"I met him once; you know when. I don't think I'll wait."

"You'd better," said her husband. "He is one of those shrewd crooks that would put two and two together and make it ten. I wonder what he wants?"

To say that Mr Smith was in a genial mood is merely to state that he was normal. He had the appearance of having come from a fashionable wedding. His well-fitting morning coat, his polished boots and white spats, no less than the silk hat he put so tenderly on a chair, were alike splendid.

"Sorry to interrupt you. You going out, ma'am?"

He looked at the door. Dora was dressed for the street, for she had been on her way out when Martin had arrived.

"I'd have got here before, but I had to shake a trailer."

Martin's face darkened.

"Might I suggest that, in those circumstances, you might have kept your trail from passing through my front doorway?"

"I shook it." Mr Smith smiled blandly. "There isn't an amateur detective in the world who can trail me, once I give my mind to the business of beating him. Not even Stormer's sleekest sleuth can get his nose down on me."

With a flourish he pulled a grey silk handkerchief from his breast pocket, patted his lips gently, and replaced the handkerchief.

"I was going out, if you'll excuse me – "

"That is unfortunate," said Mr Smith gravely. "I had a few words to say to you, and I'm thinking it will interest you, too, to know that a member of the ancient house of Bedford has joined the unholy congregation of Busy Bees."

"What are you getting at?" asked Martin.

"I'm getting at a revelation which I should like to make as dramatic as possible. Audrey, your respected sister-in-law, has joined the police."

Martin frowned. He was not quite sure about this man, except in one respect, that he could dispense alike with his cooperation and his company.

"What stuff are you giving me?" he asked gruffly. "Audrey joined the police?"

"When I say 'the police' I exaggerate although Stormer's are as near to the official blues as you can get in this country."

"You mean she's joined Stormer's staff?" asked Martin.

Mr Smith nodded.

"I discovered it by accident," he said. "Saw her going into Stormer's office with Willitt — that's the child's portion of cheese who is Stormer's vice-regent on earth. Now I know Stormer's; they seem to have had me trailed since I was so high. I don't remember the time when Stormer's didn't intrude in my life or obtrude upon my profession; and naturally I'm deeply interested in those birds. I know Stormer's methods. He's introduced into England a system that has never been here before, and isn't recognized, anyhow — the badge system. Every Stormer man has one, a little silver star with his name stamped on the back. I suppose they do it here because it is done in America. Though badges in this country mean no more than fraternity pins. I watched the girl go in and come out again with Willitt, and round they went to Lobell's, the jewellers on Cheapside, and I happen to know that Lobell's supply this Star of Hope. There wasn't any need for me to go in; you could see them inside the shop from the ring section of the window, and sure enough there was her ladyship cooing with joy. They parted at the door. Willitt went to the nearest telephone box, and what do you think he did?"

"Telephoned," said Martin laconically, and Mr Smith beamed his admiration.

"You've a brain, Elton. Yes, sir, he telephoned – to the Ritz-Carlton Hotel. Phoned to the Ritz-Carlton for a suite for the lady."

Again he drew his handkerchief, this time to dust his immaculate boots.

"Mr Brown, or Torrington, is staying at the Ritz-Carlton," he said, apropos of nothing.

And so staggered were Martin and his wife by the news that they did not simulate an ignorance of Mr Torrington.

"Thought I'd tell you. Maybe it'll be useful to know that young Miss Bedford can be very dangerous, especially to the folk that Wily Wilfred has sent chasing Torrington's millions."

Martin knew that he was referring to the spotter in these terms, and was visibly uncomfortable.

"He's a good fellow," Smith went on, "but given to syndicating his news, and that's where his value drops to nothing. I've got out of him this afternoon that he put you on to Torrington… I thought perhaps you'd like to know."

"Thank you," Martin found his voice to say. "I take very little notice of the stories these men tell."

"And you're wise," agreed Smith. His bright eyes were fixed on Dora.

"Nice girl, your young sister," he said.

Martin almost dropped. The man might have been standing outside the door, listening to the conversation that took place before his arrival. Dora was less liable to be thrown off her balance.

"You mean Audrey?" she asked, and laughed. "People invariably amuse me when they refer to Audrey as my younger sister. I am exactly a year younger than she."

Dora was a perfect opportunist.

"What makes you think we're interested in Audrey Bedford's movements, Smith?"

The crook suspended his boot-dusting operations for a second, and looked up.

"Family affection," he said, "plus the precarious nature of our mutual profession. She's going to give trouble, mark my words. The bogey-man nearly caught her the other night, and if it hadn't been for a certain person he would."

"You mean Malpas? Was she the lady at the Palace?"

Mr Smith nodded.

"That was nothing. His big try was on the Outer Circle in the park. She's popular. That's the third man who's tried to catch her, and the third man that's failed. I've an idea I shall be going to the funeral of the fourth. She's hoodoo for all honest crooks."

And that seemed to complete his business, for he found no excuse for staying.

"I'll get along now," he said, "having done what I conceive to be my duty. That young sister of yours is certainly mustard, Mrs E."

He did not emphasize "young," but Martin Elton knew that he had used the word deliberately, and when he had gone he turned to his wife.

"Smith wants a 'cut.' If we pull off this job, it'll cost us twenty thousand to keep him quiet – perhaps more. It all depends what happens to Audrey."

IN A HAYMARKET FLAT

The ceaseless thunder of traffic, the never-ending rumble of heavy buses, and the pandemonium of cab-horns and newsboys notwithstanding, Dick Shannon's Haymarket flat was a quiet spot. The ear can grow accustomed to sounds which at first deafen and bewilder, and, so growing accustomed, can filter them out of hearing.

The first intimation Dick Shannon had that the Portman Square case was getting on his nerves was the discovery that the sound-filter no longer functioned. Noises came up from the street to disturb and irritate him; the banging of a taxicab door made him jump.

He was engaged in a cold-blooded review of all the circumstances attending the disappearance of Lacy Marshalt and the death of his servant, and he had scribbled on a pad before him four links of the chain that refused to fit.

First of these was the battered man who had been recovered in the fog from the river. Second, the woman found dead in the park. Third, Tonger's death, and the fourth the passing of Marshalt himself.

Stanford was a new factor, unconsidered until then; a shadowy figure in the background, known well enough to the police, but associated with gangs that he had thought Marshalt could not have known but for his friendship with Dora Elton.

He opened a loose-leaf binder, packed tight with typewritten manuscript, and turned the leaves slowly. There was the very detailed story of the man who was evidently Laker; shorter and less satisfactory particulars of the unknown woman of the park; and the longest dossier of all was that which dealt with Tonger. He read to refresh his memory, though almost every word of the report he knew by heart.

"Tonger wore a grey tweed suit, black slippers, blue-striped shirt, white collar...pockets contained £7 in English money, 200 francs, the stub of a return ticket by Instone Line to Paris. (*Note* – Tonger went to France on the morning of his death to deliver a letter to unknown addressee, returning same day, verified by Customs, Paris, and Customs, Croydon); old gold watch, No. 984371, gold chain, two keys, pocket-case containing prescription for bromide of potassium mixture. (*Note* – Prescription issued by Dr Walters of Park Street, Tonger having described himself as in a highly nervous state and unable to sleep); three £5 notes and a triangular bodkin..."

Dick looked up at the ceiling. Triangular bodkin? That homemade bodkin had puzzled him before; but though he kept it in the house, hoping that a constant view of it would suggest to him its use, no inspiration had come.

He opened a little safe in the corner of the room, took out a flat box and examined the bodkin now with the aid of a magnifying glass. Expert engineers had already examined and measured it, and had supplied a great deal of meaningless data. He picked the tiny rod up and looked at it curiously. The instrument was four inches in length, blunt at the point, and terminating in a handle like a corkscrew. Near this the steel widened until at a place where it fitted into the wood it was nearly an inch across; and here the evidence of amateur work was clear even to the non-technical observer. Dick remembered the vise and files in the storeroom, and guessed that this queer tool was fashioned there. But for what purpose?

The almost flat handle was detachable. Nevertheless, the bodkin must have been of an inconvenient shape to be carried in a pocketbook, as the bulging leather of the case told him.

There was nothing in Laker's dossier, nor in that of the unknown woman, which offered any possible hope of identification. Nor had Marshalt's papers, before they were removed by the lawyer, given him any hint that was of value. Dick had examined the missing millionaire's banking account, but apparently he had banked with various establishments; for in the only one traceable there was nothing to suggest great possessions. Marshalt's few directorships yielded him very little income, for they were either struggling concerns, or were actually on the verge of bankruptcy.

A search of Malpas' house and an inspection of his passbook had been even less informative. He put away the casebook, filled and lighted a pipe, and, leaning back in his chair, went over and over the case until his brain reeled.

Suddenly he sat up with a start and looked toward the curtained window. He had heard a rattling of stones against the glass. It was early in the evening, and it seemed an unnecessary method of attracting attention, when a perfectly good electric bell was available.

Drawing aside the curtains he pushed open the casement and looked out, and saw nothing but passing pedestrians hurrying through the rain, about their business. A little way down the Street excavators had been laying new gas mains, and there were several heaps of gravel within reach of the nimble passer-by. He went back to his work. It might have been a few stones thrown up by the wheels of passing traffic, but he was hardly seated before the signal came again, and this time he went downstairs. There was nobody at the door, and he stepped into the street. He saw only a sprinkle of people hurrying through the downpour. Left or right there was no loiterer. He waited a moment, closed the door and went back to his room, and rang the bell for the man who was valet and chauffeur and, at a pinch, cook.

"Somebody is amusing himself by throwing pebbles up at my window, William. Go out by the back way, and come round by the opposite side of the road and keep watch," he said. "If it is a small boy, you needn't trouble to chase him – "

"*Swish!*"

Again the rattle against his window. He sprang across the room, threw open the casement and looked out. There were two men walking under an umbrella, a girl hurrying down the hill in a shining wet macintosh, a third man walking slowly with a girl, also under an umbrella, and they exhausted all the possibilities. He beckoned the servant.

"Sit here," he said, "so that your shadow falls on the blinds." He pushed a chair halfway between the window and the table, and crept downstairs, opened the door half an inch and listened.

Presently he heard the rattle of stones and sprang out. It was the girl in the macintosh, and he gripped her by the arm.

"Now, young lady, what is the joke?" he demanded sternly, and found himself looking into the laughing face of Audrey Bedford.

"What on earth – ?" he gasped.

"I was being mysterious! I hope I didn't frighten you. But I wanted to see you, and as detectives never ring bells – "

"What the dickens are you talking about? Come inside. You certainly scared me. What were you throwing up – chickenfeed?"

"I've done worse than that. I've thrown up the job," she said. "Happily, I can come in unchaperoned because you are One of Us."

He dismissed his servant, who would have preferred to stay.

"Now, young lady, having fulfilled your heart's desire, and having very completely mystified me, perhaps you will tell me what you mean by 'One of Us.' "

She dived into her macintosh pocket, took out a little silver star, and laid it dramatically on the table. He picked it up, read the inscription on the face, and turned it over.

"Stormer's?" he said, as though he did not believe the evidence of his eyes. "But surely – ? I thought you were safely installed in your journalist coop?"

"I am finished with chickens," she said, as she took off her streaming coat. "They are fatal to me. You are evidently not used to receiving lady visitors, and that is to your credit."

She rang the bell and, when the man appeared:

"Very hot tea and very hot toast, and you can boil me an egg – no, on second thoughts, I'd rather have something less reminiscent. When a lady calls on you," she explained, after the astonished valet-chauffeur-cook had gone, "the first thing you do is to ask her if she wants to drink tea, and the second thing is to ask her if she's hungry. You then push up your cosiest chair to the fire, and express your anxious hope that she hasn't got her feet wet – to which I reply I haven't. You may be a good detective, but you're a poor host."

"Now tell me your day's adventure," he begged.

Complying with her instructions he pushed forward a chair, and she stretched her damp shoes to the blaze.

She described her experience with Mr Hepps in a few pungent sentences, but her incursion into the realms of crime detection was not so easily retailed.

"I don't know what I've to do, except to live in a nice hotel, the Ritz-Carlton, and keep a fatherly eye upon an old gentleman of sixty, who doesn't even know me, and in all probability would bitterly resent my guardianship. But it is respectable, and Mr Stormer is certainly more attractive than Mr Malpas – and more human."

"How did he come to hear of you?"

"He hears of everything – he's a real detective," she said. "Honestly, I don't know, Captain Shannon. By the way, I feel I ought to touch my hat to you, you're so far above me in point of rank and influence. I'd seen Willitt before. He came to me at Fontwell the day we met – or rather, the day your car met my bus – and I had an idea afterward," – she hesitated – "that he was sent down by Mr Marshalt. I've no reason for believing this, it is sheer instinct, and I'm depending a whole lot upon my instinct to make me a good detective."

He was laughing now.

"You're a queer child," he said.

"I hate the superiority in that word 'child,'" she smiled. "As a detective I know I'm not going to be any good, but it is rather fun."

"And it may be rather unpleasant," said Dick, as all the possibilities began to appear. "This inoffensive old gentleman – by the way, what is his name?"

"He's a millionaire."

"Even that seems no adequate reason for his being watched," he said.

The man came in with tea just then, and put the tray down on the table preparatory to laying a cloth. Dick dispensed with that formality.

"It *is* a profession," he said thoughtfully, "but not a nice one for a girl, though if you're well directed, you may never see the unpleasant side. At any rate, I'm glad you're with Stormer's. I don't know exactly what to advise you," he said. "I certainly have a plan for your future, and I wish you could find something amusing and free from all possible risks, until I've settled this Portman Square mystery, and have Malpas under lock and key. And then – "

"And then?" she repeated as he paused.

"I hope then you will let me settle your affairs," he said quietly, and there was something in his eyes that made her get up quickly.

"I must go home," she said. "The tea was lovely, and thank you!"

"You haven't finished the toast."

"I'm due to eat a large and substantial dinner in an hour."

He rang for her macintosh, which had been taken to the kitchenette.

"What will you say when I take your future in hand?"

She shook her head.

"I don't know. I don't think I've reached the place where I want my future to be in anybody's hands but mine. You mustn't think I'm being ungrateful. I very much appreciate – all you've done, and could do – "

She laughed nervously. It may have been the red lampshade that was responsible for the colour in her cheeks. They were certainly the same hue. Just then the man came back with her coat, and Dick helped her. He heard the faint ring of the bell.

"Somebody at any rate knows the way to get in without breaking my windows," he said.

"Did you mind?" She laughed softly to herself. "I was a pig to do it, when you are so worried. It was so easy; nobody saw me lift my hand and throw the stones."

William was back again, and behind him came Steel.

He nodded to the girl, then to Dick.

"What are these?" he asked, and pulled from his pocket a handful of yellow pebbles of varying sizes. Some were as big as hickory nuts, one was even larger. Handful after handful he poured on the table.

"What are those, sir?" he asked again triumphantly.

"Those," said Dick carefully, "are diamonds. About a quarter of a million pounds' worth."

"And three times as many more in Malpas' room," said Steel. "The idol is full of them! Now I know why the ghost walks!"

THE IDOL

"I lit upon the cache by accident," said Steel. "Finding things were a little dull, I was making a loafer's examination of the big idol in the alcove. If you remember, Captain Shannon, this god or mumbo-jumbo or whatever he is, is supported on each side by a bronze animal that looks something between a cat and a panther. I've often wondered whether they were there as ornaments, or whether they had any especial use. This afternoon I gave one an extra strong tug to see if it was firmly fixed, and, to my surprise, it began to turn by itself with a noise that suggested that I'd started some sort of clockwork machinery on the grand scale. Nothing happened, however, except that the cat turned half-right — she had previously been facing squarely into the room. I tried the other cat in the same way, and exactly the same thing happened.

"Whether I touched a spring, or whether that jerk set the machinery moving, I don't know. At any rate, the cat on the left of the figure turned half-left; and the moment it stopped, an extraordinary thing happened. The upper part of the statue has a starved look about the ribs; all the bones show — it looks as though they had been moulded on over the figure. The moment the cat stopped, the chest of the idol opened in the centre like double doors. I got up on to the pedestal and put my lamp inside, and I swear to you the body is half filled with stones as big as, and bigger than, any of these! I took a handful and put them in my pocket, and came straight away to see you. I didn't dare to telephone, for fear somebody cut in and heard more than I wanted them to know."

242

Dick was examining the diamonds. Each bore a little red seal that showed the place of its origin.

"Malpas must have had a good haul," said Steel, "but what I can't understand is, why he didn't get rid of this stuff."

"I think I could explain that," said Dick. "There's been a pretty bad slump in the past few years in the diamond trade; the market is so loaded with stones that prices are down to their minimum. That kind of slump often occurs in diamonds. His supply was greater than his opportunities for disposal. There is another thing to be remembered: diamonds are an investment, and the most portable form of wealth. A man who contemplated a hurried retirement from the country could have no better form of swag – he could carry a couple of millions in a handbag! Have you closed the door of the idol?"

Steel nodded.

"Fortunately, there was nobody in the room but myself at the time. The inspector was on the landing outside, talking to the two men. I pushed the cats back in their positions and the doors closed."

Shannon picked up the diamonds and, pouring them into a prosaic sugar-bowl, locked the vessel away in his safe.

"The other stones must be removed tonight," he said. "We'll collect them, put them in a bag, and take every stone to the Yard."

Audrey had been a silent and amazed audience, and Shannon had almost forgotten that she was present.

"You will come along, won't you, Audrey? You'd like to see what a million pounds' worth of diamonds looks like?"

She stood undecided.

"I don't know that I want to see that room again," she said, "but curiosity is one of my weaknesses."

Giving strict instructions to his servant to remain in the sitting-room and not to move until he returned, Dick piloted his party downstairs, and, calling a taxi from the rank in the middle of the road, followed the girl and his assistant.

The drive up Regent Street was unrelieved by any kind of conversation. Each was busy with his or her thoughts. For some extraordinary reason, the bodkin with the corkscrew handle occurred and recurred to Dick Shannon's mind, without his being able to explain what association there was in that instrument with the discovery of the evening.

He had brought with him a stout leather grip to carry the stones.

"I doubt whether that will hold them all," said Steel – an idea which secretly amused Shannon.

Steel had left two policemen on duty in the room; the third was in the hall, and the inspector came down from the upper floor to meet them.

"I think we'd best get all the men in the room, in case there happens one of those curious accidents which invariably occur when we run counter to the wishes of friend Malpas."

He went up to the alcove and drew the curtain aside. It was the first time Audrey had seen the dread figure of the idol, and she shuddered at the fearful sight. It seemed to her that the emerald-green eyes of the cats were fixed balefully upon her – an illusion which most people had who had seen them.

Steel tugged at one of the animals; there was a whirr of machinery, and the cat moved slowly to the right and stopped. He did the same with the other, and a similar movement occurred. As it came to a standstill, the two breasts of the figure opened.

"Here we are," said Steel with satisfaction, and, planting a chair against the pedestal, Dick mounted.

He thrust his hand into the opening and brought out a heap of yellow stones.

"They are up to sample, I think," laughed Steel, trembling with excitement.

"They certainly are," breathed Dick. "They most certainly are!"

He got down, dusted his hands, and, opening the bag, planted it on Malpas' desk.

A sound made him look round. Both cats were turning to their original position. Presently they stopped, and the doors dosed with a click.

Steel was gaping at the statue.

"There's a mechanism there I don't understand," he said. "Wait — I'll fix it again."

He had taken a step when the lights went out and the room was plunged into darkness.

"Stand by that door," said Shannon quickly. "Let nobody in or out. One of you men feel your way along to the buffet, and keep your truncheon against the panelling. If it moves, hit out! Where are the lamps?"

He heard Steel curse softly as he groped in the darkness, and then: "The lamps are on the landing table, sir," came the inspector's voice.

"Get them. You man at the door, let the inspector pass, and make sure that it is he who comes back."

Audrey felt her heart going at double speed, and instinctively her hand sought Shannon's arm.

"What is going to happen?" she whispered fearfully.

"I don't know," he answered in the same tone. "Keep close behind me, and take my left arm."

"The door's shut."

It was the inspector again. Dick had forgotten that the secret controls affected the doors as well as the illumination.

"A match, somebody. What is happening here?"

It was Steel's voice, speaking from the floor, as he crawled toward the idol.

"Did you hear anything, sir?"

"I thought I heard a wailing sound. Can you feel the idol?"

"I am…oh, my God!"

The girl's blood froze at the cry of agony which followed.

"What is it?" asked Dick.

"I touched something almost red-hot. The base of the idol, I think."

They heard his stifled cry of pain.

"There's something burning," whispered the girl. "Can't you smell — the scent of hot iron?"

Dick had already detected the curious, sickly aroma. He put the girl gently from him.

"I'm going to discover what has happened," he said.

And then a policeman at the far end of the room struck a match, and at that moment the lights came on again.

Apparently nothing had been moved. The idol still turned its malignant face to the room; the green eyes of the cats glared unchangingly.

"What has happened to you, Steel?"

The man was nursing his hand. Right across the palm was a red and black weal an inch wide.

"It's a burn," he groaned.

Dick ran forward and felt the base of the pedestal – it was cold, ice-like.

"It wasn't that, sir," said Steel. "It was something else that came up out of the floor, a sort of hot barrier – "

"Barrier or no barrier," said Dick, "I'm going after those stones."

He jerked the cats round, the little door opened. Leaping on to the pedestal, he put his hand inside.

The body was empty!

A BAG

"This, I think," said Dick, "is where we get off. To be robbed under our eyes is just a little more than public opinion will stand."

He examined the floor carefully, even going to the length of pulling up the carpet, but there was no sign of a trap door. Where the searing hot bar came from was a mystery.

He looked round at the girl and smiled wryly.

"If you're not going to make a much better detective than I have been," he said, "you'll be a pretty poor one – we have seen the worst."

But the amazing happenings of that evening were not yet completed.

"There's nothing to be gained by whining," said Dick. "Did the panelling move, Constable?"

"No, sir; I had my stick here." He pressed his murderous-looking club against the panelling, which must have moved if the visitor had used that method of entrance.

As it proved, this way into the room was no longer practicable. "I had the elevator cables cut," said Steel. "The buffet lift doesn't move any more. Whew!"

Audrey was making an extemporized bandage with two handkerchiefs to keep the air from the raw wound.

"Jehoshaphat! I never knew a little thing could be so painful!" he groaned.

"Let every man carry his own lamp in future, Inspector," said Dick. "Better recover them now."

It seemed almost as if those words were a signal, and the unknown had decided that the arrival of the hand-lamps must be prevented at any cost, for the lights went out for the second time, and the door to the lobby closed with a thud before the nearest policeman could reach it.

"Matches, somebody, quick!" said Dick, feeling frantically in his pockets.

He heard the rattle of a box.

"Strike one, confound you!" he roared.

"I'm trying to," said the meek voice of Audrey.

A scratch, a splutter of flame, and the lamps blazed on simultaneously with the lighting of the match.

"This is uncanny," said Dick, "and — "

Audrey saw his jaw drop and his eyes open wide. He was staring at the idol. And well he might; for on the floor before the figure was a leather bag. It was big and new.

"Where did that come from?"

Dick jumped at it, and, lifting it with some difficulty, placed it on the table by the side of the grip he had brought to transport the diamonds.

"Be careful, sir," warned Steel. "You don't know what is in there!"

Shannon went over the outside of the bag with a quick, professional touch.

"If it's a bomb, it's a new kind of bomb," he said, and jerked the bag open.

He nearly swooned. The deep interior was almost filled with the yellow stones he had seen in the idol's breast!

He drew a deep breath, and beckoned Steel forward.

"I think that's about all that was there?"

Steel, dumbfounded, could only nod, and Dick, taking the bag in his hand, bowed profoundly to the gaping figure of bronze.

"You're a queer chap and a terrifying chap, but you're also a very obliging chap, and — thank you for the grip! We'll take the bag straight to my flat," he said in an undertone. "When we've collected the other stones I'll lock them away at headquarters. I shan't feel safe until they're behind shell-proof doors!"

"But how did it come?" asked the bewildered Steel, so completely knocked out by the recovery of the stones that he forgot the pain he was suffering. "They take the stuff away…and send it back in a bag! It's incredible!"

But Shannon had no inclination to discuss the matter.

"Let us get out of this place quick, before they discover their mistake," he said. "Inspector, tell your men to collect their belongings. I'm withdrawing your guard from the house."

The inspector was apparently relieved.

"That is the best news I've had for a long time, sir. I'd sooner do six months' duty than one night in this place."

They filed out into the street. Dick was reaching out his hand to pull the door shut, when it closed violently of its own volition, and through the fanlight he saw the lights go up.

"Now they've discovered their mistake, and there is going to be serious trouble." He looked longingly at the door. "I'd give something to be on the other side," he said.

"You're scared!" whispered a voice in his ear. "I'd give something to run, but I haven't the courage."

They crossed the road to the shadow of the railings. Presently a line of light showed at the window. Somebody had pulled the curtain aside and was looking out. As they did so, a devil stirred in Shannon's heart – a wild, insane desire to make a quick end to the mystery that was breaking him.

"I'll take a chance," he said.

His gun went up and three staccato shots rang out as one. There was a crash of glass; the streak of light disappeared.

"This is where I get into very serious trouble," said Shannon with a mirthless smile. "But, gosh! I hope I killed him!'

"Who?" asked the frightened girl.

But Dick did not reply.

You may not outrage the laws of the Metropolis, even though you be the highest commissioner in the land. There was a shrill of police whistles, the sound of hurrying feet; three helmeted figures appeared from nowhere in particular, and behind them the crowd that comes from the air on all such occasions as these. Doors and windows were opening in Portman Square. Such a monstrous happening had not occurred within the history of this sedate place.

Commissioner or no commissioner, Dick had to give his name, the registered number of his automatic, and his address, and submitted without protest because it was the rules of the game. The shots, at any rate, brought the taxi they wanted, and, getting in first, he planted the bag squarely on his knees. As the weight pressed on him, Shannon felt that the evening had not been wasted.

"I don't know why I shot – bad temper, or pique, or something. I used to be fairly useful with a gun, but the light wasn't as good as it might have been."

"Who is it in there?" insisted Audrey. "Who do you think it is – Mr Malpas?"

"He is one, and there are probably others," said Dick.

"But are they there all the time?"

He nodded.

"Very likely."

"Phew!" Audrey fanned herself with her hand. "I'm not going to make a good detective! I wanted to scream."

"Not so much as I did, Miss Bedford," said Steel. "Can you go out of your way to drop me at Middlesex Hospital? I must have this hand dressed."

They made a detour and dropped Steel to have his injury attended to. Then they crossed Oxford Street, and down dingy cinema-land, which in London is Wardour Street.

"You ought to have brought a policeman with you, Captain Shannon," she said with sudden gravity.

He laughed.

"I don't think we're likely to be molested between here and Scotland Yard."

Halfway along Wardour Street she saw a glow of light strike the roof of the cab through the little peep-hole at the back, and, turning, looked out. A big car was just behind them, and was drawing to the right to pass, at a place where the street narrowed so that there was scarcely room for two vehicles abreast. Almost before she could think, the inevitable happened. The car swerved quickly to the left, pinned the smaller taxicab against the edge of the sidewalk, jacking it up till, with a grind of brakes, the machine was flung to the narrow pavement.

Dick's first thought was for the girl; his arm was instantly around her, and, pulling her toward him as the cab shivered its frail windows to fragments, he managed to screen her face. At that second the door was jerked open; somebody put his hand in and felt on the floor. Dick turned in time to see the hand grip the bag, and his fist shot out. The blow caught the man's shoulder, and for a second he loosened his grip on the bag, and then, muttering something, he struck, through the doorway. Shannon saw the glimmer of steel, and, wriggling round, partly to escape the thrust and partly to get at his pistol pocket, he kicked out with all his strength, and, by luck, hit home, for he heard a grunt and the knife fell amidst the broken glass. In another instant the assailant was gone.

"Stop that man!" shouted Dick.

He had seen the approaching policeman, but his voice was drowned in the roar of engines. The car swerved to avoid the officer, and, turning into Shaftesbury Avenue, disappeared.

With some difficulty Dick Shannon struggled out of the cab, and helped the girl to her feet. The taxi was a wreck, but the driver had escaped injury to everything but his feelings.

"Did you get the number?" asked Shannon.

"No, I didn't," growled the policeman, "but he nearly got me!"

"I got it," said the frightened cabman, "you bet I got it! XG 97435."

Dick chuckled.

"I'll save you the trouble of looking that up, Constable. It's the number of my own car! Our friend has a queer sense of humour."

He made himself known to the officer.

251

"I want a taxicab, but I think I'll go with you in search of it," he said. "I don't wish to be alone with this bag."

"Something valuable in it, sir?" said the constable, respectfully interested.

"About three million pounds," said Shannon.

The constable was politely amused. He invariably smiled at his superiors' jokes, and he smiled now.

"Where is your inspector?"

"He may be here any moment, sir. He usually comes round at about this hour. Here he is, sir, with the sergeant."

He hurried forward to meet his superior, and Shannon did not lag far behind him.

A few words explained the situation, and the policeman, delighted with the prospect of getting released from his tedious beat-walking, accompanied him to the flat.

"Hallo!" Dick looked up at his window. He had left the servant with strict injunctions not to leave the sitting-room until he came back, but the lights were out.

"Come into the passage and hold this bag," he said. "Audrey, you stand behind the officer. My William is not usually a man who disobeys instructions."

There was a light switch in the hall: he turned it on, and a lamp showed at the head of the stairs. He opened the flat door. The hall was in darkness, and when he pressed the control, no light came. Reaching up, he discovered that the bulb had been removed – and recently, for the brass holder was still warm.

His gun held stiffly before him, he walked across the hall, and tried the door of the sitting-room. It was locked. Stepping back, he lifted his foot and kicked. The door opened with a crash that brought the constable halfway up the stairs.

"Anything wrong, sir?"

"Stay where you are," ordered Dick sharply.

Reaching in, he turned over the switch, and the room was flooded with light.

The first object he saw was William. He was lying half on the sofa, and half on the floor, and the trickle of blood on the sofa told Shannon all he wanted to know.

The safe was open: he expected that: blown out, and hanging on its hinges. The sugar-bowl, with its precious contents, was gone.

He lifted the man to the sofa, and loosened his collar. He was breathing thickly, and a quick examination of the wound told the commissioner that the injury was not likely to be a serious one. It told him something more: the attack had been delivered only a few minutes before he arrived.

From the sideboard he took a carafe of water and splashed it on the man's face, and presently William opened his eyes, and stared stupidly around him.

"Did you get him, sir?" he asked eagerly.

"No, my son, I didn't get him. He got you, apparently."

William groaned, and, leaving the man, he opened the door which communicated with his bedroom, and gave the apartment a quick search. A window at the back was open; he pulled it down, and drew the blinds. And here he found other evidence of an intruder's presence. Two drawers in his dressing table were open, and the contents turned over. Somebody had pulled away the pillows from his bed, evidently in search of something. He came back to find the chauffeur sufficiently recovered to sit up.

"I'll send you along to the hospital. You'll see Mr Steel there," he said, with a touch of grim humour.

Going out to the landing, he found the stairway in darkness. Somebody had extinguished the stairway light.

"Who put this light out?" he asked.

"Are you up there, sir?" said the policeman in surprise. "I thought you put it out."

"Come up, and bring the bag. Will you come up, Audrey?"

"The bag, sir? You took the bag."

"What!" shouted Dick.

"When you came down just now, you said, 'Give me the bag, and stay where you are,' sir," said the policeman in tremulous tones.

"Oh, you double-dyed goop!" stormed Dick. "Couldn't you see me?"

"It was in the dark, sir," said the policeman.

"Did you see him, Audrey?" asked Shannon.

There was no answer.

"Where is the young lady?"

"Down here, sir, near the door."

Dick turned and snapped on the light. The passage was empty except for the policeman.

Flying down the stairs three at a time, he flung open the door and walked into the street. Audrey had disappeared!

The bag had gone – that was bad enough. But Audrey had disappeared – that was the loss that turned Dick Shannon's heart to ice.

A DOMICILIARY VISIT

The cabman was still waiting. He had seen "the gentleman" come out with a bag, and then the lady came out, and that was about all he knew. He admitted he was more interested in a conversation he was holding with a brother taxi driver on the rank. He didn't know which way they went, or whether they went together. He was quite sure the young lady came out after the gentleman.

"Gentleman be – blowed!" snarled Shannon. His language was almost justifiable. "What did he look like? Was he young or old?"

The cabman did not know. He was facing the wrong way at the time to see properly. But he thought he was an elderly gentleman. He insisted upon the thief being of gentle birth and, pressed, he wasn't sure that he had seen the lady go at all.

Dick went back to his flat with a heart as heavy as lead.

"I'm sorry I cursed you, officer," he said. "It was my own fault. I should have made sure there was nobody in the flat before I attended the chauffeur. Come up. Do you know anything about first aid? You can look after my man while I telephone."

Within a minute every police station in London knew of the robbery. Motor cyclists were starting out to warn the patrolmen to look for a man with a bag, and – here the description was explicit – for a girl in a macintosh coat.

William was now recovered sufficiently to tell all that he knew, which was not much. He did, however, confirm Shannon's theory that the robbery had occurred only a few minutes before he arrived.

"I was sitting at the table, reading the evening newspaper, when I thought I heard a sound in the bedroom. I listened, but it seemed to me that it was only the flapping of the blinds, and I didn't get up. The last thing I remembered was reading an account of an Old Bailey trial."

The back of the building in which his flat was situated looked out upon the flat roof of an annexe built out from Lower Regent Street, and he realized for the first time how simple a matter it was for a burglar to gain admission through the rear of the premises.

"They were pretty quick workers," was all he said, and, leaving William to be escorted to the hospital, he went out, intending to take the taxi on to Scotland Yard.

As he crossed the sidewalk a man touched his hat. It was the plain-clothes officer who patrolled that beat, and Shannon knew him by sight. In a few words he told what had happened and described the girl. The detective shook his head.

"No, sir, I didn't see the lady, and I don't remember anybody carrying a bag. I was standing at the top of Haymarket, outside the tube station, where thousands of people pass, but I think I should have remembered anybody carrying a grip at this time of night."

"You saw nobody who might be concerned in the robbery – none of 'the boys'?"

The officer hesitated.

"As a matter of fact, I saw one," he confessed; "a man you pointed out to me a few months ago."

"Slick Smith?" asked Dick quickly.

"Yes, sir, that's he – Slick Smith."

"Which way did he come?"

"He came up the Haymarket, and I thought he was in a bit of a hurry. I said good night to him as he passed, but he either didn't see or didn't want to see me. He was wearing a dark blue trench coat, and had evidently been out in the rain for some time, for it was wet through."

"What time was this?"

"About five minutes ago. He crossed toward the Pavilion, and there I lost sight of him."

Headquarters had no news when Dick arrived. He would have been surprised if they had; and he waited only long enough to consult the chief on duty before he went in search of Slick Smith.

The American crook was not at home; had not been home since very early in the evening.

"I don't know what time he'll arrive," said the landlord. "In fact, I never hear him come in. He's a very quiet man, one of the best lodgers I've ever had."

The landlord did not protest when Shannon went up to the rooms occupied by Smith, for he was well aware of the character of his tenant, the police having conveyed information to him a very considerable time before. The door was fastened, but the lock was very easily manipulated and Dick went into the room, making a quick but thorough search for any evidence likely to incriminate Smith in the outrage.

If Slick Smith had been a Sabbath school teacher or the leader of a Band of Hope, indeed, anything that was wholly innocuous and pure, his belongings could not have afforded any less evidence of his criminal propensities. Dick was in the midst of his examination when he heard the door downstairs open and a low-voiced conversation. A little later Smith walked in, a smile on his cheery face, a very large cigar in the corner of his mouth and a twinkle in his eye.

"Good evening, Captain," he said cheerily. "If you'd sent me a note, I'd have been at home to meet you. What I like about the English people is their friendliness. Fancy your calling on me!"

Dick shut the door.

"Give me an account of your movements since five o'clock," he said curtly.

Smith scratched his chin.

"That is going to be difficult," he said. "The only thing I'm absolutely certain about is that I was in the Haymarket at a quarter to ten. One of your bloodhounds saw me, so it would be absurd to deny that I was there. The rest of the time I have been loafing around. And there's no use my telling you where, Captain Shannon," he said with evident sincerity, "because you know that, if I said I was at Boney's at four fifty-five, why Boney would swear I was sitting right there up against the stove, even if I was a hundred miles away. But if you've any doubt of my bona fides, Captain, there's an agency in the village called Stormer's, who have had a sleuth on my heels for months. I guess they'll be able to give you a schedule that will satisfy you – unless I slipped him." He chuckled. "I do that sometimes, and it rattles him to death. I'll tell you what, Captain, let's show hands. You've had a burglary at your flat tonight."

"How do you know that?" asked Dick sternly.

Again Slick Smith laughed.

"I saw a policeman on duty outside the door as I came past ten minutes ago," he said dryly, "and another policeman taking a fellow with a broken head off to hospital. A man hasn't got to be clever to know that there was sump'n doing. Unless you've gone in for the movie business, and I didn't notice a camera or a battery of Kleig lights around. Do you want me for that burglary?"

"I want you for nothing," said Dick shortly. "You are a known bad character, and you were in the vicinity of the Haymarket at the hour thieves broke into my flat. What's the matter with your face?"

From the moment he came into the room Smith had steadfastly kept one side of his face in the shadow, and now Dick gripped him by the shoulders and turned him round so that the light fell upon that side of his face. From the cheekbone to a point above the left ear was a long, ugly graze that had taken off a portion of the man's hair.

"That is a bullet's track," he said.

He touched a slight wound on the man's jaw that was skilfully dressed.

"And that is a cut – the cut that broken glass would make. Who has been shooting you up, Smith?"

"I didn't get his name and address," drawled the other. "I was in a hurry."

"Shall I tell you now you were shot, and the position you were in? You were standing behind a window; the bullet struck the glass, grazed your forehead, ricochetted alongside your head, and a splinter of the glass – "

He stopped. He saw a tiny glittering speck on the shoulder of the man's wet trench coat, and reaching forward, pulled it from the cloth in which it was buried.

"That's glass."

They looked at one another, neither speaking. The smile had gone from Slick Smith's face, but the humorous eyes still held a twinkle.

"There's the making of a good detective in you, Shannon," he said. "A violin and a shot of 'coco,' a few monographs on cigar-ash, and a scrapbook, and, gee you'd have a queue waiting outside your house in Baker Street! I was shot at – that's true. And it was through glass – through the glass of a taxi window. I've got a feud with one of those cheap gangsters from Soho. I can give you the number of the taxi I was riding in, if you want to investigate."

He took a card from his pocket and put it on the table. Dick saw the number pencilled on the back. Slick's alibi was well prepared.

Shannon was exasperated by the coolness of the man; his nerves were on edge, and he knew at the bottom of his heart that the loss of a fortune in uncut diamonds concerned him less than the question of the girl's safety.

"You make me feel a fool. I suppose I am," he said. "Smith, will you be candid with me to this extent? My flat has been robbed, and I've lost very valuable property, which belongs to somebody else. But that isn't troubling me so much as" – he hesitated – "as another matter. When I went to the flat I was accompanied by Miss Bedford. I've an idea that you've met her?"

"I saw her once," said Smith.

"Whether you were concerned in the robbery or not doesn't, for the moment, matter a row of pins to me. Will you tell me this: did you see Miss Bedford tonight?"

"Did I see her? I certainly saw her," said Smith with a broad smile, "and I'm hoping to see her again if somebody hasn't run away with her. Doughty Street is a mighty cold and windy place for a young lady to be standing all this time."

"Doughty Street!" gasped Dick. "Where is she?"

"She was outside the door a few minutes back," said Smith.

AUDREY'S STORY

Before the words were out of his mouth, Shannon was flying down the stairs. In the street he saw the figure of a girl walking up and down.

"Audrey!" he cried joyfully, and before he realized what he was doing, he had taken her in his arms. "My dear, this is wonderful!" he said, and his voice shook. "You don't know what this minute means to me."

"Didn't Mr Smith tell you I was waiting?" she asked, gently disengaging herself. "He wouldn't let me come in until he had found whether you were there."

"Then he expected me to be here?" said Dick in surprise.

"He thought so: he said that this would be the first call you'd make."

He hustled her into the house and up to Smith's room, Smith receiving his new visitor with the greatest calmness.

And then the girl told her story.

"I was near the door, when I heard you, as I thought, come down the stairs and say something in a whisper to the policeman. It was not until the man dashed past me and opened the door that I realized I was mistaken. Dick, it was Mr Malpas!"

"Malpas? Are you sure?"

"Positive," she said emphatically. "I couldn't mistake him. He wore a soft felt hat and his coat collar was turned up to his chin, and that awful nose...! My first thought was to scream. And then my hand, which was in my pocket at the time, touched the silver badge, and I began to realize a detective's responsibilities."

"And you followed him?" said Dick. "You mad woman!"

"He was across the road by the time I had made up my mind, and I flew along after him, keeping him in sight. He walked down Panton Street into Leicester Square and turned up toward Coventry Street, and I kept behind him and at a little distance. At Coventry Street he crossed the road, passed up the little street that runs by the side of the Pavilion Theatre, and, crossing Shaftesbury Avenue, walked quickly up Great Windmill Street. I saw a car waiting by the sidewalk, but didn't realize that it was his until he jumped in and started it moving. And then I did a very foolish thing. I shouted 'Stop!' and ran toward the car. Instead of going off at top speed, as I expected him to, he looked round and kept the machine going at a slow pace, just fast enough to keep ahead of me, and then he suddenly stopped, and I came up to it before I realized what danger I might be in. It was a closed limousine, and I could not see the face of the driver. The street was dark, and there was no light of any kind inside the body of the machine.

" 'Is that you, Miss Bedford?' he asked. Although all along I was certain it was he, I was simply struck speechless when I found that my suspicions were correct. 'Come inside; I want to speak to you,' he said. I turned to run, and he was out of the car like a flash. There was nobody in sight, and I was terrified. I don't know how I got away, but I did. Looking round, I saw that I was not being followed, and the car couldn't be seen, of course, because I had turned three or four corners before I lost my breath and could go no farther. Just as I was deciding that I ought to look for a policeman and tell him, Mr Smith walked into view. I had a fright; I thought it was Malpas. That is all, except that Mr Smith brought me to your flat, and on the way we met a detective, who told us you had been inquiring about him."

Dick drew a long breath.

"So the mystery of your omniscience is a mystery no longer, Smith. How came you to be in that neighbourhood?"

"I was following the young lady." Not a muscle of Smith's face moved, not an eyelid twitched. "That is what I was doing – following the young lady; though, if I'd known she was one of Stormer's women, maybe I'd not have been so anxious. *Quis custodiet ipses custodes.* That's Latin, and it means 'Who shall trail the trailer?' And now I'll guess you are wanting to go, Captain, and I'll not detain you. Nothing is missing as far as I can see, but if you find any of my property in your pocket when you get home, maybe you'll send it me by express delivery."

Dick drove the girl to her hotel, and, with the relief which her safety brought, came the reaction. Somewhere in London were diamonds of a fabulous value; and that they were in the possession of their unlawful owner did not make the situation any less serious.

A RECONCILIATION

Audrey woke the next morning, a little bewildered, to discover herself in an apartment as richly appointed as her new lodgings were plain. There was a tap at the sitting-room door; she unlocked it and scurried back to bed as a trim maid came in, wheeling a little wicker trolley on which her breakfast was laid. By the side of the plate was a letter, and, glancing at it, she uttered an exclamation of surprise. It was from Dora, and was addressed to her, not only at the Ritz–Carlton, but gave the number of her suite. Audrey smiled. Good news travels almost as quickly as bad, she thought, and opened the heavily underlined letter, wondering what had led her sister to take this unusual course. The first few lines filled her with amazement.

My Dearest Child,

I wonder if you are ever going to forgive me for all the horrid things I've done and said to you, and for my terrible and wicked conduct a year ago? The remembrance that you went to prison *innocently* for an offence which was really Martin's, haunts me. And when I recall my dreadful attack upon you, I can hardly believe that I was sane. I want you to let *bygones be bygones* and to come and see me. I've a lot to tell you – one act of mine I can at least undo. Will you be a forgiving angel and telephone me?

Your loving sister,

Dorothy.

"Dorothy?" repeated Audrey, frowning.

Yet, despite the conflicting emotions which the letter aroused, on the whole she was glad. The maid had hardly gone before she was at the telephone. Dora's voice answered her.

"Of course I'll come and see you – this afternoon if I can. And you're not to worry about the – the Holloway incident. I can't speak more plainly on the telephone, but you understand?"

"Yes, dear," said the low voice of Dora.

"You haven't asked me what I'm doing here."

"Oh, I know all about that," said Dora's dispirited voice. "You're working for Stormer's, aren't you?"

Audrey gave a gasp of surprise.

"How did you know?"

"Somebody told me; but that doesn't matter. You will come, and you do forgive me…?"

Audrey went to her bath, feeling a lightness of heart that she had not experienced for many a day. Deep down she was fond of her sister, and her enmity had been a real trouble to her. It seemed as if one of the major unhappinesses of life were dissipated. She did not, however, forget her curious mission. While she was dressing she took advantage of the maid's presence to ask about the mysterious Mr Torrington.

"They say he's a millionaire," said the maid, in that despairing tone in which people who are not millionaires speak of those who are; "but I don't see what pleasure he gets out of his money. He never goes anywhere; never does anything, sits in his room all day, reading and smoking; goes sneaking out at night – not to theatres, as any other decent gentleman would go, but just loafing around the streets. That's not what I call enjoyment. Now, if I had all that money I'd see life! I'd go to the Palais du Danse every night, and to all the good pictures you could see in the afternoons."

"Perhaps he doesn't dance," said Audrey.

"He could learn," said the girl. "A man with that money could learn anything!"

"Is he in his room now?"

The girl nodded.

"He was five minutes ago, when I took him in his breakfast. I will say this for him, that he's very polite and his habits are regular. Do you know that he's up at half-past five every morning? It is a fact, Miss. The night porter has to take him in coffee and rolls at that hour! He says he has been in the habit for years of getting up at half-past five, and he can't break himself."

"Has he a secretary?"

The maid shook her head.

"No, he hasn't got a secretary, not even a parrot," she said vaguely.

In the course of the morning Audrey got into touch with Stormer's and made her brief report. It could have been briefer, because she had nothing really to tell. But apparently the agency was well satisfied that she was on the spot. They seemed easily pleased, she thought.

At three o'clock that afternoon she knocked at the door of the house in Curzon Street, and was admitted by a new maid, and it was characteristic of Dora that the delinquencies of the old one should be the subject matter of her conversation.

"She got a little too fresh, and she admitted people without telling me they were in the house, after I had given her strict instructions that I was not at home to them." Then, realizing that the conversation was not exactly as she had planned it, she caught the girl by the shoulders and looked lovingly into her face. "You have forgiven me, girlie?"

"Why, of course, dear."

For some reason, Audrey felt awkward and gauche. It was as though there were some tension in the air that she felt without being able to define. Perhaps it was the absence of Martin which disconcerted her. She expected to see him; the reconciliation was incomplete without his presence. And it was strange that Dora made no reference to or apology for his absence.

"Sit down, my dear, and let me have a good look at you. You haven't changed very much since the old days, really you haven't. Nobody would dream that you were a year older than I."

Audrey looked up in amazement.

"A year older?" she said.

"That is why I wanted to see you. You'll have some tea?"

"But I don't understand you, Dora," said the girl, ignoring the invitation. "I am not older than you; I am a year younger."

Dora's slow smile was almost convincing.

"You're a year older, darling," she said. "Dear Mother was responsible for the mix-up. For some reason, which I bitterly regret, Mother did not like you, and her dislike took a queer expression, as we have reason to know."

"I always understood that I was born on the 1st of December, 1904 – " began Audrey.

"On the 3rd of February, 1903," smiled Dora. "I have your birth certificate. I wanted to show it to you."

She opened the drawer of the secretaire and from a blue envelope took out the long oblong slip.

"There it is, dear – Audrey Dorothy Bedford. That was mother's first husband. I told you that she never called you by your name."

Audrey was examining the document, bewildered.

"But she told me…she said you were the older – lots of times. And, Dora, I remember you were always in a class higher than I at school. If what you say is true, then my father – "

"I told you that your father was on the Breakwater, but that isn't so." Dora dropped her eyes. "It was *my* father," she said brokenly. "He was an American who came to South Africa and met Mother when she was a young widow with a child only a few weeks old. They were married three months later."

Audrey dropped down into a chair.

"How queer!" she said. "But I am Audrey! And we are both Dorothy? That must be so. But" – she shook her head helplessly – "I can't believe that I'm older than you."

Dora checked her rising anger with a great mental effort, but what she had to say was interrupted by a cry from the girl.

"I can prove I'm the younger!" she said triumphantly. "Mother told me where I was christened – at a chapel in Rosebank, South Africa!"

In the bedroom above the room in which they were talking Martin Elton, his ear to the floor, listened, and grew suddenly haggard. Audrey

Torrington must be put away! By what way, in what fashion, he did not care. He waited, listening, and when at last her foot sounded on the stairs he got up and opened the door.

Dora's voice, laughing and carefree, came up to him, and presently the street door closed and he went down to meet his wife.

"Well?" she asked, and then she saw his face and shrank back as if she had been struck.

"Martin...you wouldn't..."

He nodded.

A life stood between him and the lavish prosperity which had been his life's dream. He had taken his decision.

MR TORRINGTON'S SECRETARY

Mr Willitt was invariably nervous in the presence of Dan Torrington. He was more so now under the searching scrutiny of the old man's eyes.

"I will allow Stormer to understand many of my peculiar requirements, but when it comes to a question of appointing a secretary, I must be the best judge, Mr Willitt. Will you tell or cable your principal to that effect?"

Willitt shifted uncomfortably. He was already sitting on the edge of the chair, and any further movement would precipitate him to the floor.

"We have no desire to dictate, or even to suggest, Mr Torrington," he said awkwardly, "and Mr Stormer understands that you are quite well able to manage your domestic affairs without assistance. But he particularly wishes this person engaged."

"Let Stormer engage him, then."

Torrington was smoking a cigarette through a long black holder, his back to the fire, his thin legs outstretched.

"By all means let Mr Stormer engage him – he has my permission. I, for my part, will offer no suggestion."

"It's not a him, it's a girl," blurted Willitt.

"Then I certainly will not employ her!" retorted the other emphatically. "A girl would get on my nerves. I don't understand them, and I should be one half the time offending her and the other half apologizing." He glanced at the crestfallen face and laughed. "You seem to have set your heart on this. Who is she?"

"She is the young lady who was employed by Malpas."

"Malpas!" said the old man softly. "Is she by any chance the friend of that very engaging young man, Captain Shannon?"

"Yes, sir," said the other.

"Oh!" Torrington stroked his chin. "Is it Shannon's wish?" he asked at last.

"Shannon knows nothing about it; it is entirely Mr Stormer's idea. The truth is – " he began.

"Now we have it," said the other dryly. "I thought that you would pass through that painful process – tell me the truth!"

"She is in our employ, and we want somebody near you in case things go a little wrong."

"And is she one of those capable females who will put them right?" laughed the old man. "I'll oppose you no more. Tell her to see me this afternoon. What is her name?"

"Audrey Bedford."

The words conveyed nothing to Torrington.

"I'll see her at three – "

"She's in the hotel at this minute; won't you see her now?"

"You brought her, did you?"

"She's staying here," said Willitt. "In fact, Mr Torrington, she has been instructed by us to devote her attention to you, and she is in course of carrying out those orders."

Torrington chuckled and rubbed his hands.

"So that is it!" And then his face grew graver. "Send her along. Miss Bedford? I'm not so sure, if my recollection of the girl is right, that I shan't have all my time occupied in protecting her!"

Willitt slipped out of the room and returned in a few minutes, ushering in the girl, and Dan Torrington took her in from the crown of her little hat to the toes of her dainty feet.

"Anything less like a detective I have never seen." He shook his head.

"And I have never felt," she laughed as she took his hand. "Mr Willitt says that you want me to be your secretary?"

269

"Mr Willitt is exaggerating," said Torrington good-humouredly. "The one thing I *don't* wish is for you to be my secretary, but I'm afraid I shall be forced against my will to ask you to accept that position. Are you a capable secretary?"

"I'm not," she confessed ruefully.

"So much the better." Torrington's smile was infectious. "I don't think I could endure a capable secretary – competence is a most depressing quality to have around one. At any rate, you will not open my letters furtively and photograph their contents. And I'm equally sure I shall be able to leave money around without missing any. All right, Mr Willitt, I will talk with this lady."

He felt strangely drawn toward the girl; a curious sympathy which he experienced the moment she came into the room made the appointment not only less irksome, but even desirable.

"Your duties are nil," he bantered her. "Your office hours will be when I really require assistance – a moment which will probably never arrive. I remember you now; you were the girl who got into hot water a year ago."

That wretched jewel robbery! Was she never to be allowed to forget that year cut out of her life?

"You have a sister, too, haven't you?"

"Yes, I have a sister."

He bit his lip; the light danced on his spectacles as he stared into the fire.

"A bad lot." And then, quickly: "Forgive me if I have hurt you at all."

"I'm not very hurt; but I don't think she is quite as bad as people imagine," said Audrey quietly. "A woman is happiest when she has no history, but – "

"You're wrong," he interrupted. "There isn't a woman without a history. Character is history and history is character. Certainly she's happier if she hasn't the history which a marriage with Martin Elton would attach to her name. Oh, yes, I know the gentleman remarkably well, though he'll never guess that. You worked for Malpas, you say? A somewhat strange gentleman."

270

"Very," she said emphatically.

"Do you think they will ever catch him?" he asked after a pause. "You know there is a warrant out for him?"

"I didn't know, but I guessed," she said.

"A nice man, do you think?"

"Mr Malpas? I think he is a horror!"

A faint smile dawned in the old man's face.

"Oh, you think he is a horror, do you?" he said slowly. "Well, maybe he is. All right. You had a bit of a shock last night? – Of course, you were the girl with Shannon when the diamonds were lost?"

She stared at him in amazement.

"Is it in the newspapers?" she asked, and he chuckled again.

"No; it is in my private newspaper! You saw them, eh? Heaps and heaps of them, beautiful little yellow stones – they belong to me!"

She was speechless with astonishment. He made his claim in an ordinary tone of voice, as he might have said, "That book is mine," or "This is my room."

Three million pounds' worth of uncut stones! It was hardly believable that this man, who made so calm a statement, could accept their loss so philosophically.

"Yes, they're mine, or were," he said. "You'll find the seal of the Hallam & Coold mine on every one of them. Mention that fact to Shannon the next time you see him, though I should imagine he knows."

"He never told me."

"There's a whole lot Shannon doesn't tell you that he knows, and one day somebody is going to get a shock," he said.

Suddenly his eyes dropped to her feet, and so long did he stare down at her shoes that she shifted her feet uncomfortably. And when he spoke he said an astounding thing.

"In wet weather it hurts a little, doesn't it?"

"Yes, a little," she was surprised into saying, and then she gasped! "Hurts...? What do you mean...how did you know?"

271

He was laughing as she had never seen a man laugh. There were tears in his eyes when he finished. He saw her flushed face, and was penitent.

"Forgive me! I am distressing you. You see, I am an inquisitive man, and I made inquiries about you from the prison officials – the doctor told me a lot!"

And then, abruptly, he turned the talk into more conventional channels and nodded toward his writing table.

"There are a heap of letters there; just answer them."

"Will you tell me what to say?"

He shook his head.

"There is no necessity. To people who write for money you can say 'No.' To people who want to see me, you can say I'm in Paris; and to newspapers who write asking for an interview you can say I died last night and my end was peaceful."

He put his hand in his pocket and took out a crumpled envelope.

"Here's one that requires a special answer," he said, but did not give her the letter.

"Just write: 'There's a boat leaving for South America on Wednesday next. I will stake you to the extent of £500 and your passage. If you value your life you will accept my offer.' "

She wrote the words rapidly in longhand.

"To whom shall I send this?"

"To Mr William Stanford, 552, Portman Square," said the old man, looking abstractedly at the ceiling.

WHAT BUNNY SAW

There were certain peculiar features about Mr Torrington's suite at the Ritz-Carlton, features which the girl did not notice until she was alone that afternoon in the sitting-room, Torrington having gone out. All the doors were fitted with bolts, and, opening a window to watch a fire that had broken out on the upper floor of some premises almost opposite, she was amazed when the doors were flung open and three men came in at a run.

One, she knew, was a Stormer agent; the other two were strangers.

"Sorry to startle you, Miss," said the agent. "We ought to have warned you not to open the windows."

"What happened?" she asked. "What did I do?"

"I'll tell you later," said the man, pulling the sash carefully and snapping back the fastening.

When the other two had gone: "You touched an alarm. No, you can't see it, because you didn't really set it going until you moved the catch. There is no need to open the windows – this room has a special system of ventilation."

"A burglar alarm?" she gasped. "I never guessed I was doing anything so foolish."

"There's one on every window; there's one on every door at night. I'll show you something."

Even the most stern and inflexible of private detectives becomes indiscreet in the presence of a pretty girl. He took her into Mr Torrington's bedroom, a plainly furnished apartment, remarkable for the few articles of furniture it contained. There was a double bed with two sets of pillows.

"He sleeps that side, and fortunately he's a very quiet sleeper. If by chance he put his head on that pillow" – he pointed to the other and lifted it gingerly. Running from one corner was a thread-like wire, which disappeared under the bed. "Any pressure on the pillow would bring the night men."

"But Mr Willitt didn't tell me there were more watchers than me," she said, a little chagrined, and then laughed as she realized what little value her own assistance would be to Torrington in a moment of peril. "Is there really any danger to him?" she asked.

"Well," said the man vaguely, "you never know."

She had time that afternoon to write a hurried letter to Dora, whom she had left in a somewhat electrical atmosphere. It was all rather absurd, after what had passed, to quarrel over a question of age. Her mother was so eccentric that it was quite possible that she had taken this peculiar course of pretending that the younger was the elder. At any rate, it was not worthwhile quarrelling about, and she sat down and wrote to her sister.

DEAR DORA,
I think we were both rather foolish. I am Dorothy or anything you like, and you are my younger sister! Already I have taken that maternal interest in you which comes so natural to the head of the family! I will see you again very soon.

She signed it "Dorothy."

Dora had the letter by the evening post. She was at dinner, and passed it across to her husband without comment.

"She has more intelligence than you, my friend," said Martin, reading and putting it down. "It was lunacy to try to rush matters. You should have let the idea soak in, or else given her a chance to get acquainted with you before you sprang it on her."

"Anyway, I'm not going through with it," she said briefly. "If it came to a showdown, there's the birth registered at Rosebank. It would only take the cost of a cable to prove that Audrey was telling the truth."

He fixed his speculative gaze upon her, and, irritated by his scrutiny, she got up abruptly from the table.

"Don't go," he said. "Shall I show you my profit-and-loss account for this year. You'll have a fit when I do. Here's a letter that will interest you."

He took it from his pocket and threw it down within reach of her hand.

"From the bank?" She opened it quickly, and her face fell. "But I didn't know you were that much overdrawn, Bunny," she said. "I thought you owned stock."

"I do. The bank has got it against the overdraft, and the stock has depreciated considerably of late. We're in a pretty tight corner. I admit I've been in worse, but then, I wasn't so soft as I am now – better fitted for the rough-and-tumble of starting again. Now, I've got a little set in my habits, and I don't intend going rough, anyway. That letter means nothing, except that she's humouring you. Audrey has got to go away."

"Where?" she asked breathlessly.

"I don't know yet. We'll get her somewhere abroad until you fix things."

"But if she disappeared, and I made my claim, they'd know at once there was something wrong. You don't think Shannon's a fool, do you?"

"Shannon!" he said contemptuously. "I'm not worrying about him. I'm thinking of Slick Smith and what it's going to cost me."

"I shouldn't worry very much about him."

"You wouldn't, eh? No, I guess you wouldn't. I do. It is not only in connection with Audrey and all he knows and guesses that I'm thinking of him. You remember the night I went gunning for Lacy Marshalt? I guess you do! There are very few walls I can't climb, and I got up to the roof of Malpas' house, which is next door, just before the fuss started down below."

"You mean the murder of Marshalt?"

He nodded.

"I was there just a few minutes before, and Shannon spoke the truth when he said the police station clock saved my neck. At the far end of the roof, on Marshalt's section, there was a detective on guard. He didn't see me, and he didn't see the man who came hand-over-hand up the rope, opened the skylight in Malpas', and dropped in. I did. I saw trouble coming, and I got away quick."

"You saw the man go through the skylight? Then you saw the murderer!" she gasped.

"I saw more than that," he nodded. "When he got down below into the little storeroom under the skylight, he lit a candle and took out of his pocket a half-wig, a false nose and a chin. When he'd fixed them, why his own mother wouldn't have recognized him for anybody but Malpas."

"Malpas!" she gasped. "Who was it?"

"Slick Smith," was the answer.

MOVING AN IDOL

Sergeant Steel came to Shannon's office in response to a call, and found him in the midst of reading a very long cablegram. From the Western Union headline, which he recognized, he gathered it was from America, and expected his chief to make some reference to its contents. But apparently it had nothing to do with the case, for Dick turned the sheets upside down and addressed himself to the business for which he had sent for Steel.

"Take a plain-clothes officer with you and admit yourself to 551, Portman Square. You will probably find the controls are off. I want you to wait and watch the removal of the Malpas god. As soon as it is gone, close the house and report."

"Are you moving the idol?" asked the other in surprise.

Dick nodded.

"I've arranged with the Builders' Transport Company to have a lorry and twenty men before the house at half-past three. See that they get in, watch the loading, and escort the idol to Scotland Yard. I've told the transport company to cover it up, or we should have half London following the trolley under the impression that we're giving an exhibition. I've arranged for its reception at the Yard. When we've got it there, two of our engineers will make a very thorough examination, and I think this will throw a light upon Malpas and his methods, and – Steel!"

The sergeant turned back.

"I had a talk with one of Marshalt's servants today. She came with a whole lot of useless stuff about things that mean nothing, but she let out one interesting fact. Marshalt was really scared of the man next door. I've been thinking that all that talk and appointment of Stormer's men to watch out was sheer bunk. But it was true. One day this woman had to go into Marshalt's study to take some coal, and she just got into the room when three knocks came from the other side of the wall. You remember I told you that Miss Bedford heard the same signal. Marshalt and Tonger were together, and the effect on Marshalt was to reduce him to jelly. That's what the woman said, but I'm allowing a generous margin for exaggeration. I don't know whether you've any cut and dried theory, but remember that Marshalt and Tonger were in the room together when the knocks came. And Marshalt was scared sick."

Steel considered this new point.

"I don't see how that adds to our knowledge, sir," he said, and Dick Shannon showed his teeth in a smile.

"It adds a lot to mine. It tells me who was the two-faced villain who was on the other side! Now get along."

Half an hour later Sergeant Steel, accompanied by one plain-clothes officer, walked up the steps of 551, fitted his key in the tiny lock and admitted himself and his companion. The light was burning in the hall, and in the big room above apparently nothing had changed except that somebody had drawn the curtain over the idol.

"Pull back those window curtains," said Steel. "Let's have a little real light in this place."

So saying he switched off the lamps. In daylight Malpas' room was even more funereal than it was under the glare of the electric.

"I don't know why the chief wants us to watch the removal," grumbled Steel.

"Our people have been squealing about this job," said the other, "and they will be glad Captain Shannon has decided to cut out the guard for good."

Steel looked at his watch.

"The contractor's men will be here in half an hour, and then we'll see what this old idol looks like in the Black Museum."

"Are they moving it? Is that the idea, Sergeant?"

"That is the idea," said Steel, idly turning the pages of a book he had been reading when he had been in occupation.

The officer strolled up to the statue and examined it curiously.

"It will take some moving," he said. "It looks to be cast in one piece, and it must weigh a ton. I wonder the floor supports it."

"The floor doesn't; the wall is built out underneath. Captain Shannon had a hole knocked into it to see if there was any hidden mechanism there, but there wasn't."

"Who are doing the moving?"

"The Builders' Transport Company," said Steel. "Did you wedge open the door downstairs?" he asked, with a pretence of carelessness. The place was on his nerves.

Half an hour passed, and there was no sign of the contractor. He took up the telephone and immediately missed the familiar buzz of the receiver and tapped the hook.

"The phone is dead. Has anybody ordered it to be cut off, I wonder?"

He glanced nervously at the door, and, obeying an impulse, walked across and planted a chair so that it was impossible that it should close. The light was fading in the sky; he put on the lamps again, to find that they did not work.

"I think we'll go," said Steel hastily, "but don't touch that chair!"

He himself vaulted over it and went down the stairs quicker than he had moved since he had been a boy. The wedge at the door still held. As he stood there he heard the upper door shut.

"What was the hurry?" asked the plain-clothes man, coming out after him.

"You've never been on duty here, have you?"

"No. Not that I should mind. Our people made a fuss about it, but it looks an easy job to me."

"It would," snapped Steel. "And it would look an easy job to anybody who doesn't understand it. Go around to the store in Orchard Street and phone the transport company: ask them how long they'll be."

He himself paced up and down the pavement, keeping one eye upon the open door, his uninjured hand on the butt of the gun that he carried in his pocket.

His walk took him a few yards beyond the open door on either side, and he was turning when he saw a yellow hand come round behind the door and grip the wedge – the hand of a man, a flesh-and-blood man, and Steel was afraid of no man in the world.

Whipping out his gun, he leapt the steps, and, as he did so, the wedge was withdrawn and the door began to close. It was within an inch of coming to rest when Steel flung himself against the dark panelling, and for a second it held. And then somebody inside added his weight to the springs, and the door closed. Steel stood, panting and exhausted, leaning against the black panels and then, looking round, saw his assistant coming back at a run.

"I got on to the transport people; they say that the order was countermanded this afternoon by Captain Shannon himself."

"I'll bet it was," said Steel bitterly. He looked up at the blank windows. "When we get back to the Captain we'll learn that he gave no such order. That was a good idea of mine about the chair…go along and phone him – no, I'd better do that."

He got through to Shannon immediately, and the commissioner listened in silence.

"No – I gave no order. Let the matter stand for tonight, Steel. Tomorrow I will open the house and you'll see things happen. Go, watch the back and see what happens."

He rang off and tapped on the hook until he got the exchange again.

"Give me Electric Supply Corporation," he said, and when at long last he had reached the official he wanted: "This is Captain Shannon of headquarters. As from tomorrow afternoon at four o'clock I want all electric current to be cut off from 551 Portman Square. Precisely at that moment – can you fix it without entering the house…? Good!"

In the meantime, the disgruntled Steel and his man made their way to the mews behind that side of Portman Square on which the Malpas house was situated. They were half a dozen yards from the entrance when a well-dressed man walked out, swinging a polished Malacca-cane.

"Slick Smith!" gasped Steel. "And he is wearing yellow gloves!"

THE FLAT BURGLAR

Mr Slick Smith had developed the social craze for making afternoon calls. This new weakness of his broke into his hours of sleep, for it meant rising at an unusual hour – he was sometimes up as early as noon.

He was known by the police to be an expert hotel and flat thief, but in truth Mr Smith had attainments beyond these sordid limits. Unconscious of the sensation which his yellow gloves had excited, Slick Smith strolled westward until he came to the busy Edgware Road, and, turning northward, he strolled at his leisure into Maida Vale. In that excellent thoroughfare there are many blocks of residential apartments, some of the highest grade, rented at a price which only a wealthy stockbroker could hear without swooning. There were others where professional men who worked for their living could afford to live, but these latter, for the moment, had no interest for Slick Smith.

It was along the broad carriage drive of Greville Mansions that he walked when he left the sidewalk. This imposing block was occupied by families so wealthy that they could afford, for the greater part of the year, to live somewhere else. In other words, a flat in Greville Mansions was the accompaniment of a country house, and thirty per cent of the flats were as a rule untenanted all the year round.

There were two entrances, behind each of which was the brass grille of an elevator, attended by a smart man in livery. Into one of these sedate halls, with its redwood panelling, its neat janitor's office and perfectly carpeted floor, Slick turned. He beamed upon the janitor.

"I wanted to see Mr Hill," he said affably.

"Mr Hill is out of town, sir. Did you come about a flat?"

"Ya-as," drawled Slick. "Lady Kilfern's flat is to rent, I understand?"

"To let, sir, you mean. Yes, it is to be let furnished. Have you come from the agents?"

The yellow glove went inside the well-fitting coat, and there came forth, between two fingers, a blue slip of paper, which the janitor read.

"That is all right, sir. This is an order to view Lady Kilfern's flat. Will you come with me?"

He took him up to the second floor, unlocked a magnificent door and led the way into her ladyship's apartments. Slick did no more than glance over the sheeted furniture, and then shook his head sadly.

"I'm afraid that this is the front of the block? It is? I understood it was at the back. I am a bad sleeper, and the noise of the traffic disturbs me."

"There's nothing to let at the back, sir."

"Whose flat is that?"

They stood on the landing, and he indicated a door behind the lift cage. The janitor told him the name of the tenant − a lawyer − while Slick strolled leisurely down the passage to the big window that looked out on to the back.

"This would suit me admirably," he said. "A fire escape, too. I'm rather nervous of fires."

He leaned out of the window and took a survey of the courtyard below. He saw more than this: he noted that there were patent locks on the door of No. 9, and that a man of nerve, holding to the edge of the fire escape landing, could just reach the window of what was apparently No. 9's hall.

"I should like to see one of these back flats, but I suppose that is impossible?" he said sadly.

"Yes, sir; I have a pass key in case of fire or accident, but I am strictly forbidden to use it."

"A pass key?" Mr Smith was charmingly puzzled. "What is a pass-key?"

Displaying the satisfaction with which persons of limited intelligence explain something which is novel to others and familiar to themselves:

"This is a pass key," he said, and produced it from his waistcoat pocket with some labour.

Slick took it in his hand and examined it with interest. "How extraordinary!" he said. "It looks just like any other key. What system does it work on?" He looked the man straight in the eye.

"That's beyond me, sir," said the janitor gravely, even reverently.

He put back the key in his pocket, and at that moment the lift bell rang.

"Excuse me, sir – " he began, but Smith caught his arm.

"Can you come back again and see me? I'd like to get your opinion about this front of the house flat," he said anxiously.

"I'll be back in a minute, sir."

When he returned, having deposited a carload of people on an upper floor, Smith was standing where he had left him, a thoughtful figure.

"As I was saying, sir, these pass keys – "The janitor put his hand in his pocket, and a startled expression appeared on his face. "I've lost it!" he gasped. "Did you see me put it back?"

"I'm sure you did. Why, there it is!"

He pointed to the carpet at the man's feet.

"I wouldn't have lost that for a fortune," said the relieved janitor, and again the interruption of the bell called him to the nether regions. "You ought to go up and see the roof, sir. There's a fine view. I'll take you up."

"I prefer to walk," said Slick Smith.

He waited till the lift was out of sight, and his preference for walking took him in three strides to the door. He pushed it gently and it opened, as he expected it would, for he had unlocked the door, fastened back the catch and pulled it close again, all in the time of the janitor's first absence. Now he let the safety catch drop, and went swiftly from room to room.

The place was handsomely furnished, and evidently the plutocratic lawyer had some artistic taste, for the pictures which hung in his small dining-room included two veritable old masters. But Slick Smith was not worrying about pictures. He was after valuables of a more portable character, and in five minutes he had made a most scientific exploration of the best bedroom's contents, and all that he regarded as worth taking he took, slipping the articles into the capacious pocket of his tail-coat. This finished, he had another look round.

He was particularly interested in the kitchen and the contents of the larder, feeling the bread to discover its newness, smelling the butter, examining an opened tin of preserved milk that stood on the kitchen table; and at last, as though he were satisfied that there was nothing worth eating, he crept up the passage, and listened at the door. The whine of the elevator came to his ears, and, stooping, he lifted the flap of the letter box and caught a glimpse of it passing upward. Instantly he was out, had closed the door, and was waiting in the hall when the janitor came down.

"Oh, here you are, sir! I wondered where you'd got to."

"I have decided to take her ladyship's flat," said Smith, "but I presume that you do not attend to that side of the business?"

"No, sir, I don't," admitted the man. "And thank you, sir." He took the munificent tip which Smith slipped into his hand, and the yellow-gloved man walked out, and, some distance along Maida Vale, hailed a taxicab, and gave the driver an address in Soho.

Getting rid of the cab, he passed down a side street, and stopped outside a little jeweller's shop. Glancing left and right to make sure that he had not been followed, he dived into the dark interior, and a little man in a skull cap shuffled from behind the curtain.

"What is this worth?" He passed a ring across to the jeweller.

"If I gave you five I'd be robbing myself."

"If you offered me five I'd be murdering you," said Smith good-humouredly.

And then the door opened and a square-shouldered man walked in.

"Hallo, Smith! How's trade?"

Smith looked at the Scotland Yard man with a smile.

"Doing a little buying and selling?" said the officer pleasantly.

"I gather that you've been tailing me up?"

"How could you think of such a thing?" said the other, shocked. "Let me have a look at that ring."

"I didn't buy it, I didn't buy it!" protested the little jeweller. "He offered it to me, and I told him to take it away!"

"Where did you get this, Smith?"

"It was a present from my Aunt Rachel," said Mr Smith humorously. "In fact, it is my own ring, and Captain Shannon will be very pleased to identify the same."

"Shannon would?" said the other, nonplussed.

"Sure he would," said Slick. "Come along and see him. But I'll save you trouble; look on the inside, will you?"

The detective carried the ring out into the daylight, and read the inscription:

To Slick, from Auntie.

"Well, I'm — "

"I dare say if you're not, you will be – and I wasn't trying to sell it. I was merely – the fact is, dear lad," said Smith, with engaging candour. "I spotted you when I got out of the cab, and I felt that I ought to bring a little brightness into your dull and drab life. If you'd known your job, you'd have detained the cab to find where I was picked up. But, alas! you don't. Do you want me to go to Shannon?"

The detective jerked his head sternly.

"One of these days – " he threatened.

"A good title for a song: I wonder you don't write it," said Slick, and walked all the way back to Bloomsbury, whistling.

Until there came to him a sense of his folly. If that smart detective had arrested him and searched him… Slick Smith went cold at the thought.

THE LEVER

A man engaged in the peculiar work which was Mr Martin Elton's specialty necessarily accumulates, in the course of the years, quite a large number of documents which must be kept in a safe place, where they cannot attract the attention of the curious. For such things cannot be destroyed without risk or exposed without danger.

Martin relied very much upon the pigeon-holes of his brain for data, and in this respect he was well equipped, for he had one of those extraordinary memories that never forget the smallest detail, and in turning over the pressing problems that awaited treatment, and in searching his mind in all directions for the necessary assistance and the inducements he could offer to obtain that help, he recalled a four-page memorandum, written in the neat handwriting of Big Bill Stanford.

Stanford was something of a paper strategist. In the old days it was his delight to work out to the last button the "combinations" of every contemplated coup. Most of these had been destroyed, but there was one which had struck Martin at the time as being so ably compiled, that he had kept it, partly as a curio, and partly with an eye to the future. Papers such as these, with other intimate matters, were kept at the safe deposit. That afternoon, Martin paid a visit to the vaults, and spent half an hour examining and destroying much that was no longer of value. When he came out, he had in his breast pocket those four single sheets of notepaper which might very well prove to be a powerful lever when it came to influencing Bill Stanford to his way of thinking.

287

Reaching home, he sent for a district messenger, and dispatched him with a note to Stanford, and half an hour later his telephone bell rang. He gathered from the quality of Stanford's voice that the man was annoyed.

"See here, Martin, I can't run about like a pet dog every time you send for me. What do you want?"

"I wish to see you. It is really important."

Stanford growled something, then: "You'd better come here tonight, and see me."

"I'd better do nothing of the kind," said Martin. "You take your instructions from me, Stanford, as usual, whether you're Marshalt's nominee or not. I want you here before five."

"What's the idea?" Stanford's voice was sharp and suspicious. "I told you I was not free for anything."

"Come and tell me that," said Elton, with a touch of his old impatience. "Don't say it over the wire, with half the busies in London listening in. You don't suppose I would send for you if it wasn't urgent, do you?"

There was a long silence at the other end of the wire, and then Stanford spoke in a milder tone.

"All right, I'll come. But don't think that you've got me so that I'm obliged to take orders from you, Elton. You've got to get this right – "

Martin Elton cut him off at that point. He knew his man too well to allow him to get started on a telephone argument.

A few minutes after five, Stanford came, and he came in a cold temper. Martin was lying on the settee, a favourite posture of his, and looked up from a book as the man flung into the room.

"What in hell do you mean by sending for me, as if I were a coolie, Elton? You've got a nerve – "

"Shut the door," said Martin. "You're a bit of a loud speaker, my friend; if you want to tell your sorrows to Curzon Street, I'll lend you a soapbox."

"Do you think I've nothing to do but run about after you?"

The man was white with anger; he had that quality peculiar to criminals, and not entirely absent from more law-abiding people, an immense vanity, which was easily hurt when his own dignity was threatened. Martin waved him down.

"There is no sense in quarrelling," he said. "This is serious; otherwise, I shouldn't have sent for you."

He got up, took a cigar from the cabinet and lit it. He offered the cabinet to the other, and Stanford sulkily accepted. Then he dropped his bombshell.

"Audrey Bedford has gone to Stormer's, and that child is a fast worker."

"Audrey? You mean your wife's sister?"

Martin nodded.

"Gone to Stormer's? I should worry! Those people mean nothing to me – or to you, either. And if you've brought me from Portman Square, neglecting my duties, to tell me this, you're wasting my time!"

"I tell you she's a fast worker," said Elton slowly, "and she's a keen worker, too, Stanford. You're not forgetting, are you, that she did twelve months in Holloway for carrying stuff you had stolen – "

"Don't say 'you,' say 'we'," said Stanford angrily.

"We won't split hairs," agreed Martin. "She did the time. How do you think she's feeling about it – sore, eh? I guess you'd feel sore if you did twelve revolutions of the moon in prison for a crime you didn't commit?"

Stanford was eyeing him suspiciously.

"Well, what about it?" he asked, when the other paused. "I suppose she does feel sore, but she's got a new job now and doing fine. Why do you think Stormer's took her?"

"I'll tell you – because she's been to them and spilt all she knows about the robbery, and they've set her on to collect evidence. Don't forget that Stormer acts for almost every embassy in London."

William Stanford laughed contemptuously.

"Well, she can collect all the evidence that is collectible as far as I'm concerned," he said. "And she can start a museum, and then I shouldn't care. Is that all?"

"Not quite," said Martin. "Do you remember you wrote out a little plan of campaign for that Queen of Finland job? Do you remember how you scheduled every possibility, even drawing a little plan of the place in the park where the hold-up should be, with detailed instructions as to how the getaway was to be made?"

"I remember," said Stanford after thinking; "but it was destroyed."

"It wasn't destroyed," said Martin coolly. "It was such a perfect piece of work that I very foolishly kept it. Audrey was here two days ago – she came while Dora and I were out, and went up into Dora's room to put her hair straight. Dora keeps the key of my safe deposit in her bureau."

Stanford was looking hard at him.

"Well?" he said.

"Today I went to the deposit to get out some money that I had there. I found the money, but all my papers are gone."

Stanford went white.

"You mean that my little plan went with the rest?"

Martin nodded very slowly.

"That is what I mean," he said. "Now don't get up in the air," as he saw the blood come up to the man's face and the impotent rage gleam in his eyes. "I know I was a fool to keep it; it should have been destroyed at once, especially since, if I remember rightly, you used names. I'm as much in this as you are, and in as much danger – more, because she's got something on Dora and me that she hasn't got on you."

Stanford was rubbing his hands together, a nervous trick of his. "You've let me down, you swine!" he said in a fury. "Keeping a thing like that!"

"Who wrote the names on the paper? If they weren't there, you could snap your fingers at them," interrupted Martin. "The real fault was yours. I'm not going to pretend that I'm not to blame, but if there's a trial, and a jury say that paper is sufficient evidence against you, Stanford, it will be your own cleverness responsible for the conviction."

Stanford shrugged his shoulders. Behind his apparent strength and his bluster he was something of a weakling, as Martin well knew.

"What do you want me to do?" he asked, and for half an hour they discussed ways and means.

AUDREY GOES TO DINNER

There would be no need for her attendance that night – Mr Torrington was very emphatic on the point, though there was a kind tempering to his sternness to which the girl instantly responded.

"So if you have any theatre engagements or dinner parties, or, if you've got some plain sewing to do, you'll have all the time you want."

"Are you going out – ?" she began, and was instantly apologetic. "I ought not to have asked you that, and I really didn't ask in my role of amateur detective, but out of – " Here she floundered, seeking without success words to convey her meaning.

"Out of sheer friendliness?" he suggested, and she nodded.

"I guessed that. No, my child, I'm staying at home tonight." He looked at the clock on the mantelpiece. "After dinner I have an important interview."

He opened the door for her, and she went out, liking him. She was glad to have this time absolutely her own, for Dora had asked her to come to an early dinner. She was going out, she said, and was not dressing up, so would Audrey come as she was?

The girl had not seen or heard from Dick Shannon that day, and she searched the newspapers in vain for any reference to the diamond steal. When Torrington had spoken about the matter on the previous day, she thought the news was public property; but apparently he had some source of information which was not available to the press, for she found that no newspaper gave so much as a paragraph to the happening. She wished she could see Dick – if only for a few minutes, though there was nothing in particular she wished to say to him. But he hadn't phoned or called – she was glad of the distraction which Dora's dinner party offered.

It was her sister who opened the door to her when she arrived. "Come in, my dear," she said, kissing her. "I've had another domestic upset. My cook left this afternoon, and my new maid is out for the day! I hadn't the heart to keep her – she was visiting her sick mother. So you'll have to forgive all the deficiencies of dinner – happily, the fastidious Martin has gone to his club."

"I thought you were both going out?" said Audrey in surprise.

"So we are," smiled Dora, "and Martin is coming back to collect me. He had to meet a man, and I suggested that he should dine at the club, and return afterward."

The table was laid for two, a picture of a table, for Dora, whatever her faults, was an excellent housewife. So perfect was the little dinner that followed that Audrey might have suspected that the cook, before her departure from the scene, had prepared the meal – which was the truth; for that angry lady had only left an hour before Audrey arrived, and this was brought about by a baseless accusation of dishonesty, well calculated by Dora to wound the thickest-skinned domestic servant. She had hated parting with the woman, even temporarily, though she knew that an abject apology in the morning would bring her back, and Dora thought it no shame to grovel to a good cook.

Halfway through the dinner: "We're going to have one small bottle of wine to celebrate the family reunion," said Dora gaily.

Getting up from the table, she took a bottle from a silver bucket, and deftly nipped the wire of the cork. Audrey laughed.

"I haven't tasted wine since – " She remembered the night she had dined with Marshalt, and hurriedly dismissed that unpleasant recollection.

"I don't think you've ever tasted wine like this," Dora prattled on. "Martin has many faults, but he is a wonderful connoisseur. There aren't four dozen of this champagne in England, and when I told him that we were using a bottle tonight, he writhed!"

The cork came out with a pop, and she filled the glass till its creamy head overflowed the side.

"Here's to our next merry meeting," said Dora, and raised her glass.

Audrey laughed softly, and sipped.

"Drink!" said Dora. "That isn't the way to drink a toast."

Audrey raised her glass with great solemnity and did not put it down till it was empty.

"Oh!" she said, and gasped. "I suppose it is very beautiful, but I haven't an educated taste. I thought it was rather bitter – like quinine."

Half an hour after, Dora's new maid unexpectedly appeared.

"I thought you were going to the theatre?" said Dora sharply.

"I have a headache, madam," said the maid. "I'm very sorry, but the ticket you gave me will be wasted."

"Come in," said Dora.

"Perhaps you would like me to wait at table, to save you and Miss Bedford – "

"I've finished dinner," said Dora, "and Miss Bedford has just gone. I wonder you didn't meet her."

MR TORRINGTON SURPRISES

The visitor who called at the Ritz-Carlton was expected, and no sooner did he give his name than the clerk called a page.

"Take this gentleman to Mr Torrington's suite," he said, and Martin followed the boy to the elevator.

Daniel Torrington, in slippers and dressing-gown, shot a keen, inquiring glance at the man as he came in, and without any great show of cordiality motioned him to be seated.

"I have an idea I've met you before, Mr Torrington," said Martin.

"I'm as certain that we haven't met, though I know you very well by repute," said Torrington. "Take your coat off, Mr Elton. I had your request for a private interview, and there were many reasons why this should be granted. You are, I believe, the brother-in-law of my secretary?"

Martin inclined his head gravely.

"I have that misfortune," he said.

"Misfortune?" The old man's eyebrows went up. "Ah, I see what you mean! You're thinking of her criminal past?"

He did not sneer, but there was an undercurrent of sarcasm in his tone, which Martin, sensitive to such things, detected immediately.

"That must be a great sorrow to you and your wife. This unfortunate girl was concerned in a jewel robbery, was she not? I'm not sure whether she was the miscreant who held up the Queen of Finland in Green Park, or whether she planned the theft."

"She was caught with the jewels in her possession," said Martin.

The interview was going to be much more difficult than he had imagined.

"She was caught with the jewels in her possession?" repeated the other. "Well, now, isn't that too bad! Of course, I knew all that, before I engaged the young lady, though I presume you came here with the object of protecting me from her machinations?"

Again Martin felt that cold chill of disappointment. The old man was laughing at him despite his set face and his air of courteous concern.

"No, I didn't come with that object. I came on a very much more intimate matter," he said soberly, "and one which touches you nearly. You will forgive me if I refer to something which must be very painful to you?"

Torrington nodded. The eyes behind the powerful glasses were fixed immovably on Martin's face; his whole attitude was antagonistic. Martin felt it more keenly at that moment than he had before.

"Mr Torrington, many years ago you went to prison in South Africa for illicit diamond buying."

Torrington nodded.

"Yes, there was a frame-up, organized by the greatest scoundrel in the diamond fields, one Lacy Marshalt, who is now, happily, deceased. I was certainly the victim on that occasion, and, as you say, I went to prison."

"You had a young wife" – Martin hesitated – "and a child, a little girl, Dorothy?"

Again Torrington nodded.

"Your wife was greatly shocked by your arrest, and never afterward forgave you for the shame, as she thought, you had brought upon her. And soon after you were taken to the Breakwater she left South Africa, and since then, I think it is true that you did not hear from her?"

"Once." The word came like the snap of a whip. "Once, my friend, she wrote – yes, once!"

"She came to England with her baby and an elder daughter, changed her name to Bedford, and lived on a small income – "

"Annuity," interrupted Torrington. Whatever emotions he experienced he did not betray by so much as a twitch of muscle. "An annuity which I purchased for her before my arrest. So far you are right. Go on."

Martin drew a long breath. Every word was an effort in this atmosphere. He felt like a man striving to pick a hole in a granite wall.

"Your late wife was rather eccentric. For some reason, best known to herself, she brought up Dorothy" – he emphasized the word – "to believe that she was the daughter of her first husband, and the other girl was taught that she was the elder. I don't pretend to explain the mind of the woman – " began Martin.

"Don't," said Torrington. "Well, all these things may or may not be true. What then?"

Martin Elton took the plunge.

"You are under the impression, sir, that your daughter Dorothy died. That is not true. She lives; she is in England now, and is my wife."

Daniel Torrington was looking at him; his eyes seemed to pierce their way into the secret places of the visitor's very soul.

"Is that the story you have to tell me," said Torrington at last, "that my little Dorothy is still alive and is your wife?"

"That is the story, Mr Torrington."

"Ah!" The old man rubbed his chin. "Is that so?"

A long and painful silence followed.

"Do you know the story of my arrest – the circumstances? I see that you do not – I will tell you."

He looked up at the ceiling, licked his lips, and seemed to be reconstructing the scene in his mind.

"I was sitting on the stoep of my house at Wynberg – I always came down to the Peninsula for the summer – and I remember I was holding my baby in my arms. You know what a stoep is, I suppose? It is a broad, raised porch that runs the length of the house. I saw Marshalt coming round the shrubbery, and wondered what brought him, until I saw the two detectives who were following. He was scared of me, scared sick! As I rose and put the child down in her cradle, he pulled a gun and fired. He said I shot first, but that is a lie. I wouldn't have shot at all, but the bullet struck the cradle, and I heard the child scream. It was then I drew on him, and he would have been a dead man but for the agony of mind I was in about the child. As it was, I missed him, and his second shot smashed my leg. Did you know that?"

Martin shook his head.

"You never heard about the shot that hit the cradle, eh?"

"No, sir; that is news to me."

"I thought it would be. The child wasn't badly hurt; the bullet just nicked her little toe and broke the bone – I wonder your wife never told you," he drawled.

Martin was silent.

"My little Dorothy isn't dead – I've known that for a very long time. I've been looking for her, and, thanks to my friend Stormer, I have found her!"

"She knows?" said Martin, his face ghastly.

Torrington shook his head.

"No, she doesn't know; I didn't want her to know. I wanted to keep that from her until my work is complete. And I've pretended to everybody about me, except one man, that she is a stranger to me. Ask the innocent Mr Willitt, who almost begged me on his knees to make her my secretary."

His cold eyes did not leave Martin's face.

"Your wife is my daughter, eh? Ask her to come here and show me her left foot. You can fake birth certificates, Elton – that makes you jump, my friend – but you can't fake little toes!"

He rang the bell, and, to the man who came: "Show this gentleman out," he said, "and when Miss Bedford returns, will you ask her to come straight to me?"

Martin went home like a man in a dream, and Dora read disaster in his pallid face. She drew him into the drawing-room and closed the door.

"What is the matter with you, Martin? Did you see him?"

He nodded.

"He knows," he said huskily.

"Knows – ?"

297

"He knows Audrey is his daughter – that is all. He has known it all the time. He's had Stormer looking for her. He was going to tell her tonight. I suppose you know what this means to you and me?"

He sat with his face buried in his hands.

"It ought to mean a fortune to us," she said, and he looked up quickly.

"You wanted to do this, and I agreed against my will. It was my idea to tell the old man that she was his daughter. It was you who said you'd rather die than see her with all that money. Where is that fortune coming?"

She nodded slowly.

"He'll pay to get her back, if– "

"If what?"

"If she is still alive," said Dora Elton. "And if nothing…else has happened."

A LADY CALLS ON MR SMITH

The landlord of Mr Slick Smith was a tolerant, easygoing man. He knew that his tenant lived on the shady side of life, but that neither heightened nor lowered Slick Smith in his estimation. To him, his lodger was a man who paid his bill regularly, was invariably courteous, gave no trouble, and was grateful for any little services which the landlord, a highly respectable lawyer's clerk, could render to him.

He had had what he called a heart-to-heart talk with Smith as soon as he discovered his nefarious calling, and that conversation might be summarized into a sentence: "You may do what you like, but you must not bring me or my house into disrepute."

Visitors he looked coldly upon, for visitors savoured of conspiracy; and, to do him justice, Slick Smith seldom offended in this respect.

The landlord heard a knock that night. It was eleven o'clock — that hour which separates, in some intangible fashion, the sheep who go to bed before and the goats who frolic after. The landlord himself went to the door and found a young and prepossessing woman — a stranger to him, and, as far as he knew, a complete stranger to his lodger.

"Mr Smith?" he said dubiously. "No, I don't think he's in, Miss. Can I give him a message?"

"It's very important; I must see him," said the girl in almost peremptory tones.

The landlord hesitated. Visitors of any kind he objected to, but lady visitors at eleven o'clock at night offended him beyond measure. Nevertheless, thinking there might be some good excuse for her presence, that she might, for example, be a sister or a messenger from his sick mother, or something equally proper, he went upstairs and knocked at the door, receiving no answer. Turning the handle, he walked in. The room was untenanted, and he went back with a message that was consonant with his principles.

"Mr Smith isn't in, Miss," he said, closed the door upon her, and went back to his pipe and his law book.

After a while he thought he heard somebody walking down the stairs, opened the door and peered out. It was Mr Smith.

"I didn't hear you come in."

"I haven't been in long," said Smith in his usual genial tone.

"Are you going out?"

"I heard a knock and thought it was for me."

"There was a lady came to see you – " began the landlord.

"I expect it is she," said Smith.

His landlord felt it the moment to assert his authority.

"If you'll excuse me, Mr Smith, I don't like visitors at this hour of the night, and, of course, you'll not ask the lady in?"

"If I do, perhaps I can borrow your parlour," said Smith. "I think this is rather an important business message. In fact, it is from my friend, Captain Shannon, the Sherlock Holmes of Scotland Yard."

The landlord knew that Captain Shannon was eminently respectable, and granted the necessary permission, even going so far as to put on all the lights in the parlour.

"Come in," said Smith. "You're from Captain Shannon?"

"Yes," was the reply – all of which the landlord heard, as it was intended he should hear, and was satisfied.

He heard the low murmur of their voices in the drawing-room for a quarter of an hour, and then the girl went out, and Smith sought him.

"It is rather more important than I imagined," he said gravely. "Captain Shannon is in a serious difficulty, and has called me in – we frequently help the police out of their difficulties."

This was news to the landlord, but he was satisfied, being a simple man who knew nothing but law, and lawyers are notoriously childlike.

Slick changed from the evening dress he had been wearing when he had returned, into a lounge suit, put on a fleecy overcoat, and, taking from a drawer one of the many implements of his craft, joined the girl, who was waiting for him at the corner of the street, and walked with her as far as Southampton Row.

Glancing over his shoulder as he walked down the Row, he saw the inevitable Stormer man following him. When he called a cab, his shadow followed his example. Smith didn't trouble to look; he knew. At the Marble Arch:

"Where to, sir?" asked the cabman.

"Greville Mansions, Maida Vale," said Slick.

He came to that aristocratic block with the air of a proprietor, as he was well entitled to do, for he was the temporary tenant of a handsome suite on the second floor, and uniformed porters would, for an indefinite period, touch their hats to him.

The night liftman took him up, exchanging commonplaces about the weather, and bade him goodnight, leaving him, as he believed, to the enjoyment of that dreamless sleep which is the right of all men wealthy enough to rent a ladyship's flat at twenty guineas a week.

That same evening Sergeant Steel and his superior were two of the council of three that met at Dick's flat. The third was the inspector in charge from Marylebone Lane, and the subject of discussion was 551 and its artistic treasure.

"I am still undecided about moving the idol," said Shannon, "but the orders to the electric light company stand. I've had one of their engineers to see me, and he says they can cut off the supply from the conduit outside the house. Which means that the power that has helped Malpas and his friends will no longer be available."

"I take it you'll have the place opened before the supply is cut off? Otherwise, it may lead to endless difficulties," said the inspector.

Dick agreed.

"I'm satisfied that we shall paralyze the activity of Mr Ghost, though it is also possible that, when the current is cut, we shall imprison our friend in some secret hiding place and leave future generations to unearth the mystery."

"In that case," said Steel, "we shall never see Slick Smith again."

Shannon laughed.

"You think Smith is the king pippin of the crowd?"

"I'm certain of it," said the other emphatically. "Hasn't it struck you as remarkable, Captain Shannon, that Smith has invariably been around when we've seen these demonstrations? This afternoon I saw him walking out of the mews, immediately following the appearance of a yellow-gloved hand at the door. And he was wearing yellow gloves!"

"So do fifty thousand other people wear yellow gloves," said Dick. "It is the fashion amongst the smartly dressed men of London. You can keep Smith in mind, though I'm not satisfied that your view is the correct one."

"There's something wrong with him, anyway," insisted Steel. "I mean something out of the ordinary. He is wanted badly on the other side — I've never seen him without a Stormer man on his trail, and Stormer's don't take all that trouble unless they think they have a good kill ahead."

Dick smiled as he thought of the latest recruit to the Stormer corps.

The meeting broke up at half past ten, having decided upon the plan of operations for the following day; and at a quarter to eleven Steel made his round of the many and curious clubs that had sprung up in London since the war. There were dance clubs and supper clubs; some in gilded saloons; not a few in furtive cellars, converted at great expense into halls of gaiety by the engagement of the inevitable syncopated orchestra and a loose system of membership. He noted the normal irregularities, and checked them for future action. His tour finished, he strolled home. The clock was booming the quarter to twelve as he came into Upper Gloucester Place, where his lodgings were, and his hand was in his pocket, feeling for the key, when he saw a man walking quickly toward him on the opposite side of the road. There was nothing unusual about a quick walker at this hour of the night, nor even remarkable in the fact that he carried a bag; for Marylebone Station is within a stone's throw, and arrivals by the late trains often passed through Upper Gloucester Place on their way to their homes.

He didn't recognize the man as he came into the focus of a street lamp, but the bag certainly seemed of familiar shape. For a moment he debated with himself, and then, though every cell of his body called loudly for sleep, he turned back and pursued the bag.

There was practical reason for his act. In his then nervous state, if he had omitted to make a closer inspection and satisfy himself that his eyes had deceived him, he would have lain awake for hours, cursing his laziness. The chase was a little absurd, for one bag is very much like another, and, seen across the width of a street on a dark night, and by the unsatisfactory street light, the resemblance is even more complete. But he was determined to see that bag, and quickened his pace, as he had need to do, for the man ahead of him was walking rapidly, though the grip was so heavy that from time to time he changed his hand.

His way led down Harley Street, but he kept on, and then, at this stage of his annoyance, Steel began to run. He was within a dozen yards of his quarry when the man turned, and, seeing his pursuer, followed his example and ran swiftly, turning into a side street and diving into one of those narrow mews which abound in these parts. Bag or no bag, the fugitive had a reason for his flight, and Steel's policeman instinct aroused, he sprinted. There was no policeman in sight, and the runner with the bag evidently knew the beat so well that he could avoid the unpleasantness of meeting a representative of the law; for he doubled round again. This time he was not so fortunate; there was an officer on point duty at the corner of the street, and the quarry checked, hesitated a moment, and then, as Steel went up to him, put down his bag, and, dodging under the detective's arm, flew like the wind.

In that brief space Steel recognized him; it was Slick Smith! Should he go after him? He decided that the bag was his proper objective. At this moment the policeman, who had seen the flying man, came up.

"Go after that man and get him," said Steel, and turned his attention to the bag.

At the sight of it his heart leapt...

Dick was undressing when his subordinate dashed in, his eyes blazing with excitement, and the big leather grip in his hand.

"Look at this!" he said, and jerked it open.

Dick looked in dumbfounded amazement.

"The diamonds!" he said in a whisper.

"Slick Smith had 'em!" cried the detective breathlessly. "I spotted him going down Upper Gloucester Place with the bag, and followed him, though I didn't know it was he. And then he bolted, and when I came up with him he dropped the bag."

"Slick Smith? Where was he coming from?"

"From the direction of Park Road," said Steel rapidly. "I thought I should drop dead when I opened the bag and saw what was in it."

Dick ran his fingers through the stones.

"This time there shall be no mistake," he said. "Get a cab."

He dressed hastily, and before he had finished, Steel was back, and this time he had left nothing to chance, for when they carried the bag downstairs they found the cab surrounded by uniformed police, and with four men inside, two on the box and one officer on each footboard, the taxi made its way to Scotland Yard, and the big steel doors of the safe closed upon Malpas' treasure.

"Now let them come after it," said Shannon. "In the meantime – "

"We'll pull in Slick Smith," said Steel eagerly. "I'll go to his quarters now."

"You won't find him," said Shannon. "Do you imagine that he's going to walk back into the trap? Leave Smith to me. I think I can fix him."

The two men returned to Haymarket, to find the suspicious William at the door, eyeing a very small and very grimy boy.

"He says he's got a letter for you and he won't give it to me, sir."

"He told me to give it only to Captain Shannon."

"I am Captain Shannon," said Dick, but the boy was still reluctant to part with his message.

"Bring him in," said Dick impatiently, and the lad was brought to the sitting-room, an exceedingly ragged and grimy product of a

London slum, stockingless, almost shoeless, and his face and hands that peculiar colour which only small boys can produce.

After a great upheaval of his clothes, he produced a dirty-looking thing that looked like a newspaper cutting, folded into a cocked hat. Dick opened it, and saw that it was a piece torn from a morning journal. The message was written in pencil on its unprinted edge.

For God's sake save me! I am at Fould's Wharf. The fiend will finish me before the morning.

It was signed "Lacy Marshalt"!

FOULD'S WHARF

"Lacy Marshalt!" squeaked Steel. "Good God! It isn't possible!"

"Where did you get this?" asked Shannon quickly.

"A boy in Spa Road gave it to me and asked me to take it. Well, he wasn't exactly a boy, sir; he was a young man."

"You don't know his name?"

"No, sir. He said a gentleman had pushed it up through a grating near Dockhead and said that, if it was took to Captain Shannon, he'd pay me a pound for it."

"Why didn't he bring it himself?"

The boy grinned.

"Because he knows you, sir — that's what he said. He's been over the hills."

"Over the hills," in the argot of the class Dick understood best, meant penal servitude, and the reluctance of the unknown emissary was understandable.

"Fould's Wharf? Do you know where it is?"

"Yes, sir; it's near Dockhead; it is a wood wharf. I've been fishing there lots of times."

"Very good, you can show us the way. William, get the car out. Take this lad on the seat beside you, and disinfect him! Here's your money, my boy."

He passed a pound note to the youth, who clutched it eagerly.

The car stopped at the Yard to collect as many officers as were available. It stopped again when they crossed London Bridge, and picked up a local detective-sergeant who knew the place.

"Yes, it is a wharf attached to an old warehouse – one of the few stage wharfs on the river."

"What do you mean by 'stage wharf'?" asked Dick.

"It is built out over the water on piles, and hasn't, as is the case with most wharves, a stone and brick front."

They traversed a dismal road, skirted the dock, where the high masts of seagoing ships showed over the wall, and once they sped under a huge bowsprit that topped the wall, spanning the narrow street. Presently the detective leaned across to the chauffeur.

"This is the place," he said. "I think we can dispense with the boy now, Captain Shannon."

The small boy, to his bitter disappointment, was dropped; and the men, passing down a steep declivity, came to an old gate, which they had no difficulty in scaling.

They were on an untidy cart track that led by the side of a building, and ahead Shannon saw the glitter of the river. Turning the corner, a cold northerly wind made them pull their coats tighter.

"The wharf proper is to the right."

The detective-sergeant indicated a dreary expanse of wooden staging that thudded hollowly under Shannon's feet as he walked to the edge of the crazy structure and looked down in the water.

"There's nobody here; we'd better try the warehouse."

"*Help!*"

The voice was faint, but Dick heard.

"Where did that come from?" he asked.

"It certainly didn't come from the warehouse," said Steel. "It sounded more like somebody shouting from the river."

They stood for a moment listening, and presently they heard it again – a low moaning, and then:

"*Help! For God's sake, help!*"

"It came from underneath the staging," said Dick suddenly.

He ran to the edge of the wharf and looked down. The tide was rising; it was only a few feet below him. A little to his right he saw a boat, and feeling his way over the side, he dropped into the bottom.

"*Help!*" This time the voice was nearer.

Peering under the stage, he thought he saw a movement in the black depths.

"Where are you?" he shouted.

"I'm here!"

It was Lacy Marshalt's voice!

There were no oars in the boat, and, untying the painter, he pulled himself along by the aid of the staging until he came opposite the point where the voice had sounded. With his hand-lamp he began a search, and after a second it rested upon the ghastly face of Marshalt. The man was up to his shoulders in water, his hands, which were held above his head, seemed to be fastened to the pile.

"Put out your light — he'll get you!" he screamed.

Dick snapped back the button. As he did so, there were two quick reports. Shannon's hat flew off; he had a burning pain in his left ear; and for a moment he let go his hold on the staging and the boat drifted. Dropping down to his knees, he paddled it back with his hands, and the next moment Steel came over the edge and was by his side.

"Get out your gun and put your light on," said Dick as he guided the boat forward amidst the labyrinth of rotting props. "And when you see a head, shoot!"

In another second they were up with Marshalt. A chain was padlocked about his waist; his wrists, fastened by rusty handcuffs, were fixed to a staple high above his head. It was clear that, if he were left in this position another ten minutes, nothing could have saved him.

"A handcuff key, quick! Have you one, Steel?"

"Yes, sir."

In a second the cuffs were loosened, and then Dick turned his attention to the padlock. He had to work in the dark, while Steel searched the darkness with his lamp for the man who had fired the shot. At the back of the staging a wall showed, covered with green weeds, and three rusty iron bars that looked like the top of a grating. It was on this opening that Steel concentrated his attention, his pistol raised ready to shoot. Nothing appeared, however, and after three minutes' work Marshalt slipped down with a groan of relief, and was hauled into the boat.

They paddled him back to the river edge of the stage, and lying full length on the rotten boarding, the Southwark sergeant drew him to the stage. Marshalt was a pitiable sight; he was shivering with cold, his face was unshaven, his cheeks hollow. They rushed him into the nearest police station, where, after a hot bath, he dressed in a borrowed suit, and, save for his pallor, looked none the worse for his adventure. That he was badly shaken was not remarkable; he was in a pitiable condition, trembling in every limb.

"I don't know where I've been," he said wearily. "How long is it since I disappeared?"

When they told him he groaned.

"I've been two days in a cellar under the warehouse. If I hadn't found a scrap of paper that had fallen down from the street, I'd have been dead. When is Captain Shannon coming back?"

"He is searching the warehouse now," said the local sergeant.

Dick's inspection of the warehouse added very little to his knowledge. He found the main door unlocked, but no sign of his assailant. There were several underground apartments where the man might have been kept prisoner. He found one which communicated with the street, and it was here that he discovered something even more important. At the foot of the flight of stone steps leading down to the basement he saw a green-labelled carton, and picked it up. It was the cardboard case which had contained ammunition for an automatic pistol, and was obviously that which was missing from the box in Marshalt's storeroom when he had made his cursory inspection. He handed it to Steel without a word.

"Malpas is here somewhere," whispered the detective, and looked round nervously.

"I think not," said Shannon quietly. "Our friend only takes one shot a night."

He glanced up at the ladder-like stairs leading to the upper part of the warehouse.

"I hardly think it is worth while searching upstairs. I'll ask the sergeant to do so tomorrow morning."

The man who stood by a gap which had once been a window in the upper part of the building heard this decision with relief. It saved him from the risk which would follow a jump in the dark.

He gave Dick Shannon a very good start before he felt his way downstairs, and, peeping cautiously forth to see whether an officer had been left on duty (a disconcerting habit of the police), he went up to the edge of the staging, peered down, and, with some reluctance, lowered himself into the boat and pushed into the cavernous dark. His hand touched the cold water, and he shivered.

"War is certainly hell!" said Slick Smith.

MARSHALT'S STORY

Bt the time Shannon reached the police station, Marshalt was sufficiently recovered to talk of his experiences.

"Frankly I can give you very little information, Captain Shannon," he said, "except about the beginning of this adventure. As you have probably discovered, I was lured into Malpas' flat by a note, which asked me" – he hesitated – "to meet a lady there – a lady in whom we are both interested. I admit that it was the worst kind of folly for me not to have suspected a trap. The man hated me – a fact which is, I think, known to you. But I was curious to see him; I'd heard so much about this mysterious Mr Malpas."

"When did the note reach you?"

"About half an hour before I went out. I was dining at Rector's with some friends of mine, and, as a matter of fact, I was just leaving the house when Tonger brought the note – as Tonger will tell you – "

"I'm afraid Tonger is beyond telling us anything," said Dick quietly, and Lacy Marshalt stared at him.

"Dead?" he said in an awe-stricken whisper. "Good God! When did he die?"

"He was found dead within half an hour of the attack on you." The news seemed to strike the man speechless, but after a while he went on:

"I don't know whether it was a premonition, or whether it was a remembrance of the warnings I had received, but before going out I went up to my room, took off my shirt and put on an old bullet-proof singlet that I wore when I was in the Balkans a few years ago, looking

311

for concessions. It was very uncomfortable, but, as it proved, this precaution saved my life. I went out without any overcoat, intending to walk back to my house, and knocked at the door of 551, which was immediately opened."

"You heard no voice?" asked Dick.

Marshalt shook his head.

"No, the door just opened. I expected to see a servant there, but, to my surprise, there was nobody visible, but I heard somebody from up the stairs say 'Come up.' Naturally I followed the instructions. I walked into a big room, heavily draped with velvet, but empty. Then it was I began to feel a little suspicious, and was walking out of the room when, to my amazement, the door closed in my face. The next moment I heard somebody laugh, and, looking round, I saw a man who was obviously disguised, standing at the far end of the room. 'I've got you now!' he said.

"He had a revolver in his hand, one of the old-fashioned kind. Realizing the impossibility of getting out of the room, I ran toward him. I hadn't taken two steps before I was tripped up by a wire, and rose only to be caught again. I thought he was bluffing, and my object was to get to him and take the gun away from him. I was only a few paces from him when he fired, and that is all I remember, until I woke up in dreadful pain, and I guessed – look!"

He pulled open his shirt and showed a pink discoloration, the size of a man's hand, on the left of his chest.

"Where were you when you recovered consciousness?"

"I remember very little clearly after that," said Marshalt frankly. "I must have been awake often, and once I remember the old man jabbed a needle into my arm. It was the stab of the needle that woke me then, I think. I tried to rise and grapple with him, but I was as weak as a child. From time to time I have come to my senses, but always in a different place, until I woke one evening in that dreadful cellar, handcuffed and helpless. Malpas was looking down at me. He did not tell me who he was, and although I racked my brains I couldn't recognize him. But apparently I had done him some bad injury in South Africa. He told me that that night was my last on earth. It was when he had gone that I found the paper and fortunately there was a stub of pencil in my pocket. I awaited my opportunity. It was a terrible business getting to my feet, but eventually I succeeded and was able to push up the note to a young man who peered down; he seemed so startled at the sight of a man in evening dress – and what an evening dress! – that he nearly bolted."

"You've no recollection of being taken back to Portman Square?"

Lacy shook his head.

"None whatever. Now tell me about poor Tonger. How terrible! Who killed him? Do you think it was Malpas?"

"Tell me one thing, Mr Marshalt: is there any kind of passage or doorway between your house and Malpas'? I will admit that I have made a very careful examination without discovering any."

Marshalt shook his head.

"If there is, Malpas must have made it, but I doubt it." He frowned. "Now you mention the fact, I remember that I made a complaint once about a knocking noise that I heard. Both I and Tonger have heard those knocks from time to time. What he was doing I can't tell you. By the way, did Stanford get to my house? It occurred to me in my few waking moments that some time ago I named this man to take charge of the house in case anything happened to me."

"Why did you do that?" asked Dick.

"It happened years ago, when I knew Stanford and was more friendly with him than I am now. In fact, to be candid, before I knew that he wasn't straight and honest. It was at a time when there was a scare – you remember, a gang kidnapped a Greek millionaire, and held him to ransom? So Stanford is at the house?" He pulled a wry face. "Probably it is all right," he said, "and if I remember, the stipend would insure me against – well, I won't do him that injustice," he added, "but really, he is not the type of man I would have chosen."

He offered Dick his hand.

"I can't be sufficiently grateful to you for all you've done for me, Captain Shannon. You've saved my life. If you'd been even five minutes later…" He shivered.

Dick did not reply at once, and when he spoke he made no reference to the service he had given to the millionaire.

"Will you tell me this, Mr Marshalt?" he said. "Though you say you did not recognize Malpas, you must have had some idea as to who it was, some lingering suspicion?"

Marshalt hesitated.

"I have," he said. "My own impression – you will think it is fantastic – is that Malpas is a woman!"

WHAT AUDREY SAW

Audrey Bedford had a dream, and it was a particularly unpleasant one. She dreamt she was lying on a narrow ledge like the top of a T, the lower stalk of which was a high tower. And as she lay, her head racked with a distracting pain, the tower swayed backward and forward, and she with it. Every now and again the board upon which she lay tipped up gently, and she screamed in her sleep and clutched tightly to the edge, expecting to be precipitated into the black void below.

The reality was a headache; that was her conscious obsession. It was an ache that began behind her eyes, shot to her temples, and thence, by a million fiery routes, to the back of her head. She groaned as she turned over and buried her face in the crook of her arm. She had never had such a headache. She reached out for the bell by the side of her bed, and in a confused way went over the remedies she would use, beginning and ending with a cup of tea. She wanted that drink very, very badly; her tongue was parched, her mouth bone-dry, and she had a horrible taste. She turned over again, groaned and sat up.

It was quite dark, and she was not lying on a bed at all; she was on a mattress and there was a blanket over her, and when she reached out she touched the floor. Unsteadily she rose to her feet, leaning against the wall to prevent herself from falling, for her head was going round and round. Then she began to feel for the door, found it after a while and pulled it open. It was dark outside. At the end of what seemed to be a long tunnel she saw a little glimmer of light and staggered toward it. One half of her brain told her she was walking down a short, unfurnished corridor, and that the light she saw was a naked lamp hanging by a wire from the ceiling.

She saw a wash bowl in a little room leading off, and went toward it gratefully. When she turned the faucet, the water was brown and discoloured, but presently it ran clean, and, using her hands as a cup, she drank greedily. She washed her face; a towel was hanging from a peg – it almost looked as if it had been placed there specially for her benefit, for there was no furniture in the apartment save the mattress and blankets.

She let the bath tap run; the sound of the running water was very companionable. Then, sitting down on the projecting window ledge, she tried to get back to the beginning of this experience. The last thing she remembered was talking to Mr Torrington. No, it was later than that; she was in her room, putting on her hat to go out. Step by step she traced her conscious movements and came, with a start of horror, to the dinner table of Dora Elton, and the wine that creamed and bubbled, and tasted so vilely. Dora!

Frantically she searched the recesses of her memory to carry her beyond that last remembered period, but in vain. She was at Dora's house. She remembered now that the woman had once told her that the upper story of the Curzon Street establishment had never been furnished.

She was still stupid from the effect of the drug; but only now did she understand why it was so dark. Every window was covered with a thick shutter, the shutters being held in place by a steel bar, hammered tight into a socket. Using all her strength, she tried to lift one after the other, but though she made a complete circuit of the room, she found none that would yield.

The door was locked; she looked through a keyhole, but could see nothing. And then her exertions, on top of the drug, produced the inevitable result. She felt her knees give way, and had just sufficient presence of mind to lower herself to the ground before she again lost consciousness. She woke feeling cold and stiff, but the headache had almost gone, and she retraced her steps to where the water was.

She managed to find a light in the room where she had been when she first woke. This proved a bare apartment except for the mattress on the floor and a broken chair. By dint of tugging she managed to get a stout rail loose; it was her only weapon, and would be of little service if she attempted to use it in her present weak state. But it was something; it lent her a little more confidence. By degrees she managed to pull the remainder of the chair to pieces, until she got a stout leg and a portion of the back, and with this she attacked the bars of the shutters, but without result.

Hungry and weary, she lay down on the bed, pulled the blanket over her, and fell asleep almost immediately. When she woke, it seemed warmer, and her hunger had subsided to a numb, gnawing pain. She sat on the bed, trying to think. And then she heard the sound of a voice. A man was speaking. Was it Martin? No, it was too deep for him. She crept to the door and listened; and as she did so, she heard a stealthy footstep on the stair just outside the door.

Who was it? Her heart beat tumultuously. The voice from below came again, and, hearing it, she almost swooned.

It was Lacy Marshalt! She put her hand to her mouth to arrest the scream. Lacy Marshalt, and he was talking.

"Yes, it was somewhere here…"

She was going mad – she must be. Mad already! Somewhere below was Lacy Marshalt, and Lacy Marshalt was dead!

And then as she stood, frozen with horror, the footstep sounded again inside, and, crouching down, she looked through. A faint light illuminated the staircase, and she saw the figure of a man, but his face was turned away.

"It was somewhere here," said Marshalt's faint voice again.

The man on the landing was listening as intently as she. While she looked, he turned his head. She saw the long nose, the pointed chin and the high, bumpy forehead. Malpas! When she looked again, he was gone.

Malpas and Marshalt! What did it mean? Her limbs were trembling; she had to use the wall as a support as she crawled back to her room. She was not in Curzon Street at all: she was in the hands of

317

the devil-man! The horror of it seized her, and for a second her reason rocked. And then somebody rapped softly on the passage door.

She held her breath and waited, her eyes fixed on the place where the terror would appear.

THE MAN ON THE LANDING

The tapping was resumed after an interval. Audrey kept quiet, scarcely daring to flicker an eyelash. Did he know she was there? The thought occurred to her at that moment that Dora and her husband must be in the secret of this awful house.

Again came that dreadful tapping, and then silence. She waited for half an hour before she dared move. There was no noise; the house was as still as the grave; no sound of voice or footstep came up to her as she listened at the door, and she went back to where she had been, only to start up again at the sound of a key turning in the lock. From where she sat she could only see the wall of the passage. Something rattled, and then the door closed again.

Was he waiting in the passage for her? Her heart fluttered at the thought, and then the absurdity of the idea occurred to her. Why should he wait in the passage? Nevertheless, she had to summon all her courage to look out, and when she did, she could have cried for joy, for on the floor was a tray, holding a hot coffee pot, rolls, bread and butter, and thick slices of cold meat. She carried the tray into her room, and ate cautiously. How hungry she was, she only began to realize now; and it was not until most of the viands had disappeared, and she had drunk her third cup of coffee, that she stopped to regret that she had not looked round the corner when the man was still in the passage.

But perhaps it was Dora. No appeal could be made there, she thought. Neither did her hope lie with Martin, if hope there was.

And now she could think clearly and logically. Why had they done this? What was gained for Dora or her husband by this senseless act? That Dora hated her she knew; she would go a long way to hurt her, she was just as sure. But Dora would hurt nobody unless she profited herself, and what profit there was in shutting her up in Malpas' house, she couldn't understand. But she *was* in Malpas' house; that made her serious again.

She turned on all the switches she could find; the light, like the running water, gave her a sense of company. When would the next meal come, she wondered. Should she make an attempt to see the man or woman who brought it? Several times she made a journey to the door to listen, but the stillness was unbroken.

It was on her seventh visit to the door that the scarcely audible sound of somebody descending the stars reached her. She knelt on the floor, her eyes on the rather large keyhole, and presently she was rewarded. Something dark passed before the door and stopped on the broad landing. She saw him clearly now, or as plainly as the dim light permitted. He wore a long coat that reached to his heels; his head was covered with a black slouch hat. For a moment he stood there in a listening attitude, then he put out his hand, and a part of the wall opened – a door, scarcely more than six inches square, so well camouflaged by the design of the paper that covered the wall that Dick Shannon had passed it a dozen times without detecting its presence.

She looked, fascinated, as his hand went into the opening. She saw a flash of blue flame, and the lights in the passage went out. Then he turned. He was coming toward the door. She told herself he would pass and go upstairs again, but, even as she looked, she saw the end of the key coming into the hole, and, turning, she ran, screaming, down the passage and slammed the door of her room tight, and stood with her back against it…the outer lock clicked open…

DORA WILL NOT TELL

Dick Shannon returned to his flat at four o'clock in the morning, having escorted Lacy Marshalt back to his house, and witnessed the embarrassment of Mr Stanford at the sudden apparition.

He found two men in his sitting-room, one a sleepy-eyed but dogged William, the other –

"Why, Mr Torrington, you're the last person in the world I expected to see!"

The man was changed, his tone of light banter had gone. Dick recognized this the moment he spoke.

"I want to see you pretty badly. My daughter has disappeared."

"Your – ?"

"My daughter – Audrey. You didn't know that she was my girl? I can't go into the story now, but Audrey Bedford is Audrey Torrington, the child of my second wife."

Dick was looking at him through a haze.

"I'm dumbfounded," he said. "Audrey...she has disappeared, you say? But she has been staying at your hotel?"

"She went out last night and didn't come back. I let her go out because I had arranged to meet Martin Elton, who had something to tell me – something which I knew and something which I guessed."

Briefly he narrated all that had passed at the interview with Martin.

"Unfortunately for him, I knew all the facts and guessed what he was driving at before he'd finished; and I left orders that Audrey should be told I wanted to see her when she returned. At eleven o'clock she had not come in; at midnight, when I sent to inquire, thinking she might have gone to a dance, she was still out. Knowing that young girls nowadays keep up until all hours, I wasn't alarmed, till one o'clock came and then two. Then I communicated with headquarters; they told me you were out and that you would be notified as soon as you returned. I couldn't wait any longer, so I came here."

"Where did she go?" asked Dick.

Mr Torrington shook his head.

"I don't know. She merely said she was going out; she told nobody where. I haven't, of course, searched her room – I didn't want to take that course until I was sure."

"We'll search it now," said Dick, and drove him back to the hotel.

The night porter who opened the door to them had no news.

"The young lady hasn't come back yet, sir," he reported.

He took them up in the elevator to her room, and opened the door for them. The bed had not been slept in; her nightdress had been laid across the turned-down sheet; a glass of milk stood on the side table. Dick saw a well-worn writing case by its side, and this he opened, examining the letters quickly. There was none which gave him the slightest hint of her destination, until he saw, in the microscopic wastepaper basket with which hotels supply their guests, the torn-up fragments of a letter. Tipping the basket on to the table, he began to put the pieces together.

"This is from Mrs Elton, it was written today."

Presently he had it complete. It was a note telling her to come early, and there was a significant PS:

Please burn this letter. I hate to think that my letters are lying around, especially in a hotel, where everybody sees them.

"I will see Elton. You needn't come, Mr Torrington," said Dick quietly.

The old man demurred, but presently saw the wisdom of this course, and left Dick to go alone.

The Elton house was in darkness, but he had not to wait long before he saw a light appear in the passage. It was Martin Elton; he was in his dressing-gown, and might have just come out of bed but for the telltale evidence of cigar ash on the front of the gown.

"Hallo, Shannon! Come in. You're rather an early caller," he said as he closed the door.

"Is your wife up?"

"I don't know — I'll see. Do you want her?"

"I want you both," said Dick.

When a police officer speaks in the tone that Dick Shannon employed, there is very little ultimate profit in argument.

Dora came down in a *négligé* within a few minutes of his arrival.

"Do you wish to see me, Captain Shannon?"

"I want Dorothy Audrey Torrington," he said.

"I don't — " she began.

"You don't know what I mean, of course. Now listen, Mrs Elton. Your sister came here to dinner at your invitation. You sent her a letter which you asked her to burn, but which she did not burn, but tore up. She arrived at this house somewhere about six o'clock." And then, as a thought struck him: "Let me see your maid."

"My dear Captain Shannon, what use can the maid be? I will tell you all I know. I don't want the servants brought into this," said Dora tartly.

"Go and bring her down."

Martin went upstairs to the top floor of the house, knocked at the door, and was almost staggered when the door opened immediately and the maid came out, fully dressed, and wearing an overcoat.

"What the – ?" he began, and she laughed.

"What do you want, Mr Elton?"

"Captain Shannon wishes to speak to you," said Martin, recovering from his surprise. "He is inquiring about madam's sister. You know, she dined here tonight, and you'd better tell Shannon that you were here all the time, and you remember her going."

She made no reply.

"Here is the girl," he said as he brought the servant into the room, and Dora glared at her.

"Why are you dressed like that?" she asked angrily.

"Because I always dress like that when I'm going out," said the girl.

She was a red-faced, healthy-looking young woman, somewhat stocky of build.

"Now, my girl," said Shannon, "Miss Audrey Torrington – or as you know her, Miss Bedford – was dining here tonight, I believe?"

"I believe she was, sir. I wasn't in the house when she arrived, and I didn't see her go. Mrs Elton sent me out to the theatre, and dismissed the cook an hour before Miss Bedford arrived, so that there were only three people in the house – Mr and Mrs Elton and Miss Bedford."

"I was not here at all," said Martin, in a rage. "I was at my club!"

"You were in the house, upstairs," said the girl calmly. "I didn't see Miss Bedford go, because I was at the other end of the street, talking to one of our men. I saw a cab drive away, and by the time I got to the house I think Miss Bedford really had gone."

"One of your men? What do you mean?" asked Dick.

She made no answer, but produced from her pocket a small, five-pointed silver star.

"I'm one of Stormer's people," she said, and seeing the dismay in Dora's face: "So was your previous servant, Mrs Elton. I have been waiting for you. I expected you would come." She was talking to Dick Shannon. "The only thing I can tell you is that Miss Bedford is not in this house; I've searched it from garret to cellar."

Martin Elton's face was ghastly; it was his wife who fought to the last.

"How very romantic!" she sneered. "A woman detective! You were a pretty bad housemaid."

The girl interrupted her.

"I cleared the table" – she was still talking to Shannon – "and I put what remained in Miss Bedford's glass into this." She brought out a tiny medicine phial from her pocket; there was just sufficient wine to cover the bottom. "And this I found in Mrs Elton's jewel-box later in the evening."

324

Dora made a snatch at the little blue bottle she held, but the girl was too quick for her. Pushing her aside without an effort, she placed it in Dick's hand.

"I think you'll find it is butyl chloride. There is no label; that was washed off. But it smells like butyl."

Shannon's face was hard and set; his eyes fixed Elton's with a snaky glitter.

"You've heard what this lady said, Elton. Where is Audrey?"

"You want to know?" Martin answered him. "Well, I can tell you, but you've got to pay — no, not money I mean. I want twenty-four hours for Dora and me to get out of the country. Let me have that, and I'll tell you where she is. And you'd better pay the price, Shannon," he said meaningly. "She is in greater danger than you'll ever guess. Will you promise?"

"I'll promise you nothing," said Shannon. "Not to save Audrey's life would I let you loose! Where is she?"

"Find out!" cried Dora defiantly. "If this woman 'busy' knows so much, maybe she'll tell you some more."

Dick said nothing further. From his hip pocket he drew a steel bracelet and snapped it on Martin's wrist, and he made no attempt to escape, though, as the steel touched his flesh, his face went suddenly old. Perhaps the ghosts of his dead boyhood had arisen; the calm of cloistered walks; the green of playing fields; the tradition up to which he once strove to live.

"You'll not handcuff me!" screamed Dora as he gripped her arm. "You shan't! you shan't!"

But the woman from Stormer's slipped behind her and caught both her arms. In another second she was linked by a more material bond than that which bound her to the man by her side.

STANFORD

Dick took them to the station and ordered their detention. He could not charge either until he was certain. As he was coming down the steps, he asked the girl from Stormer's a question he had forgotten to put to her.

"Has he had any visitors lately?"

"Yes – Stanford. They had a row about something. I couldn't quite gather what it was – something about a plan, but I couldn't hear very well. Mrs Elton was standing so near the door that I dared not listen."

"Do you think Stanford is in this?"

She shook her head.

"It is difficult to say. I've an idea that they were bad friends. I heard Elton shouting over the phone to Stanford, and by his replies I gather that there was a row of some kind."

"I saw Stanford tonight," said Dick Shannon thoughtfully, "and he certainly did not seem to have anything on his conscience." He held out his hand. "I do not approve of private detectives," he said with a faint smile, "but I'm beginning to become reconciled to Stormer's!"

He thought at first that he would return to the hotel to tell Torrington what had happened, but instead he briefly explained over the phone, and, promising to call later, he went on to Portman Square. If any spot in London had earned his undying hatred, that agglomeration of stately houses certainly had. He knocked and rang, and knocked again. It was ten minutes before he made anybody hear, and then it was Stanford himself who opened the door. At the sight of the detective an uneasy look came to his face. Dick could have sworn that he was trembling.

"Where is Miss Bedford?" asked the detective without preliminary. "And consider well before you reply, Stanford. I've just taken Elton and his wife and put them inside, and there's a hell of a cosy cell on the same row that you'd just fit!"

The man stared at him stupidly; he seemed at a loss to find words to reply.

"I don't know what you mean about Audrey Bedford," he said at last. "How should I know? I've been here all evening; you saw me here yourself. She wouldn't come to this house, anyway." And then, as though divining that Shannon had no exact information, he went on more boldly: "What has Martin Elton to do with me? I quarrelled with him – you ought to know that. I had a row with him about some stuff of mine that he lost."

A voice came from the top of the stairs.

"Who is that?"

"It is Shannon," growled the man, and Marshalt came downstairs, fastening his dressing-gown.

"Did you want to see me, Shannon?"

"I called to see Stanford. Audrey Bedford disappeared last night, after dining with her sister at Curzon Street. There is evidence that she was drugged and taken away in a cab somewhere. There is every reason to believe that this man knows all about it."

"I know nothing," said Stanford doggedly.

"Come up to my room," interrupted Marshalt.

The three went up to the study, and Marshalt put on the lights.

"Now, let me hear this."

"You've heard all you're likely to hear, Marshalt," said Stanford roughly. "This 'busy' has nothing on me. I have got a clean record, and he can't bluff me into confessing up to something I didn't do."

"If it comes to a question of pulling in, I've got you!" said Dick. "Two nights ago we found certain things in the interior of an idol in Malpas' house – more uncut diamonds than I've ever seen before. Before we could remove them, something happened. The diamonds disappeared. Five minutes later the lights went out again; somebody had blundered, and we found them all in a big brown grip, that has since been recovered."

Marshalt's face was a study.

"Diamonds…in an idol!" He turned slowly to Stanford. "What do you know about that, Stanford?"

"Nothing!" snapped the man.

"Maybe you know nothing about the bag they were packed in – a new bag, bought from Waller's, of Regent Street, the same afternoon – bought by you!" Dick's accusing finger pointed at the man. "Waller identified you tonight. We've had him on the phone at his house at Eltham. He remembers selling the bag; it was soiled inside, and he sold it cheaply. And the man he sold it to was you!"

Stanford did not reply. He stood, one arm resting on the marble mantelpiece, looking down into the big empty grate.

"Did you hear what Captain Shannon said?" Marshalt asked sharply.

"I heard. I've nothing to say."

"Where is Audrey Bedford?"

"I've nothing to say," said Stanford. "You can pull me in if you want. And as for the bag, why, you're in dreamland! I've never bought a bag in my life. I steal all my grips!"

"Do you know Slick Smith?"

"I've seen him," said the other sulkily. Then, in a sudden rage: "If you want to take me, I'll go. If you're bluffing, I'll call your bluff!"

Dick shook his head.

"I'll not take you now. I'm going to have that bag question thoroughly threshed out tomorrow. You can be where I can get you, and if I find that you're concerned in this abduction, you will be too sick to be sorry!"

Short a distance as it was, Dick Shannon fell asleep between Portman Square and the Ritz-Carlton, and had to be wakened by the cabman.

"You're all in," said Torrington when he saw the detective, and then anxiously: "Do you think those people really know? They are not lying?"

"You mean the Eltons? Yes, they know." Torrington paced his sitting-room. "Could I see them?" he asked.

Dick hesitated.

"They are under arrest, of course?"

"Technically, they're detained. I've not charged them yet," said Shannon. "There is no reason why you shouldn't see them."

He did not ask Audrey's father why he wished to interview the Eltons. He knew, and yet did not want to know. The information he had failed to secure by threats Torrington would obtain with money.

"Can you get them out? I know I'm asking something that you hate to do, and I know, Shannon, that there is nobody in the world to whom Audrey's safety means more than it does to you."

The struggle in Dick Shannon's mind was short.

"Come with me," he said, and they returned to the police station.

To the station sergeant:

"You can release those people I've detained," he said. "If I want them I know where to find them."

He left the station premises before Elton and his wife had appeared and walked wearily up the stairs to his flat as the clock was striking five.

The faithful William was waiting.

"Get the alarm clock and set it for nine. You needn't bother to get up," said Dick.

He kicked off his shoes and his collar, and putting the clock on a chair within a few inches of his head, he lay down on his bed fully dressed and was asleep in a second.

At nine o'clock he woke to the sound of a musical earthquake, and went, half asleep, to his shower, and even the icy cold water did not have its usual effect, for he nodded as he stood. He might have gone to sleep on his feet if William, peeping in at the door, had not brought him to his senses.

"You'd get a better shower, sir, if you took your clothes off," said William respectfully.

Dick woke with a start, to find himself clad and saturated. He had a hasty breakfast between telephone calls. Torrington had not returned to his hotel, and the watchers in Doughty Street had seen no sign of Slick Smith; which fact did not bother Dick. If they would only leave Slick Smith alone.

He had rung the bell for William to clear away when Torrington appeared.

"I tried every inducement with them," he said, sitting down wearily, "and the man is willing to help me. But the woman!"

"She dominates him, eh? Do you think they know?"

"They know all right," said old Torrington drearily. "Her hatred is terrible to see. It is as though all the loathing which her mother developed for me had been inherited and passed on to poor Audrey. I offered them money – I offered them what was tantamount to safety," he added frankly, "though I knew you wouldn't approve of this. I said I'd give them enough to live luxuriously for the rest of their lives, and put an aeroplane at their disposal this morning to carry them to France. But nothing I said could shake her. The man is at the end of his tether, but Dora seems to grow in strength as her position grows in danger. Stanford knows."

"Have you see him? What makes you say he knows?"

"Elton let it out by accident. Just the first syllable of the name, but I am sure he is in it."

"I'll see him again," said Dick. "I have to go again this morning. I am taking Lacy Marshalt into Malpas' house to see what I can get from him first-hand."

"You wouldn't like me to come?" asked the old man anxiously.

"I'd like you to sleep," said Dick, putting his hand on Torrington's shoulder. "I can stand this a little better than you."

Torrington shook his head.

"I couldn't sleep. Old people require less than others. Do you mind if I wait here? I can't bear to go back to the hotel."

Dick's cab had scarcely disappeared round the corner when there stepped from the shelter of an all-night druggist's almost opposite the man who had been an interested spectator of his departure.

"Atta!" said Slick Smith.

He, too, would have given a thousand dollars for ten hours' sleep.

BY THE BACK WAY

Slick Smith had to exercise unusual caution. He knew that every plain clothes officer in London was on the lookout for him, and he was not the type on whom a false beard sat with any dignity.

The weather was in his favour; the rain continued and continued and still continued. Mr Smith inwardly blessed the inclement elements; they gave him an excuse to walk under the very noses of men who were watching for him. He pulled down the brim of his soft felt hat, turned up his collar to his eyes, and crossed the road.

Taxicabs are scarce on rainy days, for what the drivers call the "amateur riders" dig up their pennies and indulge in orgies of locomotion of which they would not dream on other occasions. But luck was with him; he found a fast brand of taxi disengaged.

"Pick up that long yellow car. You'll overhaul it in the traffic of Regent Street. Keep it in sight," he said, and was, in fact, on Dick's trail before he was clear of the block which accumulates even in the early hours of the morning on Oxford Circus.

As the crook suspected, Shannon was making for Marshalt's house. When he was sure on this subject, he varied his directions, and was dropped within fifty yards of the square, at a point beyond observation. The mews at this hour of the morning was filled with noise, for the chauffeurs were tuning up in their garages, and one or two trolleys, less delicately constituted, were being prepared for the day's work in the open.

All the men were sufficiently engaged in their own business to be incurious, and they did not notice the stocky man who strolled aimlessly along the wall separating the courtyard at the back of the square; nor did they see him dive through the door that brought him to the back of Malpas' house. And if they had, so many strange men had loafed about the mews these days that they would have marked him down as a detective, and taken no further notice, for interest in the Portman Square murder had almost evaporated.

Dick, neither knowing that he was being followed, nor caring, was shown in by one of the maids, and immediately taken up to the study, where Mr Marshalt sat alone, gloom on his face, which was not dispelled by the announcement of his visitor.

"I want to see Stanford, Mr Marshalt, but in the meantime I'd like you to accompany me to this house of mystery and tell me just what happened to you."

The man got up with some reluctance.

"I hate the place," he said testily, "but it is due to you that you should know just what happened. Can you get in?"

"I have a key, if the controls are off."

He explained the system under which the doors were opened and closed.

"I guessed that, of course, when I went there," nodded Marshalt. "In fact, I've had the system offered to me, but rejected it. It would be very awkward if the current failed."

"The current will fail this afternoon," said Shannon. "I'm arranging to have it cut off at the main. Will you come now, or would you rather wait until you've had your breakfast? I'm in no hurry."

"I'll come now," said Marshalt, rising.

He went down with the detective, put on his macintosh, and they left for the house together. The key turned in the lock of Malpas' front door and it opened. Dick saw a wedge of wood lying in the hall, and kicked its thin edge under the open door, Marshalt watching interestedly.

"You would like me to tell you just what happened on the night I was shot? I came in here," he said, "and, as you know, there was nobody to receive me."

He led the way up the stairs, talking all the time. On the landing he stopped.

"I was somewhere about here when the voice bade me come in. I think I said I was at the bottom of the stairs – no, I am more correct in saying that I was somewhere here."

They went into the long room and Dick pulled open the curtain. "Now, will you describe to me where Malpas stood when he fired? Place yourself in that position, Mr Marshalt."

Lacy walked to the end of the room until his back was to the hidden statue.

"He was here," he said, "and I was where you are standing."

"The whole thing is perfectly clear to me." Dick was speaking very deliberately. "I think I had the solution a week ago – it's – "

Bang! The door had closed.

"What was that?" asked Lacy, startled.

Shannon didn't turn a hair. He was inured to these happenings.

"Look as though the door's closed on us."

He strolled across and tried to pull it open, but without success. Then: "Where is Stanford?"

"He's in my house somewhere," said Marshalt slowly. "Who did that?"

"That is what I am going to find out – today," said Shannon, "and you will help me. And there goes the door!"

It was opening slowly.

"That's queer," muttered Marshalt.

He walked quickly from the room and looked over the banisters.

"That is very queer! But you told me about an idol – where is that?"

Dick went back with him into the room and pulled aside the curtains, and started back with a cry. The idol was there – and something else. Lying limp across the black marble pedestal, his head hanging down on one side, his feet on the other, was Big Bill Stanford!

THE LAST VICTIM

Dick jumped forward and made a quick examination.

"He's not dead," he said, "but he soon will be unless we get help. Will you run back to your house and phone the Middlesex to send an ambulance? This telephone isn't working," he said as he saw Lacy looking at the instrument on the table.

After he had gone, Shannon made a quick examination of Stanford's injuries. There were three bullet wounds, one through the shoulder, one that had its entrance under the heart, a third that had ripped the neck. The man was unconscious, and might or might not be dying. Shannon examined the pedestal: it was thick with blood, and he had hardly finished his inspection, and stanched the flow that was coming from the shoulder wound, when the shrill bell of the ambulance sounded in the street below, and in a few moments the white-coated attendants were lifting the unconscious figure to the stretcher.

"How did it happen?" asked Marshalt with a perplexed frown. "I left him in my storeroom – the place where I keep odd things. The truth is, I'd had a few sharp words with him. I'm not satisfied that he knew nothing about Audrey Bedford, and I told him so, and he answered me to the effect that he was leaving the house. I'm perfectly satisfied that he was killed there after you and I came out. It is terrible, terrible! What is this man Malpas? He must be a fiend incarnate!"

"You are safe in saying he's that," said Dick. He looked thoughtfully at the door. "I'm so tired of searching this house after these kind of happenings that I don't think I'll trouble again. Stanford wore no collar and tie. Did you notice that?"

"Yes; I thought that was strange. When I saw him he wore both."

"Just show me where he was," said Dick, and they came out together and into the house next door.

The first thing he saw, hanging on a peg in the storeroom, was a collar and tie.

Shannon saw one of the two remaining maids. Stanford had been seen that morning; the girl who had let Dick in said that she had seen him in the storeroom from five minutes to a quarter of an hour before the detective's arrival, and that was the total extent of the information he was able to get. The man had occupied Marshalt's room until the owner of the house had returned, and he had shifted his things up to the suite which had been occupied by Tonger in his lifetime.

The commissioner had seen these apartments before, and he found nothing now that helped him in any way. Stanford's meagre baggage contained only a few articles of clothing, a Continental time table, and a few toilet necessities.

Dick came down again, bitterly disappointed, for there was nothing in his hand that brought him any nearer to the mystery of Audrey Bedford's disappearance.

He had sent Steel to the bedside of the wounded man, with instructions that he was to remain there until he was relieved, and check any statement the wounded man made, either in his delirium or upon recovering consciousness, a contingency for which the hospital authorities were not prepared. As soon as he had made his report, he drove to the Middlesex Hospital, and was admitted into the private ward to which Stanford had been taken. Steel was standing beside the bed, looking down at the unconscious man.

"He knows where that girl is," said the sergeant.

"Has he talked?" asked Dick quickly.

"Only in his sleep; when they were giving him an anaesthetic before probing down after the bullet, he cried out, 'I won't tell you where she is!' "

"That's not much; he probably thought he was speaking to me. There's nothing to be gained here."

He stood indecisively on the steps of the Middlesex Hospital, with the sense of being a beaten man, wondering which way he should turn next. He could not believe that she was in Lacy's house – it was impossible that she should be taken to the house of mystery, every room of which was open to search. So he argued, and precisely at that minute Audrey Bedford was running, screaming, down the passage, and behind her the sinister figure of Mr Malpas.

THE PIVOT WALL

For a long time after Dick Shannon's departure Lacy Marshalt sat at his desk, his head in his hands. Presently he leaned back and pushed a bell. One of the maids answered after a long delay.

"Who else is in the house?" he asked sharply.

"Milly, sir."

"Tell her to come here."

From his pocket he took a crumpled handful of notes and Treasury bills, selected a few and smoothed them out. By the time the girls returned there were two little heaps before them.

"There is your salary and a month in lieu of notice. I am shutting up the house and going abroad."

"When do you want us to go, sir?" asked one of the girls in surprise.

"I want you to go at once. I intend to leave in half an hour." He himself watched from the head of the stairs while their luggage was being removed, and at last saw their cab pass out of sight. Then he walked down, put the chains on the door, double-locked and bolted it, and returned at his leisure to the study. His face was set in a smile from which all humour had vanished. He was thinking of the man who had tried to rob him once, and would have betrayed him, the man who, with a belated return to decency, had refused to speak until...

For half an hour he gave himself up to his thoughts. Lacy Marshalt was something of a dreamer. The tinkle of the doorbell, followed by a thunderous knock, aroused him. He walked to the window and peeped out. On the doorstep were Elton and his wife. And Torrington – yes, he recognized Torrington, though he had not see him in years. An inspector of police and four men, who were obviously detectives.

He took his letter case from his pocket, extracted a flat handle and a bodkin, and fitted the one into the other. Then he walked to the mantelpiece and thrust the bodkin deep amidst the wood foliage that framed the fireplace. He turned his wrist, and, without a sound, mantelpiece and fireplace swung round on a central pivot. He had the profile of the huge idol to the right, the fireplace in section to the left. Then, opening the bottom drawer of his desk, he lifted a false bottom and took out a little box, and for a second busied himself. A half-wig, a long, pendulous nose, a pointed chin, so perfectly coloured to his face that even an expert would not know where nature began and art commenced – he fixed them with deft fingers.

Then he turned the bodkin again and the mantelpiece swung back to its place. The knocking on the door was continuous, and presently he heard the smash of glass. He had taken the key out, and that would not help them, he thought. Stepping inside the semicircular fender, he pushed the bodkin home and turned again, this time to the left.

As the hearth and wall swung round, he put down his foot to ease the little shock which came when the fireplace came to rest. Once a clumsy Tonger had let it stop with such a jerk that a hot coal had been flung out into the Malpas room. Again the bodkin came into use, and, standing aside, he saw the fireplace turn back to its proper position. He unfitted the steel blade with curious deliberation, replaced it in his pocket, and then went up the stairs very slowly.

Audrey Bedford was there. Reluctantly, painfully, Stanford had told him. And now all that began this tragedy which had overtaken him, and had robbed him not only of the fortune he had accumulated, but promised to rob him of life itself, was to end as it began – with Audrey Bedford!

He paused at every landing to anticipate his grim final triumph over the hounds of the law, who were baying at his door, eager to seize him and to drag him to that dreadful dock, where the red-robed, white-haired man gave judgment of death. Lacy's smile was fixed: it had become frozen on his face. All his plannings…his strivings, his clever manoeuvres –

And then he remembered something that struck away the smile. Why had the door controls operated while he was with Dick Shannon? Was there a reason for that? He shrugged. The climate – a score and one things might affect an electric connection…

Now he was outside the door and bent his head, listening. He heard a light footstep in the passage and smiled again. Half the fierce joy that came to his heart was in the anticipation of the terror his appearance would strike when her fearful eyes met his.

He opened the little cupboard in the stairs and turned a switch, and knew that at that moment the lights had gone out in the empty room through which he would soon be passing in search of his prey. He needed no light, not even the trick lamp he had carried to illuminate his face, to terrify all who saw him. The darkness belonged to him, and to her.

He turned the key. As he did so, he heard her light steps fly along the passage, heard her babble something, and the slam of a door. In another second he was inside; the key was pushed into the lock and turned. He was alone with her.

His sensitive hands touched the wall. Slowly he crept along until he reached the first door and opened it. He could hear no sound of breathing, but he must be sure. Round the walls he went, across the centre, his arms outstretched, and again reached the passage. A second room – this was where she had been. He felt the bed with his foot, but heard no sound, and again made a circuit of the room. He stopped at the opening of the third room and listened. She was there! He sensed the presence, heard somebody breathing.

"Come here, my little dear. You can't get away from me this time! We have an appointment; it has been a long time delayed, but you must keep it today!"

He heard the sound of feet on the floor, and somebody slipped past him; but he was too quick, and again stood in the entrance.

"Your lover is downstairs, my beloved – the dunderheaded Shannon and his confederacy! And your father! You didn't know you had a father, but he's there. He'll see you…later. You and I are going out together. That's a good end for the man he hates, but he'll find no joy in it."

Suddenly he lunged forward and caught an arm. It was not the arm he expected. As he stood, a strange and terrifying green light showed level with his breast. He was looking into his own face – nose, chin, head!

Another Malpas – fearful, monstrous – had him by the arms.

"God! What is it?" he screamed, and tried to get himself free.

"I want you," said the hollow voice.

With a yell, Lacy Marshalt struck at the hideous figure, and, turning, ran. As he did so the lights came on, and, looking back, he saw a replica of himself! Malpas! But he was Malpas!

"Damn you!" he sobbed, and pulled his gun.

The automatic spat once, twice.

"Save yourself a whole lot of trouble, my friend," said his double. "Your cartridges are blank – I changed them nearly a day ago!"

With a howl of fury, Lacy flung the pistol at him. The man ducked, and the next minute had Marshalt by the throat.

And somewhere in the dark background stood Audrey, her hands clasped in an agony of fear, yet in her heart a newborn life.

THE DOUBLE

Dick had joined the group at the door, and now the knocking had ceased. A requisitioned jemmy had been forced between the lock, and the lock was creaking loose as the last blows were being hammered home.

"She is here – you're sure?"

Martin nodded.

"Stanford took her away last night. He said he would get her into Malpas' house."

Shannon had already tried the front door of 551, but the controls were on.

"Do you know what has happened to Stanford?"

"I've just learnt," said Elton in a low voice.

At that moment the lock broke and they poured into the hall. Dick led the way upstairs. The study was empty, and this time he went straight to the fireplace and began looking for the aperture which he knew existed there somewhere. The way in that must be through the fireplace and nowhere else.

Presently he found the hole, fitted poor Tonger's homemade bodkin, and the triangular sides gripped on the sensitive mechanism. As he turned the handle, the fireplace swung, and those who stood behind him had a clear view past the statue of Malpas' room.

"Don't touch that handle," he warned them, and ran across the gap, stopping only at the table to switch over the controls.

He was dashing through the open door when he heard the two shots fired. Dick stopped, his face as white as death. Only for a

342

moment did he pause, and then went on. Fast as he ran, it seemed to him that his feet were leaden.

As he reached the door it was flung open. Two men came out – two men so identically alike that he stared from one to the other.

"Here's your bird, Captain Shannon," said the shorter of the two, and flung the handcuffed prisoner into the hands of the waiting detectives.

Then, with one sweep, he removed wig, nose, and chin.

"I think you know me?"

"I know you very well," said Dick. "You are Slick Stormer – or, as you prefer to be known to the London police, Slick Smith!"

"Got me the first time – but when did you recognize me?"

Dick smiled.

"A clever detective like you ought to know," he said.

Dick saw somebody else in the passage, a timorous somebody who kept as far away as possible. In another minute he had raced down the corridor and had caught her in his arms.

Slick took a quick glance and closed the door.

"Maybe you'd like to see your daughter, and she'll be glad to see you, but she knows this fellow better than you, I guess," he said, and Torrington nodded...

WHAT SLICK SAID

"I've never been quite sure whether you took me at my own valuation, or whether you were one of these reserved Englishmen who believe nothing very much, and only then to oblige a lady," said Slick Smith, a magnificent host, sitting at the head of a dinner table that night.

"I came into this case nineteen months ago, when I had a letter from Mr Torrington, giving me all the facts he possessed, and asking me whether I could trace his wife and verify the story of his daughter's death. Incidentally, he told me a great deal about Mr Lacy Marshalt that interested me both as a detective and a human being.

"I've got some experience of the unpopularity of private detective services, especially in England, where they are regarded as a joke, and a joke in bad taste at that. And I knew that, if I was going to do any good in this business, it was vitally necessary that I should pass into the underworld with the necessary credentials. I therefore communicated with Captain Shannon, in my capacity as Stormer, telling him that a notorious American crook was expected to arrive in England almost any minute, and favoured him with a very vivid description of what this hideous scoundrel looked like. I got the usual warm-hearted 'Your communication shall receive our attention' from headquarters, but I happen to know that, the moment Slick landed, he was picked up, trailed to London, warned, cautioned – in fact, all the things happened to him that usually happen to the imported article.

"Fortunately, very few people in London know me. I've always made it a rule, since I established my agency in London, to come into

344

no case personally, and only three or four of my best staff would be able to identify me on oath. But those three or four are mighty useful, for they not only can identify me, but they *can't* identify me, and that is valuable!

"Another important advantage was that, as Slick Smith, I could always have one of my men with me without attracting the suspicion of the criminal classes. You remember I was invariably trailed by one of Stormer's men – he'd have lost his job if he hadn't!

"My other job was to discover the whereabouts of a very large number of diamonds which had been stolen from Mr Torrington's mine in the past few years, and which both his police and the South African force were certain had been brought to England. And I was able to unearth a very considerable traffic. In South Africa, as you know, Captain Shannon, it is a penal offence to be found in possession of a diamond, unless you can account for it to the satisfaction of a magistrate – I'm talking about uncut diamonds now. For years Lacy Marshalt has been such a trafficker. He was engaged that way when he was acting as detective for the Streams Mining Corporation, and when he framed up a charge that sent Mr Torrington to the Breakwater. He's been that way ever since. But the trading of diamonds in South Africa is a dangerous game, both for the seller and the buyer; and he hit upon the idea of coming to London, establishing himself in a big house, and arranging a regular courier service to bring the stones over. But obviously he couldn't do this as Marshalt, because, sooner or later, somebody was going to squeal. And the day the squeal went up to heaven, Lacy Marshalt, who in the meantime had scraped into the South African Parliament, and had been scraped out again when the electors came to their senses, would go down to the dark hulks where the bad men go.

"He bought the two houses in Portman Square at a time of great depression in house property, and they were bought in different names. No. 551 was purchased through a bank. Engaging a good Continental firm to fix the electrical fittings, he left the principal, and to my mind the cleverest, piece of mechanism to the last.

"Lacy Marshalt is an engineer. He is one of those people you read about every day, who might, had he chosen an honest path, have made a fortune, not that they ever would, but judges have those illusions.

"The control was too fiddling a job and too much like hard work for Lacy. The fireplace and statue were a labour of love. The statue he bought in Durban: I traced it nearly a year ago, and knew all about its mechanical thorax. But the pivot opening was entirely his own. He lived alone in his house – Tonger at that time was still in South Africa, acting as his agent – for four months before the work was completed, and then he brought his man home. And just before he came, Malpas appeared in the London directory. Malpas, the buyer of diamonds who could never be caught!

"Tonger is the real tragedy of this story. He married rather late in life a youngish woman who died and left him with a daughter of whom he thought the world; and it was real bad luck for Tonger to have her come into contact with Lacy Marshalt. You'd think that Tonger, being his friend and helper, would make a difference. No, sir! Nothing ever made a difference to Lacy, and when the inevitable happened, and Tonger wanted to know certain things, Lacy seized on the arrest of Torrington as a heaven-sent opportunity for shifting the blame, persuaded the girl to name Torrington as her lover, and got her away to America, where he allowed her a reasonable sum a week, threatening that, unless she did as he wished, which was to write to her father regularly and tell him how happy she was, he would stop the allowance and ruin Tonger, who as she believed held some responsible position in Marshalt's office.

"New York is no worse a place for a woman than any other big city: that is my experience," said Slick thoughtfully. "I guess the same old devil perches on the top of the London Monument as sits on the fifty-fourth floor of the Woolworth building. The girl went her own way – drank a lot, got into debt, but dared not tell Lacy. Then one day, in a panic, she jumped the boat and came to London. I think you saw her that day you had your first interview with friend Malpas?"

Audrey nodded.

"She was the woman who knocked at Marshalt's door."

"Yuh! Poor Tonger must have nearly died when he saw her. At any rate, as I have reconstructed the matter, he took her in, hurried her up to his apartments and kept her there for days probably trying his best to induce her to tell him the truth – he may already have guessed it. Then one day Lacy found out she was in the house, and knew that, once Tonger got on his track, he was doomed.

"He decided to act then and there. Tonger was sent to Paris with a letter that meant nothing – I've seen it. It was to a man who did business for Marshalt. While he was away Marshalt got the girl out of the room, and probably told her to go to the park and wait for him. Consider this" – Slick raised his finger to emphasize the point – "Tonger's daughter was a dipsomaniac. She was drunk when she was first seen in London, and we've got evidence from the servants that, the week before he died, Tonger had an extraordinary amount of whisky in his room – he who hitherto had never taken drink. It was she who soaked – not Tonger.

"When Marshalt found that she had this craving, it was easy to give her a flask with enough cyanide to kill a regiment, and tell her to go into the park, well knowing that, sooner or later, she would drink from that flask and never move further. But he tried to do too much. He intended that night seeing Miss Bedford – Torrington. He wanted to see her pretty badly, so badly that he wouldn't put off the engagement. Then Tonger came back.

"There was no need for Marshalt to explain the disappearance of the woman, as he knew nothing about her: she might have gone out by herself. You may be sure that she went out by the back way – the way a certain lady used to come in when she paid her surreptitious visits to Lacy. It wasn't likely that Tonger would learn that very evening that his daughter was dead, and yet that is exactly what did happen! Tonger made his discovery at the very moment Marshalt was waiting in Malpas' room for the arrival of Audrey Bedford.

"What Marshalt intended, I don't know. I guess he would have produced the letter making an appointment in that apartment, but that is mere speculation – we shall never know. At any rate, he did not meet Miss Torrington. Maddened by his discovery, Tonger, who knew the secret of the mantelpiece, and had fashioned a key to it, opened it, passed into Malpas' room, and confronted his treacherous employer. He was, I think, armed with an old-fashioned pistol, and Marshalt spoke the truth there. He fired twice, and Lacy went down. The bullet-proof shirt he wore – not because he had been in the Balkans, but because he was scared to death that some day Torrington would come on the scene – saved his life. While Tonger, half demented, was searching the desk, Marshalt recovered, staggered back to his own room, and shot Tonger in his tracks.

"The controls of Malpas' house are fixed in many places. There is a switch on the stairs, there is a set of switches below, one on the desk and another in Lacy's study.

"What happened immediately afterward is also a matter of speculation, unless Marshalt spills it. He was going to make his escape when he heard the servant scream, and probably saw Captain Shannon run down the area steps. That was his opportunity; he slipped out. If you remember, the door was open."

Dick nodded.

"Now, Marshalt had already prepared a hiding place for himself. In the character of a lawyer or something of the sort, he had a gorgeous flat in Greville Mansions, where he was called 'Mr Crewe.' I happen to know because I have occupied an adjoining suite to some purpose. He got there that night, nursed his bruise – he had a slight wound, too – and then came back to get the diamonds. I know, because I've seen him."

"Who was the man whose face I saw through the skylight on the night of the murder?" asked Shannon.

"Mine," said Slick Stormer calmly.

"But your men on duty on the roof said – "

Slick laughed.

"Why do you think they were on the roof? They were my alibis and protectors! The last time you were questioning one of them I was crouching behind a chimney pot not a yard away from you. Of course they hadn't seen me! They'd have lost a good job if they had! I was always around that roof. Climbing is my specialty, though I'm not such a good climber as Martin Elton, who didn't have a rope lowered to him as I did.

"Marshalt's job was to scare everybody out of the house. He hated like poison that police guard, because he wanted to get at the diamonds that were in the idol's tummy, and naturally he could only do that by getting rid of the police. Wearing his evening dress and a made-up face, he appeared – as himself! The poet says that we can rise on stepping stones of our dead selves to better things. Tennyson, was it, or maybe Browning? It's good enough for Longfellow. That is how Marshalt figured it out – that he could rise on that stepping stone to handle all these good and sparkling gems. He got desperate after the hiding place was discovered, and with the help of Stanford, who had to be taken into the secret, he cleared the idol under your eyes. But Stanford was a bungler, and unused to the mechanism, and after the diamonds had been put in the bag, he started monkeying with the mechanism to see how it worked, switched out all the lights, and incidentally brought the statue round into the room. He must have had the bag in his hand at the time, and put it down in a fright on the pedestal, and naturally, when the statue turned again, it took it back."

"What was it burnt my hand?" asked Steel.

"The fireplace! When you reached out, the thing had revolved, and you'd put your hand on the hot bars of the grate from which the coal had only recently been removed. You recall, Captain Shannon, that there was generally a smell of hot iron in the room when these demonstrations occurred.

"After you'd got away with that, he followed you. Stanford went down to the Haymarket and did his little burglary – I saw him come out, as a matter of fact, but I thought it was unnecessary to tell you – while Marshalt followed you in his car and engineered an accident. The honour and glory of recovering the bag goes to Stanford, who was still in the flat when you found your man knocked out.

"The money retrieved, Marshalt's first thought was to get the bag away. He took it to his flat in Greville Mansions: this I know, for I found it there when I broke in to look for Miss Torrington. I didn't find her, but I saw the bag, and only gave it up when I saw I could turn it over to good hands without being arrested myself.

"Now, Marshalt is a suspicious man. He found that the bag was gone, and naturally he suspected his confederate. The shooting of Stanford, you'll find, occurred just before you arrived this morning – I understand he was artistically draped round the pedestal. That nearly completes the story. Again we must guess what happened between Stanford and Marshalt. The probability is that Marshalt only found then that the young lady was concealed on the premises, and, knowing that the game was up and the fortune was lost, he went to have his revenge on the daughter of the man he best hated. Unfortunately for him, I have made a practice for a long time of being in that house when the people that came in from the Cape brought their diamonds. I was there once in broad daylight, tapping the walls, and Marshalt heard me – Miss Torrington heard me, too – I wanted to know all about that pivot door. I have twice impersonated the mysterious Mr Malpas and got away with it. It was a hobby of mine to be Mr Malpas whenever I broke in, for I knew that a day would come when he and I would meet face to face, and I was hoping that he suffered from a weak heart. I scared one young lady all right," he said, and Audrey could smile at the recollection.

"I screamed, didn't I?" she said ruefully. "I didn't hear you calling my name for a long time."

"I scream myself sometimes," said Slick, "or want to! There is only one thing left to tell you, and you know that already, Shannon. You knew it before you got that summons to Fould's Wharf. Once he recovered the diamonds, it was up to Marshalt to make a dramatic reappearance. It was very nearly too dramatic, let me tell you! He got into the water under the pier, locked the handcuffs himself, and with the key of the cuffs in one hand and a gun in the other, waited for you to turn up, as he knew you would, within a specified time. But you were delayed five minutes on the road, and in that five minutes a tragic thing happened: by accident he dropped the key of the handcuffs in the water, and couldn't release himself! If you hadn't got there when you did, he'd have drowned. When you came, it was easy. He had his gun in his hand – if you'd kept your light on him you would have seen it, but he asked you to take the light off, and immediately you shut down your lamp he fired two shots at you, dropped the pistol in the water – I've since recovered it – and the rest you followed. If he had killed you – there was the proof of his innocence – he couldn't have done it.

"And now, Miss Torrington, I'll thank you for that badge."

She gave a gasp of surprise, felt in her bag and produced the silver star.

"Thank you," said Slick gracefully; "and I hope you're not offended. I never allow anybody to keep a star after they've passed out of my employ and gone into the establishment of a rival."

His eyes met Dick's, and they were laughing.

"That is a joke," he said. "You won't see it because you're English! But do you mind if I indulge in one private laugh? Ha! ha!"

EDGAR WALLACE

BIG FOOT

Footprints and a dead woman bring together Superintendent Minton and the amateur sleuth Mr Cardew. Who is the man in the shrubbery? Who is the singer of the haunting Moorish tune? Why is Hannah Shaw so determined to go to Pawsy, 'a dog lonely place' she had previously detested? Death lurks in the dark and someone must solve the mystery before BIG FOOT strikes again, in a yet more fiendish manner.

BONES IN LONDON

The new Managing Director of Schemes Ltd has an elegant London office and a theatrically dressed assistant − however Bones, as he is better known, is bored. Luckily there is a slump in the shipping market and it is not long before Joe and Fred Pole pay Bones a visit. They are totally unprepared for Bones' unnerving style of doing business, unprepared for his unique style of innocent and endearing mischief.

Edgar Wallace

Bones of the River

'Taking the little paper from the pigeon's leg, Hamilton saw it was from Sanders and marked URGENT. *Send Bones instantly to Lujamalababa… Arrest and bring to head-quarters the witch doctor.'*

It is a time when the world's most powerful nations are vying for colonial honour, a time of trading steamers and tribal chiefs. In the mysterious African territories administered by Commissioner Sanders, Bones persistently manages to create his own unique style of innocent and endearing mischief.

The Daffodil Mystery

When Mr Thomas Lyne, poet, poseur and owner of Lyne's Emporium insults a cashier, Odette Rider, she resigns. Having summoned detective Jack Tarling to investigate another employee, Mr Milburgh, Lyne now changes his plans. Tarling and his Chinese companion refuse to become involved. They pay a visit to Odette's flat. In the hall Tarling meets Sam, convicted felon and protégé of Lyne. Next morning Tarling discovers a body. The hands are crossed on the breast, adorned with a handful of daffodils.

EDGAR WALLACE

THE JOKER

While the millionaire Stratford Harlow is in Princetown, not only does he meet with his lawyer Mr Ellenbury but he gets his first glimpse of the beautiful Aileen Rivers, niece of the actor and convicted felon Arthur Ingle. When Aileen is involved in a car accident on the Thames Embankment, the driver is James Carlton of Scotland Yard. Later that evening Carlton gets a call. It is Aileen. She needs help.

THE SQUARE EMERALD

'Suicide on the left,' says Chief Inspector Coldwell pleasantly, as he and Leslie Maughan stride along the Thames Embankment during a brutally cold night. A gaunt figure is sprawled across the parapet. But Coldwell soon discovers that Peter Dawlish, fresh out of prison for forgery, is not considering suicide but murder. Coldwell suspects Druze as the intended victim. Maughan disagrees. If Druze dies, she says, 'It will be because he does not love children!'

OTHER TITLES BY EDGAR WALLACE AVAILABLE DIRECT
FROM HOUSE OF STRATUS

Quantity		£	$(US)	$(CAN)	€
	The Admirable Carfew	6.99	11.50	15.99	11.50
	The Angel of Terror	6.99	11.50	15.99	11.50
	The Avenger	6.99	11.50	15.99	11.50
	Barbara on Her Own	6.99	11.50	15.99	11.50
	Big Foot	6.99	11.50	15.99	11.50
	The Black Abbot	6.99	11.50	15.99	11.50
	Bones	6.99	11.50	15.99	11.50
	Bones In London	6.99	11.50	15.99	11.50
	Bones of the River	6.99	11.50	15.99	11.50
	The Clue of the New Pin	6.99	11.50	15.99	11.50
	The Clue of the Silver Key	6.99	11.50	15.99	11.50
	The Clue of the Twisted Candle	6.99	11.50	15.99	11.50
	The Coat of Arms	6.99	11.50	15.99	11.50
	The Council of Justice	6.99	11.50	15.99	11.50
	The Crimson Circle	6.99	11.50	15.99	11.50
	The Daffodil Mystery	6.99	11.50	15.99	11.50
	The Dark Eyes of London	6.99	11.50	15.99	11.50
	The Daughters of the Night	6.99	11.50	15.99	11.50
	A Debt Discharged	6.99	11.50	15.99	11.50
	The Devil Man	6.99	11.50	15.99	11.50
	The Door With Seven Locks	6.99	11.50	15.99	11.50
	The Duke In the Suburbs	6.99	11.50	15.99	11.50
	The Feathered Serpent	6.99	11.50	15.99	11.50
	The Flying Squad	6.99	11.50	15.99	11.50
	The Forger	6.99	11.50	15.99	11.50
	The Four Just Men	6.99	11.50	15.99	11.50
	Four Square Jane	6.99	11.50	15.99	11.50
	The Fourth Plague	6.99	11.50	15.99	11.50

ALL HOUSE OF STRATUS BOOKS ARE AVAILABLE FROM GOOD BOOKSHOPS
OR DIRECT FROM THE PUBLISHER:

Internet: www.houseofstratus.com including author interviews, reviews, features.

Email: sales@houseofstratus.com please quote author, title and credit card details.

OTHER TITLES BY EDGAR WALLACE AVAILABLE DIRECT
FROM HOUSE OF STRATUS

Quantity	£	$(US)	$(CAN)	€
THE FRIGHTENED LADY	6.99	11.50	15.99	11.50
GOOD EVANS	6.99	11.50	15.99	11.50
THE HAND OF POWER	6.99	11.50	15.99	11.50
THE IRON GRIP	6.99	11.50	15.99	11.50
THE JOKER	6.99	11.50	15.99	11.50
THE JUST MEN OF CORDOVA	6.99	11.50	15.99	11.50
THE KEEPERS OF THE KING'S PEACE	6.99	11.50	15.99	11.50
THE LAW OF THE FOUR JUST MEN	6.99	11.50	15.99	11.50
THE LONE HOUSE MYSTERY	6.99	11.50	15.99	11.50
THE MAN WHO BOUGHT LONDON	6.99	11.50	15.99	11.50
THE MAN WHO KNEW	6.99	11.50	15.99	11.50
THE MAN WHO WAS NOBODY	6.99	11.50	15.99	11.50
THE MIND OF MR J G REEDER	6.99	11.50	15.99	11.50
MORE EDUCATED EVANS	6.99	11.50	15.99	11.50
MR J G REEDER RETURNS	6.99	11.50	15.99	11.50
MR JUSTICE MAXWELL	6.99	11.50	15.99	11.50
RED ACES	6.99	11.50	15.99	11.50
ROOM 13	6.99	11.50	15.99	11.50
SANDERS	6.99	11.50	15.99	11.50
SANDERS OF THE RIVER	6.99	11.50	15.99	11.50
THE SINISTER MAN	6.99	11.50	15.99	11.50
THE SQUARE EMERALD	6.99	11.50	15.99	11.50
THE THREE JUST MEN	6.99	11.50	15.99	11.50
THE THREE OAK MYSTERY	6.99	11.50	15.99	11.50
THE TRAITOR'S GATE	6.99	11.50	15.99	11.50
WHEN THE GANGS CAME TO LONDON	6.99	11.50	15.99	11.50
WHEN THE WORLD STOPPED	6.99	11.50	15.99	11.50

Hotline: UK ONLY: 0800 169 1780, please quote author, title and credit card details.
INTERNATIONAL: +44 (0) 20 7494 6400, please quote author, title and credit card details.

Send to: **House of Stratus Sales Department**
24c Old Burlington Street
London
W1X 1RL
UK

Please allow for postage costs charged per order plus an amount per book as set out in the tables below:

	£(Sterling)	$(US)	$(CAN)	€(Euros)
Cost per order				
UK	2.00	3.00	4.50	3.30
Europe	3.00	4.50	6.75	5.00
North America	3.00	4.50	6.75	5.00
Rest of World	3.00	4.50	6.75	5.00
Additional cost per book				
UK	0.50	0.75	1.15	0.85
Europe	1.00	1.50	2.30	1.70
North America	2.00	3.00	4.60	3.40
Rest of World	2.50	3.75	5.75	4.25

PLEASE SEND CHEQUE, POSTAL ORDER (STERLING ONLY), EUROCHEQUE, OR INTERNATIONAL MONEY ORDER (PLEASE CIRCLE METHOD OF PAYMENT YOU WISH TO USE)
MAKE PAYABLE TO: STRATUS HOLDINGS plc

Cost of book(s): —————————— Example: 3 x books at £6.99 each: £20.97

Cost of order: —————————— Example: £2.00 (Delivery to UK address)

Additional cost per book: ———— Example: 3 x £0.50: £1.50

Order total including postage: ——— Example: £24.47

Please tick currency you wish to use and add total amount of order:

☐ £ (Sterling) ☐ $ (US) ☐ $ (CAN) ☐ € (EUROS)

VISA, MASTERCARD, SWITCH, AMEX, SOLO, JCB:

☐ ☐ ☐ ☐ ☐ ☐ ☐ ☐ ☐ ☐ ☐ ☐ ☐ ☐ ☐ ☐ ☐ ☐ ☐ ☐

Issue number (Switch only):

☐ ☐ ☐

Start Date:

☐ ☐ / ☐ ☐

Expiry Date:

☐ ☐ / ☐ ☐

Signature: _____

NAME: _____

ADDRESS: _____

_____

POSTCODE: _____

Please allow 28 days for delivery.

Prices subject to change without notice.
Please tick box if you do not wish to receive any additional information. ☐

House of Stratus publishes many other titles in this genre; please check our website (**www.houseofstratus.com**) for more details.